"We didn't know if there were any sparks between us. So we tried a kiss to find out if we had chemistry."

"And?"

"And there wasn't. Not like . . ."

Sabina trailed off, biting her lower lip. Roman clenched his fists. That lip shouldn't be pinched between her teeth. It ought to be pressed up against his mouth, that tender flesh responding to his hot kiss.

"Like what?" he asked in a low growl, demanding she finish her sentence.

"Like . . . um . . . like there ought to be." She dropped her gaze, so he knew she'd censored herself.

"That's not what you were going to say."

"You don't know what I was going to say."

"Yes, I do." He stepped close to her and took her head in both his hands, tilting it until her eyes caught dancing sparkles from the streetlights. "You meant, there wasn't any chemistry like *this*."

And he claimed her mouth like a lion claiming its prey.

Romances by Jennifer Bernard

The Fireman Who Loved Me
Hot for Fireman
Sex and the Single Fireman
One Fine Fireman: A Novella

SEX *and the* SINGLE FIREMAN

A BACHELOR FIREMEN NOVEL

Jennifer Bernard

AVON
An Imprint of HarperCollins*Publishers*

This book is a work of fiction. References to real people, events, establishments, organizations, or locales are intended only to provide a sense of authenticity, and are used fictitiously. All other characters, and all incidents and dialogue, are drawn from the author's imagination and are not to be construed as real.

AVON BOOKS
An Imprint of HarperCollins*Publishers*
10 East 53rd Street
New York, New York 10022-5299

ISBN 978-0-06-208898-7
www.avonromance.com

First Avon Books mass market printing: February 2013

Printed in the U.S.A.

10 9 8 7 6 5 4 3 2 1

This book is dedicated to the firefighting community, especially the three hundred and forty-three fallen on 9/11. We will never forget you. Many thanks to Rick Godinez, Fire Captain II of the Los Angeles Fire Department, for sharing his expertise. I'm so fortunate to be able to work with Tessa Woodward, Jessie Edwards, the Avon team and my agent, Alexandra Machinist. Special thanks to the readers who have embraced the Bachelor Firemen and who chat with me on my Facebook page. And to my wonderfully supportive family, who cheer me on from Maine to Rhode Island to Alaska, I love you.

SEX *and the* SINGLE FIREMAN

Chapter One

Revenge, decided Sabina Jones, was a dish best served on the side of the road to the tune of a police siren.

It had all started with Sabina doing what she always did on Thanksgiving—hitting the road and blasting the radio to drown out the lack of a phone call from her mother. Thirteen years of no Thanksgiving calls, and it still bothered her. Even though she now had her life pretty much exactly how she wanted it, holidays were tough. When things got tough, Sabina, like any normal, red-blooded American woman, turned up the volume.

In her metallic blue El Camino, at a red light in Reno, Nevada, she let the high-decibel sound of Kylie Minogue dynamite any stray regrets out of her head. She danced her fingers on the steering wheel and bopped her head, enjoying the desert-warm breeze from the half-open window.

So what if she had her own way to celebrate

Thanksgiving? This was America. Land of the Free. If she wanted to spend Thanksgiving in Reno letting off steam, the Founding Fathers ought to cheer along and say, "You go, girl."

The honk of a car horn interrupted Kylie in mid–"la-la-la-la." She glanced to her left. In the lane next to her, a black-haired, black-eyed giant of a man in a black Jeep aimed a ferocious scowl her way. He pointed to the cell phone at his ear and then at her radio, then back and forth a few times.

"Excuse me?" Sabina said sweetly, though he had no chance of hearing her over the blaring radio. "If you think I'm going to turn my radio down so you can talk on your cell phone while driving, forget it. That's illegal, you know. Not to mention dangerous."

The man gave an impatient gesture. This time Sabina noticed that his eyebrows were also black, that they slashed across his face like marauding Horsemen of the Apocalypse, that his eyes were actually one shade removed from black, with maybe a hint of midnight blue, and that his shoulders and chest were packed with muscle.

She rolled her window all the way down, pasted a charming smile on her face, and leaned out. With her window wide open, the noise from her radio had to be even louder. "Excuse me? I can't hear you."

He yelled, "Can you please turn that down!" in a deep, gravelly voice like that of a battlefield commander sending his troops into the line of fire.

Despite his use of the word "please," it was most definitely not a request. Sabina guessed that most people jumped to obey him. An air of authority clung to him like sexy aftershave. But she'd never responded well to orders off the job. At the station she didn't have a choice, but here in her own car, no one was going to boss her around, not even a gigantic, sexy stranger. She reached over and turned up the volume even higher.

"Is that better?" she yelled through her window, with the same sweet smile. With one part of her brain, she wondered how strict the Reno PD was about noise ordinances.

She couldn't hear his answer, but she could practically guarantee it included profanity.

For the first time this miserable Thanksgiving, her mood lifted. Her childhood holidays had always been spent fighting with her mother. In her mother's absence, she'd have to make do with bickering with the guy in the next car over. As someone who prided herself on never complaining, she'd much rather fight than feel sorry for herself.

It occurred to her that he might be talking to a family member. Some people had normal families and celebrated holidays in a normal fashion—or so she'd heard. She moved her hand toward the volume dial, ready to cave in and turn it down.

The man rolled his window all the way up, stuck one finger—a very particular finger—in one ear, and yelled into his phone.

Sabina snatched her hand away from the dial. If he yelled at his family like that, and had the nerve to give her the finger, he deserved no mercy. Besides, the light was about to change and she was going to make him eat her El Camino's dust.

She stared at the red light, tensing her body in anticipation. The light for the cars going the other direction had turned yellow. The cars were slowing for the stoplight, and the last Toyota still in the intersection had nearly passed through. She poised her foot over the accelerator.

Then something black and speedy caught the corner

of her eye. The Jeep cruised through the intersection. The big jerk hadn't even waited for the light to change. It finally turned green when he was halfway through the intersection.

Indignant, she slammed her foot onto the accelerator. Her car surged into the intersection. He wasn't too far ahead . . . she could still catch him . . . pass him . . .

A flash in her rearview mirror made her yank her foot off the accelerator. A Reno PD cruiser passed her, lights flashing, siren blaring. It crowded close to the Jeep, which put on its right-turn signal and veered toward the curb. She slowed to let both vehicles pass in front of her. As the policeman pulled up behind the Jeep, she cruised past, offering the black-haired man her most sparkling smile.

In exchange, he sent her a look of pure black fire.

Sweet, sweet revenge.

Sabina's cell phone rang, flashing an unfamiliar number. For a wild moment, she wondered if it was the man in the Jeep, calling to yell at her again. Of course that was impossible, but who would be calling from a strange number? She'd already wished the crew at the firehouse Happy Thanksgiving. She'd already called Carly, her "Little Sister" from the Big Brothers Big Sisters program.

Was her mother finally calling, after thirteen missed Thanksgivings? Annabelle wasn't even in the U.S., according to the latest tabloid reports. But still, what if . . .

Her heart racing, she picked up the phone and held it to her ear. "Hello."

Clucking chicken noises greeted her. She let out a long breath. Of course it wasn't her mother. What had she been thinking?

"I can't talk right now, Anu. I'm in Reno."

"Yes, skipping Thanksgiving. That's precisely what I want to talk to you about."

"I'm not skipping it. I'm celebrating in my own way."

"I located a potential partner for you. A very obliging guest here at the restaurant. He's letting me use his phone so you can install his number in your contacts." Anu, who was from India, claimed pushy matchmaking was in her blood.

"Seriously. Can't talk." Especially about that.

"Very well. You go to your soulless casino filled with strangers, drink your pink gin fizzes, and pretend you're celebrating Thanksgiving."

In the midst of rolling her eyes, Sabina spotted the police cruiser in her rearview mirror.

"Gotta go." She dropped the phone to the floorboards just as the police car passed her. The cop cruised past, turning blank sunglasses on her.

A sunny smile, a little wave, and the officer left her alone. A few moments later, the black Jeep caught up to her. The gigantic black-haired man looked straight ahead, either ignoring her or oblivious to her. For some reason she didn't like either of those possibilities. Or maybe she just wanted another fight.

She reached for her volume control and turned the radio up full blast. The man didn't react, other than to drum his fingers on his steering wheel. Fine. She rolled her window down to make it even louder, knowing how ridiculously childish she was being.

Thanksgiving brought out the worst in her, she'd be the first to admit.

The corner of the man's mouth quivered. Good. She was getting to him. The sounds of Kylie filled the El Camino, high notes careening around the interior, bass line vibrating the steering wheel. Adding her own voice to the din, she sang along at the top of her lungs.

She might as well be inside a jukebox, especially with that gaudy light flashing in the rearview mirror . . .

Oh, *crap.*

One hundred and twenty dollars later, she pulled up in front of the Starlight Motel and Casino. Why couldn't she experience, just once, a peaceful Thanksgiving filled with love, harmony, and mushroom-walnut stuffing? Her mother had always dragged her to some producer's house where she'd be stuck with kids she didn't know, rich, spoiled, jealous kids who mocked her crazy red hair and baby fat. She'd always ended the evening in tears, with her mother scolding her. *This is what we do in this business, kiddo. Would it kill you to make a few friends? Those kids could be getting you work someday.*

Her mother had gotten that part wrong. Sabina had found her own work, thank you very much. And it meant everything to her.

The setting sun beamed golden light directly into her eyes, mocking her with its cheerful glory. Thanksgiving always messed with her, always bit her in the ass. On a few Thanksgivings, she'd tried calling her mother, only to get the runaround from her assistant. But now Annabelle was in France and none of her numbers worked anymore.

Damn. Why hadn't she just signed up for the holiday shift at the station and spent the day putting out oven fires?

She grabbed her bag and marched through the double front doors, only to stop short, blocked by a giant figure looming in her path. Even though she couldn't see clearly in the dimmer light of the lobby, she knew exactly who it was. A shocking thrill went through her; she should have guessed the man in the Jeep would turn up again.

"Well, this is a lucky coincidence," the man said in a voice like tarred gravel. "The way I figure it, you owe me three hundred and sixty-eight dollars. Cash will be fine."

"Excuse me?" She peered up at him, his black hair and eyes coming quickly into focus. Her stomach fluttered at the sheer impact of his physical presence. He was absolutely huge, well over six feet tall, a column of hard muscle contained within jeans and a black T-shirt. "If you're referring to your well-deserved spanking from the Reno PD, don't even start. No one made you run that red light."

"Sorry, did you say something? I can barely hear you over the ringing in my ears."

Sabina lifted her chin. If he thought he could intimidate her, he didn't realize who he was dealing with. She worked with firefighters all day long, not one of them a pushover. "Maybe you should try not yelling at your family for a change."

"Excuse me?" He glowered down at her, looking mortally offended. "What the hell are you talking about?"

Realizing she'd probably crossed a line, Sabina scrambled to recover. "Anyway, you already got your revenge. They gave me a ticket too. We're square."

"I wouldn't have had to yell if you'd had the common decency to respond to a perfectly reasonable request."

Sabina felt her temperature rise. He wasn't making it easy to make peace with him. "Request? Something tells me you never make requests. Orders, sure. Requests, dream on."

"You think you know me?"

"Why should I want to know you when all you do is scowl and shout at me?"

"Shout?" He shook his head slowly, with a stupefied look. "They told me the people were different out here. I had no idea that meant insane."

Sabina tried to sidestep around him and end this crazy downward spiral of a conversation. "I wish the police gave tickets for rudeness, you'd have about three more by now."

He blocked her path again, so she found herself nose-to-chest with him. Sabina imagined him as a Scottish laird or a medieval warrior hacking at enemies on the battlefield. The man was fierce, but annoyingly attractive. He even smelled nice, like sunshine on leather seats.

"How about drowning out a man's first phone call with his son in two thousand miles? How's that for rudeness?"

He had a point. But a surge of resentment swamped her momentary pang of conscience. So some people *did* talk to their children on Thanksgiving. Normal people, irritatingly, aggravatingly, unreachably normal people. People who were not her or her mother.

"Fine," she snapped. "Here." She dug in her pocket and took out a handful of change. "We're at a casino, right? Play your cards right and you'll get your precious three hundred and sixty-eight dollars. Good luck."

She lifted one of his hands—so big and warm—and plopped her small pile of change into his palm. With the air of an offended duchess, she swept past him, deeply appreciating the way his black-stubbled jaw dropped open.

So maybe she'd been wrong before. Maybe revenge was a dish best served in a hotel lobby with a side of loose change.

Chapter Two

In room 602, as Sabina was untangling her hair from its braid, her cell phone rang again. Once again, the call wasn't from her long-lost mother. "Don't worry, Anu, I'm not teetering on the edge of my motel balcony with a bottle of cheap gin in one hand."

"I am thoroughly reassured."

"You really shouldn't worry so much."

Anu made a skeptical sound. For someone like her, who was surrounded by family, Sabina's single existence seemed incomprehensible. Every time Sabina tried to explain that the San Gabriel firehouse was like a family, Anu made scornful snorting noises.

"Do you promise you will avoid alcohol?"

"No."

"Anonymous strangers?"

"Too late."

"What?"

"I'm joking. There was an anonymous stranger, but

I got a ticket thanks to him, so you can cross him off the list."

"This sounds fascinating, but I must go. I'm at the restaurant. A big crowd just arrived and my mother is becoming perfectly flustered."

After she ended the call, Sabina stared at her silent cell phone. So much for any sort of contact from her mother. A dull ache settled in the pit of her stomach. She'd worked so hard to leave the past behind, to become a San Gabriel firefighter, to create the life she wanted. But on days like today, none of it seemed to mean anything. The energy that had fizzed through her during her bouts with Sexy Jeep Guy felt more like a hangover now. Maybe she needed another verbal brawl with the man. A run-in with him might work even better than a pink gin fizz in terms of forgetting her Thanksgiving blues.

It had taken a long time for the giddy vibrations from that one short encounter to fade away. She kept remembering the look he'd given her before striding out of the Starlight lobby. Offended and scorching, as if she'd screwed up during boot camp. She didn't like that scornful look at all, not one bit. If she saw him again, she'd tell him exactly why he'd been completely in the wrong and how a little loud music was vitally necessary on certain occasions. He'd apologize for his behavior and . . .

She snorted. Of course she wouldn't see the guy again. It was a big, anonymous hotel where everyone minded his own business. That's what she liked about Reno. Here, everyone was a stranger never to be seen again, no matter how much they made your nerve endings vibrate.

She finished brushing her hair and decided to leave it loose, just for tonight. Her hair didn't get out much.

Normally she wore it in a braid so it didn't cause trouble on the job, and so no one would recognize her. Speaking of which . . . she peered into the mirror. A tiny sliver of tawny red-gold shone at the roots of her hair. Time to visit the salon again, even though it broke her hairstylist's heart every time she had to dye Sabina's hair dust-bowl brown.

Sabina examined her reflection in the way she'd honed over the years, making sure there was absolutely no resemblance to the person she'd been until the age of seventeen. As Sabina Jones, she never wore makeup. Not on the job, and not on a date. As Sabina, she was tall, lean, and known for the distinctive brown braid that hung down her back—the polar opposite of her former self.

The only similarity was her eyes. She'd considered colored contact lenses but decided that was a little too "witness protection program" for her needs.

In all these years, no one had recognized her yet.

She pulled on a slinky tank top in a teal color that made her eyes glow. That and tight, white jeans gave her a feeling of flirty confidence. If the Jeep guy saw her now, he'd eat his heart out. That scornful look would change to desire, to hopeless longing, to begging for forgiveness on his knees . . .

She rolled her eyes at her reflection. If Sexy Jeep Guy didn't make requests, for sure he'd never beg forgiveness on his knees. Anyway, enough was enough. If she saw him again, she'd have to apologize—she knew perfectly well she'd been in the wrong—and that would be tough to do on an already crappy Thanksgiving. Fingers crossed, they'd manage to avoid each other until she headed back to San Gabriel.

* * *

In the restaurant on the ground floor, Brad, the blond, multitattooed maître d', greeted her with his trademark devilish smile. "Must be Thanksgiving again. Our little holiday tradition." He kissed her on the cheek, took her elbow, and steered her toward the booths along the wall. "Mind a hot tip?"

"Depends," said Sabina warily. He had a knack for getting into trouble, and she'd been along for the ride a couple of times.

"A big, juicy hunk of prime-ass male came in here tonight. All alone. Completely single. I asked. I'm putting you in the booth next to him."

"You sure he's not on your side of the ledger?"

"My gaydar is as reliable as a windsock. Not even a little gay. Almost makes me wish I was a woman. Almost."

A funny suspicion crept into Sabina's mind. "Hang on. Is he really tall and . . . big?"

Brad smirked. "I didn't check that closely, more's the pity."

"I mean, you know, huge and dark-haired and kind of mean-looking."

"Alpha all the way, babe. Hot stuff. Better jump him or I'm banning you from the Starlight for life."

"Seriously, Brad, I think I know him already and this is a very, very, *very* bad idea. He doesn't want anything to do with me, and besides, I owe him an apology and I'm really not in the mood."

Brad stopped suddenly and turned her so she faced the booth on her right. There sat the now familiar, large form of the man from the Jeep. A wicked smile spread across his face as he rose to his feet. It seemed an endless process, tall as he was. When he'd unfurled himself to his full height, well over six feet, he took her breath away. "An apology. Imagine that. This ought to be good."

The man sure knew how to take command. With one huge but knowing hand, he guided Sabina into the booth across from him. She cast a murderous look at Brad, who ignored it, briskly placed a menu in front of her, and disappeared.

Across the table, the giant took a sip of his drink.

"What are you drinking?" she murmured. "Revenge on the rocks?"

"Excuse me? Whatever you said, it didn't sound like an apology."

Sabina closed her menu with a thump and rested her elbows on the table. Time to take charge of this ridiculous situation. "All right. I suppose I was a tad bit impolite earlier."

"Hmm. Does that constitute an apology out here?"

Sabina ground her teeth. "I'm sorry I played the radio too loud. I'm sorry I turned it up when you wanted me to turn it down. I'm sorry I gave you all my spare change."

The man gave a sudden laugh. A deep groove appeared on his left cheek and he looked, well, outrageously sexy. Again, that treacherous shiver snuck into Sabina's belly.

He took a long swallow of his drink. "Thank you. I suppose three hundred and sixty-eight dollars isn't too high a price to pay to talk to my son."

Did he have to rub it in like that? "You know it's against the law to talk on cell phones while you're driving."

"Yes, the nice officer explained that to me, as he wrote out *ticket number two.*"

She couldn't help it; she snorted. "Well, that's one more than I got. You win."

He laughed again, a deep, rumbling sound. That laugh did fascinating things to his face.

She glanced down at her menu, hoping to banish the tug of attraction. Not that she had any intention of ordering. One drink and she'd leave. "So I screwed up your conversation with your son."

"Yep. It went a little like this. 'What did Grandma say? She's taking you to France?' 'She's. Buying. Me. New. Pants. Geez, Papa, are you deaf?' "

Sabina suppressed a smile. It wasn't funny, really. She'd been very rude, every step of the way. "I really am sorry. I blame Thanksgiving, but I know it's no excuse."

One black eyebrow rose, but before he could say any more, Brad returned with Sabina's usual, a gin fizz. Then he disappeared in record time, mumbling something about sending the waitress to take their order.

The man picked up his glass. The light from the red globe lantern on the table made the amber liquid glow. "To Reno's finest."

Sabina clinked her glass against his. "May they forget we ever existed."

They both sipped from their drinks. The fizzy taste of the gin danced through her system, and she felt herself relax for the first time this weird Thanksgiving.

She lifted her glass again. "To Kylie Minogue."

He tilted his head in a "touché" gesture. "To Kylie." Another clink. Another sip.

Even more relaxed by now, Sabina regarded the man with a certain amount of satisfaction. The guy wasn't so bad, now that she'd seen him smile. She'd found him sexy before, but that groove in his cheek gave his appeal a whole new dimension.

"Hey. I don't even know your name," she said suddenly, surprised. Somehow it felt as if they'd traveled way past introductions.

"Ha. I don't know yours either." He lifted his glass. They clinked again.

Sabina sipped her pink gin. "Of course, they're on file with the Reno PD."

"And I'd almost managed to drown the memory."

Laughing, she swallowed more gin fizz. The man had something about him, an edge, a spark. The tangy drink made Sabina glow with well-being and issue another apology. "Sorry for accusing you of yelling at your family. That was uncalled for."

"Well, I did yell. But I'm from New York. We're used to yelling just so people can hear us over the din."

"New York?"

"Brooklyn, born and bred. I'm only moving to California for my son. He's into baseball. He's flying out after spending Thanksgiving with his grandparents."

That news made her nervous. But it was a big state, after all. One of the biggest. She eyed him over the rim of her drink. He wore a white open-collar shirt that did nothing to hide his physicality. Every line of his body, every speck of five o'clock shadow, screamed testosterone. If she was smart, she'd get out of here before she did something stupid.

But somehow her body didn't budge.

"You can call me Jones," Sabina told him.

"Jones? That's your name?"

"Close enough."

One black eyebrow went swooping up. "I see. Fine, then. You can call me Rock."

She choked on her drink, sending a spray of gin fizz into her napkin. *Rock*. It wasn't possible.

He wore a wounded look. "You find that funny?"

"Well." She dabbed at her eyes, which were tearing up from the gin stinging her sinuses. Great way to impress the guy. Even better than causing him to get two tickets. "It's just that you're . . . well, you're a big guy. Very . . . manly. Rock is . . . Well, I guess it suits you."

"My family would appreciate that. Of course, they'd go with Rocco, the Italian version."

Rocco. That seemed even more hilarious. She fought back her helpless laugh and raised her glass in another toast. "To Rocco and Jones. Sounds like a law firm you don't want to mess with."

"Or a TV show from the eighties about two renegade detectives."

"You lost me there." Mention of TV shows always made her nervous. "I never watch TV."

She put her glass down, the pink liquid sloshing resentfully, as if she'd hurt its feelings. "Well. Apology accepted, I assume?" She rose halfway to her feet.

"Absolutely not."

"Excuse me?"

"I'm not sure we're done yet."

She stared at him. His eyes glowed black and daring in the soft light from the globe lantern. The look in them made her dizzy, as if he were a magnet and she was a helpless safety pin being drawn closer, closer . . . Unwelcome thoughts filtered into her mind. What would this man, so huge, so outrageously virile, be like in bed? *No, Sabina, you're not going there. Bad, bad idea. What's gotten into you?*

The waitress appeared with a bread basket and a menu pad. "Ready to order?"

The man kept his gaze on Sabina. "Ms. Jones, would you please do me the honor of joining me for dinner?"

She swallowed. *Walk away, walk away.*

"Just to be clear, this is a request, not an order." He gave her a slow smile, the groove deepening in his cheek.

Good Lord Almighty, he was one sexy man. She sank back onto the vinyl seat.

Chapter Three

Rick Roman, occasionally known as "Rock," cursed himself for a fool. Jones—the name suited her, in a weird sort of way—was the kind of woman he had no business tangling with. Even through his fury at the interrupted phone call with Luke, he'd noticed how the Nevada sun picked out strands of bright gold in her toffee-brown hair. Now, close enough to touch, it looked so soft, like spun sugar, as it tumbled past her shoulders down her narrow back. But most of all, those eyes, shimmering somewhere between turquoise and teal . . .

He gave himself a mental kick in the shins. Dinner with the beautiful if obviously incognito "Jones" wasn't going to lead to the bedroom. He didn't do that sort of thing. He'd been living the life of a single father slash virtual monk for the past decade, after all. But when she'd started to leave the booth, he'd had the feeling she was about to take all the light with her. He couldn't bear to see her go.

But now what? He hadn't spent much time having dinner with gorgeous women lately. "I'm having the steak, medium rare. Two?"

She nodded and smiled at the waitress. That smile had struck him like a blow to the chest when she'd aimed it from her El Camino. It did something similar now. "Make mine bloody."

Roman grinned at her. "That's what I like to hear. If you'd said grilled catfish or veggie burrito I would have given you a ticket myself. My worst fear about California is the food."

"Not the earthquakes? Carjackings? Cult murders?"

"Nope. It's the guacamole salad."

She laughed, and the dim little world of their booth seemed to glow. Even when she'd been goading him from her car, he'd been intrigued despite his irritation. The look in her eyes, feisty but a little haunted, made him want to catch her like a firefly and find out all about her.

He leaned forward, creating an intimate space between the two of them. "So what do you do, Jones? Do you live here in Reno?"

Her expression went wary. She lifted her glass as if it were a shield.

"Never mind. I have a better question. What's wrong with Thanksgiving? You said you blamed Thanksgiving."

At first he thought she wasn't going to answer. Molten candlelight pooled between them, contrasting with the dimness outside the booth. Beyond it came the quiet hum of flirtatious voices and clinking silverware. It all created a sort of intimate magic. Maybe she felt it too, because finally she tilted her head, smiled with a sort of crooked defiance, and said, "I'm missing one important element of Thanksgiving. A family."

"No family at all?" This was hard for him to imagine, having lived within subway distance of his family all his life.

"I had one, of course. But I haven't spoken to my mother in a while."

"How long is 'a while'?"

"Oh . . . not long. Thirteen years."

He calculated quickly. She appeared to be around thirty. She must have been a teenager then. "Falling out?"

She took a long swallow of her drink and lifted one shoulder. Light bounced off the pink liquid in her glass to glimmer in her eyes.

"Must be rough. Especially on Thanksgiving. If I'd known . . ."

Jones made an impatient gesture. "Doesn't matter. I'm a big girl. Enough about me and my family. What about you? Is there a Mrs. Rock?"

"There was. Luke's mother. She died about ten years ago," Roman answered. After all this time, the answer came easily, so easily Jones didn't even react. "How about you?"

"Same. I mean, no one."

Their eyes met, and suddenly the air between them tensed with possibility. He found himself leaning closer to her, trying to pin down the shades of aquamarine and sky blue and even a dash of gold in her eyes that combined to such brilliant effect. Close like this, he breathed in her scent—warm, feminine flesh with a hint of jasmine.

It went straight to his groin. He wondered if he was drunk, but it usually took more than half a Scotch to accomplish that.

"What are you doing?"

He realized he was staring. Blinking, he sat back. "Sorry. Your eyes are . . . uh . . . spectacular."

"Oh." She lowered her eyelashes over them, which gave him a moment to get a grip on himself. "Thanks. But I can't take any credit. It's all in the genes. Gift from my mother. You know, before she stopped talking to me."

So she wasn't vain. Which seemed odd for such a gorgeous woman, with those high, elegant cheekbones and that perfectly oval face. She had a taut energy about her, as if she was poised for action at any given moment. He hoped that action wasn't to flee. He really, really didn't want her to leave.

The waitress appeared with their steaks, breaking the mood. They both turned their attention to their slabs of meat. For once, Roman barely noticed that it was overcooked and that they'd tried to disguise an inferior cut of beef with manufactured sauce. He was too aware of Jones's vibrant, graceful presence across the table. Too aware of the expressions that played across her face. Pleasure at her first mouthful of meat. Thoughtfulness as she chewed. Speculation as she glanced his way.

It was that speculative look that really got to him. Was she thinking the same thing he was? Two unattached adults with high-octane chemistry. One night in Reno. Could they? Should they? *Would she?*

No. This was nuts. He didn't do that kind of thing. She probably didn't either. Though maybe she did. Hard to say, when he'd only set eyes on her a couple of hours ago—and not in the best of circumstances.

But still, two single people, alone on Thanksgiving, far from home, undeniably attracted to each other . . .

Intellectually, Sabina knew her steak was a little overcooked. But most of her brain was taken up with another issue. Inconvenient sexual tension. Not long ago this man had been yelling at her to turn down her music. Now she was fantasizing about him sweeping her into his massive arms and whisking her off to his hotel room.

And she hadn't told anyone about her mother in . . . well, she never had, not since she'd made her escape. Dinner was almost over now. And the thought of leaving the booth, of no longer being able to feast her eyes on his black-eyed magnificence, didn't appeal to her one bit. She scrambled for a safe topic.

"So your son likes baseball?"

"Oh yeah. He's a star pitcher back in Brooklyn, but he wants to play year round. We were hoping to move at the beginning of the school year but we had to wait for my replacement to start."

"How old is he?"

"He just turned thirteen."

Silence fell between them. Not a normal silence, but the kind in which naughty thoughts careened like monkeys in a cage. She could mention Carly, who also loved baseball. It would provide a way to continue a nonthreatening line of conversation. They could talk about batting averages and crazy sports parents and the kids' favorite players and . . .

She cleared her throat. "Are you here for just one night?"

The question came out in an unexpectedly husky tone that sent his gaze flying to meet hers. Her belly tightened with a sudden spike of arousal. He was too damn attractive, this man. No one could blame her if she let down her hair, figuratively speaking, for one night.

"Yes." He fiddled with his silverware. "You?"

She nodded. Her eyes dropped to the big hand wrapped around his fork. He had workingman's hands, complete with calluses and a white scar over the middle knuckle. Little black hairs curled at his wrists. How one man could pack so much potent masculinity into one body boggled her mind.

"Jones. Listen." His voice dropped down to an even deeper register, one she felt in the pit of her stomach. "I never do this sort of thing."

Her throat tightened in excitement. She could have pretended she didn't know what he was talking about. But instead she said in a low voice, as hot lust speared through her, "I don't either."

"I shouldn't even be thinking about it. But I am. We're two single adults alone on Thanksgiving. And I'm very attracted to you. Extremely so. It's throwing me for a loop, honestly." He smiled ruefully. Between the groove in his cheek and the desire in his eyes, Sabina felt herself melt.

"I am too," she said faintly.

"You're . . . attracted or . . . thinking about it?"

"Both. But I shouldn't either. I mean, I don't." Great, now she was babbling. "Usually."

"Usually." His head lifted, eyes flaring. "Does that mean . . . ?"

Impulsively, she reached over the table and ran her finger across the scar on his knuckle. "How'd you get that?"

He went completely still. Time seemed to stop while he looked at her hand on his, then back up slowly, deliberately, his eyes glittering. "Playing with fire."

Like a match tossed onto lighter fluid, those three little words ignited all that simmering lust into action. Sabina grabbed her purse. Rock threw some bills on the table, not seeming too concerned about which ones or how many. He took Sabina's hand and guided her through the restaurant while she glanced pityingly at the other patrons who weren't them, who weren't heading toward the mind-blowing sex she absolutely *knew* was coming. She felt thrillingly alive, on fire, half crazed.

She caught a brief glimpse of Brad's delighted wink on the way past. And then they were racing hand in hand up the stairs to his suite.

Inside, Rock put his hands on her shoulders and looked searchingly into her eyes until she thought she'd melt.

"You sure about this? I'm leaving tomorrow."

"I'm sure." To prove it, she boldly put her hands on his chest as she'd been dying to do since she first saw him in the booth—no, in the Jeep, to be completely honest. He felt just as rock solid as she'd imagined—ridges and valleys carved from living stone.

He ran his outsize hands down her sides, shaping the slope of her waist. Tingles shot all the way to her toenails.

"Sure as sugar," she added.

It sounded so goofy, she put a hand over her mouth to stop the laughter. Rock cocked his head and chuckled along with her. The movement of his strong throat muscles made her dizzy. Everything about him made her head spin. When their laughter had died down, he raised his hands to cradle her head in his warm grip. He had the hands of a million-dollar massage artist, magical, powerfully gentle hands that held her steady while he lowered his mouth to hers. Time seemed to stop during that long journey; at any rate, her breath did. She lost herself in the fierce black eyes coming closer and closer, the firm mouth set on claiming its prize; he was a marauder, an ancient conqueror come to life.

When their lips touched, it was as if firecrackers

exploded in a July sky. After the initial shock, she gripped his wrists and leaned into him, giving back stroke for stroke, pressure for pressure. He growled, the sound rumbling deep in his chest, and tilted her head to take even more thorough possession of her mouth. He explored it with a dedicated intensity that wiped her mind clean of any thought except him. Him and more him, and the taste and feel and scent of him.

As she surfaced from the drugged glory of that kiss, she congratulated herself on not having collapsed on the floor. Then she realized there was a good reason for that; her feet were no longer on the floor. Just as she'd fantasized in the restaurant, he'd swooped her up in his arms and cradled her like a baby.

"You're . . . quite strong," she pointed out, in a husky voice that seemed to drip with sexual need. It would have embarrassed her, if she hadn't been beyond embarrassment by now.

"The better to pleasure you, my dear." He waggled his black eyebrows.

"I'm not exactly a lightweight." Her friend Vader had picked her up a few times, but he'd always complained and held his back in mock pain afterward.

"You're perfect." Further proving his superior strength, he held her with one arm while he used his other hand to run his fingers through her hair. "Down to the last hair on your beautiful head."

The tenderness in his voice gave her a quick pang. What would it be like to have a man like Rock *actually* love her? Actually be tender with her, as part of a, well, a relationship?

She shoved the thought to the back of her mind. This wasn't about a relationship. This was about hot, sweaty sex at its finest. She extracted herself from his grasp so she could reach for his belt buckle. When that was undone she pulled his shirttails from under the belt and snuck her hands into the firm heat that lurked underneath. Muscles carved from iron rippled under her touch. She followed the bulging ridges up his chest to his massive shoulders, luxuriating in the rough curls she encountered along the way.

Rock made a harsh sound and set her on her feet. He ripped his shirt off and stood before her in all his muscular glory. Holy Mother, he was incredible. Like an ancient statue of some discus thrower twice the size of a normal person. His chest rose and fell with his rapid breaths. His eyes practically burned holes through her thin tank top.

"Can I please take your top off before I die?"

Between the two of them, clumsy with lust, they got rid of her top and the plain cotton bra underneath. Naked to the waist, she quivered under his blazing black scrutiny. He made her feel like a goddess come to life, as if she'd been formed solely to bring this powerful man to his knees.

"You are the most beautiful thing I've ever seen," he said in a heartfelt tone.

She swallowed hard. "So are you." She couldn't stop devouring every detail of his physique. Her gaze followed the line of black hair that marched past his half-open belt buckle. Underneath, boxers. Under those . . . Good Lord Almighty. The thick rise of his jeans, the unmistakable arousal underneath, made her body vibrate with anticipation. Her nipples hardened to fierce little peaks.

He put his hands to his zipper. She held her breath. Then he stopped.

"Damn it." With a wild look, he ran his hand through his hair. "I don't have protection with me. I never even thought about it."

Well, damn. "I don't either."

Breathing fast, half naked, they stared at each other.

"Brad!" Sabina said suddenly.

"What?"

"The maître d'. He'll have some. He parties every night after his shift. Be right back."

Sabina would never forget the smug look on Brad's face, or his efforts to extract a promise to tell him every detail in exchange for a handful of condoms. "Waste not, want not," he said with a wink.

She stuffed them in her purse and raced back up the stairs, too anxious to wait for the elevator. What if Rock had changed his mind? What if this wasn't such a good idea? What would he think of a woman who rushed off to get condoms from a gay maître d'? Was this the craziest way to spend Thanksgiving ever?

As she reached the third floor, her steps slowed. Was she really about to have sex with a man known only as "Rock"? A man who was clearly hiding his real identity and knew her only as "Jones"?

By the time she reached his door, she was in an agony of regret and pure sexual frustration. Of course she couldn't do this. She didn't have sex with strangers. Besides . . . a man like that . . . he'd be too hard to forget come morning.

She scrabbled in her purse for a piece of paper but all she found was the ticket from the Reno PD. She tore it in half, making sure she kept the part with her name, found a pen, and scrawled one word.

Sorry.

Not much of an explanation, but it was all the ticket had room for. She pushed it under the door of Rock's suite and fled.

Chapter Four

It could have been worse, Roman decided as he performed a slow circle in the middle of his new house, a cozy tract-style home with a shake shingle roof, two bedrooms, and French doors leading out to a sunny backyard. "Jones" could have *actually* cut off his balls. He'd been straight with her. He'd admitted his attraction. Even though he'd known better, he'd given in to it. But she must have been planning to make a fool of him the entire time. At least she'd done it with flair.

He stepped into the backyard. He'd have to put on a new roof, of course. Shake shingles were a fire hazard—so was all of Southern California if it came to that. Eighty degrees at the end of November. No amount of backyard sprinklers could disguise its true desert nature. The thought of sprinklers led to thoughts of a shower, which made him remember the cold shower he dove into when he'd realized he was alone in his suite with a gigantic boner, a ticket, and a fake apology.

Damn, why did every thought lead to the ruthless tease Jones? If she'd been trying to get revenge for her ticket, she'd chosen a uniquely frustrating way. Though funny enough, he had to admit. The humor had finally sunk in after his massive hard-on had died down—hours later, it seemed.

So this pleasant, sunny bungalow was his home for the next . . . well, for as far as he could see into the future. Luke would like it—or at least the Luke of a year ago would have. The current, thirteen-year-old version of Luke was a lot harder to please. Roman devoutly hoped this move to California would be a new start for the two of them. He'd already scoped out the neighborhood, delighted to discover a park with a couple of ball fields filled with kids and a potentially acceptable Italian restaurant.

Speaking of Luke . . . He dialed his parents' number.

"How's the house, Papa?"

"I think you're going to like it. Your bedroom looks out on the backyard."

"A yard. Awesome. What are the people like there?"

Gorgeous, sexy cock teases.

"Like people anywhere," he said instead. "Maybe a little tanner. They seem to smile more here."

As they're making an ass out of you.

"Did you have a nice Thanksgiving with Nonno and Nonna?"

"Yeah. Nonna made that pork dish you like. And pignoli tart."

Roman's mouth watered. Suddenly he missed New York so much he wanted to hit something. His punching bag would do. But it was in the moving truck along with the rest of their things and not due to arrive until tomorrow.

"Nonno wants to take me to a Green Day concert next summer."

"*What?*" He'd misheard that, right? "You're barely thirteen. And your grandfather's over sixty."

"And you're way too strict. He likes them. And he says you're too 'stodgy' for a single father. You need to loosen up."

"He said I need to loosen up?" Roman knew for a fact that phrase did not exist in his Italian father's vocabulary.

"Not exactly. But he said something about *la dolce vita*. Doesn't that mean relax and enjoy sh— stuff? And not be so strict?"

Roman decided to ignore the whole line of conversation. "Did they book a cab for the airport yet?"

"Don't worry, Papa, of course they did. Nonna's been cooking food for the trip the last two days."

"Good. And you'll have a flight attendant watching out for you too." He already knew how stressful Luke's solo flight would be—for him, not for Luke.

"I'm not a baby, Papa." Luke heaved a mortified sigh. Roman supposed it wasn't the easiest thing to be the son of a hyper-protective single father. But nothing in this world was going to bring harm to his son if he could help it.

"I better go, kid. Gotta get to the uniform store."

"Give 'em hell, Papa."

"Excuse me?"

"Didn't Harry Truman say that first? If it's okay for a president, why not me?"

Roman grumbled. *"Ti voglio bene, Lucito,"* and hung up before Luke could protest the Italian diminutive he hated.

* * *

Sabina stopped by La Piaggia on the way to work. Anu bustled around the kitchen, badgering the breakfast chef, who looked grateful to see Sabina arrive.

"Get yourself a double espresso, I'll be out in a minute," Anu ordered, tossing her black braid over her shoulder. A tiny diamond dot sparkled in one nostril, and the red *bindi* on her forehead proclaimed she was married, though Sabina rarely saw her husband. Apparently he worked a lot, and they had a friendly if passion-free marriage.

Typical Anu, specifying the drink Sabina was to have. What if she'd changed her usual order and opted for a cappuccino instead? But Sabina didn't mind; Anu was the only person stubborn enough to insist on being Sabina's friend despite her constant wariness.

She took a gulp of espresso and looked at her watch. Her shift started in ten minutes. A warning nagged in her memory, telling her today something important was happening and she shouldn't be late. But Anu plopped down in the seat across from her in a flurry of saffron-yellow sari silk.

"I believe I have talked my parents into adding mango lassi to the menu."

"Really? An actual Indian dish? Should I call the Channel Six news?"

"Very amusing. We're going to call it mango gelato." Her full lips quivered with humor. Anu had the brightest, most intelligent eyes of anyone Sabina knew.

Sabina snorted. "I think your parents need to give San Gabriel more credit. Have you forgotten about Bombay Deluxe?"

Anu's eyes sharpened. "Be quiet. Do you want my parents to overhear?" San Gabriel's only Indian restaurant, run by Pakistanis, was a sore point with Anu's family. "So . . . did you meet anyone interesting in Reno?"

Sabina nearly swallowed the lemon twist that came with her espresso. "You're freaking eerie."

"I knew it! As soon as I saw you I knew it. You have that perfectly dreamy look."

"I have to go." Sabina set down her tiny cup on its saucer and rose to her feet.

"What was his name? What does he do? Would I like him?"

"Don't know, can't imagine, and have no idea."

Anu stared, her shining eyes going wide. "Didn't I tell you about anonymous strangers?"

"So you did. And look—I have a few of these left over." She pulled out the stash of condoms she still had in her purse.

"Put those away," hissed Anu, whipping her head around to watch for her highly conservative Hindu parents.

"Fine. More for me." Sabina smiled, feeling like a cat with a bowl of cream. Teasing Anu was always so much fun.

Anu shook her head scoldingly, trying hard not to laugh. "You now owe me every detail, Sabina Jones, you wicked girl. Come tonight and I'll make you some chana masala."

"Throw in some naan and you've got a deal. But it'll have to be tomorrow. I'm on shift tonight."

"Patience I will practice."

They parted after a quick hug. Sabina dashed to her car. Damn, she was going to be late. That bit of memory lurking in her brain raised the alarm again. Today was a big day for some reason.

Her cell phone rang, but she let the call go to voice mail.

At Fire Station 1, she screeched her El Camino into her usual parking spot and flew through the side door, which opened into the apparatus bay. It was empty but for the sparkling fire engines and a spooky silence. She took Brent's coat out of Engine 1, stashed it in his locker, and put her own gear in its place—the official signal that she was now on shift and he could go home.

She checked her watch. One minute after the start of lineup. No problem, she'd just sidle in the back, join the guys as they listened to Captain Kelly talk about new safety bulletins and who was getting overtime this week . . . Suddenly she remembered the nature of the big thing happening today. The new training officer was starting.

He was rumored to be a total hard-ass. They'd been told they'd meet him at lineup.

She rushed to her locker, grabbed her uniform, ran to the female dorm area, and changed in record time. From the kitchen she heard a deep, unfamiliar voice. Tightening her belt, she dashed down the corridor. Maybe she could sneak in at the back of the crowd. Maybe the new training officer would never notice her. Maybe . . .

She skidded to a halt next to Vader, pinned to the spot by a pair of smoldering black eyes glaring at her from what seemed an impossible height.

"You're in trouble now," whispered Vader out of the corner of his mouth.

He had no idea.

It took every ounce of the self-control he'd developed from being the most feared fire captain in the history of Brooklyn fire stations for Roman to hide his reaction to the sight of the elusive Jones.

She looked different, of course. Her lovely hair was constricted into a braid that flew behind her as she dashed into the room. Her uniform hid the lithe figure that had haunted him every night since she'd run out on him. But he'd never forget those eyes, which were now wide with shock in a face gone suddenly white.

Good, he thought savagely. Let her quake in her shoes for a while. Captain Kelly continued going over the names of the crew members who hadn't yet introduced themselves. They were all a vague buzz until it was Jones's turn.

"I'm Firefighter Jones," she said in a subdued voice.

So at least she'd given him her real last name. That made things a little better.

"Are you in the habit of being tardy?"

"No, sir."

The big guy next to her spoke up. "I can second that, sir—"

"This isn't a democracy," Roman barked. "This is a firehouse. Firehouses require discipline." He stared down the assembled firefighters, who looked slightly shocked. He had to admit they were a good-looking bunch, save for one older man who had quite the belly on him.

Captain Kelly, a mild-mannered veteran who was filling in as the scheduled overtime duty, better known as "SOD," captain until a permanent replacement for Captain Brody was named, finished introducing the crew and gestured for Roman to take over.

Roman stepped forward. "I'm Battalion Chief Rick Roman, the section commander in charge of the Training Section, specializing as the department's safety officer and hazmat specialist. Fire Chief Renteria has asked me to run the section and act as the training officer at Station 1 for the time being. I'll be riding with all the companies as needed for training purposes and to observe.

"I'm here for another purpose as well. I'll be filling in for Battalion Chief Drake, who will be stationed here as soon as he recovers from knee surgery. Which brings me to my real job, which is to whip this place into shape. The fire chief wants more discipline here. This firehouse has become a national joke. I hear they call you the Bachelor Firemen of San Gabriel. You've even been on *America's Next Top Model.* Girls infiltrate the premises so they can meet you."

The big-bellied guy spoke up. "The girls don't do that so much now that Ryan's gone." He added under his breath, "More's the pity."

Roman drilled him with a long stare, which had the result of making more words flow from the rattled fireman's mouth.

"That's Ryan Blake, Hoagie to us. You probably read about his wedding. They had it on the news. Marzipan cake with butter cream frosting. Him and Katie are on their honeymoon right now. Camping in Mexico—"

He closed his mouth abruptly as Roman stalked over to him. "Have you read the Rules and Regs, Section D, subsection 24 lately?"

The man's eyes scuttled from side to side, as if searching for a manual. Roman didn't enjoy making people uncomfortable, but the issue was an important one.

"Firefighter Breen, you know the regs, right? Remind Firefighter Lee of this section."

Stud looked as though he'd rather throw himself into a tar pit. But under Roman's relentless gaze, he mumbled, "Firefighters shall maintain a level of fitness suitable for performance of their duties. Regular testing of such shall be administered at random intervals determined by the station commander."

"Random intervals," Roman repeated. "Could be today. Could be tomorrow. Are you ready, Firefighter Lee?"

A wave of red slowly crept up the man's face. Roman took a step back; he'd made his point. He addressed the entire group. "After lineup, we'll do some drills. Over the next few weeks, I want to see how each of you performs basic fire ground operations—hose lays, ladders, search and rescue, ventilations, rapid intervention, forceful entry. I want to be impressed. I expect to be impressed. Station 1 is a top-performing fire station, despite the tabloid crap."

Finally, some pride lightened the tight faces of his new crew.

"I will require you to act like it in every respect. Dismissed."

An audible sigh of relief swept across the line of men and one woman. Jones's glittering turquoise eyes were fixed on him with a look close to hatred. How dare she? He was the injured party, not her. A torn ticket with the word "sorry" on it? It still lurked in his wallet, a deliberate reminder to avoid all beautiful, deceitful strangers.

"Firefighter Jones, in my office," he barked at the end of lineup, as the other firefighters all rushed to the workout room.

A quiver of alarm passed over her face, instantly hidden behind a defiant mask. He spun on his heel and stalked toward the office they'd assigned to him. It used to be the captain's office until they switched things around for the incoming battalion chief. He held the door until she'd ducked under his arm, then closed it behind them.

He sniffed. Funny smell in this office. He'd been too preoccupied with preparing himself to put the fear of God into the crew to notice before now.

Never mind. He had more important things to think about. Unfortunately, under Sabina's angry stare, all rational thoughts scattered. She folded her arms over her chest, which made him remember every detail of her pale pink nipples and supple, sun-kissed skin with its dusting of freckles, the way her lovely breasts swelled so proudly on her graceful torso, the sounds she made when he skimmed his hand over her waist . . .

"You should have told me," he said.

"No, *you* should have told *me*."

Standoff.

Her cell phone rang. She didn't look at it, keeping her eyes on his until it stopped. Each ring increased his irritation, until his next words burst out without conscious permission from him.

"You blew me off by way of a *ticket*?"

"It was all I had. I didn't even have a receipt. I thought it was better than nothing, *Rock*."

At her tone, which implied he was a liar, his temperature rose another degree. "For your information, the guys at my old station called me Rock."

"You mean the ones you didn't humiliate in front of the whole crew?"

There went his temperature, up another degree. "Don't question my methods."

"Really? Is that one of your rules?"

"Yes," he said flatly. "And if you'd told me you were a firefighter, we wouldn't be in this awkward situation."

"It's not awkward at all." She uncrossed her arms and marched toward him. She poked a finger into his chest. "It never happened."

She'd poked his chest. No one ever poked him. He was Chief Roman the Hard-ass, the Intimidator, the Feared. "The hell it didn't. I have your handwriting on a ticket to prove it."

"You *kept* it?" She went slightly pale.

"If you wanted revenge for your ticket—"

"*What?*" Now she looked just as out-of-her-mind furious as he felt. "As if I would ever do something as low-down as that. It could have been worse, you know."

"Oh yeah? How's that?"

She leaned toward him with a wicked look. "I could have gotten you completely naked. Then I could have tied you to the bedpost and left you begging . . ."

Dio. He reached for her, pulled her against his chest, and fastened his mouth to hers. It was just to shut her up, really it was . . . until he felt her lips under his. Then insane lust bolted into his groin, blotted out every intention except touching this woman, devouring her mouth, running his hands up and down her sleek back. And it wasn't just him. She was kissing him back just as fiercely, her coffee-scented lips opening under his invasion, her tongue battling with his. A force field of sexual electricity zinged around them. In two seconds he could have her naked up against the desk . . .

"Ow!" He yelped and lifted one leg. Something latched to his ankle. Something painful and growling. "What the hell?"

"Stan." Jones wrenched herself away from him. "Down, Stan."

The hard pinch on his ankle released. A beagle-ish looking dog looked mournfully up at him.

"You've got to be kidding me."

Jones gave a spurt of shaky laughter and smoothed her hair with a hand that trembled just a bit, he was savagely happy to see. She looked flushed and shaky, and damn if he didn't want to grab her and do it all over again. "Stan's the firehouse dog. He was very attached to Captain Brody. And he's very protective."

"Good doggy." Partly to hide the shocking lust that still cruised his bloodstream, Roman reached down to pet him, but the creature backed away. The dog had a point. He'd been way out of line with his behavior. He probably ought to thank the pup.

He straightened up, hoping his boner wasn't visible in the new uniform. Clearing his throat, he faced Jones. "You're right. Nothing happened in Reno. Or here in this office. More to the point, nothing will happen in the future that isn't completely by the book. I . . . uh . . ." He decided to quote the ticket. "Sorry."

A rapid series of expressions chased across her face. Many things seemed to be on the tip of her tongue, but she restrained herself. "Yes, sir."

When she was at the door, he stopped her with a curt "Wait."

She paused.

"You can let the crew know that firefighter fitness is a top priority of mine. I've seen men killed because they got soft."

Her shoulders tensed, but she gave a tiny nod before slipping out of the office.

After she left, he met Stan's soulful brown eyes. The dog still looked wary. Roman noticed one of his ears looked mangled, as if it had been chewed up and spit out. He could relate. "You and I might have more in common than you think, Stan."

Chapter Five

"I'm going to apply for a transfer," Vader grumbled as he hoisted two hundred pounds of metal over his head. "I don't need this shit."

"Yeah, right." Sabina was working out her aggressions on the treadmill next to him. She'd set it to the highest level; sweat dripped off her. "Leave the Bachelor Firemen? I'll bet you a soda you never even bother to get an application."

Sodas were the common currency of the firehouse, actual gambling being forbidden. Sabina couldn't even keep track of how many sodas Vader owed her.

"He's going to ruin this station. Acting like he owns it. I can't wait for those drills. I can't wait to go mano a mano with the dude. I'm going to obliterate him. He'll wish he was back in his pansy-ass New York station. I want Brody back."

"Vader, don't be a baby. Brody's not coming back. I heard he loves his new job at the academy. Besides,

Chief Roman's a training officer, he won't be here forever."

In the corner, Double D made a strangled sound as he attempted a sit-up. His feet rose into the air and he toppled backward. Sabina stepped off her treadmill and ran to help him.

"I'll hold your feet down, D."

"Little thing like you couldn't hold down a parakeet."

She glared at him. Double D was old school and still resisted the very concept of a female firefighter. "Try me. Or I'll peck your eyes out." She knelt between his legs and pressed on his feet.

Double D leered. "Two, you don't look so bad from this angle."

She narrowed her eyes at him until he stopped snickering and attempted a sit-up. He barely completed one before collapsing back to the mat.

"I'm fucked," he panted. "He's going to write me up."

"No, he won't. Come on, try again."

Wheezing, Double D struggled through another sit-up. "Chief Roman's the king of hard-asses." Pant. "Called my buddy from the Bronx this morning." Pant, pant. "Ever since his wife got killed in 9/11, he's been hell on his crews. Scariest bastard on the Eastern seaboard."

In her shock, Sabina let loose her hold on his feet and he crashed into a clumsy backward somersault, contorted twist sort of move.

Vader cackled. "Nine point two from the German judge."

Sabina crawled to Double D's aid. "Sorry, D. His wife was killed in 9/11?" He lay like a plump beetle stranded upside down, legs wiggling. She offered him a hand.

"'Swhat I heard. She was like *you.*" Clearly not a compliment, from the tone of his voice.

"What do you mean?"

"Female on the job." He was still trying to catch his breath. "Shows what happens. Wife and mother of a young kid, going inside that tower, getting herself killed." Under Sabina's fierce scowl, he backtracked. "Not to say she ain't a hero. They all were. All three hundred and forty-three."

Every firefighter in American knew the exact number of their fellow firefighters and paramedics killed during 9/11. Sabina felt ill at the thought of the way she'd yelled at Chief Roman.

"We should give him a chance," she said. "So he's not Brody. So what? We'll get used to him. And he'll get used to us."

"Firefighter Lee," came a harsh voice from the doorway. "Nap on your own time. I want ten sit-ups, starting . . . now!"

Sabina scrambled back to her position at Double D's feet. She watched, amazed, as he reeled off a rapid-fire set of ten semi-decent sit-ups.

When he was done, he didn't flop down as he had before. He stayed upright, looking at Chief Roman, who gave a brusque, unimpressed nod, then scorched the rest of the room with a hard stare.

"Firefighter Jones, you're not working out today?"

"I was helping—"

"A hundred sit-ups, starting now."

Sabina hid a smug smile. A hundred sit-ups . . . piece of cake. She'd always worked hard to keep her former baby fat at bay, for fear of resembling her old self too much. She launched into her crunches, aware of his eyes on her. Self-consciousness flooded her face with crimson. Under her San Gabriel FD T-shirt, her nipples pushed against her sports bra. He'd seen her naked from the waist up. Oh God. The new training officer knew exactly what her nipples looked like. He knew the sounds she made when she got turned on. Was he thinking of it right now? Because it sure felt that way, with his stern gaze surrounding her, bathing her in hot awareness.

Her breath came fast, and it wasn't only from the exercise. Squinting her eyes, she willed herself to ignore his mountainous, commanding presence in the doorway of the workout room.

"Chief Roman, what do you lift?" Vader asked in a squeak. Sabina glanced over and saw his pecs quiver with the effort of holding two hundred and fifty pounds above his chest.

"Enough," Roman answered in a tight voice.

Sabina imagined him stripping down to T-shirt and shorts and lying back on the bench press. Bulging muscles and mighty legs danced in her vision.

"You all right there?" Roman asked Vader. She glanced over at her friend.

"Ye-es." Vader seemed to have no air in his lungs. The veins on his neck bulged. His eyes popped.

"Vader!" Sabina jumped to her feet. "Someone do something!" She was strong, but she couldn't lift that amount of weight. She ran to help him, but before she got there, Chief Roman reached down with both hands and plucked the iron bar out of Vader's loosening grip as if it were a cheerleader's baton. He set it back on the rack.

"Don't hurt yourself, Firefighter Brown."

"No, sir," Vader gasped. "I'm fine, sir."

"We need you functional." He addressed all of them. "Carry on. Drills start this afternoon, barring any calls, of course." He left the room.

Sabina pounded Vader on the back while he wheezed and coughed. He clutched at her.

"Off day," he managed. "I skipped my energy drink."

Sabina rolled her eyes. Vader was her best bud at the station, but his obsession with his muscles had always struck her as ridiculous. "You'll beat him next time."

His eyes glittered. "I'll beat him, then I'll transfer. And he'll beg me to stay on hands on knees. Fucking hands and knees!"

"Sure, Vader."

He hoisted himself off the bench and lowered his voice to a hoarse whisper. "Need to talk to you about something private, Two. Tomorrow after work?"

She shrugged and nodded, and he went to work out his triceps. Sabina had to give Roman credit. She'd never seen either Vader or Double D this worked up. The man sure knew how to piss people off.

While Sabina was doing squats, which she hated, her cell phone rang again. She didn't recognize the number, but anything was better than squats. "Hello," she answered warily.

"It's Max. Don't hang up, munchkin," said a nicotine-drenched voice.

"Max?"

"Max Winkler. Uncle Max. Your childhood mentor. You quit answering your phone? This is the third time I called you."

"What are you—" She darted a glance around the workout room. She couldn't talk to Max here. "Hang on."

She darted out of the gym and into the bathroom, making sure to slide the sign so it said "Women." "Why are you calling me?"

"It's about your mother. When can we talk?"

"We are talking. Is she okay?"

"Yeah, yeah, she's fine. How about lunch?"

"No, Max. I'm not even in LA. I'm not that person anymore. Just tell me or I'm hanging up." As a child, she'd fallen for Max's tricks every time. Hopefully she'd learned a thing or two since those days.

His deep-throated laugh, which inhabited the bottom-dwelling register of a bass line, made her pull the phone away from her ear. "Playing hard to get, huh?"

"I'm working, Max. I actually have a job that means something to me now, and . . ."

But she was talking to emptiness. She knew what that meant. A more important call had come in and Max had switched over without bothering to mention it to her. She ended the call and turned off her phone. As long as her mother was fine, she had nothing to say to Max.

She splashed cold water on her face to calm herself down. Was Max going to make trouble for her? He didn't know where she lived. No one from her old life did.

Don't be paranoid. She'd told him to get lost, and Max never wasted his time. Everything would be okay.

Stepping out of the bathroom, she gratefully inhaled the beloved smell of the firehouse—a hint of gas drifting from the apparatus bay, coffee from the kitchen, varnish from the ladders they'd been working on. And for the millionth time she gave thanks for the one-hundred-and-eighty-degree turn that had landed her at San Gabriel Station 1.

For his first overtime shift filling in as battalion chief, Roman made a brief appearance at dinner, which was prepared by Fred the Stud. The easy flow of conversation was clearly hampered by his presence, so he returned to his paperwork as quickly as possible.

"Thanks for the meal," he told Stud, scraping his chair back from the table.

"Sure thing, Chief Roman. We never had a battalion chief at the station before. What about the dinner rotation?"

"Stud," said Captain Kelly sharply. "Chief Roman will not be cooking." He shot a glance Roman's way. "Unless he wants to, of course."

"No," said Roman, more brusquely than necessary. "No cooking."

As he disappeared into his office, he heard a few mutters. "Of course not . . . hard-asses don't cook . . . Chief Bighead . . . Brody always made pot roast . . ."

He ignored the complaints. He wasn't here to make friends.

Victor Renteria, chief of the San Gabriel Fire Department, called soon after dinner. "Heard you're already making an impression over there."

"Just doing my job."

"I knew I got the right man. If you can keep those guys out of the news for two weeks, I'll buy you a bottle of Jameson's."

"I don't foresee any problems."

Chief Renteria gave a long, ironic chuckle. "Glad to hear it. Have they briefed you on the curse yet?"

"No one's mentioned it." He'd heard about it, of course. Virgil Rush, the 1850s volunteer fireman jilted by Constancia B. Sidwell, his mail-order bride, had been so tormented by his crewmates' teasing that he laid a curse on all San Gabriel firemen, dooming them to disaster in their love lives.

Since he didn't have a love life, he couldn't care less about the "curse."

"Media eats it up. We used to like the publicity—bunch of good-looking, single firemen landing in *People* magazine—good for the image. But it's gotten out of hand. The opinion pages are making mincemeat out of me. Did you see their nickname for me? Chief Rent-a-Mirror. They've taken this too far, Roman. It's personal now. I can't think about those bastards without a stiff drink in my hand. Get this damn thing under control, that's all I ask."

"I'm on it, Chief. Total media blackout."

"You can make exceptions for fires, of course," said Renteria dryly. "But only for fires."

As Roman hung up, Stan opened one eye and bared his teeth. For a beagle who slept most of the time, he sure was feisty. He gave Roman a long, meaningful look, then collapsed himself into a ball on the floor.

So the dog didn't like him. Why the hell should it bother him?

Only two calls came in that night, both handled perfectly well by the men and woman of the B shift. Roman got almost no sleep, tossing and turning on the narrow bunk, which was six inches too short for him and about seventy-five feet too close to Sabina Jones. Although he'd tried not to acquire this information, he knew exactly where she was sleeping. And now he knew her first name. *Sabina*. Unusual. Kind of romantic-sounding. Of course, everyone at the station called her Two. Of all ridiculous names. She wasn't the second of anything; she was one of a kind. Even after such a short acquaintance he knew that much.

As he fell into a brief snooze, his last thought was about what the fire chief would say if he knew that he and Sabina had been one second thought away from hot, naked, sweaty, spectacular sex.

* * *

Luke raced across the San Gabriel Airport terminal and launched himself at Roman, who caught him in a tight hug. Being mostly Italian, their family had never been shy with physical affection. Roman loved ruffling his son's hair, giving him random bear hugs, slinging his arm around his shoulder as they walked. Like a flashback to the old Luke, he talked a mile a minute as they waited at the outdoor baggage carousel in the glaring sunshine.

"Nonna gave me money to rent a DVD player and I watched ten movies, fast forwarded right through the boring parts, where's our house, did our stuff come, cuz I wouldn't mind camping out a couple nights, I think it would be fun, maybe we'd see some coyotes, Ben knows someone whose cat was eaten by a coyote, do you think we could get a dog now that we have a backyard, I was thinking maybe a Great Dane, like a huge dog, because we're Romans and our family is big, even Nonno is huge he says it's because we're part Cherokee but I thought we were part Viking, do you know, Papa?"

Roman just shook his head, shouldered two of Luke's duffel bags, and handed him the third. Hopefully, Luke's excitement meant this move was the right step. For the first time in a year he didn't seem irritated or angry.

"One thing at a time. Are you hungry? Did you eat anything on the plane?"

Luke reeled off every snack he'd had on the flight, including the homemade cannoli his grandmother had given him.

"I had an extra but I gave one to the girl next to me," he finished, looking guiltily up at Roman. "She looked really thin and hungry. She hadn't even eaten breakfast."

"You've got a good heart, Lukey."

"Not really. I had two myself before I even talked to her."

Roman grinned down at his son. Honest to a fault, his Luke. Except for his height, he didn't look much like Roman; his exuberant brown eyes and sandy hair came straight from his mother's side of the family. Tall for his age, he used his wiry strength to whip fastballs past gawking batters.

"Home, then food?"

"I can't wait to see the house!" And he was off again. He chattered nonstop through the tour of the little beige house. Luke's bed had gotten broken during the move, but for now Roman had plopped the mattress in the center of his bedroom. Luke chose to shove it up against the window that looked out on the backyard.

"Can you believe how warm it is?" he kept saying. "It's like summer vacation every single day!"

"Don't you believe it. I've registered you at the toughest school in San Gabriel. The teachers are all ex-marines from Company F. Stands for Flunk."

"Papa. Not funny. Don't you think a Great Dane would love it here? Or maybe a Great Dane and a Newfie."

"I'll have to introduce you to the dog at work. You might change your mind about getting one."

"Never," Luke vowed.

In his joy at having his son back to normal, Roman forgot about the station, the awkward situation with Jones, and his sense of being a fish out of water—an enormous one. Maybe a shark.

For dinner, he took Luke to the neighborhood Italian

restaurant, La Piaggia, whose stucco façade glowed a lovely apricot pink in the sunset. But when the hostess, an energetic young Indian woman in a hot-pink sari, brought him his penne al'arrabiata, his good mood disappeared.

He gagged on the thick, cloying tomato-ish sauce. Luke put his fork down, eyeing him nervously.

"Papa. It's just pasta."

"No. No, it isn't. You can't call this pasta. Arrabiata is not a challenging sauce. That's why I ordered it. If they can't do—"

The sharp-eyed hostess hurried to their table. "Is there a problem?"

"Yes. This sauce. It tastes like ketchup. I don't think it has a single speck of red pepper in it."

She raised her chin. "Our customers don't enjoy spicy food. More's the pity, because there are some excellent North Indian dishes that—"

"But it's arrabiata! Do you know what that means?"

"I await enlightenment." She joined her palms in a gesture somewhere between spiritual and sarcastic.

"Angry. It means angry. Fired up. Inflamed."

"Inflamed?"

"And it's not hard to accomplish."

"Clearly." She eyed him pointedly. "You are inflaming me at this very moment. And not in the good way."

"Papa, *please*."

Roman struggled for calm. "Here's the thing. I'm new in town. You know the fire station nearby?"

Surprise flashed in her eyes and she nodded.

"That's me. Respectable, law-abiding, life-saving citizen. So work with me here. If I show you how to make a proper arrabiata, will you try it out on your customers? I promise you they'll love it. Everyone does. Right, Luke?"

"You'll probably want to marry him," said Luke, resigned by now.

"Highly unlikely," the hostess said, gesturing to the red mark on her forehead. "Once is more than enough."

"And another thing. Why is your restaurant named after a beach?"

"I'm Indian. You think I know?"

Roman lost his capacity for words. Luckily, she didn't. "Come along then."

"What? Really?"

"You offer to cook for me, I would be crazy to say no, would I not?"

Roman leaped to his feet, nearly upending the table in the process. Of all the times he'd offered to make a real sauce at an inferior restaurant, this brisk Indian woman was the first to accept. He loped toward the kitchen, Luke hopping after him.

Maybe San Gabriel had some potential.

Chapter Six

Sabina couldn't wait to tell Anu all about her terrible day, her horrible new sort-of-boss, and the god-awful coincidence that had ambushed her. How was it possible that the random man in the Jeep next to her, a man who then showed up at the same Reno casino, a man so wildly attractive she'd nearly fallen into bed with him, would turn out to be her new training officer? *What were the chances of that?*

The words started pouring out of her the second she walked into the kitchen.

"You will not believe what an utter jerk—" A hand was clapped over her face and someone dragged her back into the dining area. She yanked her head free and found Anu behind her, in full, hot-pink, Indian hostess garb.

"What the—"

Anu slammed the swinging kitchen door shut and

blocked it, arms folded. "No yelling. You might upset my special guest."

"What?"

"Smell that. Take a deep breath."

Sabina breathed in and caught a waft of some magical, tomatoey scent floating through the cracks in the door.

"New cook?"

"No. Some crazy customer who took over my kitchen for the night. Take a look. Just don't let him see you. I don't want him distracted."

Bewildered, Sabina crept up to the diamond-shaped window in the door. Inside the kitchen, the regular cook leaned against the dishwashing station, his arms folded sullenly across his chest. The kitchen assistant, who hated the cook, smirked as he diced onions. The heavenly smell made her stomach growl.

She craned her neck to see all the way to the stove. A tall figure loomed over it, giving his complete and total attention to the large stainless steel pot he was stirring. A sandy-haired boy stood next to him, peering over his arm and taking enthusiastic sniffs of the sauce.

Oh my God. It couldn't be. But it was. *Was Chief Roman haunting her?* She whirled around, her back to the door, and put her hands to her temples, which were starting to throb.

"Does he work at your station?" Anu asked with avid curiosity. "Is he wasting his talent putting out fires? You must tell me everything you know."

Sabina groaned. "He's my new training officer. And he must be an even bigger jerk than I thought. Yesterday he announced he wasn't going to be part of the dinner rotation. We figured he couldn't cook. But here he is, making the most incredible sauce I've ever smelled. I suppose he thinks he's too good for us. I suppose we're not worthy of his New York culinary expertise." The more Sabina thought about it, the more worked up she got.

Anu made a gesture Sabina interpreted as complete agreement.

"Who does he think he is?" She paced back and forth. "You should have heard how he lectured us today. He thinks we lounge around all day eating bonbons and calling the tabloids. And now this! He's the most arrogant, rude, patronizing *ass*, the whole crew hates him already . . ."

Finally Anu gave up on the gestures and clapped her hand over Sabina's mouth again.

Sabina squealed in outrage. Then went silent as a deep voice spoke from the half-opened kitchen door behind her.

"Firefighter Jones. Hungry?"

"If the *Encyclopedia Britannica* listed all the ways to piss off your new training officer, I've hit them all. And made up some new ones." Sabina kicked her feet up on her glass-topped table and gave Vader a morose look. They'd planned to grab a bite at La Piaggia but she'd fled in agonized embarrassment after spewing every abject apology she could think of. None of them had helped. She'd never forget Roman's expression. Or the look on his kid's face as he glared at her from behind his father. Or the endearing sight of such a big, powerful man bent over a stove, his son at his elbow.

Chief Roman, she now knew, was undoubtedly the most attractive man she'd ever met. But he must despise her after that scene in the restaurant. She'd insulted him in front of his son, for God's sake. Every time she thought about it, she cringed.

With a groan, she dropped her head in her hands. "I called him arrogant and rude. And more bad things. It's all a blur."

"You only said the truth. I can't stand the dude."

Oddly, Sabina found she didn't appreciate hearing someone else insult Roman.

"That's just because he's stronger than you."

Vader's jaw clenched tight and the tendons in his neck stood out.

"Just teasing," Sabina said quickly, before he popped a vein. "You could probably bench-press five of him. Single-handed."

Vader emptied his beer can and crushed it in his fist.

"Vader! Must you?"

"I must. I'm a man."

"I know you're a man. You don't need to prove it by demolishing things."

Vader got to his feet and circled restlessly around her comfiest armchair, then sat back down. Something must be bothering him. She knew Vader's rhythms well. He was an outstanding friend, loyal, devoted, unquestioning, goofy—kind of like a golden retriever. The other guys saw him as a steroid-obsessed bodybuilder, but she knew he was more than that.

"Something happened over Thanksgiving."

"You went out drinking, went home with twin models, and now you can't remember their names?"

"I wish."

She did a double take at his tone of deepest misery. "Well, spill it. You know me. I don't judge."

He did another circuit of her living room, which she'd decorated in a neutral palate of ecru and sage green to give away absolutely nothing about herself—as if it were an impersonal, upscale hotel room, comfortable but anonymous. Long silence followed while he played with her pleated window shade. She crossed one leg over the other, trying to contain her impatience.

"I want to help you out, but you're going to have to tell me what it is," she finally said.

"Fine." His Adam's apple worked as he tried to bring forth the words. He shifted from one foot to the other, shoved his hands in the pockets of his black jeans, made his biceps twitch the way he did when he was nervous. "The thing is, I got dumped. This chick, Cherie, called me a . . ." He dropped his voice to a hoarse whisper. "Homophobe."

"What?" Sabina wondered for a wild moment if Vader actually knew what it meant. "That's a big word, Vader, don't hurt yourself."

"This isn't a joke."

"Sorry." Sabina quickly sobered. Maybe it sounded ridiculous to her, but Vader deserved her sincere attention. "You'd better tell me the whole story."

"I went out with this girl over Thanksgiving. Cherie. We were out playing pool and this dude made a pass at me. I told him to bug off. Politely and all. But Cherie got offended because her brother's gay. She said I was a homophobe and that she couldn't possibly date one of *those*."

Sabina considered the best approach to take here. She loved Vader, but some of his ideas about men and women dated from the Stone Age. "Do you think . . . well, maybe you are?"

He shifted around some more, cracked his neck, clenched his jaw. "If I tell you something, you have to keep it on the down low. Not one word, ever."

"Geez, Vader."

"Promise?"

"Yeah, of course."

"At my rookie station, the guys thought I was gay because I like to work out. They made fun of me every single freaking shift. Probably trying to break me down. I nearly quit, but I stuck it out just to rub their faces in it."

Sabina sucked in a horrified breath. "Vader, that's wrong. Someone should have stopped it. That's called harassment."

"Nah. I just put in my time and moved on. But it opened my eyes, you know. I don't want anyone thinking I'm like those homophobic dickheads."

His brown eyes glittered, and for once, he looked completely serious. It occurred to Sabina that there was a lot she didn't know about Vader. He never talked about anything too personal and was especially mysterious about his family.

He assumed his usual leer. "Especially if it keeps me from boning Cherie."

Then again, maybe she'd imagined that brief moment of reflectiveness. "Why don't you just move on to someone else?"

"I would, but she's hot. Stacked, and it's all natural, I checked—"

"Okay, okay." Listening to Vader talk about women could be unnerving. "So you want to date her, but she won't go out with you because you might be a homophobe. No problem. Just prove to her that you aren't."

Vader sank into the armchair, opened a new can of Pabst Blue Ribbon, then plopped it back on the coffee table without even a taste. "I was thinking you could talk to her. Tell her I'm cool with the gays. But not actually gay. You can tell her, you know, what a stud I am."

"Excuse me?"

"It wouldn't be a lie, because I am a stud." He winked with his usual goofy-macho spirit.

"You know I don't want anyone thinking I sleep with guys at the station." One of the hazards of being a female firefighter was the dating issue. One, so nicknamed because she was the first female to join the crew, kept to herself and spent her downtime doing Sudoku. But Sabina liked hanging out with firemen. She loved the banter, the pranks, the traditions, the bets, the teasing, the back-and-forth. She admired, loved, and respected her fellow firefighters. And she was extra careful not to mess that up with sex. That's why the close call with Roman was so . . . But never mind him.

"Okay, then tell her I'm not a homophobe. Tell her I'm manly but enlightened. She won't believe me, but maybe she'll listen to you. For some reason she thinks I just want to get into her pants."

He looked so indignant that she burst into laughter. Vader, goofy but sweet to the core, never failed to entertain her.

"Sounds like Cherie's no dummy. I'll help you come up with some ways to impress her, how's that?"

A text message popped up on her phone. Max. *You can't avoid me forever,* it read. She could practically hear that rusty saw blade voice of his. *Just watch me, Max!* She ignored this text as she had the last four and reminded herself to look into changing her number.

"Come on, big guy," she told Vader, jumping to her feet. "Let's go get some very manly but enlightened pizza."

Roman arrived for his next overtime shift walking as if he had lead in his boots. It had taken him a while to reassure Luke that the whole station didn't hate him and that they didn't need to escape back to New York. And that he shouldn't fire Sabina.

"She should take back every word," Luke kept saying. "If she doesn't, I'm going to sneak into the station and put spiders in her bed."

"She's probably encountered worse. It's not easy being a female firefighter. Your mom had some stories to tell. Cut her some slack, would you? She apologized."

He had no idea why he was defending her. Clearly Sabina Jones despised him. Which was absolutely fine as long as she did her job and showed him the proper respect.

At lineup, he kept his expression hard as concrete as he surveyed the crew. Everyone was on time. Everyone looked well turned-out. No one was on his cell phone to *People* magazine setting up a photo shoot. He wondered if they got a bad rap. Once the news media got hold of something, no one could shake it loose. He'd seen enough of it after 9/11 to know.

Sabina met his gaze with a completely professional demeanor, though he thought she looked a little tired. Savagely, he hoped she'd tossed and turned all night. Her words at the restaurant had hurt more than he wanted to admit. Did he really come off as some arrogant ass?

"Okay, troops," he said when lineup was over. "More drills today. Show me how fast you can suit up in full turnout and breathers on air."

The firefighters obediently headed for the apparatus bay. As Roman strode after them, a movement caught his eye.

Firefighter Brown, the muscleman known as Vader, was whispering in Sabina's ear. Roman's hackles rose as he looked more closely at the two of them. That was no professional whisper. It was personal. Intimate. Unacceptable.

"Firefighter Brown," he barked. "Can you run a stopwatch?"

Vader looked offended. The muscles in his jaw bulged as if they had a mind of their own. "Yes, sir. Of course I can. What do you think, I can't tell time . . ."

"Sit this drill out and take this." He tossed Vader his stopwatch, which forced the guy to take a step away from Sabina. Instant relief settled over him, as if the world had turned back on its proper axis. "I'll catch more errors if I don't have to time. Come on."

Vader followed him, muttering under his breath, but Roman was too glad he'd separated him from Sabina to mind.

He reminded himself that he and Sabina despised each other. Or at least, she despised him. He could accept that, he supposed. That didn't mean he was okay with watching her get cozy with someone under his nose.

But as the day went on, he kept catching other little moments between them. Sabina and Vader were both part of the engine company. Vader was the hose man who hooked up to the hydrant, Sabina the nozzle person. They worked smoothly together—suspiciously smoothly. After one drill, performed to perfection, they took a little too long to emerge from behind Engine 1. "Jones! Brown!" He nearly went in after them with a hose. When they appeared, Sabina looked a little flushed and Vader wore a smirk. He swore he heard Vader saying something to her in French, something that sounded like an endearment.

Later, after demonstrating a new technique with the two-line rope system for rappelling during rescues, he caught Sabina whispering in Vader's ear. His hand rested intimately on her back.

A shocking, volcanic surge of irritation rocketed through Roman. He pictured himself ripping Vader away from her and tossing him through a window. Sabina would jump into his arms and cling to him, gazing up at him with lovely, adoring turquoise eyes and sighing over his manliness.

He gritted his teeth so hard he tasted blood. *Dio,* why had he let this woman get under his skin so quickly?

Forget Sabina and Vader. Firefighter romances were common. That's how he'd met Maureen, after all. Whatever they had going on, it had nothing to do with him. He was here to do a job. With a superhuman exercise of will, he erased the image of Sabina and Vader from his mind.

"Okay, let's switch gears. Let's look ahead to hazmat procedures. How many hazmat calls have you responded to here?"

The firefighters all seemed to pipe up at once.

"There was that explosion at the treatment plant . . ."

"An oil truck turned over on Highway 90, that was a mess . . ."

"What about the time Ella Joy set the turkey on fire?"

Laughter broke out, until Roman shut it down with one hand gesture. "Hazmat calls are among the most dangerous situations a firefighter can face. These days, you have to consider the possibility of terrorist involvement. They're no laughing matter."

All the smiles disappeared. *Bravo, Roman. Chief Hard-ass, bringing down the hammer. Doing the job they pay you to do.* That didn't mean it felt good.

That night Sabina woke up suddenly on her little bunk in her home away from home. She spent two to three nights a week in this room and never had trouble sleeping here. She swung her legs over the side of the bed and stuck her feet into the fuzzy slippers she kept here. Shaped like ladybugs, red with black spots, they inspired endless teasing from the guys. She called them her firebug slippers and claimed they prevented fires from breaking out at night during her shifts.

In her ribbed tank top and cotton shorts, she padded out to the hall. A light at the end of the hallway guided her in the direction of the bathroom. Someone must be in there. Too much of Ace's sweet iced tea, no doubt. They'd all guzzled it down with their fried chicken and collard greens, along with frequent toasts to Southern mothers who sent their homesick sons their family recipes.

Yawning, she leaned against the cool plaster wall of the hallway, waiting her turn in the bathroom. Finally the toilet flushed, water ran in the sink, and the door opened. The light was immediately entirely blocked by a towering figure emerging from the bathroom. It could only be Chief Roman.

Immediately Sabina snapped to attention. "Good evening, sir."

She could barely see his face, silhouetted as he was against the light from the bathroom, but it seemed as though his mouth twitched in a smile.

"Buona sera."

"Buona sera," she repeated.

He gave a visible start. "You speak Italian?"

"Not at all." *Crap.* Her knack for accents always came back to bite her at the wrong moments.

"Are you sure?"

"Absolutely. Are you finished in there?"

"Yes. Sorry." He came forward, holding the bathroom door open for her. As she passed him, she surreptitiously scanned him from head to toe, hoping to God he didn't notice how she devoured every detail of his nighttime wear. His loose drawstring pants hung low on his hips, revealing the taut, pale-skinned valley between his hipbones. His stomach muscles marched in double formation up his long, long torso. Her tongue tingled. How she'd love to put it just there, at the point of his hipbone, and go for a wild roller-coaster ride up his spectacular musculature.

She dragged her eyes away before he caught on to her completely inappropriate lust.

He looked embarrassed. "I'm not used to the heat here yet. I always seem to want to take something off."

That didn't help her temperature one bit. *Thanks a lot, mister.*

"Don't worry about it," she mumbled, imagining him taking off his one remaining piece of clothing—his pants.

Once inside the brightly lit bathroom, she turned to smile her thanks and caught him doing exactly what she'd been doing one moment earlier. Checking her out. His gaze seemed to be trapped by the stretch of bare skin between her shorts and her top.

Then he snapped his eyes up to meet hers. His jaw was black with stubble. A crease on one cheek showed how he must have been sleeping.

"Good night, Sabina." He nodded formally, as if they were at a ball. She almost curtsied back.

"Good night, Chief—"

"Roman's fine."

"Roman."

He left, closing the door behind him. She slumped onto the toilet, the sound of his voice saying her first name echoing in her mind.

Chapter Seven

The next morning, as the early relief guys were showing up, Roman passed by the apparatus bay, where two of the crew, Stud and Psycho, were checking their equipment.

"Everyone knows him and Two are hot for each other," Psycho was saying.

Roman went dead still. Was Psycho talking about him? Had the crew already picked up on the tension between him and Sabina? And . . . *was* she still "hot" for him?

"That's a load of baloney," said Fred. "They're just friends."

"Oh yeah? I heard they were making out in the backseat of the pumper. Pumper. Get it?"

Roman frowned. They couldn't be talking about him. He hadn't gone near the pumper.

"You're lying. Two would never do that."

"What, does ickle Fweddy have a crush on the

pwetty girl?" Psycho, whose name suited his insanely bright blue eyes, made girly faces at Fred.

"I don't!"

Roman smiled. Of course Fred the Stud had a crush on Sabina. It was a common condition at Station 1.

"Why wouldn't you? She's hot. Did you see her doing Pilates in the workout room? I wanted to crawl onto that mat and sex her up, Psycho-style. Talk about working your core . . . ooh, yeah, baby . . . lift and tighten . . ."

Roman knew ruthless goading when he heard it, but Fred had an unbroken record of falling for a tease.

"Don't talk about her that way! She's not like that!" The clatter of equipment being tossed to the floor told Roman it was time for the hard-ass to step in.

When Roman strode into the bay, Psycho had his hand on Fred's forehead and was laughing as Fred wheeled his feet helplessly, unable to get close. Psycho dropped his hand as soon as he spotted Roman. Fred staggered.

"What's going on here?" asked Roman in the voice that had terrified ten years' worth of Brooklyn probies.

Fred scrambled to his feet. "Psycho was . . ." Fred sputtered, then went silent. Clearly he didn't want to mention Sabina.

Roman turned to Psycho, who he knew to be an excellent firefighter with a dangerous taste for living on the edge. Tattoos covered his torso and upper arms; he was a battling-his-demons type. Roman could relate, except for the tattoos. "Psycho?"

"It was my fault, Chief. I was speaking inappropriately about two of my fellow firefighters. It would be entirely understandable if you elect to administer punishment."

Oh yeah. And the guy had most of a psychology degree from Princeton.

Roman raised an eyebrow. "Just out of curiosity, what punishment would you consider appropriate?"

Psycho's brilliant blue eyes flashed in surprise. He gave a resentful shrug.

"I overheard the word 'Pilates.' Maybe a Pilates demonstration for the crew would be a good start."

Psycho choked out an extremely reluctant "Yes, sir." Hatred radiated from him in near-visible waves.

"And Stud?"

"Yes?" The kid's face was contorted from the effort to hold back his laughter.

"Come with me. I have a job for you."

Roman ushered Fred out of the apparatus bay. The youngster skipped alongside in a way that reminded Roman of Luke. "Chief, I just wanted to make him shut up, I wasn't going to hurt him. But he was saying things he shouldn't. I don't know why he gets like that . . ."

"It's okay, Stud. You were defending your fellow firefighter. I have no problem with that."

"So you heard what he said? It's a lie, Chief." Fred seemed to have forgotten where they were. His voice rose passionately. "Two and Vader are just friends. She never goes out with guys from the station, she always swore she wouldn't and I believe her no matter what they say . . ."

He snapped his mouth shut as they rounded the corner into the training room and caught sight of Sabina perched on the couch.

Too late. Obviously she'd overheard him; a slow wave of pink traveled up her cheeks. She looked sleepy-eyed and groggy. Steam rose from the coffee mug gripped tightly in her hand. Stan leaned his head against her knee in a state of apparent bliss.

An awkward silence encompassed the three of them. Roman couldn't read her expression. Curious?

Furious? She must hate being the subject of rumors. Her hands tightened around the mug. A glance at Fred told him the kid had gone a painful red.

Finally Sabina summoned a bright smile. "This coffee tastes different. *Good* different. I can actually swallow it for once. I was trying to find Ace to tell him so. Anyone seen him?"

"I made the coffee," said Roman brusquely. The rookie, Ace, had yet to brew a decent pot. Unable to stomach his sludge one more time, Roman had brought in the best Italian roast the Lavazza exporters could provide.

Sabina's eyes widened. "*You* did?"

"I can put up with a lot, but not bad coffee." Or with the way Sabina kept throwing him off balance. He couldn't afford to be off balance. He had to do something about it. "Fred, have yourself a cup. Jones, in my office, please."

Roman shut the door behind her with a sharp click.

Sabina assumed an at-ease military posture, her hands clasped behind her back. Roman looked about as happy as a granite cliff. His usual firehouse expression, in other words. He'd been different in Reno. More relaxed, more sociable, more attractive . . .

She watched him cross his arms over his massive chest. Even under his shirt she could see the muscles of his upper arms flex.

No. His attractiveness level hadn't changed one bit. If anything, it had increased in the short time she'd known him. The sight of him walking into the training room, with fresh stubble on his jaw and his black hair a tiny bit sleep-mussed, had nearly knocked her off the couch. She hadn't even noticed Fred, until he'd turned red as a maraschino cherry. Whatever they'd been talking about, it must have been embarrassing.

The chief cleared his throat. "Romances between firefighters are bad for station morale."

A shock wave of heat flashed through her. *Firefighter romances.* Why was he bringing that up?

"Yes, sir," she answered faintly.

"I checked department policy. There are no rules against it."

Good Lord, was he talking about the two of them? Her heartbeat picked up speed, as if she were headed into the first curve on a roller coaster. Was he was going to ask her out? "That's true. There aren't."

If he did ask, what would she say? Did she want to go out with him? How quickly would they end up in bed together? The constant nearness of Roman had rattled her nerves and disturbed her sleep all night. The only relief had come when they'd been called out on a fire. At least it had distracted her from Roman's magnetic presence and midnight eyes.

And now he was talking about firefighters dating.

When he opened his mouth to speak again, she blurted, "Yes."

"Yes. That's your answer?" If anything, his expression looked even grimmer. It occurred to her he'd never asked her a question. Her face flamed.

"It might be," she said cautiously. "That depends."

His black eyebrows drew together like the wings of a crow. He rubbed his forehead. "In Reno you told me you were unattached."

Her mind raced. Why was he talking about that? It had to be the preface to an invitation. But he didn't act like a man trying to ask a woman out—more like a man trying to get a hairball out of his throat.

"That's true."

"True that you told me that, or true that you're unattached?"

Suddenly the whole thing felt like a trap. All her highly developed wariness kicked in.

"Chief Roman, may I ask why you're asking about my personal life?"

He reacted as though to a slap on the face. Matching her stance for stance, he locked his hands behind his back and nodded, suddenly all business. "Yes, you may. The reason is this. If you choose to get involved with another member of your company, think hard about all the ramifications and the potential for trouble. If you want Captain Kelly to change your shift or your assignment, he will do so. Obviously, we can't forbid you to date a fellow firefighter. But since I'm charged with bringing discipline to this fire station, I'm asking you to be discreet."

Sabina felt a wave of mortification sweep from her head to her toes. The man wasn't asking her out. Of course not. What was she thinking? There *were* rules against firefighters of different ranks dating. As a Battalion Chief, he was her superior. What an idiot she was. Good Lord, he was probably talking about *Vader*. Everyone knew they were just friends.

Everyone but the new guys.

She flashed back to the bit of conversation Roman and Fred had been having when they'd walked into the training room. She'd been too busy ogling Roman to decipher it. They'd been talking about her. She was used to it, of course, but somehow it felt different with Roman involved. What did he think, that she slept around? With her fellow firemen? Then again, she nearly had, in Reno.

She drew herself up to her most correct, most

military posture, spine straight, jaw jutting forward. "Chief Roman, this conversation is completely uncalled for. You should know not to listen to firehouse gossip. I have a strict policy against dating fellow firefighters."

He rubbed his jaw. "So, in Reno . . ."

"I didn't know you were a firefighter. It wasn't a date. And besides, we . . . well, we didn't."

"True. Good thing, too," he said thoughtfully, though his narrowed, sidelong look suggested something different.

A vision of Roman, chest bared, hands on his belt buckle, flashed through her brain. "Good, yes," she agreed, her voice only a tiny bit squeaky. She cleared her throat. "Satisfied?"

"Mmm," he answered, although she didn't think "satisfied" quite described his expression. He looked more as if he'd stumbled into a very confusing hornet's nest. She jumped on the opportunity to take him off guard.

"Answer me this, Roman. Why don't you cook for the firehouse? You can cook circles around most of us."

One eyebrow lifted. "Most?"

Sabina raised her chin. "Hoagie used to make a pretty good Thai curry."

A gleam of interest flashed in Roman's eyes. "Sorry I missed that."

"You haven't answered the question," Sabina said, after a short silence.

Roman looked away, fussing with some paperwork on the desk. "I don't have an answer. Cooking is . . . well, it's . . . personal."

She watched, fascinated by his embarrassment, as he straightened a pile of folders, placed a paperweight on top, glanced over at Stan's empty dog bed.

"What about cooking at La Piaggia? That's not very personal."

His head swung up, fire in his eyes. "It certainly was. I took that arrabiata atrocity very personally. How any self-respecting restaurant could serve something one step removed from ketchup and call it— Are you laughing at me?"

"No, sir." Sabina pressed her lips together to keep away the smile that wanted to spread across her face. Roman might be intimidatingly huge and powerful, but right now, he was . . . well, adorable. "I just think it might help the crew warm up to you a little if you cooked for them."

He straightened to his full height and glowered at her. "Why would I want that?"

"No reason. Just station morale. Teamwork. That sort of thing."

"Discipline. Authority. Respect. That's what I care about." Each word dropped from his mouth like a heat-guided missile.

Someone knocked on the door. "Come in," Roman barked, all trace of the passionate defender of arrabiata gone. Fred poked his head in, Stan worming his way between his feet. The dog headed for his corner after an indignant look at the two humans keeping him from his morning nap. "Psycho says his Pilates demo is about to start."

Roman gave a sharp nod. "Discipline," he repeated as he ushered her out the door. As she passed in front of him, she could have sworn he winked.

A warm, fizzy feeling spread through her, as if at any moment a hot air balloon might lift her off the ground.

That delicious state of mind disappeared the instant her shift ended and she spotted the beige Mercedes parked in front of the fire station. A man leaned out the window and called to her in his three-pack-a-day voice, "Munchkin! Over here."

She skidded to a stop. *"Max?* What are you doing here?"

"We need to talk."

"You shouldn't be here." She looked desperately over her shoulder, where the other members of her shift were beginning to filter out of the station. How did he know where she worked? How had he found her, and why?

Max grinned at her, his white capped teeth gleaming in the sunshine. "Better get in if you don't want anyone to see you."

"This is kidnapping."

"Semantics, my little munchkin." His raspy laugh sounded like coffee percolating. "You look fabulous, by the way. I always told them they should let you grow up on the—"

Sabina yelped and ran to the passenger side. "Don't say anything. I'll get in if you shut up until I say you can talk."

"Your wish is my command. Haven't I always done whatever you asked? Didn't I get you that tutor—?"

"Shut up!"

Max cackled and put the Mercedes into drive. It purred forward like a beige panther in heat. Sabina ducked down to avoid the openmouthed stares of the B shift.

"Sorry for the ambush. You forced me into it. Bad idea, ignoring my calls and texts. A power player like me isn't used to that."

Sabina cursed at him, using every inventive swearword she'd picked up during ten years on the fire lines.

Max cocked his head, showing off the sculpted

waves of his artificially chestnut toupee. "Now *that* I am used to."

Sabina peered out the window and saw they'd put a healthy distance between them and the firehouse. She sat up. "Okay, what's the deal, Max? This is completely out of line. How'd you even find me?"

Max gave her a thorough, appreciative once-over. "I have to hand it to you, Sabina. I wouldn't have recognized you if I didn't know better. Where's the adorable imp Taffy McGee, that chubby mischief maker, the modern-day Shirley Temple with curls like morning sunshine, according to *USA Today*? See how I still know all your reviews? My God. The most famous child actress in America, hiding in plain sight in a California firehouse. Who'da thunk it?"

Chapter Eight

She should have known. *She should have known.* Of course ignoring a manipulative Hollywood agent wouldn't make him leave her alone. "What do you want, Max?"

"I take it your Bachelor Firemen don't know who you are? Love the concept, by the way. Bachelor Firemen. Mmm. I bet Lifetime would snap that up in a second."

Desperation ate at Sabina's gut. "If I promise to play nice, will you forget about the station? My life has nothing to do with Hollywood anymore. And I don't want them knowing. Please, Max. You were never an asshole. Well, you were, but not about everything."

"Make sure you put that on my tombstone," he said in a dry rasp. *"Here lies an asshole, but not about everything.* Where can I take you out to lunch that won't blow your cover?"

Sabina played with the end of her braid. The feel of

it grounded her; as Taffy, she'd always had short curls. "We'll have to get out of San Gabriel. And I have to be back by three." Today she was taking Carly, her "Little Sister," to baseball practice, but that information was off-limits to Max. "Mind driving to Camino Ranch?"

"What's another hour on the freeway?"

"I'm going to nap until we get there. I just got off a twenty-four-hour shift and I don't have the strength for this."

"Go right ahead, munchkin. When you wake up I'll ply you with sweets like the old days. Hello, darling." She started, until she realized he was now talking into his Bluetooth. He ought to get a phone chip implanted in his brain.

She tilted her seat back and closed her eyes. Max's rocks-on-chalkboard voice was surprisingly soothing. Max had always been decent to her, in a half-assed, when-it-suited-him kind of way. For years he'd been the next best thing to family. And sometimes more reliable than Annabelle, who had a bad habit of falling for hot new directors and forgetting she had a daughter. Being with Max now felt kind of . . . nostalgic. As long as he didn't mess with her new life, she could handle him.

When she woke up, they were outside the La Farfalla Bistro in Camino Ranch. Little white ironwork chairs and tables were scattered under a green canopy. She scanned the early lunch crowd for familiar faces. When she spotted no one from San Gabriel, she relaxed. "Good choice, Max. Thanks."

Over Arnold Palmers and chopped salads, her former agent finally got to the point. "Your mother has hired me to revive her career."

"I thought she was living in Paris."

"She's coming back. The Turkish director dumped her."

Sabina shoved aside the familiar pang of worry. She'd been through enough of Annabelle's breakups to know what happened next: some fabulous new project that would consume her life—and her daughter's. Not this time. "If anyone can get her career going again, you can. Have you found something for her?"

He put up a hand and made her wait while he wiped salad dressing off his cheek.

"Your manners haven't improved even a little, have they?"

He shrugged, totally unconcerned. Max Winkler's hyperactive brain could engineer a multiparty, multimillion-dollar Hollywood deal, but it had no neurons to spare for mundane details like table manners.

Sabina concentrated on buttering her roll while he washed down a huge mouthful of salad with iced tea. Maybe this wasn't so bad, going out to lunch at a fancy bistro, the kind of place she used to go with her mother. "You know, I always thought Annabelle should do some kind of independent film to really show her range, you know? Everyone still sees her as Peg McGee, but she's so much more than that. She needs to play an older woman who becomes obsessed with a younger man, or a crusading Irish mother of ten trying to end the IRA bombings, or maybe a nun, she'd be a great nun. She could out-nun Meryl Streep any day of the week—"

Max rapped on the table, making her jump.

"Who's the Hollywood genius here, munchkin? And who's the girl who turned her back on fame and fortune?"

He leaned forward, quivering like a gerbil on the hunt.

"Two words, Sabina. Reunion show."

Sabina's jaw dropped. A sort of paralysis gripped

her, as if she was in one of those dreams where no matter how hard she screamed, no sounds issued from her mouth. The clatter of dishes at nearby tables, the valley-girl cadence of the waitress—"You still working on that?"—filled the sudden silence.

"What?" she asked, or tried to. Only a whisper trickled from her lips.

"I know exactly what you're thinking. You're thinking where would we get a script, what director would be interested, would CBS even go for a reunion show."

She shook her head, helpless to stop his flow of words. She was thinking none of those things. Her thoughts were more along the lines of whether it was too early for a double vodka tonic.

"Well, Uncle Max has been busting his nuts on this project. *You and Me* was groundbreaking in its time, but now everyone's doing the dramedy thing, so what better time to bring you, your mother, and the other principals back together? I've got Sean Flaherty working on a script, and so far he's knocking it out of the park, baby. Did you know Taffy's a single mother too now? You married a rodeo star and traveled the circuit with him while you raised your adorable little munchkin, Tyler. Sadly, your husband got gored, off camera of course and now it's Taffy and Tyler against the world. You're only visiting your mom for Christmas—did I mention it's a Christmas reunion show? That's like the trifecta wet dream of TV shows. We'll set it up for follow-up shows, of course, if the ratings are good. And they will be. Your mom still gets fan mail for you two."

Sabina couldn't make the nightmare stop. She stood up, knocking her iron filigree chair backward onto the flagstones. The crash made everyone in the restaurant look their way. She placed her hands on the table and leaned in. "How can we have a reunion show when we haven't even *had a reunion*? I haven't seen or spoken to my mother in over ten years."

"Munchkin. Don't be dramatic. Sit down and eat your lunch."

"I'll be in the car." She put her sunglasses on and stepped over the hedge that separated the seating area from the sidewalk. The Mercedes, of course, was locked. Fine. She'd window shop until Max got his ass out here. Gulping deep breaths of air, she stared blindly at a display of gadgets in an electronics store.

"You're not thinking this through." His caustic, screeching-gears voice came from just behind her.

She turned to face him. She needed to put a stop to this. Now.

"I'm not an actress anymore, Max. I'm a firefighter. I put out fires. Save lives. Risk my life. I've worked like a dog to make my life here and I'm *not* giving it up."

He picked up on her serious tone. "It's just one show. Two hours of prime time. It's for your mother. One show, and then you can walk away."

"I already walked away. And it cost me nearly a million dollars. Have you forgotten I signed all my earnings over to her? I'm not going back. Ever."

"But munchkin, how can we do a reunion show without you?"

"Get creative. Taffy died in the same rodeo accident that killed her husband. Grieving Peg McGee befriends a young neighbor who happens to be a single mother with a little boy. Or lo and behold, the baby she gave up for adoption before Taffy was ever born comes looking for her mother. You're the Hollywood genius, remember?"

"Yeah, but those ain't bad." Max gave her a look of sneaking respect. "You're wasted on a fire engine."

"No, I'm not. I'm a damn good firefighter." She

clung to the thought. Firefighter Jones, that's who she was now. Affectionately known as Two. Much as she hated that nickname, she'd pick "Two" over "Taffy" in a white-hot second.

"Hmm." Max scratched his chin. "Problem is, CBS won't do it without you."

"What?"

"I told 'em you weren't available, but they say no Taffy, no show. Most of the fan mail's for you, chickie. America loved Taffy McGee. So did Poland and Thailand, but that's just icing on the cupcake. They want to know what happened to you. You left so suddenly and barely gave the writers a chance to cobble together a storyline that made sense."

"I was growing half an inch a month. They had to bring in a body double."

"I know, I know."

"And I needed out. I'm not going to apologize any more for that."

"I get it. No apologies needed. But are you going to deep-six your mom's big comeback and, by the way, pass up a million-dollar payday, for your precious fires?"

She spun around and marched toward the Mercedes. "Take me back, Max, we're done. I'm not doing it."

"Just think about it."

"If you mention it again, I'll call CBS myself and tell them to fuck off." She brandished her phone. "I still have contacts."

"Fine, fine. Just tell me you'll think about it."

"I'll think about what an asshole you are, how's that?"

"It's a start."

Carly was waiting on her front steps, baseball glove in hand, when Sabina drove up. She raced to the passenger door and hopped in with the car still rolling.

"Hey."

"Hey."

Carly's ponytail hung over her shoulder in rich, fudge-colored waves. She was some mixture of black, Irish, and Mexican, Sabina had never determined precisely. Reserved, quiet, given to occasional moments of explosive fury, she'd crawled into Sabina's heart the very first day the Big Brothers Big Sisters program had matched them four years ago, when Carly was nine.

"Home situation as usual?" Sabina asked as she steered her El Camino away from the curb.

"Hangover's right on schedule."

"How much longer do you give the boyfriend?"

One slim shoulder hunched. "Couple months. She really likes him. But he's a loser. She knows it."

Sometimes Sabina thought the parallels between their lives were eerie, even though their worlds were completely different. Did it matter if the boyfriend was a Turkish film director or a truck driver, if the same broken heart resulted? "Sorry."

Carly didn't answer. She didn't like talking about her family, and Sabina didn't push her. As a "Big Sister," her role wasn't to interfere but to provide other experiences and influences to Carly. They'd done all kinds of things—seen *Wicked*, gone to the state fair, attended the *Nutcracker*, attempted ice skating—but more than anything, Carly wanted to play baseball. She was so good, she'd won a spot on a co-ed team and played alongside some wickedly skilled boys. Lately, Sabina's role in her life had mostly revolved around practices.

Sabina sped through the sunny streets of San Gabriel toward Los Feliz Park. She listened to the hoarse roar of her El Camino, so different from Max's purring Mercedes. This was the soundtrack of her life now—rough and real. She loved the life she'd created here because it had nothing artificial in it. She did real things here. Fought fire. Hung out with real guys who weren't playing a part. Helped out a girl who needed her.

Why did the past have to come back and threaten all that? Damn Max anyway.

Carly didn't seem to mind her distracted silence. When they reached the park, she shot out of the car. "You'll be in the stands, right?" she called over her shoulder.

"You know it."

Sabina made her way toward the bleachers around the field. She waved and smiled at a few parents. She spotted Diane, a single mother whose son played second base, and clambered across knees and purses to sit next to her.

Diane waved and pointed to her ear. She was talking into her headset—she sold real estate and spent every practice on a constant series of calls. Sabina watched lazily as the players did their pregame warm-ups. The sun beat down on her forehead, urging her eyes to close. She put both elbows on the bench behind her and leaned back, tilting her face to the warmth. Everything would be okay. She'd escaped from Hollywood once already. She'd figure it out. She'd get used to Chief Roman. Their awkward history would be ancient history before long. Everything would be fine.

Diane's voice penetrated her consciousness. "All right, doll face. Let's have lunch tomorrow. Holy Mother of Pearl, who the crap is that?"

Sabina thought she was on her call until Diane poked her in the ribs. She sat up with a start. A tall man in jeans was striding toward the field, one arm slung around the shoulder of a tall kid in uniform. Make that a huge man. Make that—what kind of freakishly awful luck did she have?—Chief Roman.

He wore sunglasses and a simple black T-shirt speckled with white paint.

She suddenly remembered him talking about his son at the Starlight. That's why they'd moved here . . . for the year-round baseball.

For the first time since she'd arrived in San Gabriel, she considered the possibility that the station actually *was* cursed. Or at least she was.

With a knot forming in her stomach, she watched the pair stroll to the coach and engage in a long discussion. The boy looked wide-eyed and eager, his sandy hair standing up on end. The last time she'd seen him, he'd looked horrified by her thoughtless words.

"That's . . . um . . ."

"Wait, you *know* him? It was more of a rhetorical question." Diane was staring at Roman as if he were dancing naked on the pitcher's mound. "That is one incredible-looking man, if you like them dark and hulking. Is he single? Where'd he come from? Who *is* he?"

"He's, well, actually, he's . . ." Before she could finish, Roman looked into the stands and went still. With his sunglasses on, she couldn't tell if he'd seen her or not. But he must have, because after he finished with the coach, he gave his son a squeeze on the shoulder and took the steps two at a time until he reached her row.

"Firefighter Jones," he murmured. "Baseball fan?"

"I . . . uh . . . mentor a girl on the team. Carly. She's the pitcher."

He raised his eyebrows; black swoops above his sunglasses. "This could be interesting then. My son's got a helluva curveball."

Sabina bristled. "Carly's fastball's been clocked at seventy miles an hour. Fastest of any girl in Southern California."

"Like I said, this should be interesting. Luke wants a spot on the roster, but he's got to earn it."

"Carly's been working for this since she was nine," Sabina said hotly.

"Then he'll have some competition."

Next to her, Diane's head whipped back and forth between them. "No need to get worked up over it," she said. "Why don't you sit down, mysterious stranger?"

Roman hesitated. Then shook his head. "Luke and I have a tradition. I need to sit in a certain spot, ever since he hit three home runs in one game."

"Then we'll . . ."

Sabina tugged at Diane's arm. "Enjoy the practice. I hope your son does well."

He nodded and made his way past them, down the top row to the far end. Sabina knew this because Diane gave her a blow-by-blow account, using her sunglasses as a mirror.

"Let him be. He's my new training officer," Sabina hissed.

"At the station? That's just not fair. You already work with the hottest guys in town, and now him?"

"You're welcome to him. As far as I know, he's unattached."

"You're nuts. Single, gorgeous, sexy father, and heroic fireman. You sure that's not worth breaking a few rules?" Luckily, another real estate call came in. Sabina blocked out the sound of "two bedroom, one bath" and focused on the field.

Carly and Luke were put on opposite sides for the practice. Carly's side took the field first. As she stepped onto the pitcher's mound, she looked nervous. She couldn't seem to find the strike zone until the third batter, but once she had two players on base she settled down and threw two strikeouts and fielded a feeble grounder for the third out.

Sabina couldn't help it. She turned and tossed a triumphant told-you-so glance in Roman's direction. He gave her a thumbs-up and a nod of respect. At least he wasn't a poor sport.

The teams switched, and Luke took the mound. Sabina searched for similarities to Roman and found them in his height and a certain confident—bordering on arrogant—presence. But his sandy, gold-streaked hair and wide smile must have come from somewhere else. He looked excited enough to bounce off the field. He exchanged a few practice pitches with the catcher, trying to get his rhythm. He looked into the stands a few times, always relaxing when he saw his father.

Sabina wondered how many times father and son had done this. Many, she guessed, with a sudden pang. Her own father was a struggling actor who'd signed away his rights without regret. She'd seen him a few times, growing up, until he'd gotten married to a powerful agent who wanted a family of her own. No more daddy outings after that.

Even as little as she knew Roman, she couldn't imagine him ever signing away custody of his son.

Luke's first pitch was a fastball. At least, it looked like a fastball until it swerved at the last second, leaving poor Jack Cassen lurching into the dirt, bat spinning down the foul line.

Every player on both teams went quiet and alert. The coach's eyes goggled. A buzz spread through the stands.

The next pitch caught the outer edge of the strike zone, but it went so fast Jack never even swung. One pitch later and Jack trudged back to his teammates.

Sabina searched for Carly, who looked shell-shocked. She got up and grabbed a bat, practicing her swing in case she got a turn. She batted fourth.

No such luck. The first three players went down in about five minutes.

Sabina dared a glance back at Roman. He showed no reaction, no cheering or gloating.

Carly looked fired up when it was her turn to pitch again. Sabina had never seen her hurl the ball with so much focus and fire. But the players knew her pitches and managed a hit and a walk before she shut them down.

Good going, Carly. Keep your cool. One pitch at a time, Sabina chanted under her breath. When Carly trotted off the field, she looked fairly pleased with herself. She glanced up at Sabina, who clapped her hands and whistled enthusiastically.

Carly was up first. She let the first few pitches pass, assessing Luke's style, trying to get a feel for the new pitcher. Sabina's heart was in her throat. Watching a kid play carried a lot of stress. No wonder some parents lost it. She stole another look at Roman. He leaned forward, elbows on knees, watching from behind his sunglasses. The sun glinted in his dark hair, picking out bits of deep brown in the thick waves.

Gah. She yanked her attention back to the field.

Carly balanced on the balls of her feet, drew her bat over her shoulder, stared down the line at the mound. When the next pitch came in, she pounced. The sharp crack of aluminum on leather echoed through the air. The ball zoomed straight at Luke, who was still in the downswing of his pitch. Sabina jumped to her feet. The crowd of parents roared.

Luke stretched to his full height, caught the ball after one bounce, vaulted to his feet, and raced to first base. He launched himself toward Carly and touched one flying heel with his glove before rolling back onto the ground, the ball still in his grip.

Carly stumbled but continued her headlong rush to first base. Even when the umpire signaled she was out, she clung to the base, arguing her case. Finally she got to her feet, angrily brushing the dirt off her shorts. Luke trotted next to her, as if checking to make sure she was okay. She ignored him, instead breaking into a run to rejoin her teammates.

Luke shrugged and veered back toward the mound. The inning ended two batters later.

Sabina sank back to her seat. Diane ended her call. "What happened? What'd I miss?"

"Nothing yet, but something's off. Carly's not usually like this." She glanced over her shoulder at Roman, who was watching the field closely, eyebrows drawn together in an ominous frown. He shifted his head slightly to look her direction. A wordless flow of communication passed between them. *Keep your eyes open for trouble.* Along with a substantial dash of: *You sure look good in civilian clothes.*

Chapter Nine

Roman didn't like the way Luke's first practice was shaping up. He was proud of Luke, who was pitching his usual stellar game. But the girl pitcher, Carly, though extremely talented, seemed to have some issues around sportsmanship. When she pitched to Luke, her fastball veered right at his head. Luke would have been beaned if he didn't have incredible reflexes. She didn't even look apologetic. He didn't blame her for being rattled.

Sabina looked worried too. No matter how hard he tried, he couldn't stop checking on her every few minutes. Her hair gleamed honey-bright in the afternoon sun. Her braid flowed down her narrow back like an intricate tawny river. She wore a tight sky-blue top that showed off her graceful, toned shoulders. He knew how strong she was from the drills. Strong, fast, lean, capable. She could spring into action quick as a leopard when she had to. But here, on her day off, she was simply a sexy woman and he couldn't take his eyes off her.

Good thing he'd given in and acquired sunglasses.

The crowd oohed, and he realized he'd missed a play. Luke and Carly, bat in hand, circled each other halfway between the pitcher's mound and the batter's box. What had happened? Had Luke returned the favor and brushed her back?

Then, so quickly he barely caught it, all hell broke loose. The bat flew out of Carly's hand, Luke tossed his glove, and Carly took a swing at Luke, who grabbed her arm to stop the blow. Horrified, Roman surged to his feet as everything seemed to shift into slow motion. The bat went winging across the grass. The coach went running toward the two kids. The two kids yelled at each other and grappled awkwardly, as if trying not to actually fight. The coach shouted at them as he closed in, then suddenly he flipped up into the air, arms and legs flailing wildly.

What the hell? Roman squinted at the field. *The ball.* The coach had slipped on the ball. He landed with a hard thump on his butt. Then the bat, which had been bouncing across the field, hit something—Luke's glove?—and boomeranged onto the poor man's thigh.

The coach held his leg and yelled, very loudly, a word most definitely not approved by the co-ed Little League.

The entire crowd leaped to their feet, shouting. Luke and Carly, still locked in their battle, hadn't seemed to notice their coach's disaster.

Roman jumped off the side of the bleachers, landing with a heavy thud, and ran toward the field. He didn't think twice about running into the thick of it. A good firefighter was never really off duty. He spotted Sabina running from the opposite side of the bleachers. "I'll deal with the kids, you take the coach," he called to her.

She shot him a burning look, but didn't argue. Roman ran to the two screaming kids, reached in, and plucked them apart, one in each hand. Both were red-faced and out of breath.

"What the hell happened?" Roman said in a dangerously low voice. Luke pressed his lips together and refused to answer. He turned to Carly, whose eyes filled with tears.

"Nothing! He . . . he . . ." She swiped a shaky arm across her face. "Nothing."

"Nothing? Is that why your coach is flat on his back over there?" He gestured toward the man. Sabina crouched over him, assessing his condition. She gently rotated his leg, listening attentively to his responses. Roman watched with appreciation. She clearly knew what she was doing.

"Oh shit," whispered Carly. "I killed the coach."

"You didn't kill him. But you could have. What kind of a bonehead move was that, throwing a bat and attacking someone on your own team?"

"Papa."

"You two are a mess and Lord knows what's wrong with the coach . . ."

"Papa!" He looked at Luke to find his son glaring at him. "It was just a fight. It was my fault too. Leave her alone."

Carly didn't seem to appreciate Luke's gesture. With a snort of disgust, she turned away from them and headed toward Sabina, who was helping the coach to his feet.

"No big harm done," Sabina announced to the crowd of players and families. "No concussion, a little bruised, but nothing an ice pack can't cure. To be safe,

I've called an ambulance to take him to the ER. But I think he'll be just fine."

Everyone applauded in relief. The coach gave a little bow, then winced. "This doesn't get you out of the team meeting at Chili's. Mandatory discussion topic will be the fact that we're all on the same side. Jimbo will lead. And many thanks to Sabina Jones and the San Gabriel Fire Department."

Another round of applause. Roman glanced sidelong at Sabina, who waved off the cheers and helped the coach toward the sidelines. She'd handled the situation well, coolly, capably, professionally. Not that he was surprised, but damn, he'd enjoyed seeing her in action.

Roman steered his shaken son off the field. "We're making friends left and right here in San Gabriel," he said under his breath.

At Chili's, a chain Mexican restaurant with plastic cactuses and waiters in sombreros, Jimbo, the coach's assistant, stuffed all the players in a big corner booth and launched into a lecture about sportsmanship. The parents pulled a few tables together and discussed the drama. Sabina's friend kept asking Roman questions, but he evaded her, waiting for Sabina to show up. As soon as he spotted her walking through the door, with that graceful, long-legged stride, he jerked his head toward the bar in the other room.

When she joined him, after updating the others on the coach's condition, he had a shot of tequila waiting for her.

"Luke never fights. Never," he said after downing his. "What the hell happened?"

Sabina raised her chin. It occurred to him that, unlike most people, she'd never once shown signs of being intimidated by him. "No clue. Carly fights, but not during baseball. It's always been her safe haven."

"Same for Lukey."

Their eyes met. An electromagnetic pull pulsed to life between them, as if a cone of intimacy closed around the two of them. "That's the way firefighting is for me," he said, surprising himself. He never talked about personal things like that.

"Me too." She tilted her head, catching light from a chain of chili pepper twinkle lights dangling over the bar. Even their dim red glow flattered her. "I never feel completely right outside the fire station."

"What made you become a firefighter?" He regretted the impulsive question as soon as he'd asked it, because her whimsical smile instantly hardened into a wary shield.

"Why do you ask?"

"Curiosity. For me it was a family tradition."

One corner of her mouth rose, as if she was laughing at some secret irony. "Kind of the opposite, for me. I . . . uh . . . I was at work, at my old job. A fire broke out, and some firefighters showed up and put it out in about two seconds. It made my . . . well, my former job . . . look pretty pointless. This was right after 9/11, and—" She broke off. He realized, with a chill, that she knew his history. Of course she did; news traveled fast from station to station.

"And you felt the call," he finished for her.

"Yes. I quit soon after and enrolled in the academy."

"Our gain," he said, tilting his shot glass her direction. Her face lit up, creating a warm glow in the pit of his stomach.

"To fighting fires," he said, draining the last drop.

"And stopping brawls," she added. They both tipped their glasses, gazes meeting over the rims.

"Papa." Luke tugged at his elbow.

"Yeah, son."

"What are you doing talking to *her*?" Luke glared at Sabina.

"Great game." Sabina smiled tentatively, her cheeks turning an adorable pink.

"*Great game?* That was the worst game ever."

Just then Carly rounded the corner of the bar, stopping short at the sight of Luke.

"What are you talking to *them* for?"

"Carly!" Sabina shot her a glare, but Carly flounced away, her long brown ponytail flying behind her.

Sabina sighed. "I better go."

Roman prodded Luke until he said a sullen goodbye.

"That's two strikes against her," Luke hissed after Sabina had left, the restaurant suddenly dingy and dull without her. "The Italian place and that girl."

"You're not the umpire here, buddy," said Roman sharply, though it beat him why he felt the need to come to Sabina's defense. "And you have a lot of explaining to do."

No matter how hard he tried, Roman couldn't pry the whole story out of Luke, who wouldn't say a word against Carly. "You wouldn't understand," he kept saying. But when Roman suggested switching to another team, Luke flatly refused. Roman finally gave up and took him to Home Depot to pick out lumber for a new bed, the movers having destroyed his old one. They spent the evening measuring boards and drilling screw holes. The French doors stood wide open and the scent of orange blossom floated through.

"If you consider man-hours, it would be much cheaper to get you a bed at IKEA," Roman observed.

"That's no fun. You always make my beds."

"Yep. From cradle on up. When you go to college, you're on your own."

"She's pretty," said Luke, his head bent over the measuring tape.

"Huh?" Roman had a feeling he knew exactly who Luke was talking about.

"The one at Chili's."

Roman glanced sharply at Luke. They'd never discussed this sort of thing before. There had never been much cause; he'd kept his involvements few, far between, and secret. "Firefighter Jones. I suppose she is. Not that pretty comes into play on the fire lines."

Luke stretched out the metal tape, then let it snap back into the casing. "My mom was pretty. She was a firefighter."

"True enough. Why do you mention that?"

"I don't know. You looked different with her. Kind of . . . never mind."

"Kind of what?"

Luke scratched his face with the metal end of the tape measure. "Don't take this wrong, Papa, but usually you look kind of mean."

Roman brandished his cordless drill with a terrifying scowl. "You mean, like this? Avast, ye hearty! Walk the plank or I'll drill holes in yer head!"

Luke snickered. "You were looking at her all happy, the way you look when you're eating kalamata olives."

Roman raised an eyebrow. "Jones is not an olive."

"So you don't like her?"

Roman grunted and shifted his position on the hardwood floor. "Jones and I work together." A non-answer, but the best he could do.

"Yeah, but . . . so did you and Mama."

The drill slipped in Roman's hand and the bit pierced the floor, sending a spew of sawdust into the air before Roman shut it off.

Luke scrambled to touch the little hole he'd made. "Geez, Papa. Why'd you do that?"

Roman didn't even have a non-answer for that one. He never knew what to say when Luke started talking about Maureen. It rattled him every time, the need to get it exactly right. What sort of father was he? Shouldn't he have the proper words by now?

"Hand me those screws."

Luke gave him the screws and changed the subject. "Papa, I've been thinking. I feel stupid having a babysitter when you're working overtime."

"Don't even start that. I'm not leaving you alone."

"But I'm thirteen!"

"Fuggedaboutit, kid. And no arguing."

"No arguing?" He sat back on his heels.

"I won't change my mind, Luke. Your grandparents aren't here, so it's got to be a babysitter."

"I could stay with a friend."

"When you have a friend whose parents I've met and approved, whose room I've inspected, and whose grades are off the charts, we'll talk."

"You're joking, right?"

Partly. The "babysitter" was a professional nanny with three pages of references. It would be hard for a friend to compete with that. Roman stood the bed upright. "What do you think?"

"Not bad for a prison bed," said Luke bitterly, flinging himself onto the couch and flipping on the TV.

Roman sighed. Lord, he hoped this move was the right thing. So far, nothing about San Gabriel was as he'd imagined.

"Help me carry the bed into your room, Luke."

"Yes sir, Battalion Chief Roman." One more degree of sass, and Roman would have grounded him.

Max called that night, the next morning, and again at lunchtime. He'd booked himself a room at the San Gabriel Inn and seemed to have no other purpose in life than to pester Sabina.

He tracked her down during her evening jog, cruising next to her in his Mercedes while he sucked down a large Slurpee.

"Watch out, you might stain your seat covers," Sabina panted, rounding a corner.

"I never thought you'd end up such a knockout, Sally Hatfield."

"I don't know who that is." She'd dropped her stage name like a discarded snakeskin when she'd left the show.

"Lots of people do, though. All it takes is a search on Netflix."

"Are you threatening me?"

"I'm working it, baby, I'm working it."

"Doesn't matter how many DVDs you rent. I look nothing like Taffy anymore."

"I'm not talking about Taffy."

Sabina stumbled. He couldn't be talking about . . . no, not even Max would be that low. "You wouldn't."

"I don't want to."

"Max, you're not playing fair."

"Who says show business is fair? Is it fair that a knockout, talented woman like your mother can't get a part? Is it fair that she has to start from square one after all she's accomplished?"

Sabina spotted the park up ahead. As soon as she reached the corner, she'd cut through the playground and lose the Mercedes. Unless Max chose to embark on some James Bond sort of car chase.

"Skip the feminist manifesto, Max. I hate show business and everything about it. Actresses are supposed to love the camera. I despise it. I'd ruin your production."

"Such drama. Such angst. You've still got it, munchkin, you've still got it."

Sabina clenched her jaw and picked up her pace.

"Annabelle's landing tomorrow. I'm picking her up at LAX. This is your last chance. Imagine how happy she'd be if I met her on the tarmac with a done deal."

Sabina reached the corner of the park. Green grass stretched like an oasis in the brown desert landscape of San Gabriel. Children glided down the twisting slides, parents chatted over baby carriages. Purple bougainvillea spilled over a gateway into a nearby home. It felt so normal—idyllically normal. Max had no idea how perfectly he'd expressed everything wrong between her and her mother. Annabelle wouldn't be happy to see her; she'd be happy to see a deal.

She stopped running and leaned over, panting, hands on knees. "Max . . ." She fought for breath. "Did you know the only playground I ever saw, before I moved here, was part of a movie set?"

"So? Playgrounds. Dime a dozen."

"Did you know I threw up before every single shoot? Did you know I had nightmares about missing lines and forgetting my pants on national TV?"

He snorted. "CBS would never have gone for that."

"All I ever wanted was a normal life. Scratch that. All I ever wanted was *my* life. The right to do what I wanted instead of what I didn't want, day after day after day. If you had any conscience at all, you'd leave me the hell alone."

Max lifted his Ralph Lauren sunglasses. "Munchkin, don't forget who you're talking to."

"Right. Conscience is a dirty word to you. But I'm not a kid anymore. And I won't be threatened or blackmailed."

"No one's talking blackmail. Be reasonable, Sabina."

"Be a man, Max. Stop doing my mother's dirty work for her." Between her oxygen deficit and her fury, her whole body was shaking. "If Annabelle wants me that badly, she should stop hiding behind a Hollywood weasel in an overpriced Mercedes."

She'd gone too far. She knew it even as she rode the high of her rage. Max, his lips white at the edges, flipped his sunglasses over his eyes and floored his accelerator. He screeched around in a tight turn, spewing a cloud of exhaust in her direction. She covered her mouth to keep from breathing it in and watched the Mercedes disappear down the street.

Uh oh.

She thought uneasily about the video Max had referred to—her one brief error in judgment after she'd signed all her money over to her mother and was floundering around like a lost puppy. But Max wouldn't sink that low, would he?

Chapter Ten

Ominous silence reigned over the rest of Sabina's time off. Max left town, presumably to pick up Annabelle. Sabina didn't hear a word from either of them, even though every ring of her cell phone made her jump. Vader kept calling, but she didn't have time for his homophobia phobia, so she didn't answer.

She dropped in at La Piaggia once, checking very cautiously to make sure no irresistibly sexy training officers were on the premises. Anu hadn't seen Roman since that first night. She offered her a plate of samosas and a dire glare.

"It's all your fault. He's afraid of you," she accused Sabina.

"Glad to hear it. Maybe he'll lighten up on the drills."

"This is no joking matter. I had a genuinely brilliant cook in my kitchen for one brief, shining moment and now I'll never see him again. You never even tasted that sauce. And by the way, did you know this restaurant is named for a beach?"

"Well, yes. I thought it was intentional."

"I asked my parents, but they no longer remember why they chose that name. I'm pretty sure they'll soon forget it's an Italian restaurant altogether."

Sabina dipped a samosa in a spicy mint chutney. "So what was the sauce like?"

"Sensational and sensual. You cannot even imagine. His son was right. I nearly considered divorcing Pradeep and marrying that fireman. But my poor parents would never recover from the shame."

"Maybe they'll forget you're married."

"One can always hope. Besides, I have him earmarked for someone else." She winked one bright eye.

"Oh no." Sabina dropped the last samosa back on the plate and backed away as if from a cobra about to strike. "Keep your crazy Indian matchmaking skills to yourself."

"Me? I don't need to do a thing. Just do me one favor. When he's your husband, will you allow him to cook here, say, once a week? Friday nights would be best."

Sabina fled to the tune of Anu's delighted laughter.

She'd checked in with Carly a couple times since the disastrous practice, but could extract no explanation for the strange incident. The coach was just as mystified as everyone else. But he was determined to keep them both on the team as long as they behaved themselves.

"Why should I quit the team because of some new kid?" Carly shouted into the phone when Sabina informed her of the coach's decision.

"Coach won't tolerate any misbehavior."

"Tell him, not me."

Between one thing and another, it was a relief to

start her next shift. Never mind all the issues with Roman—she could handle that. She could handle anything as long as she had San Gabriel Fire Station 1 and the guys.

During lineup, she ignored Vader's wounded sidelong looks. "Cherie still won't bone me," he hissed at her as they broke off for proficiency exercises. "And you're not helping. These blue balls have your name all over them."

"That's disgusting."

"And uncomfortable." He sulked as they filtered into the apparatus bay. "You said you'd help me." Sabina ignored him, clasped her hands behind her back, and watched as Roman took Ace, the ridiculously good-looking blond surfer-boy rookie, through his paces on the breathing apparatus.

The kid was practically shaking as he gave a breakdown on the apparatus, then explained to the assembled veterans how buddy breathing worked. Sabina remembered that deer-in-the-headlights feeling—multiplied by ten in her case, knowing that female firefighters had an extra burden to prove themselves. Thanks to her TV training, she'd never lost her cool. She'd gained a lot of respect that way, and supposed she ought to thank Annabelle, though her mother didn't even know about her new career. They'd stopped talking after one last epic battle in which an enraged Annabelle started counting the "woman-hours" she'd put into raising Sabina. "And now you want to walk away whenever you please? You owe me. You owe the show!" Maybe that's what had bothered Sabina the most—the fact that Annabelle cared more about the show. Shortly after her mother had cut off communication, Sabina had signed over her earnings so she couldn't possibly owe her mother anything.

Ace stumbled his way through the exercise, with Roman offering only a few corrections. When he was done, Psycho shouted, "Hey Acie, this your first time breaking down the breather?"

Ace swallowed and nodded proudly.

"It's a first! Ice cream for the crew."

Cheers erupted, and even Roman displayed a grim little smile. "Don't mess with tradition."

Just then the long tone that signaled a fire call sounded. "Reported structure fire at 1500 South Mall Plaza. Task Force 1, Task Force 2, Engine 4, Engine 5, and Battalion 1 respond to the reported structure fire at 1500 South Mall Plaza. Incident number 306, time of alarm 10:32."

Everyone hurried to don turnout gear. Roman climbed into Engine 1 ahead of her, taking a spot in the backseat. The top of his helmet nearly brushed the roof of the engine. She put on her headphones.

"Training opportunity," said Roman. "I'll be taking notes, guys."

Wonderful. Sabina tried to ignore his imposing presence, but her position, squished between him and Vader, made it impossible. Actually, it would have been impossible if he'd been across a room behind a glass wall. The man could not be ignored.

Double D, the engineer, punched the address into the GPS as the big door of the apparatus bay lifted. Sabina rolled her eyes. Everyone knew where the mall was, but Double D loved that GPS. He turned the sirens on and they zoomed out of the bay into the street.

Vader looked as nervous as she felt. So did Double D. Even Captain Kelly looked tense. For the first time, Chief Roman would be working a fire alongside them, watching their every move.

When they screeched to a halt outside the mall,

they saw a small crowd outside the double door of the entrance. It didn't look like an emergency was in the works. People lounged against the concrete retaining walls, a few people were smoking cigarettes, a couple of kids were playing with skateboards. On the tactical channel, someone said, "False alarm? Kids playing a prank, maybe."

What an anticlimax. Sabina debated donning her face piece but didn't see the point based on the lack of a fire. But she supposed they had to go through the motions. Roman spotted a security guard and headed off to question him. Sabina forged through the crowd at the door, ignoring a whistle from one of the skateboarders.

Inside the mall, she finally spotted a wisp of smoke. So there actually was a fire. Luckily, the wide, echoing central corridor of the mall was already emptied of people. Either it was a slow day or the security guards had already evacuated everyone. She sniffed, picking up a very odd scent.

She spoke into her mic. "Visual confirmation of the structure fire. Unable to identify the smell, but the smoke appears yellow."

"The smell?" Roman's deep voice rattled her helmet. "Where's your face piece?"

Holy Mother of . . . She snapped her face piece into place. "It's on. Now."

"Jones." His voice scorched the radio. "You went into the hot zone without your face piece. You've been exposed."

"But . . . there wasn't a fire . . ." She trailed off, knowing anything she said now would make it worse. She'd let down her guard—and her face piece. What a boneheaded, rookie, idiot move.

"Come on out of there, Jones. Hazmat's on its way."

Sabina looked around desperately. Wasn't there something she could do to fix her horrible mistake? Maybe some recon? "The smoke appears to be coming from Charmed, I'm Sure. It's a shop on the left, halfway down. It caters to the tween crowd, selling charms for bracelets and such. I appear to be experiencing no ill-effects from ingesting the smoke, no burning throat, no stinging eyes."

"Anyone still in there?"

"I don't see anyone. Wait, there's someone coming out of the shop." She ran toward a skinny girl with spiked hair and a pierced eyebrow, who was being chased by a billow of smoke the color of a yellowing bruise. When she reached the empty hall, she stumbled to her knees, coughing.

Sabina ran to her side. "Are you all right?" Even though Sabina spoke through her face piece, the girl seemed to understand, and nodded.

"Come on." Sabina hauled her to her feet and dragged her down the hall. "You have to get out of here."

Tears streamed down the girl's face. "I'm *so* going to get fired."

"Don't worry about that right now. Can you identify the chemical?"

"I followed the instructions!" the girl wailed. "I swear."

"What instructions? What were you doing?"

"It was a . . . a . . . I mean, it's just henna or something . . . maybe sage . . . then I lit a candle for ambience, you know, and it caught on a Glamour Kitty shirt and . . . here."

She thrust an empty package into Sabina's gloved hand and ran for it. Sabina paused to scan the package. She squinted at it through her face piece, then gave up and raised it again. What the hell, she'd already been exposed. She was already in trouble.

When she pushed open the entrance door and stepped outside into the clean air, she found herself face-to-face with Chief Roman. He looked even grimmer than usual behind the shield of his face piece.

"Firefighter Jones. What the hell are you doing?"

"You can call off the hazmat team, Chief. She was making a love potion."

Back at the station, the firefighters gathered around the TV to watch the local news.

"Check it out, Ella Joy's talking about the mall fire."

Roman glanced at the TV, which displayed a graphic reading "The Sunny Side of the News." An exquisite part-Asian news anchor was speaking.

"San Gabriel firefighters rushed to the South Desert Mall today after receiving reports of an unknown chemical spill. Fears of a potentially deadly hazmat threat fizzled when an employee of Charmed, I'm Sure admitted she'd been brewing a love potion in the back room. The brave firefighters quickly dealt with the situation. The question remains, did the potion actually work?"

The anchor winked as a graphic unfurled beneath her. It read, "The Bachelor Firemen of San Gabriel."

"Did her love potion magically summon the nation's most desirable firefighters to the scene? No word yet from Charmed, I'm Sure as to whether they're planning to brew any bigger batches of the concoction."

Dio. Exactly what the fire chief didn't want.

"Turn that crap off."

The firemen jumped and someone scrambled for

the remote. In the silence that followed, Roman gestured for them to gather around.

"That performance was unacceptable. You've gotten lax. You've gotten slow. A bunch of probies back in New York could have done better. A hazmat situation is one of the most dangerous any firefighter can encounter. Procedures must be followed to the letter, every single time, no exceptions."

The crew nodded, though he detected resentment on a few faces.

"We'll be conducting hazmat drills until you can do them in your sleep. If any of you need a refresher before we start, grab a manual from my office. Firefighter Jones."

She met his gaze with her chin up.

"I'm going to have to write you up."

Her lips tightened, but she offered no other reaction. Vader, on the other hand, swung his head from side to side like a prizefighter. "But Chief, it wasn't a hazmat call. It was a freakin' love potion."

"I'm aware of that."

"You're going to write her up for a love potion?"

"We didn't know what it was. It could have been a chemical attack by persons unknown."

"At the *mall*? What, eighth-graders gone wild?"

"Shut up, Vader," Sabina snapped. "The chief's right. I screwed up." Clearly she didn't enjoy admitting that. Her turquoise eyes glittered.

Roman dismissed the meeting and headed into his office, where the phone was already ringing.

Chapter Eleven

As predicted, Fire Chief Renteria was furious about the Bachelor reference. Roman listened to him rant in stony silence. He refrained from pointing out that while he could control his crew—mostly—he had no say in what the TV reported.

He hung up and ran his fingers through his hair. Charmed, I'm Sure. Love potions. A news channel called the Sunny Side of the News. What sort of place had he landed in?

He cast a glance at Stan, who was snoring. Opening a drawer, he scrabbled for the doggy treats he'd brought in. He knelt down next to Stan and placed one right next to his moist, black nose. It twitched. Then his tongue slurped out and gathered up the treat without opening his eyes.

"You don't play fair," Roman told the sleeping dog. "Try another one."

He offered another treat, this time waving it under

his nose. This one seemed to work. Stan's brown eyes sprang open and he flipped to his feet, his whole body vibrating with joy.

But he ignored the treat, ran right past Roman's hand of friendship, and shot toward the door.

Roman jumped to his feet. In the doorway, a solidly built, dark-haired man in his thirties was bent over, scratching Stan behind the ears.

"Stan never was much for treats," the visitor said with a laugh before rising to his feet. "You could offer him a rubber eraser and he'd be just as happy."

The man was probably a head shorter than Roman and inspired an instant sense of respect. He surveyed Roman with cool, gray eyes.

"And you are?"

"Sorry. Captain Brody. Former resident of this office." He offered his hand.

"Pleasure to meet you." Roman strode forward and shook his hand, noticing his powerful grip and level glance. A man to be reckoned with. "I heard you're over at the new academy now. How's that going?"

"So far, so good. We have twenty cadets, half of them from some pretty nasty environments. That's our ultimate mission. We train good firefighters and at the same time try to help some kids who need a little discipline and a purpose in life."

"Can't argue with that." Roman gave Stan a disgusted look. The dog was rubbing his jaw adoringly on Brody's pants leg. "What can I do for you, Captain?"

He ought to offer the captain a seat, but something told him not to. Maybe it was the reserved, assessing look in the man's eyes.

"Well . . ." For the first time, Captain Brody looked uncomfortable. "I spent a lot of years at this station and I know the crew here like family."

"That happens."

"I've been hearing some rumblings. Grumblings, is more like it. I know it's bound to happen with a new training officer in the mix, but I thought you should know about it."

"Why?"

"Well, it's a fine line we all walk. Authority versus community. You don't want to be too much of a hard-liner because then the men won't follow you."

"I don't anticipate any problems in that regard." Roman had never had trouble getting men to follow him.

"I'm sure you don't. But that doesn't mean it's not coming. For the safety of the station, I felt I should warn you."

Roman aimed his most authoritative stare at the captain. "Completely unnecessary."

"I disagree," Brody answered quietly.

So the man wasn't easily intimidated. He shouldn't be too surprised by that. In another situation—if Brody hadn't stepped way out of line by coming here—they'd probably be friends.

"Not only unnecessary, but unwelcome. I have a job to do here. I'll do it the way I see fit."

Captain Brody met him stare for stare. His eyes narrowed to gray slits as he took Roman's measure. At that moment, Roman would have willingly died before he blinked first. He held his ground. Brody had no call to question his leadership style. And he wasn't about to allow it.

Finally Captain Brody nodded. "Have it your way."

"It is what it is."

"I won't come here again."

"That would be best."

At Brody's feet, Stan whined. "I can take the dog off your hands, if—"

"The dog stays."

"All right, then." Brody gave another brief nod, bent down for a quick scratch of Stan's ears, then left.

It took several minutes for the tension to leave Roman's body. Was there some kind of rebellion afoot out there? Was he that harsh in his methods? He didn't think so. Overall he'd been restrained because these guys didn't know him. Back in New York, when he'd been a captain, he'd let some real tirades fly. But the guys knew to take it with a grain of salt.

He looked down at Stan, who looked bereft. Realizing he still held the doggy treat in his fist, he knelt down and offered it once again. Stan gave it a half-hearted sniff, then dragged himself back to his corner.

"Fine." Roman sniffed it himself and made a face. No wonder the dog wouldn't touch it unless he was asleep. What did they put in these things, anyway? He should try making his own doggy treats—dry some veal or marinate some lamb.

He knew writing up Sabina would make him even less popular. Had he done the wrong thing? Hell no. He could still summon the terror that had shot through him when he realized she was in the hot zone with no face piece. Un-fucking-acceptable.

"Vader, you're starting to piss me off. What kind of firefighter would I be if I complained about a perfectly fair notice to improve?"

Vader dribbled the basketball, hammering it like a yo-yo. He'd dragged her to the backyard for some hoops after they'd spent a couple of hours poring over the section of the manual that dealt with hazmat protocol.

He shot the basketball, it bounced off the backboard, and Sabina leaped to catch it.

"It was a *love potion*. You got reprimanded over a love potion."

"I'm not reprimanded." A reprimand would be in her file forever. Roman had only given her a notice to improve, which would go away in six months.

"Close enough. The guy's a prime asshole. I heard Brody came in today to mellow him out and Roman gave him the boot."

Sabina shot and missed. The ball hit the edge of the backboard and dribbled into the bushes. Sabina fisted her hands on her hips. "Who called Brody, I wonder?"

Vader's strong jaw twitched the way it always did in uncomfortable situations. "A concerned citizen."

"Vader, you shouldn't have done that. Don't you think we should give the guy a chance?" Why was she defending Roman? He'd shredded them after the mall fiasco, especially her. But for whatever reason, she couldn't bear to hear Vader talking about him like that.

"We did. He's a dickhead."

Psycho, who was doing a hyperactive series of laps around the backyard, dove for the ball and came up balancing it on one finger. "I'm in, Vader."

"In what?"

"In on whatever we gotta do to take Roman down."

Sabina marched over to him and snatched the ball from his hands. "You're both nuts. He's been here, what, a week? Two weeks? Get over yourselves." She noticed that Psycho was giving her an odd, wicked look. "What?"

"Nothing."

His brilliantly blue eyes flicked down to her chest, then back up, so quickly she thought she might have imagined it. A demented smile stole over his face.

"What is wrong with you, Psycho?"

"Oh . . . nothing . . . I'm sweating like a pig here. Think I'll go take a shower."

"Fine." She frowned at him as he turned his back and walked away, whistling a soft tune. It sounded familiar, that song. She was racking her memory, trying to place it, when he slowly raised one arm and pretended to sensuously soap his chest, running his hands across his pectorals as if they were breasts.

Oh my God.

Max had done it. He'd gotten her most mortifying on-screen moment into the hands of a San Gabriel firefighter. Not just any fireman, but Psycho, who had no mercy.

She raced after him. With a flying tackle, she toppled him to the ground. "Where'd you see it? Who else saw it?"

Psycho shook with evil laughter under her. "Who *didn't* see it?"

Vader ran up next to them. "See what? What are you guys talking about?"

Sabina raged at Psycho. "I'm going to kill you. Strangle you and feed you to Stan. Who has it now?"

"The Sunny Side of the News, for all I know." Psycho cackled. "Why didn't you ever tell us you liked to whistle in the shower, Two?" He whistled the tune again, until Sabina squished his face into the grass.

"Whistle in the shower? Everyone likes that, what's the big deal?"

"Jones, Vader, Psycho." Roman's harsh voice made them all jump. Sabina rolled off Psycho and scrambled to her feet. It wasn't really Psycho's fault anyway. It was Max's. How could he be so cruel?

"Psycho, if you don't bring me that video in the next two minutes, you'll be polishing the pumper for the next two months. Vader, do some push-ups, you're getting soft."

Roman sure had Vader's number. Her muscle-bound best friend instantly dropped to the ground and began pumping up and down.

"Jones, in my office."

Sabina had to call on every ounce of her rusty acting skills to walk through the station with her head held high. Sidelong glances and a few smirks followed her, but Chief Roman's commanding presence kept outright snickering from breaking out. Sabina knew her fellow firefighters like brothers. Brothers loved to tease. And this . . . this was even more tease-worthy than Vader's baby-blue truck.

Roman ushered her into his office and shut the door. She'd spent more time in the captain's office in the last week than in the previous two years. A sense of utter demoralization swept over her. In one day she'd screwed up at a fire scene and been seen topless by smirking firemen. Everything she'd worked so hard for was falling apart around her.

And all this humiliation was taking place under the gaze of Chief Roman, the most attractive man she'd ever known.

He leaned against his desk, which looked tiny in comparison, and folded his arms over his massive chest. His midnight-black eyes took her in, not unsympathetically. "You know, I heard all the chatter and thought it was about me and my dictatorial ways."

She felt pink creep up her cheeks. "They're just getting used to your leadership style. I have no problem getting written up. I made a mistake. A big one."

She wasn't sure if she was referring to the mall fire or to her stupid decision at the age of nineteen.

"At any rate, it turned out they were talking about you, not me, and a certain video that was delivered to the station this morning and viewed by a certain portion of the crew."

Had he seen it? She couldn't tell from his impassive expression.

"What can you tell me about it?"

"Well . . ." Sabina put on her movie critic voice. "*Zombie Nights IV* is the fourth in the critically panned but commercially successful Zombie Nights series. Some even call it groundbreaking in its depiction of the angst faced by those unfortunate souls turned into zombies."

Not a trace of amusement crossed his rugged face. "And your role?"

"I played a naïve waitress whose last pre-zombie moments take place in a shower. I shot the scene . . . oh, probably eleven or so years ago."

He ran one hand through the thick black hair. "The chief isn't going to like this. If the media gets hold of it, we're screwed. I can confiscate the video. I can forbid the guys from mentioning it outside the station. But it will be like trying to put water back into a waterfall. The damage is done."

She licked her dry lips and rubbed her hands, damp from Psycho's sweat, on her thighs. He was right. She was in for it. Cue umpteen million shower references and renditions of the tune she'd whistled during that brief but everlasting topless scene.

But she didn't think Max would take it to the media. Complete exposure would destroy all his leverage.

"Do you want to take some time off until this blows over?"

Time off . . . hiding out in her house, curled up in a fetal position, watching talk shows and eating barbecue potato chips . . .

No. She was not going to let a Hollywood jackass derail her career.

Snapping her spine straight, she glared at Roman. "Absolutely not. I can handle the guys. A little teasing won't kill me. They can blab about it all they want. And the scene's probably online somewhere anyway. I'll deal with it."

Her composure nearly faltered under his long, thoughtful scrutiny. But it was worth it to see grudging respect dawn in his eyes.

"If you need some help—"

"I don't."

He nodded, then gave a gesture of dismissal. At the door, she turned.

"But . . . um . . . thank you. I do appreciate it."

A nod of acknowledgment.

"And just so you know, it was only that one time, and you don't really see anything, no nipp—" She snapped her mouth shut, knowing she'd turned bright red.

He'd seen her nipples, after all. And he was remembering them right this second—she could see it in his eyes. "No need to explain anything to me, Jones."

"Right." She wheeled toward the door again, then hesitated, bracing herself. On the other side of that door lay endless teasing and mortification.

But for once, luck was with her. A loud tone rang throughout the station as the dispatcher announced a structure fire. To Sabina, it might as well have been the voice of an angel.

Roman left the station in a terrible mood the next morning. He'd never forget the look on Sabina's face when she fled his office. And even though he'd confiscated the video, it was a pointless move. *Zombie Nights IV* was available in any video store. And Sabina was right, the shower scene was probably viewable online somewhere.

Worst of all, as soon as he'd caught a glimpse of that shower scene—Sabina's sleek, wet, naked back, her pretty profile when she turned her head, the way her nose perked up at the very end—memories of that night in Reno came flooding back.

He needed to unwind. Forget about the station. Forget about everything.

"Lukey, you feel like crappy Italian food tonight?" he asked when Luke slid into the passenger seat of the Jeep. Picking Luke up at school was one of his favorite things to do when he was off shift.

"Only if you make your sauce."

"Deal."

Anu was only too delighted to have him back in the kitchen of La Piaggia. Luke set himself up with his math homework in a corner while Roman lost himself in dicing onions and simmering tomatoes. Nothing relaxed him like cooking. The sharp scent of garlic, the heady fumes of the red wine bubbling from the pot, the sensual slide of the green peppers under his fingers . . . for the first time all week, he could breathe freely.

"Papa, what does it mean when you can't stand someone, but when you see them you feel funny?"

So much for relaxation. "What?"

Luke, usually so bouncy, sat at the counter with his head propped on one hand, a shadow across his face. "It's just weird. Usually I either like someone or I don't. But now I'm just confused."

"This isn't . . . a girl, is it?" Roman asked cautiously.

Luke lowered his head. "Kind of," he grumbled. "Not a girly girl like at school."

He must be talking about Carly, the girl pitcher, Roman realized. According to the coach, the two of them managed to avoid physical combat, but jabbed at each other in every other possible way. On the bright side, both of their batting averages were up and their earned run averages were down. Their team was the talk of the league.

"Well . . ." Roman cleared his throat. "What was the question again?"

"Never mind."

Roman cursed himself. A mother would have a much easier time with a conversation like this. But that was no excuse.

"I think you just go with it. Roll with the punches."

Luke pushed aside his calculator. "I didn't punch her."

"I didn't say you did, I meant—"

"Never mind. You don't understand."

Luke seemed to be saying that more and more often lately. Roman gritted his teeth and stirred the pot so hard that the thick red sauce splattered up the sides. "I'll tell you this much. When it comes to women, throw the rule book out the window and hang on for the ride."

Chapter Twelve

Sabina jogged around the San Gabriel Reservoir as if ten thousand zombies were chasing her. Hollywood zombies like Max Winkler. She'd spent too much time in the down-to-earth world of firefighters. She'd forgotten the shameful depths to which someone like Max would stoop.

She'd known *Zombie Nights IV* was a mistake, but after she'd signed all her earnings over to her mother, she'd been flat broke. Giving all her money to her mother had been an easy choice—it was the only way she could free herself from her guilt over leaving *You and Me,* and effectively ending the show. Signing on for an uncredited performance on *Zombie Nights* had given her enough cash to put herself through the academy and get a job as a firefighter.

Since neither her stage name nor her real name had appeared on the credits, and they'd given her a long blond wig for the role, no one would ever link *Zombie*

Nights and little Taffy McGee. Her biggest secret was still safe.

So, no regrets. The guys had been pretty easy on her, probably because Roman kept throwing hazmat drills at them. Vader had actually seemed impressed.

"You're like, a scream queen. And you never told me, Two. What the fuck? That was one of the best zombie killings ever shot. Did you see how that blood spurted? How'd they do that?"

Her mood lightened as she reached the three-mile mark, which was a willow tree that drooped graceful branches into the still water. Maybe everything would be okay. Max had exposed her embarrassing shower scene to the crew and she'd survived. They'd all seen her naked back and a slight bit of the under curve of her right breast. So what? She'd seen more of Vader during his workouts. She was still a proud member of San Gabriel Fire Station 1. Nothing had really changed.

By the time she got to work the next day, she was absolutely sure the worst was over.

"Morning, Zombie," Double D greeted her.

So she'd acquired a new nickname. Big deal.

"Cute, Doo-doo. But you don't want to piss me off. I haven't had breakfast. I might go for some scrambled brains."

His belly laugh followed her to her locker. She hid a smile. That was how to handle the guys. Give it right back. Don't let them see they got to you.

Vader, a few lockers over, hissed at her. "We got Saturday night off this week. What are you doing?"

"You mean after I buy every DVD of *Zombie Nights* in Southern California and destroy it?"

"What are you talking about? That shit's classic. I still can't believe you didn't tell me. I tell you everything." His deep-set brown eyes looked a bit moist. "Even . . . you know."

"How's Cherie?" asked Sabina, desperate to change the subject.

"She made me watch some documentary about bullying."

"Good for her. I'm starting to like that woman."

"At the end she let me touch her boobs. But the damn movie had me so freaked out I didn't even enjoy it. Give me *Zombie Nights* any day."

So much for a subject change. She ducked into the bathroom to get into her uniform. So far, so good. Her first post–*Zombie Nights* shift wasn't going too badly. She brushed out her hair and braided it with quick fingers.

Everything would be okay, she told herself for the millionth time. She'd weathered the storm. She hadn't caved in to Max. Her world hadn't been completely destroyed. Sure, a few things had changed, and part of her longed to turn back time to when Brody was still captain, Carly had the prime spot on the team roster, and no one had seen her half naked.

But then she wouldn't have met Roman.

When she emerged from the bathroom, she paused. Something was different. Something was happening. A hyperactive, excited buzz of voices came from the training room, as if a bunch of guys were all talking at the same time.

Not an unusual phenomenon, but she also detected a low female voice in the mix. Ella Joy, the Channel Six anchor? Melissa Brody, the captain's newly pregnant wife, along with her little girl, Danielle? Smiling eagerly, she hurried down the corridor to say hi. Danielle was a cutie, and she hadn't yet congratulated Melissa on her big news.

In the training room, the guys were all gathered in a tight knot in the middle of the room. She caught snatches of what they were saying.

"Can you sign one for my mom? . . . My little sister loved your show . . . I liked the episode with the pet ferret . . . What was that phrase you always said . . . *Why Taffy McGee, what were you thinking?"*

A throaty voice echoed that last phrase, along with a husky chuckle that sounded like skilled fingertips stroking velvet.

Sabina stood rooted to the floor of the corridor, completely unable to make sense of what was going on here. Had someone put on one of Annabelle's movies? She hadn't heard that voice in so many years, thanks to her nearly complete avoidance of TV.

Then Double D shifted to one side. There stood Annabelle Hatfield. She looked the same, but . . . tighter. Like a jewel that someone had been polishing for ten years. Her dark red hair—Annabelle always told her colorists to make it "Merlot"—cascaded in tumbling waves down her wiry form. She crackled with energy, as she always had. A firecracker of a woman. She'd always drawn attention without even trying, as if the spotlight was her natural habitat.

On the show Annabelle's character had been vivacious and scattered, always trying to make ends meet and rein in the troublemaking Taffy.

Off the show, she and Sabina had fought over everything from breakfast cereal to how long Sabina could grow her hair. Not past her ears.

Their eyes met. Annabelle's widened just a bit as she took in Sabina's plain blue SGFD uniform and long, brown braid.

"Why, there's little Taffy now!" Her mother laughed and blew an air kiss at Sabina, as if this weren't their first encounter in thirteen years . . . as if she weren't in the process of destroying years of obsessively cultivated anonymity.

As one, the other firefighters, mouths agape, all swung toward Sabina. Watching their expressions was like witnessing the five stages of death. Shock, denial, confusion, glee . . . well, maybe the five stages of disaster didn't exactly conform to stages of death.

Double D's mouth flapped like the flag in front of the station; for once he had no nasty dig. Psycho scratched at his buzz cut. Fred looked as if she'd killed his favorite puppy. Vader still hadn't really caught on. Ace gazed at her with a look of awe. Apart from the group, in the doorway of his office, stood Roman. She was afraid to look too closely at his expression.

She ought to go greet her mother, say hello for the first time in thirteen years. But she couldn't move. If ever she felt like a zombie, it was now. "Lineup," she blurted desperately.

Roman blinked. Then he stepped forward. "Ms. Hatfield . . ."

"Annabelle," she purred.

"Annabelle, it's time for lineup, when Captain Kelly talks about tedious things like staffing and overtime and who has vacation coming up. I'm going to have to ask you to—"

"I'd be delighted to watch. All these years and I've never seen my darling daughter do her firefighter act."

Sabina gritted her teeth. "Act, my ass," she growled under her breath, taking her position. The guys were fighting to line up next to her, but Vader won. "I don't get it." His jaw muscle clenched. "You're Taffy? The kid in the show?"

"Shut up." The fact that her mother was here, that

she'd outed her as Taffy in front of the crew, still hadn't completely sunk in.

"But Taffy was a chubster. And she had red hair."

"Vader!" Roman barked. "Focus."

Vader snapped to attention along with the rest of the crew. Sabina had never seen everyone's posture so perfect. They listened attentively as Captain Kelly went through the staffing over the next nine days and talked about vacation time over Christmas. Focused quiet reigned in the kitchen. It seemed her mother had inspired the best lineup ever.

Roman took his time talking about the drills scheduled for that week, and Sabina could have kissed him for it. She dreaded the end of the lineup when she would have to face her mother, who had perched herself gracefully on the arm of the couch. With her still-toned legs crossed, a determined smile on her lips, her jade peg-leg trousers glowing under the fluorescent lights, Annabelle watched every moment as if she'd never seen anything so fascinating.

Sabina wished lineup would last forever. Or that a call would come in. Or that the firehouse would explode. *Something.* Of all the ways she'd imagined seeing her mother again, this one had never crossed her mind.

Roman hid his fury during the longest lineup he'd ever experienced. This morning he'd fielded a phone call from Chief Renteria asking about a rumor about a female firefighter who'd done some kind of porno. Roman had set him straight, but the man still hadn't been happy.

"I don't like the sound of this. If the news got hold of it, San Gabriel would be plastered all over the media again. Deal with it, Captain Roman."

"It's already dealt with."

But *this* wasn't. How did you deal with the sudden appearance of a world-famous movie star at the station? How did you deal with the fact that one of your firefighters turned out to be a world-famous child star? Not only that, but the star of one of your favorite back-in-the-day shows? Sabina was *Taffy McGee*!

No wonder she was so damn beautiful. No wonder she'd blown him off. Fuck, he was *pissed*.

Captain Kelly droned on. "If you haven't put in a request for time off over Christmas, talk to me by the end of the week and I'll see what I can do."

Sabina gazed off into the distance, refusing to meet his eyes. She'd better be afraid. If this got out—if the media knew that this firehouse was home to Taffy McGee—all hell would break loose. And Renteria would have his ass.

As lineup concluded and the guys peeled off to go work out and prepare for the hazmat simulation scheduled for later, Annabelle Hatfield applauded. "Bravo, San Gabriel. Well done, boys. And girl."

He caught a desperate look from Sabina, an unmistakable plea for rescue. Silently he groaned and beckoned to her. "Come help me in the apparatus bay, Jones."

This wasn't a rescue, he told himself savagely. It was a chance to vent his fury.

In the apparatus bay, he strode to a secluded spot behind the pumper, as far as possible from the rest of the crew. She followed warily. When they were safely hidden from view, he clamped his hands on her shoulders and scowled ferociously at her.

"What are you trying to do to me?"

Her turquoise eyes widened. "Excuse me?"

"I'm trying to bring some order to this place, but

every day it's something else. A surprise video. Now a visit from a movie star to her daughter, who turns out to be Taffy McGee. How am I supposed to explain this to the brass? Are you doing it on purpose?"

A fury equal to his twisted her elegant features. "Yes, of course," she hissed. "First I dug up an incredibly embarrassing moment from my past and made sure all the guys could see it and laugh at me. Then I demanded that my movie-star mother visit me at the station so no one would ever look at me the same again—" She stopped suddenly, pressing her lips so tightly together they went white at the edges.

Something clenched deep in Roman's gut. He watched her, so proud, fighting so hard to control her emotions, to put on a brave face, and knew he would have thrown himself in front of a speeding fire truck to make it better. He fisted his hands to keep from touching her, though every fiber in his body screamed to.

She bit her lip hard. Unshed tears turned her eyes the misty green of a Scottish lake at dawn. A smothered sob rippled through her body, tight as a drawn bow.

And he couldn't take it. He reached out and hauled her against him. Enfolding her tense body in his arms, he soothed her with long strokes down her back and low murmurs in her ear. She felt wonderful against him, warm and vulnerable and soft. "It's okay. It'll be okay. Shh."

She shook against him, refusing to release her tears. "They'll all think I'm a freak now."

"No, they won't."

"They won't act normal. They'll treat me different. Nothing will ever be the same."

"If anyone treats you different, I'll put their ass on suspension."

She gave a snorting, piglike sob. "Don't you dare. It's my problem, not yours."

Roman smiled into her fragrant hair, breathing in the elusive scent of jasmine that clung to her. Even on the verge of a meltdown, Sabina Jones gave as good as she got.

After what seemed like far too short a time, she drew away from him. The loss of her supple body in his arms gave him a physical pain. It had been so long since he'd comforted a woman. He longed to yank her back against him so he could take care of her.

But clearly she didn't want that. She didn't want his soft side. No one did. They all wanted the tough captain.

"I'm so sorry, Chief Roman," she said stiffly. "I'm not usually like this."

"I realize that."

"I don't want you to think I'm some sort of overemotional female who can't handle the pressure."

He clasped his hands behind his back to keep from touching her again. "You can handle everything by yourself, is that it?"

"Of course."

"You never need a helping hand? A shoulder to cry on?"

She straightened her spine. "Of course not. I've been taking care of myself for a long time."

He examined her for a long, serious moment. "Firefighters work together, Jones."

"I know that."

"Do you?"

She went pale with fury. "I have an excellent record. I've never even gotten a reprimand. I've gotten the Hot Shot Award and several other commendations. I've always been a good crew member."

That was more like the stubborn Sabina he knew.

"Deal with your mother, Jones. I want no more disruptions here. Understand?"

Her face worked. Then she saluted with a military precision that screamed mockery. "Perfectly, sir."

As he watched her go, he swore he could see the hot rage rolling off her body in waves.

God, she detested Chief Roman. He was arrogant, annoying, interfering, unfair, unfeeling . . .

Okay, it had been nice of him to try to comfort her, not that she needed it. For one brief, glorious moment she'd allowed herself to bask in the warmth that radiated from him, the strength that dwelled in his bones, the steady thump of his heart.

But then he had to turn into an arrogant jerk again and get her all riled up.

Filled with furious energy, she hurried back to the training room to find her mother, who was chatting with some EMTs who had just happened to drop by. Word about the surprise visiting movie star was already spreading. Sabina waved a cup of Roman's special coffee under Annabelle's nose and managed to drag her mother off to her room in the female dorm.

"This is where you sleep?" Annabelle gazed around in astonishment. "This is the size of your toy box at our Beverly Hills villa. Remember that place?"

No trips down memory lane. Not now. Sabina struggled for calm, but it was like trying to right a rowboat after a tsunami. "Annabelle, why are you here?"

For as long as Sabina could remember, she'd called her Annabelle, never any version of "mother," unless they were in character.

Taffy called Peg Mom. It had always felt so unnatural.

"Max said you wanted me to come."

Sabina stared into her mother's eyes, the vibrant green of a hummingbird feather—similar to her own, but with the addition of curled eyelashes and a slight uptilt at the corners. Her words to Max came back to her. *If Annabelle wants me that badly, she should stop hiding behind a Hollywood weasel in an overpriced Mercedes.*

Oops.

"But . . . why here? I never wanted anyone in San Gabriel to know I used to act."

"Max didn't know where else to find you. Your address is unlisted. I don't know how he found you here in this dinky little place."

Sabina narrowed her eyes at her mother, who perched on the edge of her bed. Annabelle had photogenic features, a respectable amount of talent, a ton of charisma, and the relentless drive of a spawning salmon. She wouldn't have come to San Gabriel without a very good reason. "I didn't know you were looking for me. I only heard through the tabloids that you'd moved to Paris."

"Yes, well, that's done now." Annabelle drummed her fingers on the jade-green fabric covering her knee. Reflected light from her many rings danced around the drab space. "It was time to come home. Or . . . close enough."

Sabina paced to the far corner of the room, though it took only three steps. Still, that put her three extra steps away from a brawl with her mother. "Why didn't you call me first? Or anytime in the past thirteen years? Max knows my number."

"You're angry?"

"You've destroyed my privacy, my anonymity, everything I've worked for over the past ten years. You never think about me. You *never* did. It was always what you wanted."

"Are you starting in on that old tune again? It might make more sense if you weren't here." Annabelle cast a revolted look around the tiny room. "You can't possibly really want *this*."

"Yes, I can. It's exactly what I want. I want to work here and fight fires and save lives and make a difference in the world."

"Entertaining people doesn't make a difference?"

Sabina felt the tendons at the back of her neck go taut. How did this always happen? It was as if the past ten years had never occurred and she was right back where she'd started, arguing endlessly with her mother. "Of course it does," she managed through clenched teeth. "But that's not what I want to do. I want to do this."

"Who says you have to stop doing this?" Annabelle opened her purse and pulled out a cigarette.

"No smoking. Have you forgotten this is a fire station?"

"I don't smoke them. I chew on them. Keeps my weight down." She inserted it between her lips, which she'd painted the color of freshly washed plums. "Did Max tell you how much they're offering for the reunion show?"

"Yes. They could offer me a billion dollars and I wouldn't do it."

"But what about me? Can't you spare a thought for me?"

"Excuse me?"

"One little show, what harm could it do?"

"One little— After everything I—? Annabelle, you haven't heard a word I've said. *Since I was born.*"

Annabelle waved her unlit cigarette at her. "Look at you, kiddo. My gorgeous daughter. You could be the new It Girl. You could work with the biggest stars in Hollywood. Your pick of roles. The cover of *People*. Cover of everything. Instead you're hiding out in this odd little town where no one even knows who you are."

Sabina ground her teeth together. "They know now, thanks to you."

"You're welcome."

"I was being sarcas—"

"Do you know who asked about you over lunch at the Ivy? Greg Harrington."

Sabina shuddered; after all these years, that name still had the power to unnerve her. "Are you referring to the creep you made me date at the age of sixteen, who broke my heart and nearly raped me?"

"Oh please, don't exaggerate. He's a superstar now. I always knew he would be. He still remembers you."

This couldn't get worse. It just couldn't. Mention of Greg Harrington had to be rock bottom. Sabina cast her eyes to the ceiling and prayed for patience. "Think logically here, Annabelle. You don't need me to get your career going again. Forget the reunion show. Do a movie. Find some really cool director to work with. Quentin Tarantino always liked your work."

Annabelle tilted her head thoughtfully. "Max said your fear of public exposure was keeping you from committing to the reunion show."

A horrible thought occurred to Sabina. "Annabelle. Did you show up here *on purpose* to expose me?"

"Of course not! If I wanted to expose you, there are so many simple ways to do it. But they wouldn't include so many handsome firemen." She gave a naughty wink. "Did I detect some sparks between you and that big one?"

Just like some horrible lost episode of the *Twilight Zone*, it kept getting worse, and worse . . .

"But now that the cat's out of the bag, I don't think any of your fireman friends would mind if you did one more appearance as Taffy. We can bring a few on as extras. They're very sexy."

That did it.

Sabina stalked to her mother's side and hauled her to her feet. "Go away, Annabelle. I won't do the show. Ever. Leave me alone and let me do my job in peace."

Annabelle yanked her arm out of Sabina's grasp. "You're being pigheaded. As always."

"If that's what you want to call it, fine."

Annabelle whirled around and headed for the door. Halfway there, she paused. The fiery expression in her tilted emerald eyes would have made grown men quail, but Sabina just folded her arms and gave it right back.

"You can't hide forever, Sabina. You're making a mistake."

"*Fine.* At least it's my mistake!"

As soon as Annabelle had whisked herself from the room, Sabina sank onto the bed, quivering. She'd seen her mother. Her *mother.* After thirteen years. And nothing had changed. *Nothing.*

Annabelle hadn't even tried to give her a hug or a kiss on the cheek. All they'd talked about was the reunion show. In one hidden part of her heart, Sabina knew that if Annabelle had opened her arms and welcomed Sabina like a daughter, she would have given her mother anything.

Had Annabelle really burned through all the *You and Me* money already? Just how desperate was she?

At that thought, uneasiness snaked through her. Annabelle had always been extraordinarily stubborn and resourceful. And "no" was her least favorite word.

Chapter Thirteen

To Luke's disgust, it had taken an absurd amount of time to get their cable TV service hooked up. Now Roman wished he'd never bothered. He squinted at the TV, wincing, as the Sunny Side of the News displayed a cute graphic over the head of the gorgeous anchorwoman.

"The Bachelorette Fireman of San Gabriel."

Which didn't even make sense, but why should that be a surprise?

Ella Joy's china-blue eyes glittered as she read the story. "Our favorite Bachelor Firemen of San Gabriel had a brush with fame yesterday, when none other than actress Annabelle Hatfield visited the firehouse. She caused a sensation, but not for the obvious reasons. Channel Six News has learned exclusively that she was there to visit her daughter, Sabina Jones, who, believe it or not, is a firefighter at Fire Station 1. But you know her better as Taffy McGee in the long-running TV series *You and Me*."

The visuals switched to a horrifying montage in which shots of Taffy alternated with shots of the adult Sabina. A clip of Taffy skateboarding into a swimming pool was followed by one of Sabina running toward Engine 1 in full turnout gear. Taffy eating a hot fudge sundae with no hands was replaced with Sabina doing drills in her workout clothes. One had to look hard for the resemblance, but when they put up a split-screen shot of two close-ups, the turquoise eyes were a dead giveaway.

"When asked if any of the firefighters knew Ms. Jones's true identity, the answer came down to this."

Vader's bony face filled the screen. "*Bleep*, no."

That was one bright spot: Sabina and Vader couldn't be that close if she hadn't even told him her true identity.

Ella Joy cruised toward the end of her story. "After all the talk about the sexy Bachelor Firemen of San Gabriel, it's nice to see the tables turned. The only question now is, does the curse also apply to the Bachelorette Fireman of San Gabriel? My sources tell me Ms. Jones is still single, so there's a good chance it does. Which means, gentlemen, that you just might have a chance with her."

Roman scowled. What a stupid way to end the piece. He clicked the remote. Luke, sprawled in an armchair with his homework, was staring at the TV in fascination. "Taffy's the one in that show, right? That we watched a million episodes of when we were both home sick?"

"Right."

A *You and Me* marathon had been playing that week, a few years ago. They'd watched in a Tylenol-hazed stupor until all the plotlines blurred together and they loopily sang the theme song out loud when each new episode began.

"So Taffy is Carly's Big Sister?"

"Yep. But she's not Taffy, she's Sabina. I think." On the show, the credits had always said, "Annabelle and Sally Hatfield in *You and Me.*" Which was her real name? Who was Sabina, really?

"I wonder if she still gets into trouble all the time," Luke mused.

"I'd have to say that's a yes."

At the very least, she was going to get *him* into trouble. Right on cue, his cell phone rang.

"You're supposed to keep that damn station off the news." Chief Renteria sounded every bit as furious as he'd expected.

"This one came out of left field."

"A child actor one of our firefighters? We're going to be a freaking joke. Even more than we already are."

Roman got to his feet and walked the phone into the living room. "Hang on there, Chief. She went through the academy like anyone else. She's an excellent firefighter. It's not her fault the media got hold of this. As far as I know she was trying to keep it quiet."

"See that she does. Or I want her out."

"That could be tough." Union issues, bad publicity . . . any number of things protected firefighters from unjust firings.

"Find a way. Or stop this before it gets worse."

"I'm on it."

Roman viciously tossed his cell phone into the couch cushions. He didn't blame Renteria for being pissed. This was exactly the kind of thing he'd hired Roman to stop. Sabina and her mother had created a huge mess that Roman would have to fix.

He stalked into the kitchen. Hamburger night, Luke's favorite. Too bad all his fancy cooking was wasted on his son. He pulled a package of hamburger meat out of the refrigerator and began making patties.

Damn that Sabina Jones. Having her on the crew was like trying to put out a brushfire that kept flaring up again. If Renteria found a way to get rid of her, Roman's life would be a hell of a lot easier. But he couldn't help feeling bad for Sabina. Obviously she'd valued her anonymity, and now it was gone forever. Maybe he should call her and see how she was doing.

No. She wouldn't want to hear from him. She'd assume he was calling to chew her out. Or worse, offer to help. When he'd tried to comfort her at the station, she'd pulled away in record time. She was so damn independent. Right now she was better off leaning on her friends. Like Vader. At the thought of Sabina curled up on Vader's couch, pouring out her troubles, a current of irritation made him slap the hamburger meat harder than necessary.

He put oil in a cast-iron pan and waited for it to heat. *Get over it, Roman. You can't be Chief Roman the hard-ass and a friend.* Not that he wanted to be her friend, precisely. What did he want?

The images that flashed through his mind in answer to that question were hot enough to make the frying pan sizzle.

Ever since Ella Joy had anointed her the Bachelorette Fireman of San Gabriel, Sabina's phone hadn't stop ringing. Most of the calls were from reporters. "This is Jamie Gold from *Us* magazine, we're doing a full-length feature on you and would like to get a quote" . . . "I'm the assistant to the producer of *The Bachelorette* on ABC and we'd love to invite you on the show" . . .

"I'm doing a piece on the tough times faced by former child actors, please call me back at . . ." She didn't answer a single one of those calls.

Her mother called. She didn't answer that one either. Now that her name was back on TV and her life lay in Humpty Dumpty pieces around her, she was too angry to speak to Annabelle.

Vader called too. She knew he was wounded by her secrecy. No doubt about it, she owed him an explanation. But if she knew her friend, he'd get over it quickly. He'd never been one to hold a grudge.

She didn't get a call from Chief Roman, but then why would she? At least he wasn't yelling at her; then again, maybe he was waiting until next shift.

Determined not to let the media uproar derail her life, she picked up Carly after school and took her to the South Desert Mall for ice cream. Supposedly it was a treat for Carly, but really she was the one who needed the time. Being with Carly put things into perspective. At least she was a grown woman with control of her life—sort of. Carly still had years of putting up with other people's crap before she could strike out on her own.

As they walked into the mall, Sabina realized her Little Sister seemed down. Her wide brown eyes didn't shine with their normal brash spark. She walked with shoulders slouched, feet dragging.

"Are you up for this, hon?"

"Sure," Carly answered listlessly.

"Are you upset because I didn't tell you?"

Carly frowned. "Tell me what?"

Sabina shook her head, laughing at her own presumption. The world didn't revolve around a silly TV report about her past. "Nothing. Well, I suppose I should tell you. Before I was a firefighter, I was a child actor in a TV show. The news just found out and they're all excited about it."

That snapped Carly out of her funk. "Really, you were an actress? Damn, woman. If I was an actress I'd be telling the whole world."

"Should you really be saying 'damn'?"

"Like anyone cares what I say."

"I care."

"Whatever." Carly's gloom returned. She didn't say much more as they made their way through the food court to Cold Stone Creamery. She didn't even get excited about her chocolate-coated waffle boat. Something was definitely up.

They grabbed a pair of orange plastic chairs and settled in to enjoy their ice cream. For the first time in years, Sabina was wearing a baseball cap crammed low on her head—her old disguise when she hadn't wanted to be noticed. When she'd played Taffy, going out in public had been a trial. Her mother had welcomed the attention, parading like a queen through the crowds, while Sabina had trailed behind, hating the feeling of people staring at her.

Now she realized she'd unconsciously chosen a table in the corner where no one would notice them. She was keeping her head down, her eyes hidden so no one would catch a flash of turquoise. Silently she cursed Ella Joy, her mother, her terrible bad luck.

"Are you okay?"

She looked up to meet Carly's warm brown eyes. "I'm supposed to be asking you that."

"I'll answer if you will."

"I'm fine."

"So am I."

They both laughed and returned to their ice cream. Sabina took a long, soothing dose of rocky road. "Okay, fine, I'll go first. I didn't want the whole world to know I used to be Sally Hatfield. I liked being plain old, ordinary Sabina Jones. I didn't want my past life to get in the way of my firefighting career."

"Why would it do that?"

"Because when you're famous, people treat you differently."

Carly tilted her head and twirled her spoon in her mouth. "Like how?"

"It's hard to explain. People treat you like you're in a different world, behind some kind of magical veil. They want to be part of it, but they also hate you for it. When I was young I could never understand it. It was hard to trust anyone."

Carly was listening with complete attention now. "I know about that part. The not trusting part."

"I know you do." Sabina offered a smile that came out crooked. "We have a lot in common, if you think about it. It's hard for us to trust. We're always on guard. We've had to grow up fast."

"I still can't believe my Big Sister is a celebrity."

Sabina snorted. "*Was.* Definitely past tense. They might take me on *Dancing with the Stars*, but that's about it."

"Seriously? *Dancing with the Stars*?" For the first time, Carly actually looked impressed.

"What, running into burning buildings isn't exciting enough for you?" Sabina teased.

But Carly's face had suddenly gone tense. Her eyes narrowed to dark slits as she aimed a death stare at someone. Sabina turned to see Roman's son, Luke, walking through the food court with a few other boys; he towered over the others by at least a head. At the sight of him, a vicarious thrill washed through her, as if Roman might be right behind him. A quick check told her he wasn't, but it still took a moment for the adrenaline to subside.

Luke glanced over at them, his step hitching as he recognized the two of them. At first all he did was wave. Sabina gave him a friendly salute in return, but Carly didn't respond.

"What's wrong with you?" Sabina hissed. "He's on your team."

"They all are."

Luke said something to the others, who shook their heads and kept on walking. Luke shrugged and veered away from the group. He headed toward Sabina and Carly. He wore an old-style, blue Brooklyn Dodgers T-shirt and jeans. His light brown hair stood up in random spikes. He looked clean-cut and well-behaved. Chief Roman wouldn't tolerate anything less, Sabina imagined.

"Hey," he mumbled to Carly when he got close to the table.

"Hey," she muttered into her ice cream.

Sabina looked from one to the other. "Hi, Luke," she said with a big, bright smile. "What are you up to today?"

His gaze switched to her. "We're getting pizza."

"I'm sure it's nowhere near as good as New York pizza."

He shrugged, his gaze sliding back to Carly. Sabina had seen enough of Roman's son to know this wasn't his normal demeanor. Obviously Carly made him uncomfortable.

"We're going to go throw the ball around after we eat, if you want to come," he said to her.

Carly scooped out a spoonful of ice cream. "No, thanks. I'm hanging with Sabina today."

"Oh, that's . . ." Sabina trailed off at a sharp look from Carly.

Luke nodded, as if he wasn't surprised. He turned to go, then swung back around to face them. "That's a killer curveball you've got. Do you hold it across the seams, more like a knuckleball? Or the regular way?"

Carly let out a snort. "Wouldn't you like to know?" Sabina noticed that her face had lit up in the way only talking baseball could accomplish.

"Well, yeah, that's why I asked." Luke rolled his eyes sarcastically. Now that was more like the live-wire kid Sabina remembered. She sat back, hoping they'd forget she was there.

"I'll tell you if you explain how your fastball jumps at the end."

"I can't do that."

Carly went back to death stare mode. From experience, Sabina knew it hid hurt feelings more than anything else.

"I'm serious. I can't tell you because I don't know. One of these days it'll stop jumping and then I'll be screwed." Luke shot Sabina a guilty look. "Oops. Don't tell my father I said that word. He hates it."

Carly sneered. "Sabina's cool. She's not a narc."

Risking loss of coolness, Sabina clarified. "If you were doing drugs, I most certainly would become a narc."

Luke stuck to the main point. "I wish I knew why my fastball works. If I ever figure it out I'll tell you."

"Cool."

"See you at the game?"

"Well, duh. I'm starting." Smugly, Carly slurped up a giant spoonful of ice cream.

"Yeah, well, don't worry, I'll be there as backup just in case. So don't screw up."

"In your dreams."

Luke left with a last friendly wave to them both.

Sabina stared at Carly, whose face was a dusky pink color she'd never witnessed before. "You like him."

"No, I don't." The girl blinked. "I hate him."

"Maybe you hated him, past tense, but not anymore. He's a nice kid. It took guts to come over here when the others wouldn't."

That reminder made Carly push aside her ice cream and cross her arms over her chest. "Of course all the guys hang together. It's so unfair. They practice together and get better and better. None of the other girls wants to practice with me."

"Then why didn't you go along with them?"

"He didn't really mean it."

"So? You think the other firefighters invited me in at first? No way, kiddo." Sabina put down her ice cream, the better to focus on her point. "I had to barge my way into their workouts and their ski trips and their barbecues. I fought hard for every last ounce of respect from those guys, and I earned it too. They didn't like me at first, but damn it, I made them respect me. Sorry."

Carly, having heard much worse since the age of two, didn't even blink.

Sabina waved her pink plastic spoon. "I'm not about to let some bimbo TV reporter and some Machiavellian agent, not to mention my own mother, take that away from me. You know what, Carly?"

"What?" The girl had forgotten all about her ice cream, which dripped onto the table.

"Maybe it's a good thing this happened. It's a reminder of what I really want out of life. I want my job. My spot on the force. My right to put on that gear and throw myself into mortal danger. Is that too much to ask just because I was born to a mother who was obsessed with movies? No! It's not. Right?"

"Damn, chica. What's got into you?"

Carly's dark eyes brimmed with laughter. She put a hand to her mouth to hold back the giggles.

"Sorry, I guess I just had to get that off my chest." Sabina sank back in her chair. She glanced around, realizing she'd been ranting in a raised voice that had drawn glances from the neighboring tables. "Oops."

"Um . . . weren't you saying something about being anonymous?" Carly rolled her eyes to indicate someone approaching.

"Shit."

"It's a good thing Luke's father isn't here, you'd be in trouble with that language," Carly chastised with glee.

"Excuse me." A plump, pretty older woman stood next to their table, an eager look in her eyes, a pen and notebook in hand. "Aren't you the one on the news? The Bachelorette Fireman?"

Sabina couldn't bring herself to lie in front of her Little Sister. What kind of mentor would that make her? She forced her head into a reluctant nod.

"Well, I just think it's so wonderful that you became a firefighter. What a great role model you are for young people. I never really liked your show much, to be honest."

Sabina's gaze slid to Carly, whose eyes went wide in an oh-no-she-didn't kind of look.

"Could I get your autograph?" the woman asked.

On autopilot, Sabina took the pen and pad. She looked at the woman blankly. "I have no idea what to sign." Taffy McGee? Sally Hatfield? Sabina Jones? Two? Her various identities swirled around her in a vortex of confusion.

"Can you sign it from the Bachelorette Fireman of San Gabriel?"

Sabina nearly choked. That was the one name she refused to claim. She wrote, "Best Wishes from San

Gabriel Fire Station 1. Check your fire extinguishers! Firefighter Jones."

When she handed it back, the delight on the woman's face made her wonder if she was onto something. Maybe this attention could be used for a good purpose. Spread the word about fire safety. Encourage people to clear the brush from around their houses, keep their chimneys cleaned out, not leave burners unattended . . .

"Now," said the woman, crouching next to the table with a girlish giggle. "What I really want to know is, what's it like working with all those handsome, single Bachelor Firemen? And is that new one from New York as sexy in person as he is on TV?"

Chapter Fourteen

In the days before Roman, Sabina would have found the woman's question about the Bachelor Firemen easy to answer. Working with all those sexy firemen was like hanging out with a gang of brothers. She loved feeling like one of the guys. But now that Chief Roman was around, everything had changed. Now she had a different answer, though she'd kept it to herself at the mall. Working with all those single firemen—and that sexy new guy from New York—was like riding a stomach-churning roller coaster that you never wanted to stop.

At six o'clock the next morning, she arrived at the station even before the early relief guys. Chief Roman was already working his magic at the coffeemaker, still yawning. The scent of Italian roast made her nostrils flare and her lower belly quiver. She would always associate that smell with Roman.

"Can I have a word, Chief Roman?"

He turned, his dark gaze encompassing her in one swift glance. She noticed a tiny nick on his jaw where he'd cut himself shaving. Raising one black eyebrow, he gestured for her to precede him into his office.

She spoke before he'd even made it to his desk. "I can't apologize enough for exposing the station to another media blitz," she announced, standing stiffly at attention and gazing somewhere over his left shoulder. His broad, powerful left shoulder.

"Duly noted," he said gruffly. "Are you all right?"

"If you mean do I need sympathy or time off, the answer is no."

"No, you're not all right?"

"Define 'all right.' "

He answered with a slight smile and a silence that was somehow comforting. It lasted for a long moment, during which Sabina's emotions churned. "I'll do my best to keep this from affecting my job here. If you need me to speak to the fire chief, I can do that."

"Don't worry about the fire chief. That's my problem."

His air of calm, unworried authority made something break loose inside her. Besides, it wasn't fair to keep him in the dark.

"You deserve to know what's going on. My mother wants me to do a *You and Me* reunion show," she said, wincing at how ridiculous it sounded. "And she's pulling out all the stops, Annabelle Hatfield–style."

"A *You and Me* reunion show?" Squinting, he leaned one hip on his desk. "I'm pretty sure Chief Renteria might have a problem with that one."

"No shit. *I* have a problem with it. But my mother's got her heart set on it. And she's a force of nature. She's stubborn like you wouldn't believe." Sabina's military posture flagged; her shoulders slumped. She tried to straighten them but it felt like lifting the weight of ten fire trucks. She stared down at the floor, willing herself to keep it together, then felt a firm hand squeeze her shoulder.

"Sit down. I can't have my firefighters all churned up."

He steered her toward a chair. She sat, vibrating from the effect of his touch, while he disappeared out the door. "Churned up." That's exactly how she felt when he was around. She took a deep breath and inhaled the familiar scent of the office mixed with the added freshness of Roman's aftershave. It smelled delicious to her, sort of spicy and exciting, like cappuccino and Greek olives. She smiled at the image, as if Roman were some kind of exotic gourmet market.

He returned with two mugs of coffee and a handful of sugar packets and kicked the door closed behind him.

"I like mine black but extra sweet. How about you?" Balancing the coffee cups, he stepped carefully toward her. Something inside her melted at the sight of such a mighty specimen of manhood cradling the cups as if they were baby chicks.

"Only when no one's looking."

One marauding eyebrow quirked upward. "You have a secret sweet tooth?"

"The guys would tease me if I poured too much sugar in my coffee. You know what my rookie nickname was?"

"What?" He hoisted one hip onto the desk and blew on his coffee. He had nicely shaped lips. Firm, with a sensual curve. And they had felt so good when they'd closed over hers . . .

Stop it.

"Sweet'N Low. Annabelle never had sugar in the

house. I grew up with the little pink Sweet'N Low packets. The guys thought that was hilarious. So when I came to this station I started drinking my coffee black."

"And then you became Two."

She made a face and poured three packets of sugar in her coffee, one after the other. Who the hell cared now? Besides, if that mountain of masculinity known as Chief Roman could put sugar in his coffee, so could she.

"Just curious, why'd you give up acting?" He took a sip of steaming coffee. "Seems like you could have had quite a career if you'd stuck to show business."

She bristled. "What are you implying?"

Another eyebrow raise. Those strong, sweeping eyebrows did something to her body temperature.

"Absolutely nothing," he said. "It was a simple question."

Suddenly weary, she lowered her cup and rubbed a hand across her forehead. "Sorry. I'm getting paranoid. I just want everything back how it was."

He shrugged his massive shoulders. "Waste of energy. No matter how much you wish it, things never go back to how they were."

Oh God. She was an idiot, complaining about her stupid problems when nothing she'd faced in her life compared to losing a wife on 9/11. She curled both hands around her coffee mug and wondered if she should offer sympathy or condolences. He never mentioned his wife at the station, but he must know it was common knowledge.

Silence stretched between them, taut as a tightrope.

"I hated acting," she blurted. "But it was the only thing my mother ever wanted. If I complained about it, she'd yell at me about how lucky I was to be rich and famous and still have my whole life ahead of me. That really scared me—a whole life of makeup and cameras and directors pushing me around? When I was seventeen I filed for legal emancipation and quit the show."

Those simple words hid a lot of angst, a lot of legal maneuvering, yelling on Annabelle's part, and white-knuckle fear.

"And never looked back? So long, Hollywood?"

"Well, it wasn't quite that easy. I had no skills and a pretty sketchy education. I'd never been on my own before. I went a little wild and burned through my money. That's why I did *Zombie Nights*—I needed the cash. And that's when I decided to become a firefighter."

"Zombies inspired you to join the force? Now that's a story I'd love to hear."

She laughed, feeling herself relax, and took a long drink from her extremely sweet coffee. "I told you a little bit of it. I was hanging out on the set waiting to shoot the scene after I'd been turned into a zombie. Full makeup and everything. I looked disgusting, as you'll find out if you ever watch the movie. Which I beg you not to do, by the way. Anyway, the lead zombie, I can't even remember his name, was all hopped up on something and kept blowing his lines. I'd been there about twelve hours and there was no end in sight."

From behind the shield of his coffee cup, Roman watched Sabina tell her story, trying to hide his fascination. She was such a puzzle. A celebrity kid who had turned her back on it all. A beauty who preferred to be one of the guys. He wanted to jump under her skin and figure her out. Or at least stroke that skin, especially right there along her throat where her pulse danced . . .

He realized he was staring and snapped back to attention.

"All of a sudden people started screaming from the parking lot where the trailers were. We all ran out there. Flames were pouring out of the star's trailer. The security people called 911 and a fire engine zoomed onto the lot. They jumped out and had the fire out in about half a minute. They couldn't have cared less that they were on the set of a Hollywood movie. They came in, did their job, worked together like a perfect machine, no egos, no temper tantrums, no arguments over who gets the bigger trailer or who gets more close-ups. I almost cried when they left. I wanted to go with them so badly. I wanted to *be* them. Do something that mattered in the world."

Roman forced a smile through the ache in his heart. He felt as if he were truly seeing Sabina for the first time. The passionate light in her eyes, the determination in her voice—and Renteria wanted her out. He'd just gotten another phone call from the angry chief. A cameraman had ambushed Renteria at headquarters looking for a sound bite about the Bachelorette. "Bite me" made for a damn good sound bite, if you were the evening news.

Renteria wanted blood. But he hadn't seen the light in Sabina's eyes as she talked about the job.

"So you decided right then and there to become a firefighter?"

"More or less. On the way out, one of the firemen stopped and looked at me. Mind you, I was in full zombie mode. You know what he said?"

"Can't imagine."

"He said, 'Suffer a sea change into something rich and strange.' *Shakespeare.* He quoted Shakespeare at me. Turned out he taught drama as a second job. Right then, I was hooked."

Roman shook his head with a frown. "What does

Shakespeare have to do with anything?" Either she wasn't making much sense or he was too distracted by the way her vivid eyes lit up the bland office.

"The sea change. It occurred to me that I could give myself a sea change. I didn't have to be stuck doing zombie movies forever." She rose gracefully to her feet, still clutching her mug. "Thanks for the coffee, Roman. And the distraction. I need to make a call before lineup. I have to get a handle on this crap before it gets too out of control."

After she'd left, Roman spent a long time staring at the chair she'd abandoned, breathing the air that still carried a whiff of jasmine-scented shampoo. He felt woozy. Her words, her expressions, the way her fingers wrapped around her mug, the way her eyes lit up . . . her presence, her spirit . . .

He was in very, very big trouble.

"Max, you're stooping to new lows here. What is this, blackmail by local news?"

Max cackled. "Local's just the beginning, munchkin. I got big plans."

Sabina paced around the backyard of the firehouse. The crew was starting to gather in the kitchen for lineup. "It doesn't matter what you and Annabelle pull, I'm not going to do the show. Everything you try is only going to make me more determined never to get in front of a camera again."

"You're being stubborn."

"Yes." She could live with stubborn. Like mother, like daughter, after all.

"Are you trying to make me play hardball?"

She clenched her jaw. *Don't fall for his bait, don't do it.* "You don't scare me. You're running out of skeletons to pull out of my past."

"This one's not in the past. It's right there in your firehouse."

"Excuse me?"

His voice hardened. "A little birdie tells me you were spotted behind a fire engine setting off some major sparks with the new guy from New York. I checked your department regulations. He's several levels above you and that's strictly a no-no. Grounds for disciplinary action."

Sabina's mind raced. Behind the fire engine. She and Roman had talked. Intimately, sure, but nothing had happened. Except . . . that hug. He'd embraced her, to comfort her. It had lasted what, a few, admittedly blissful, seconds? But it didn't matter—if people started talking, she'd be toast. So would Roman. She couldn't do that to him.

The only answer was to go on the attack.

"You complete, utter jackass, it wasn't Chief Roman. It was Vader. Everyone knows Vader and I are into each other. It's the hot gossip around here, surprised you haven't heard about it since you're suddenly so interested in Fire Station 1."

"Vader?" The uncertainty in his voice gave her a savage glee.

"Yeah, Vader. Big, ripped guy. Works out a lot. Could snap you in two with one hand behind his back. And since we're both the same rank, perfectly within regulations."

Max, for once, didn't have a comeback.

"And I was wrong, *Uncle Max*. Now you've hit a new low. The absolute bottom of the barrel."

She hung up and raced across the lawn toward the kitchen, where everyone was assembling for lineup. Had it really come to this? After all these years protecting her reputation, now she was actually spreading false rumors about herself. Suddenly it felt as if she were in a bad dream, the kind in which no matter how fast she ran, she kept slipping farther behind. The men gathered inside the kitchen belonged here at this firehouse. Did she? Did she really? Or had she been living a lie for the past ten years?

For Sabina's sake, Roman was almost happy when the next call came in. He knew nothing would improve her state of mind as much as a structure fire. The dispatcher had barely finished talking when she was into her turnout and onboard Engine 1.

Quiet descended on the station after the engine and the truck roared out of the apparatus bay. Perfect time to focus on the reports Roman needed to deliver to Chief Renteria. He had a feeling his job was a precarious thing right about now. The chief wasn't happy with him, and the crew hadn't exactly warmed up to him. Nor had Stan, although he occasionally condescended to eat a doggy treat.

Roman grabbed another cup of coffee, tossed a sausage-flavored, bone-shaped biscuit Stan's way, and settled down to work.

"Why, Chief Roman, you look so sad and lonely sitting by yourself like that," said a throaty voice.

Roman looked up sharply to find Annabelle Hatfield posed in the doorway. Black sunglasses held glorious red waves of hair away from her face. In cream-colored linen slacks and jacket, she brought a whiff of winter glamour into the office.

"Ms. Hatfield." He found himself rising to his feet. Such was her power. "What can I do for you?"

"I sure do like the way you put that. And my, you're tall." She winked. All his hackles rose. Whatever had brought her here, along with a slight Southern accent that was definitely new, it was bound to mean trouble.

"Would you like some coffee?"

"Sounds delightful." She waited, with an expectant smile.

"It's right outside. Help yourself."

The smile evaporated. Now she wore that look that meant little Taffy McGee was in trouble. Yes, this was a formidable woman. Then again, he'd expect nothing less from the woman who'd given birth to Sabina Jones.

"Or you can just tell me why you're here."

"Fine," she said, advancing into the room, bringing a strong, exotic fragrance with her—papaya or mango, something vaguely tropical. She glowed with a kind of sparkling energy that made it hard to look away.

"I was hoping to see Captain Kelly."

"He's out on a call. Fighting a fire," he added, when she didn't seem to know what that meant. "But I'm the section commander, also filling in for the battalion chief."

"I suppose you'll do, then. I'm worried about my daughter." Although he hadn't invited her to do so, she lowered herself into the same chair Sabina had occupied and crossed her legs.

"I can understand that. It must be tough to see her so upset about her privacy being violated."

His dry tone made her narrow her eyes. "If you want my opinion, she shouldn't be here. She doesn't belong on a fire engine. She doesn't belong with a sweaty, steroid-bloated gym rat called Vader."

At the mention of Vader, he tightened his fist around his pen. Had he missed something? Had Sabina changed her "policy" about dating firemen? "What's your point?"

"My point is, as her mother, I can't simply stand by and let her ruin her life like this."

"She's a grown woman, Ms. Hatfield. She can make her own decisions. From what I understand, she's been doing that since the age of seventeen."

Annabelle tossed a shank of red hair out of her face. He sensed she was trying to hide the fact that he'd hit a sore spot. If so, she recovered quickly. "But, Chief Roman, you have responsibilities of your own. Are you going to stand by and let her ruin the station?" She zeroed her gaze on him, so he felt the force of her furiously strong will. "I know the media. I know how to play the media. They won't let go if something is juicy enough."

Dio, this was the woman Sabina had grown up with? No wonder she was stubborn. "Or if someone keeps feeding them."

"Exactly. But I have a solution that will stop the madness."

A solution. As if she weren't the cause of the entire problem.

"I also know my daughter, Chief Roman. And she won't give in. She's far too stubborn for her own good. She'll tear this station down before she considers stepping aside. For your sake, for her sake, cut it off before it's too late."

He fiddled with his pen, uneasy at the direction she appeared to be taking. "What exactly are you suggesting?"

"Suspend her. Just for a couple months."

"You want me to suspend your daughter?" he repeated in disbelief. He wasn't Sabina's captain, but Annabelle didn't need to know that.

"She's bad for morale, I should think. She deceived her fellow firefighters about her true identity. She's apparently dating a fellow fireman. No wonder I'm worried about her. She needs a couple of months to think about things."

And to shoot a TV show. Disgusted, Roman decided he'd endured enough of this absurd conversation.

"Sorry, Ms. Hatfield. Firefighter Jones has done nothing to merit a suspension. She's needed here on the job. Have a good day." He gave her a brisk, dismissive nod and turned back to his paperwork.

Out of the corner of his eye, he saw her mouth fall open. Maybe she was hoping to get in the last word. He decided to beat her to it, and lifted his head again.

"Piece of advice from a blue-collar guy who's never set foot on a red carpet and doesn't care if he ever does. You could try being proud of your daughter. She's a helluva firefighter."

The last he heard of Annabelle Hatfield was the swish of her linen slacks against the doorjamb as she stalked out of his office.

Something told him he'd be seeing more of her.

Chapter Fifteen

Over the next couple of days, Roman realized he should have kept his mouth shut. Upping the ante, Annabelle Hatfield went on a pre-Christmas blitz of national media appearances. On CNN she talked about her grief over the rift with her daughter.

"We were always so close. I never thought it would come to this." She dabbed at her eyes with a handkerchief. "Even though we worked together almost every day on the show, we rarely fought. It was just the two of us against the world." She raised beautiful green eyes, fogged with tears, toward the camera and delivered the kicker.

"If only she knew how proud I am of her."

Fanculo! He'd handed her a weapon and she'd snatched it up and run with it. Roman cursed again and picked up the remote control someone had left on the couch. The Engine 1 crew was out on a call—grease fire at a fast-food joint at the edge of town. The Truck 1 crew was in the apparatus bay, cleaning the remaining rigs and planning a Christmas skiing trip. He was the only one in the training room. He switched the channel to another station, where Annabelle was chatting with a reporter in an intimate living-room setting.

"My daughter chooses to risk her life every day to save others, how can I not be proud of her? Any mother would be. But it also terrifies me. She's my only child, and as a single mother, our bond was especially strong. Every time I hear sirens my heart races. That could be my baby in that fire engine, riding to some poor family's rescue. It's so very hard. I'm sure everyone with a loved one who's a police officer, firefighter, or a member of the armed forces shares my feelings. I'm here to tell you, I feel your pain. I understand your fears. Let's keep on praying and hoping and believing in our sons and daughters."

The reporter leaned forward and held her hand. "What a moving speech. You just brought tears to my eyes." She dabbed at her face with a tissue. "Do you have any message for your daughter today?"

"Darling, I love you and I'm very, very proud of you. In the spirit of Christmas, let's come together and work out our differences. Just you and me." At this point shots of the San Gabriel firehouse flashed on the screen, followed by a montage of clips of Sabina on the job.

Roman let out a growl. Annabelle Hatfield's message to her daughter was perfectly clear. *You and Me*? Come together? Work out their differences? Despite her tender manner, Annabelle knew exactly what she was doing. One way or another, she was going to get the attention she wanted, no matter the cost to Sabina.

He switched off the TV, then went a step further and unplugged it. If he could somehow program the

TV set to avoid all mention of the Hatfield family, he'd do it. If he had to ban TV watching until all this blew over, he'd do that too. He wasn't about to let a media-hungry actress disrupt his station.

"Enjoying the show?" Chief Renteria strode into the training room.

Roman bit back another curse. "Not one bit."

"Neither is anyone else. What do you plan to do about it?" The chief was a gruff, businesslike man with striking, Aztec warrior–like good looks, a graying buzz cut, and a sharp manner.

"Ride it out. Ignore it." He'd thought about it long and hard and couldn't think of any other good plan.

"Have you talked to Firefighter Jones about it?"

"Yes."

The chief gestured impatiently. "And?"

"She's as annoyed as the rest of us. She's just trying to do her job."

"She's making it damn difficult for anyone to do their job. I nearly tripped over a cameraman in the bushes out front."

Psycho strolled into the training room, then stopped short at the sight of the fire chief.

"Chief," he said with a sharp salute and an ironic click of his heels.

"This ain't the army," growled Renteria. "Chief Roman, in your office."

Nothing for it but to grit his teeth and ride it out. Roman led the way into his office and closed the door.

Renteria launched right into his lecture. "In all the years Captain Brody led this station, we never had this much media attention. I thought the Bachelor Fireman crap was bad; well, this is ten times worse. The Bachelorette Fireman? Next she'll be handing out roses and picking a wedding dress. We have a movie star who won't shut up and a firefighter whose every move gets a damn press release. Do you know how many calls our public information officer is fielding about Jones? One every fifteen minutes."

"Decline all interview requests."

"It gets worse. The dispatchers are getting fake calls. People requesting Taffy McGee to get their cats out of their trees."

"Press charges. That's illegal."

"You know why I'm here. It's time, Roman. I can't trust a temporary captain with this."

Roman tamped down his churning anger. He'd known this was coming. Renteria was just doing his job, watching out for the force. He'd do the same himself. In fact, maybe he'd be saying the exact same thing, if he didn't know Sabina, if he didn't . . .

He didn't finish the thought. Instead, he picked up a paperweight from his desk. Left by Brody, it was shaped like a volcano, and for some reason he found it soothing. He hefted it in his hands, shifting it from one to the other.

Renteria went on. "I checked her records. You just gave her a notice to improve. But generally, she's perfectly adequate. Couple awards. No disciplinary problems. Above average in all performance categories. But not spectacular."

Roman stifled the urge to wing the paperweight at Renteria's head. Sabina, adequate? That word didn't fit. In fact, in his opinion, "spectacular" worked pretty damn well. "I have to be honest here. She's done her job faithfully and well ever since she joined the station. We have no grounds to take any action against her. She'll have her lawyers all over us and I wouldn't blame her."

"Section 4B in the Rules and Regs."

Section 4B. Roman's mind raced. He'd had to learn a whole new set of regulations when he'd taken the job here. What was 4B again? "The public appearance section?"

"'No firefighter shall bring discredit to the department.' That's why we turned down *Playgirl* when they wanted to do a Bachelor Firemen spread."

"Sure, but Jones hasn't done anything like that."

"No?" Renteria raised one arm. Roman watched, shocked and bemused, as the grizzled chief pretended to soap his chest while he whistled a tune. "The shower scene heard round the world?"

"That was years before she came here. She hadn't even applied to the academy yet. The regulations don't apply."

"Those regulations were written before YouTube. It might be a matter for the lawyers, but it's worth looking into. Doesn't matter how you do it, but take care of it, Roman. This is why you were hired. To crack down and hold their feet to the fire. Provide an extra layer of authority. Consider this test number one."

The man wheeled around and headed for the door.

"Chief Renteria—"

"I told you I'm done with this crap. The guys here say you're a hard-ass. Now prove it."

Roman watched his superior officer stride through the training room with barely a glance for the firemen gathering for the next drill. He put the paperweight down before he was tempted to end his career with one swing of the arm. He knew some guys called him a hard-ass, but he didn't see it that way. He aimed for tough but fair, harsh but never capricious. By the book. Disciplined. Rigorous.

When Renteria was gone, Stan shuffled in, licking his chops. Apparently the dog had been snacking while Roman had been having his ass handed to him. Stan plodded toward the dog bed in the corner, cast one scornful glance at Roman, curled up, and instantly dozed off.

The dog disliked him. His crew called him a hard-ass and might even be on the verge of mutiny. Instead of improving the situation he'd been hired to fix, he'd made it infinitely worse in just a couple short weeks. And his fire chief had just issued an ultimatum.

Savagely, he tossed the paperweight into the waste-basket, where it landed with a satisfying clunk.

Psycho snagged Sabina as soon as she hopped off Engine 1. "Renteria was here."

"The fire chief?" She frowned, peeling off her brush jacket. "So?"

"He yelled at Roman about you. I loitered around the kitchen to listen."

"Classy move."

"Thought you'd appreciate it."

Reality returned in a miserable rush. While hauling the hose to fight the grease fire, she'd been able to put all the Bachelorette drama out of her mind. It was the only time she'd felt like herself lately. But she couldn't be on the job every single minute.

"What did he say?"

"I heard something about Bachelorette, something about Roman proving himself. I think Roman threw something. Stan came running out of there like the office was on fire."

"He threw something at Stan?"

"No. But you know how Stan is. I think he has post-traumatic stress disorder."

"Whatever, Dr. Psycho."

"Don't mock. I've got a diagnosis for your mother too."

Sabina stepped out of her boots and pulled off the suspenders of her pants. Her T-shirt was soaked with sweat. "She'll be thrilled. I'll give you her number, you can discuss it with her."

"Yeah, like I want to talk to someone with narcissistic personality disorder."

"Shove it, Psycho." It was one thing for her to criticize her mother, but she didn't want to hear it from Psycho. She arranged her turnout for the next call and shouldered her way past him.

"That's the thanks I get for warning you?"

Vader strolled over. "Warning her about what?"

"Renteria showed up. A case of soda says Two's going down."

Vader's eyes went wide. "Shut the fuck up."

Sabina flung herself away from them and shut herself into her room to strip off her T-shirt and change into a new one. Fine, she'd been warned. Not that she needed it. As soon as she'd seen the new *True Hollywood Story* thrown together by the E! Network, she'd seen the handwriting on the wall. They'd shown her shower scene over and over again. They'd replayed bits of various Bachelor Firemen stories. They'd managed to find a scene from *You and Me* in which Taffy had set the kitchen on fire while lighting a candle for a séance. And they'd shown an interview with Annabelle in which she tearfully expressed her regret over the mistakes she'd made as a single mother, and pleaded for a Christmas reunion with her only daughter, the light of her life, the brave, death-defying Bachelorette Fireman.

How could the San Gabriel Fire Department possibly continue to put up with this? Sabina had seen so many video cameras at fire scenes lately, she was starting to think she was back in Hollywood.

She slipped into a new SGFD T-shirt, wondering if this would be one of the last times she did so. A sick feeling ate at her insides. If the fire chief knew how much her job meant to her, maybe he'd show some mercy. But he wouldn't care about that. With hundreds of firefighters under his command, why should he give a crap about one especially troublesome one?

Her feet felt like lead as she dragged herself out of the bathroom and toward the training room. It was almost time for dinner. It was Stud's turn to cook. That meant meatball soup. After the other recipes he'd attempted, they'd taken a station-wide vote and restricted him to his only successful dish. At least Stan would enjoy it.

Would this be the last firehouse dinner she got to make fun of? Would this be the last meatball she'd slip into Stan's dish?

When she reached the training room, the other firefighters were milling around in the kitchen. A quiet buzz of whispers filled the room, but she couldn't make out any words. Probably teasing Stud about the meatballs. She glanced around the room. For once, the TV was off, which was a small mercy. One more shot of Annabelle's tearful, soft-focus face and she'd follow Roman's example and throw something.

Vader glanced up and met her eyes. He looked so serious she barely recognized him. Then the others turned and saw her as well. No one smiled. Why did they look so grim? Her gaze traveled from one to the other, scanning the faces of the guys she'd spent the past ten years with. Double D's usually jovial face might as well have been a Kabuki mask. Double D had never liked her, no matter how hard she'd worked to prove herself to him.

Suddenly she understood. They'd had it with her

and the chaos she'd brought down on the station. She couldn't blame them—she was sick of it too. But the pain of that realization hit deep. She actually brought her hands to her stomach, afraid she might throw up on the spot.

Rooted to the ground, she watched helplessly as Double D marched to the door of Roman's office and pounded on it. Everything seemed to be moving in slow motion. His chubby fist banged on the door. The other firefighters shifted nervously, but they hung together as a group. They were clearly united. United against her.

She tried not to think about all the times they'd had each other's back on the fire lines. No sense in torturing herself.

The office door opened and Roman stepped out, looking like a giant greeting supplicants at his castle. He scanned the crowd of firemen, and his face took on a forbidding scowl. "Yes?"

"We got something to say," said Double D. "And I'm saying it because I've been here the longest."

Under the daunting weight of the chief's glare, he hesitated. A couple of the other firemen murmured, "We're with you, D. Spit it out."

"Good advice. Spit it out," Roman barked.

Sabina couldn't take it another second. She couldn't bear to listen to her fellow firemen reject her in public. Besides, they shouldn't have to put up with this crap. They were collateral damage in the war between her mother and her, and that wasn't fair. She opened her mouth and forced some strangled words out of her tight throat. "There's no need for this. I don't want to hurt the firehouse. Chief Roman, I'll submit my resig—"

Roman held up his hand in a brisk motion so commanding her mouth snapped shut.

"Firefighter Jones. You'll have your say. Right now Firefighter Lee has something on his mind and I want to hear it. Continue."

Double D shot Sabina a look of utter outrage. Why was he angry at her when she'd been trying to save him the trouble of kicking her to the curb?

Double D stiffened his shoulders, sucked in his belly, faced Chief Roman, and launched into his speech.

"Chief Roman, it's about Two."

She knew it. She squeezed her eyes halfway shut, unable to bear it in full screen. Here it came. The end of the best years of her life. The end of everything she wanted.

"That is"—Double D indicated Sabina—"Firefighter Jones is a top-notch fireman in every respect."

What? What? Sabina didn't understand. What was he saying?

"Even though she's a woman and used to be a TV star, she's no different from the rest of us. She does her job, she works hard, she's saved my ass and everyone else's here. She ain't done nothing to deserve suspension or anything else. If you and the rest of the brass try to get rid of her, you're going to have an empty firehouse because if she goes, we all go. We stand by our own, and Sabina Jones is one of our own."

Once the crew had been called to the scene of an apartment fire that turned out to involve a meth lab. Something had exploded, and Sabina had felt the shock waves travel through the air, through her body, before the sound struck her eardrums. That's exactly how this felt.

She stared, uncomprehending, at the firemen, until the words came crashing into logical sense around her.

Double D was standing up for her. They all were.

Her vision went blurry as she fought a doomed

battle against tears. If she cried in front of them, she'd never hear the end of it. Blinking furiously, she gripped the closest support, the back of an armchair.

Say something, Sabina. Say something.

But she couldn't. Her throat muscles worked, but no words came. Emotion swamped her. This had never happened to her before. No one had ever taken her side, had ever stood behind her. With her.

Say something.

Like a lifeline, Chief Roman's deep voice resonated through the room, capturing the crew's attention. "Duly noted."

"Duly noted? That's all?" Vader shouldered his way to the front of the group. Sabina took advantage of the distraction to swipe her forearm across her face and clear the tears away.

"I've heard your perspective, and I will take it under advisement. There are a lot of factors here."

"What factors? You can't blame any of this on Sabina. She tried to keep it secret so it wouldn't affect us. She didn't even tell me!"

Sabina blinked away more tears. Vader got it. He really got it. She didn't have to explain anything to him.

"I'm not saying otherwise."

"What are you saying?" Vader took a step forward until he stood nose to chin with Roman. "That you'd deep-six one of your own firefighters just to make the brass happy? We won't let you do that."

"You don't have a say in it," snapped Roman.

Oh God. This was exactly what she didn't want to happen. She didn't want the station torn apart over her.

"This isn't necessary." She croaked the words, then cleared her throat to repeat them more loudly. Everyone looked in her direction. She summoned every bit of acting skill she'd formerly possessed. "As I was about to say before, this station means a lot to me. I don't want to be the cause of anything that distracts from doing our job. We're supposed to put out fires, remember? Not dodge camera crews and reporters. I'll . . ." God, it was hard to say. She was about to hand over her life, her precious, hard-won job, like a lamb to the slaughter. But it had to be done. "I'll step down. I'll resign."

"Your resignation is not accepted," snapped Roman.

She gaped at him. So did everyone else. You could have heard a pin drop in the kitchen. The only sound was the low murmur of the police scanner in the training room.

"As I told Fire Chief Renteria a few minutes ago on the phone, I see no grounds for action against Firefighter Jones. Anything less than full support for Firefighter Jones would reflect badly on the department and on us as firefighters. Jones, you represent ten years of experience and training. You're needed here. In fact, if you so much as request time off, I'll consider it a dereliction of duty. You're a firefighter, and you'll damn well stay here and put out fires with the rest of your crew. Got it?"

By the end of his speech, his voice had risen to a thunderous level. He pinned them all with a glare of fire, like a warrior inciting his troops to battle.

Stunned silence vibrated through every corner of the fire station.

"The media can do whatever they want. We do what we always do. *Our job*. Are we all clear?"

A rumble of "yes, sirs" followed. All eyes were riveted to Roman, who had transformed from grim hardass to mighty leader right before their eyes. Sabina called on every ounce of willpower she possessed to stay upright and not make a fool of herself.

Roman relaxed his stance. "Now is that meatball stew I smell?"

Just like that, the atmosphere loosened. Roman strolled away from the office door and joined the firemen, who clapped him on the back and shook his hand. Stan trotted behind him, sniffing the air eagerly. Sabina forced her shaking legs to carry her forward.

Never had she loved anyone as much as she loved the San Gabriel firemen at that moment. They'd had her back, every single one of them. Even the new guy from New York.

Chapter Sixteen

Roman had made one of his problems a lot worse—Renteria had hung up on him after a few choice curses—but he'd solved another. The firemen of Station 1 had swung one hundred and eighty degrees in the other direction, from outright mutiny to something like adulation. He had to admit, it felt good. No one wanted to be a hard-ass all the time.

For the first time since his first night at Station 1, he joined the crew for dinner. Stud's meatball stew could have used some oregano and a dash of burgundy, but otherwise, he couldn't complain. He sat at the head of the table and listened to the guys talk about the Christmas ski trip to Big Bear.

"Captain, you like to ski?"

"Never tried it."

Stud's fork clattered to the ground. "You gotta come with, Romeo. You can start at the bunny slope, we swear we won't laugh. They give us a discount cuz we're firemen. It's a blast and a half—"

Roman let him rattle on until he paused for a breath. "Back up, Stud. Romeo?"

Fred turned pink. "Well, you know, it's close to Roman and kinda fits with the bachelor thing, and—"

"No."

"Really? Because you don't have a nickname yet and—"

"No."

Fred gave in. "You're right, you're right."

Roman let his grim expression relax. A line had to be drawn, but that didn't mean he had to be a jerk. "You can keep working on the nickname, but back in New York they called me Rock."

At the other end of the table, Sabina choked on a meatball. The fact that only she knew his former nickname made it seem like a secret bedroom name, or something he called his penis.

Fred tilted his head. "I don't know. Rock's sort of . . . one-dimensional."

Psycho chimed in with a hoot. "Like most of our nicknames are layered and complex?"

"Rock," said Vader enviously. "I like it. Rock-hard abs, rock-hard bod, rock-hard . . . whatever."

Sabina seemed to be really struggling with her meatball.

"But he can't have the same handle as he had back East," said Fred plaintively.

"Why does it matter?" Roman kept an eye on Sabina. Should he vault down the table and administer the Heimlich maneuver?

"I can't explain it. It just does. We'll think of something. We need to get Hoagie back in here, he was always good with nicknames."

They launched into a dissection of the etymology of the various nicknames, but he didn't pay much mind. His attention was on Sabina, who finally got a grip on herself and managed to swallow her meatball. He smiled in relief, then nearly got knocked off his chair by what came next. A full-hearted, genuine, grateful smile encompassed her entire face, curved her lips into a perfect half moon, found a dimple in one cheek, made her eyes glow like crystals in a sunbeam, and generally transformed her elegant face into something that deserved an angelic choir singing along.

Good God Almighty.

His grip on his spoon loosened so it plopped into his stew. The tips of his ears tingled, then his scalp, the way it did when he was in the presence of something truly spectacular. It had happened only a few times, mostly in Italy when he'd heard a snatch of opera whistled by a man on a bicycle, or passed a glorious Florentine church.

Helpless, he gazed back like a fly trapped in a rapturous web. This was how Odysseus must have felt when his ship passed the island with the sirens. Weak and drugged, as though nothing mattered, nothing existed, except the sweet bliss beckoning him to his doom.

What had he done? By standing up for Sabina, what had he unleashed? If she kept smiling at him like this, instead of offering him that familiar wary, defiant expression, he was a dead man. If he had any chance of conducting himself like a proper training officer, he'd have to lash himself to the mast the way Odysseus had.

Maybe the aerial would do.

He wrenched his gaze away without returning her smile. Balling up his napkin, he piled it in his bowl and rose to his feet.

"I'll get that," said Ace, the rookie, scrambling to help him.

Roman stopped him with a gesture. "I'm not king here, I can clear my own plate."

"That's it!" Fred bounced in his chair. "Your nickname. King. Or King Roman."

"No."

"You're right, you're right."

"I'm going to pass on the ski trip," Roman said over his shoulder as he carried his plate to the kitchen. "No new tricks for this old dog."

"Old Dog . . . that's not bad . . ." Fred mused.

"No."

"Right."

Even though it caused him a near-physical pain, he managed to avoid the fading meteor of Sabina's smile until he reached his office. No ski trips for him. No outings of any kind where Sabina might be present. No smiles, no friendliness, no more lectures in his office. No, no, no. Face it, he couldn't handle it.

Then he remembered. Luke had a game tomorrow. Damn his luck.

For the first time, he gave serious consideration to the rumors of a "curse."

Fine. She could take a hint. As Sabina drove Carly to the game, she ticked off the facts. Roman didn't want her gratitude. He didn't want her friendship. She knew the feeling all too well. Bianca, the makeup artist's daughter, for instance. All she'd wanted was an invitation to the Kids' Choice Awards. Sabina had wanted to invite her, since she was fun and liked to snowboard and together they had giggle fests like normal girls. But instead her mother had invited the leader of a hot new boy band—long gone now—and Bianca had dumped her.

Of course, Roman could probably pick up cute, pink-haired Bianca with one finger. The point being, Sabina knew better than to trust just anyone with her friendship. And even though he'd stood up for her, he clearly wanted nothing to do with her.

She could live with that. In fact, it made life a lot easier. After she wished Carly a good game and climbed into the bleachers, she could just ignore the smoldering hulk of masculine hotness seated on the top bleacher to the left. She didn't have to wave or pretend she was glad to see him. She could ignore the fact that he didn't look her way, that his gorgeous head didn't move one micro-inch in her direction, that his neck was starting to tan. She could ignore the thin sliver of pale skin under the edge of his T-shirt and the way it contrasted with his strong, brown neck. His forearms looked darker too, under their light covering of black hair.

A flash of memory—the black hair covering his burly chest, swirling below his belt—weakened her knees and made her sink onto the bleachers a moment before she was ready.

"Sorry, lost my balance," she muttered to the woman in whose lap she'd nearly landed.

Yes, she could ignore all those things. It was such a relief.

Diane, farther down the bleachers, quickly switched places with the woman. "I wasn't sure you'd show up today," she whispered.

"Why wouldn't I?"

"All those crazy news stories. Everyone keeps asking me about you. I have to tell them I don't know a thing." She gave a sniff of pique.

"I'm sorry, Diane. I didn't tell anyone. I was trying to start a new life."

"Whatever," Diane grumbled, then obviously decided not to hold a grudge. "Did you hear about the Dane twins? They're going to do a clinic for the league in a couple of weeks."

"Really? Carly will be so excited."

The Dane twins felt like family—they were Katie Dane's brothers, and now that Ryan Blake had married Katie, that made them virtually brothers-in-law to the entire San Gabriel firehouse.

"Yeah, well, it's not like they're celebrities like *some people*."

Sabina decided to ignore that.

"On the bright side, I'm getting lots of new clients because the word is out that we're friends."

"Glad I could help."

"But you could have told me, you know," Diane hissed as the players ran out onto the field.

Sabina directed her attention to the game, but her mind kept wandering. Her job was safe, thanks to Roman and the crew—unless things got even crazier. But what else could Max and Annabelle do? They'd done the media blitz. Pretty soon some other hot story would take over and no one would care about Taffy McGee. All she had to do was ride out the storm. With the guys behind her, she could do it.

What an incredible thought—she wasn't alone. It was almost too much to take in.

The game went fast. The team was finally clicking. Carly started and pitched four great innings, then Luke was brought in to shut things down. Carly stood in the "dugout" cheering with everyone else. Sabina even spotted Carly and Luke with their heads together between innings, comparing batters, perhaps.

She couldn't help it; she glanced over her shoulder

to see if Roman noticed too. But his sunglasses made him as inscrutable as a Secret Service agent.

After the game, Carly dashed to Sabina's side. "Can we go to Chili's? Please, please, please?"

Out of the corner of her eye, Sabina saw Luke mounting a similar assault on Roman. "I don't know, Carly. I'll just be a distraction."

"Huh?" Her Little Sister gazed at her blankly. "Oh, that. Don't worry, everyone's over it. Most people never saw that show anyway."

"Right." Properly humbled, Sabina agreed to a short stop at Chili's.

At the restaurant, Carly made a beeline for Luke. Bright-eyed and revved up from the win, he offered her some chips and guacamole and they immediately began dissecting the game. When had they become new best friends? Did she need to monitor this development? But she couldn't, not when a small army of parents, led by Diane, was converging on her.

She looked around for Roman, who sat at a table in the corner, long legs stretched out, listening to the chatter of one of the single mothers. Catching his eye, she gestured to Luke and Sabina.

After quickly assessing the situation, he gave her a short nod—*I'm on it*. She relaxed. If Roman was on top of it, she didn't need to worry. The crowd of parents surrounded her and began tossing curious questions at her, as if they were photographers at a red carpet premiere.

Like a good little former actress, she answered them all.

"My acting days are over . . . I didn't want to be a distraction to the San Gabriel Fire Department . . . Reunion show? Really, my mother said that on FOX? No, there's absolutely no truth to that rumor." Through a fixed smile, she gritted her teeth. Oh, her mother was clever. She was probably hoping to stoke the public's anticipation of a reunion show so high, Sabina would be hounded into participating.

Someone asked her about the firehouse. Before she could answer, someone else asked whether she was dating a fellow fireman. It was turning into a free-for-all, everyone tossing out questions without waiting his turn. Press junkets were a lot more organized. Maybe she should rent a hotel suite and hire a PR assistant.

She ignored the dating question and answered the first one. "Everyone's being very supportive, but it's definitely hard to do our jobs when people keep aiming cameras at us." She smiled pointedly at the second baseman's father, who'd been taking pictures of her with his iPhone the entire game.

He did not look apologetic. "Must be nice to be famous."

"Well, I wouldn't—"

"You must have made a fortune playing that girl."

"Um . . ."

They closed in on her like buzzards over a fresh kill. "Why did you quit the show? Why don't you get along with your mother? What was it like dating Greg Harrington? Have you heard from him?"

At press junkets, one glance at the coordinator would bring an uncomfortable interview to a close. But here she was on her own. "I'm trying to move on so I'd rather not talk about the show . . ."

"Is Annabelle staying here in town? Will you spend Christmas with her?"

"Uh . . ."

"Okay, that's it." A giant hand landed on her upper arm and plucked her away from the crowd. "Leave her alone," growled Roman.

Everyone fell back, shocked. The man with the iPhone looked outraged. "We're just talking to her."

"Not anymore."

Roman propelled her toward a small table sheltered behind a plastic cactus. He pressed his hand on her shoulder until she sat. From far, far above, his black eyes studied her. "You okay?"

"Yes. You didn't have to do that. I was handling it." He'd already rescued her from losing her job. This felt like overkill.

"Yeah well, I didn't like it. It was damn rude."

"You're not my appointed guardian."

"I am for now." His tone left no room for more argument. Strangely, she didn't mind. It felt too good to let him take charge like this. Too good to have someone on her side.

She gave up and sank back in the chair. "I'd forgotten how funny people can get around someone they've seen on TV. They ask such personal questions."

"They were out of line." He shot a scathing glance at the small knot of chattering parents. "You need anything from the bar? I'm getting some nachos."

"Nachos sound good," she said gratefully. "Extra sour cream. And Roman?"

Already halfway past the cactus, he paused and looked at her over his impossibly broad shoulder.

"Thanks. For this and the other." Tentatively she started to smile, but he crammed his sunglasses onto his face.

"You can thank me by not doing that anymore," he growled.

She gaped after him. That? What was *that*? A harmless smile? The man was deranged.

Her cell phone rang. Vader's name popped up on her screen. "Yo," she answered.

"Yo yourself. Are you busy later? It's Saturday night."

"No." Not unless you counted eating Mexican comfort food and hiding from the public.

"I suppose you're too big a celeb to hang out with me now."

"We can hang, as long as I don't have to buy my own drinks. We celebrities never do, you know."

His laughter rumbled across the line. "Let's do it. I want to see what it's like going out with a famous chick."

"Jesus, Vader, that might be the shallowest thing you've ever said. And that's saying something. What about Cherie, how's it going with her?"

"Hit a roadblock. Her brother came to visit and she uninvited me for dinner. Said she didn't trust me not to say something stupid."

"I'm starting to like this woman."

"Nice, Two. Way to stick up for me. She says I better get used to other gay guys before she lets me meet her brother."

"Hmm . . . Vader, I just had a brilliant idea. You still want to go out tonight?"

As he returned with a plate of nachos, Roman speared Luke and Carly with a laserlike inspection. Nothing inappropriate was going on, as far as he could tell. Hell, Luke was barely thirteen and still acted like a boy, despite his height. Carly was laughing at Luke's attempts to eat a burrito without spilling beans everywhere. Then she showed him how to hold a tamale so the oil didn't drip all over his lap. No need to panic. Luke had a level head on him. He wasn't likely to get all crazy over a girl—unlike his father.

Behind the cactus, all he saw of Sabina was her

long, shapely legs, one crossed over the other, the denim of her jeans kissing each curve. Since she couldn't see him, he allowed his gaze to travel from her red cowboy boots up the length of her shin to her lovely kneecap. Knees weren't normally a turn-on for him, but hers were so nicely shaped, such a perfect hinge between the long bones above and below. She bounced her foot lightly, up and down, the motion hypnotizing him.

He heard her laugh and realized she was talking on her cell phone. As he came closer, he made out her words.

"Hmm . . . Vader, I just had a brilliant idea. You still want to go out tonight?" The low, teasing sound of her voice, like a brook flowing through a forest, sent shivers up his spine.

His pace slowed. He didn't want to interrupt her conversation, nor did he want to eavesdrop. But it might look odd if he suddenly turned on his heel and marched away with his nachos. And truth to tell, he *did* want to interrupt her call. He wanted to rip the phone out of her hand and dump it in a pitcher of margaritas. She could get it back when she promised never to call Vader again. He stood still, uncertain.

"We can go out tonight on one condition, hot stuff," she said into the phone.

Hot stuff. Roman tilted his head one way, then the other, to ease the sudden tension in his neck. *Dio,* he was getting possessive over a woman he hadn't even slept with. One who'd dumped him via a ticket.

"I get to pick the place."

From the other end of the line, Roman caught a loud, grunting protest.

"Oh yes, big guy. That's the deal. Take it or leave it."

Big guy. She was calling Vader "big guy"? Roman

could bench-press two of him. And maybe he would, next time he saw him.

"I'll be there to hold your hand, don't worry. And ply you with drinks. You'll survive, cupcake."

Cupcake? Hold Vader's hand? Roman had heard enough. In one long stride, he reached the cactus. Sabina looked up, and it felt like falling into the Caribbean at sunrise. Sparkling turquoise welcomed him with beams of dancing light. He felt riveted. Unmanned.

He plopped down the plate of nachos, scraped half of them onto a napkin, and gathered it up in one hand. The hot cheese burned through the paper, but he didn't care. It was one thing to stand up for Sabina against Chief Renteria or rescue her from a throng of gossips. But standing around like a dick while she made a date with Vader—flirted with Vader—no fucking way.

"Roman!"

He ignored her and stalked to Luke's table. "Time to go, buddy."

"But Papa, I'm spending the night with Alex. You said I could, remember?"

Vaguely, the memory returned. It had nothing to do with Sabina, which was perhaps why it had faded so easily. Luke had pestered him mercilessly until he'd consented to an overnight at Alex's—only after an extensive conversation with his parents, of course. "You have all your stuff?"

"I have extra clothes in my gym bag. And I have my backpack for school."

"Fine. Have fun. Be safe. Make sure you call me later. Love you."

"Bye, Papa. Love you too."

Roman ignored his son's perplexed look and strode to the parking lot, where he took deep gulps of dry, sage-scented air. So he'd be home alone tonight, while Sabina went out with Vader. He ground his teeth. Blame it on his Italian ancestors, but something about Sabina brought out his barely suppressed, primitive, possessive nature. Maybe he should crash their date and get started on that bench-pressing project. Show Mr. Vader Brown just who really deserved to be called "big guy."

Chapter Seventeen

Sabina met up with Vader on Grove Street outside their favorite bar, Firefly. Vader was waiting, hands shoved in his pockets. He wore his usual uniform—jeans, muscle shirt, jaw stubble, and a goofy grin.

"Hey, superstar," he greeted her.

"Shut up." She followed that up with a big hug, remembering how he'd stood up for her at the firehouse. As she felt the bulge of his muscles swell against her chest, she wondered at the mystery of attraction. If Roman's body was this close to hers, her heart would be stuttering and her blood would be sizzling. She'd never experienced so much as a tingle in a single fingertip over Vader.

She pulled out of his embrace. "Ready for this?"

"Beer and a chick from TV? Hell yeah." He headed for the entrance of Firefly. She snagged his beefy wrist.

"We're not going to Firefly."

"Why not?"

"That won't prove anything to Cherie. I have a plan."

Vader looked uneasy, his warm brown eyes narrowing under his bony brow. "All I want is a beer."

"What happened to proving you're not a homophobe?"

"I think I'm good."

"Oh no, you're not backing out now. You asked for my help and now you're going to get it." She tucked his hand under her elbow and they headed down the street. "We're going to Lush. The gay bar."

He stopped short. "Oh shit, Sabina—"

"Think how impressed Cherie will be. A real homophobe would never go in a bar like that."

Uneasiness rippled across Vader's jutting brow. "I have a bad feeling about this."

"It'll be good for you. And I'll be right there with you the whole time."

He gave in and let her lead the way down Grove Street, in the heart of San Gabriel's shopping district. Ropes of silver tinsel draped the lampposts, along with the occasional harp-playing angel. Around Christmastime, San Gabriel city leaders remembered the town was named after a saint, and angels suddenly began appearing everywhere. A string of lights traced out the shape of an angel on the façade of the new, temporary City Hall, a converted office supply warehouse. The storefronts had all acquired Christmas decorations and little knots of window shoppers.

Sabina's childhood Christmases had been just as Hollywood-weird as her Thanksgivings. Annabelle had been a Christmas-brunch-at-the-Polo-Lounge type of mother, but she'd spent lavishly on presents once they were making money. One year she'd given Sabina diamond earrings. Sabina had been eleven at the time and had really wanted a snowboard.

Why did it seem like the crew at the firehouse understood her more than her mother ever had?

Sabina squeezed Vader's arm to her side. "I really appreciate what you guys did yesterday. Never got a chance to tell you."

Vader shrugged as if it was no big deal. "Do it for anyone. Turns out Roman had your back anyway."

"Does that mean you like him now?"

"No fucking way." His muscles clenched under her arm. "Jury's still out. But I'll give him some time before I kick his arrogant ass."

"Yeah, right."

"Where's your loyalty, Two? Me versus Roman, who would you put your money on?"

"Oh for God's sake." They turned down the side street where Lush was located. "I don't bet on cockfights."

"Funny. Real funny."

"But I'd give you some money not to fight him. You're both on my thumbs-up list at the moment."

Up ahead, the retro neon Lush sign lit the street with an orange glow. The pumping beat of electronica filtered from the vine-covered building.

"You like the dude."

"He's okay. He stood up for me."

"No, you *like* him. As in, you wouldn't kick him out of bed."

Roman in her bed. For a moment, she couldn't answer. She summoned a whiff of composure. "Oh please," she said weakly.

Vader spun her around with one hand on her shoulder. "For real? You like him? I was just messing with you."

She tried to drag him toward the club, but that amount of sheer male muscle didn't budge unless it wanted to. "This isn't about me. This is about you and your alleged homophobia."

"Don't change the subject."

"Don't distract us from our mission." She marched toward the club. "Maybe I'll see if I can find a gay best friend in there. Since my own best friend is being an idiot."

Vader caught up with her in two steps. "I bet if I was gay, I'd already know all about you and Roman. I'd pick up on your feelings more. They're more sensitive, right?"

"More than you?" She snorted. "That lamppost is more sensitive than you."

"Hey. I do have feelings, you know. I'm not just a hunk of meat."

She yanked open the door of Lush, unleashing a blast of electronic sound. A bouncer in a black leather jacket perched on a stool just inside the door. "Something wrong with meat?" he asked in a voice of deepest gravel. "ID, please."

Vader snapped his mouth shut. Sabina thought he turned a bit pale, though it could have been reflected orange neon. She showed the bouncer her driver's license. "Busy night?"

"Always."

Vader nervously took out his ID. The man aimed a flashlight at it. "Derek Brown. You work out?"

"Yes," he said in a squeaky voice.

"Have a good time, meat."

"I'm not—"

"Thanks, we will," said Sabina, dragging Vader behind her. She'd never been to Lush, but she'd been to plenty of gay bars in Los Angeles. Ear-splitting trance music made the place thump like the inside of a drum. Flashing colored lights glistened off bare male chests as several men writhed on the dance floor. She wasn't the only woman here, but most of the customers were men, some hunky, some not.

Vader, in keeping with the meat theme, seemed to have turned into a hunk of lamb. He clung to her, crowding close behind her as she threaded a path to the bar. At Firefly, he strutted in as if he owned the place, which he could probably do if instead of buying drinks he'd been saving for a down payment. Here he looked completely out of his element. She had to keep a tight grip on his wrist to keep him from fleeing.

"I'll get drinks," she yelled to him, unable to hear herself over the music. Vader nodded jerkily. She wormed her way between two burly biker-type guys and held up two fingers to the bartender, then pointed to a beer bottle. She planned to give both to Vader. It would take at least two beers to make a dent in his first-time nerves.

The bartender brought her two bottles of dark ale and mouthed an amount she couldn't make out. Digging in her pocket, she pulled out a twenty. Hopefully that would cover it. The bartender seemed happy, anyway. She picked up a bottle in each hand and squeezed back the way she'd come, looking around for Vader.

He was talking to three men. He didn't seem to be saying much, just looking from one to the other, eyes growing wider and wider.

She eyed the three men. They looked decent enough, like guys she might see at the gym. They looked much like Vader, in fact, all wearing some variation of a muscle shirt. She'd peg their age at late twenties, same as Vader. All three were in great shape. Maybe they were talking about muscle fiber and the best brands of energy drinks.

She dawdled, trying to decide if she should leave Vader alone so he could get to know the men. Her job was done—she'd gotten him in here. She'd encouraged an actual conversation with a gay man. He could tell Cherie all about it, and maybe learn something from the whole experience. Maybe she could go home now and snuggle under the covers with a book. Some kind of serial killer thriller that would give her nightmares about something other than the reunion show.

She was about to donate the two bottles of beer to the guys at the bar when Vader shook his head violently and said something she couldn't hear. Something was wrong. With a crazed light in his eyes, he swung around in a circle. When he spotted Sabina, he went after her like a bull after a red cape. Before she could back away more than half a shocked step, he snatched her into an embrace and mashed his mouth against hers.

"Vader!" Her angry protest didn't make it past the mouth that was grinding against hers. With her hands full of beer bottles, she couldn't even push him away. Had he gone nuts? She tried to knee him in the groin, but her leg was trapped between his thick thigh muscles. She dropped the beer bottles onto the floor. One of them rolled away, but she heard the other shatter. Ignoring it, she pounded her fists against his chest in a rapid-fire beat.

Then she felt his hand on her ass.

"Stop it!" she shrieked into his mouth. This was going too far. They were friends, they had no spark, neither wanted the other sexually, so what the hell was he doing? At least it wasn't a full-on, tongue-entwining kiss . . . more of a fake Hollywood-movie lip-lock. But it didn't matter. She didn't want to be kissing Vader.

Suddenly, she wasn't. Someone was lifting him away from her as if he were an extra-buff G.I. Joe doll.

Behind him stood an even bigger version of G.I. Joe. One with night-black hair, a black leather jacket, smoldering eyes, and flexing muscles. Roman.

Roman had spotted Sabina and Vader by sheer chance. He'd gone home, eaten a little pasta e fagioli, watched a little ESPN, then decided it was a fine night for a drink at one of the little outdoor patios he'd spotted downtown. He'd cruised into town with the windows rolled down, enjoying the warm desert breeze. He'd picked out a nice, civilized wine bar where he could find a glass of Chianti and maybe a pleasant conversation or two. But before he'd even parked the Jeep, he'd spotted Sabina and Vader as they turned off Grove Street and headed into a dark alley.

His own personal alert system, the little hairs on the backs of his hands, had prickled in warning. If two of his firefighters were walking into trouble, he ought to provide backup. He parked and hurried after them.

The dark alley turned out to be a respectable side street. And the bar they slipped into, Lush, didn't look like the sort of place that would harbor roofie-wielding rapists. But the backs of his hands were still prickling, and he still wanted a glass of wine, so he followed them in.

What he saw—when his eyes had adjusted to the flashing lights—made him nearly lose his mind.

Someone was attacking Sabina. The bastard was mauling her; he even had his hand on her ass. Sabina beat her fists against his chest but no one helped her. No one was doing a damn thing. Through the roar of blood in his ears, he vaulted across the room with the speed of a superhero. Pouncing on the man attached to her lips, he wrestled him away from her, no easy task because the man weighed more than a block of cement.

When he finally got every part of the despicable bastard away from Sabina, Roman stood, arms akimbo, legs braced, panting like an angry bear, ready for all comers. For all he knew, the man had friends with him. Didn't matter. He could take them, whoever they were. And where the hell was Vader? Why wasn't he helping Sabina?

Through the din of pounding music and shouting voices, he heard Sabina yelling, "Roman, Roman."

"Are you okay?" he yelled back.

"Yes." She pointed behind him. "Help him."

What? Help the guy who'd been manhandling her? Incredulous, he looked around at the man he'd just ripped off her body. Vader glared back at him, face red, muscles quivering, like a dog about to pounce. Two guys were going after him, trying to hold him back, but he kept shaking them off.

"Vader?"

Vader snarled and lifted his fists. Roman sidestepped a hard punch, then readied himself for attack. Had he misunderstood what he'd seen? Had Sabina wanted that kiss? But it didn't matter. If Vader wanted to fight, he'd fight. He jackhammered a left hook into the fireman's jaw. Vader fell back for a moment, then raised his fists and came after him with a ferocious snarl.

Sabina threw her body between them before either could throw another punch. "Stop it! Take it outside, you idiots."

"Go," Roman growled at Vader. Vader's eyes glittered in the flashing lights, red, green, yellow. Then he whirled around and stalked toward the exit. Sabina followed, kicking aside some broken glass.

The bouncer glared at them as they passed. "What the fuck are you guys doing?"

"Stay out of it," Roman growled. He had a feeling Vader was teetering on the edge; he might be too.

"Stay out of my bar from now on, and I will."

"No problem."

Roman shepherded his two firefighters out the exit, and the bouncer slammed the door behind them. Immediately Vader took a martial arts kind of stance, feet wide apart, hands raised into some sort of claw shape. Roman braced himself for the attack.

"Vader, would you knock it off?" Again Sabina put herself between the two of them and addressed him. "You shouldn't be mad at Roman. You had no right to kiss me like that. I was trying to make you stop."

Roman experienced a moment of grim satisfaction. So he hadn't misread the situation. Sabina hadn't been kissing Vader by choice. But that meant Vader had been forcing himself on her, which called for a serious ass-kicking.

Vader relaxed his posture. The rabid, crazed look turned into something more like confusion. "Oh, fuck me. Sorry, Sabina. I didn't know what else to do."

"Excuse me?" She put both hands on her hips.

"Those guys were coming on to me."

"You couldn't just tell them no?"

Roman shot Vader a puzzled look. "I'm a little confused here. Men were coming on to you, so you kissed Sabina?"

Vader roared. "They were talking to me! I had to make them stop."

"The whole point of going there was so you could talk to them. Are you insane?" Sabina shoved her disheveled hair behind her ears. Two spots of pink rode high on her cheekbones. "And that's not a good reason to kiss me without my permission."

"It was all I could think of."

"Vader," Roman said in a warning tone. "I still need something to make sense here. So far nothing does."

The big guy ducked his head. "I'm trying to prove I'm not a homophobe. So Sabina brought me here. She was trying to help."

"Yes, but making out with you was not part of the deal." She swiped her hand across her mouth with a disgusted expression that made Roman's heart sing.

"I said I'm sorry."

Sabina's level gaze showed what she thought of that apology. "If Cherie could see you right now, she'd be through with you for good. I'm starting to think you *are* a homophobe."

"It was too much, too fast," argued Vader. "I had flashbacks to my rookie year. I need baby steps. Let's go somewhere else, somewhere easier. Like a . . . a . . . I don't know, an antiques shop."

"*Vader!* Total stereotype. You're hopeless."

"Forget it," said Roman. "Sabina's not going antiquing. She's coming with me."

"Excuse me?" She wheeled on him, her hair flying behind her like a neon-lit fan.

Implacably, he repeated, "You're coming with me. Vader, get lost. No more bar brawls. And make sure whoever you kiss wants it."

"They'll want it." Vader puffed out his chest with some of his former bravado. "I'm a good kisser, right, Sabina?"

Roman didn't need to hear the answer to that, although judging from Sabina's flared nostrils, it wasn't likely to be kind.

"We're done here. Good night, Vader. I expect you back in top form next week."

Roman took Sabina's hand, which settled into his lion-size paw as if it belonged there. He drew her down the street.

"Chief Roman," Vader called after them.

"Yeah?"

"No one needs to know shit about this, right? I mean, that we went to a . . . place like this?"

Roman ignored him and kept stalking down the street. Firehouse gossip wasn't his style, and if Vader didn't know that by now, he really ought to slash his steroid intake.

Sabina didn't say much as they walked toward Grove, where he'd left his Jeep. But neither did she pull her hand from his grasp. She did mutter something about her car but he ignored that. He had no intention of letting her go until he got a few things straight.

When they reached his Jeep, she finally reclaimed her hand and folded her arms across her chest. "What's this all about?"

"You and Vader. Nothing to it?"

"We're friends. He *was* my best friend but he might be on temporary suspension after tonight." She drew in a shaky breath.

"Are you all right?"

"Yeah, I'm fine. It's just . . . I feel stupid. I shouldn't have taken him in there. I should have known he couldn't handle it. But I never thought he'd react like that."

"You're blaming yourself now?"

"I mean, it's not the end of the world. I know he was rattled. He didn't mean anything by it, he just freaked out. We kissed before, back when we didn't know any better. But once you're friends with someone for a few years, kissing them isn't really on the agenda."

Roman sorted through the buzz of kissing-related statements and latched on to one fascinating comment. "What do you mean, when you didn't know any better?"

"We didn't know if there were any sparks between us. So we tried a kiss to find out if we had chemistry."

"And?"

"And there wasn't. Not like . . ."

She trailed off, biting her lower lip. Roman clenched his fists. That lip shouldn't be pinched between her teeth. It ought to be pressed up against his mouth, that tender flesh responding to his hot kiss.

"Like what?" he asked in a low growl, demanding she finish her sentence.

"Like . . . um . . . like there ought to be." She dropped her gaze, so he knew she'd censored herself.

"That's not what you were going to say."

"You don't know what I was going to say."

"Yes, I do." He stepped close to her and took her head in both his hands, tilting it until her eyes caught dancing sparkles from the streetlights. "You meant, there wasn't any chemistry like *this.*"

And he claimed her mouth like a lion claiming its prey.

Chapter Eighteen

Sabina clung to Roman's broad shoulders as a feverish sort of madness overloaded her senses. With one iron arm banded around her middle, Roman bent her backward and kissed her with ferocious intensity, as if nothing else existed in all of San Gabriel but the two of them. Blood pounded in her ears to the rhythm of *yes, yes, yes.*

His shoulder muscles felt like boulders. The phrase "built like a brick shithouse" zipped through her mind. He was all rock-solid man, through and through, and the way he kissed her . . . ravenously, lavishly, as if every corner of her mouth had some secret to discover. She returned fire with fire, kissing him back until her lips tingled and her insides went hot and liquid.

He wrenched himself away from her, panting. "We shouldn't do this."

But in the next second he was on her again, cupping

her face in his huge, calloused hands and consuming her mouth with devastatingly thorough greed.

This time she pulled away. "No, you're right. We should stop. Right?"

He stared at her with burning eyes and swept his hand through his black hair, more rattled than she'd ever seen him. "I don't know. I've been trying to stay away from you. You don't know how hard it is to be around you and not toss you on the training room couch and ravish you."

"*Ravish* me?" She liked the sound of that.

"Okay, fuck your brains out."

She gulped, speechless.

He lowered his voice to a hot, secret growl. "Or back you up against the wall in the apparatus bay. Do you know how many times I've pictured it? If the department could read minds, I'd be out on my ass by now."

Sabina slid her palm across his wide chest, edging her fingers under his black leather jacket. It made him look tough, all man, very Italian, and extremely sexy. "I wish I could read your mind right now."

"Jones, you don't have to be a mind reader to know what I want."

She glanced around to make sure the street was empty, then slid her hand down his firm stomach, feeling the heat of his body through his shirt, down past his belt buckle, to the hard, rigid lump beneath. When she touched him, he groaned, low and gritty.

"I give you three seconds to stop doing that. After that I can't answer for the consequences."

Slowly, deliberately, she traced the long shape pushing against his jeans. "One." With her hand firmly on his erection, she found an opening in his shirt and licked his chest. "Two." Moving the heel of her hand down his hard length, she whispered hotly into his neck. "Three."

In a voice as thick and hot as a triple espresso, he growled, "You were warned." He swooped her up, caveman style, opened the passenger door, and tossed her into the Jeep. He scrambled to the driver's side, using one hand to half vault himself over the hood.

She'd never seen a car take off in such a hurry. It seemed to be moving before the key had even been inserted into the ignition. Electric tension hummed between them, as if they were both holding their breath, hoping the other wouldn't back out before they came together. Neither said a word until they reached a sweet little house on a street lined with jacaranda trees.

Roman stopped the Jeep and gave her a long, serious look. She knew what the look meant. He was giving her one last chance to back out, but he couldn't bring himself to say the words. The sheer masculinity of him, the way he filled the Jeep with his presence, his power, the lust simmering under that black leather jacket—it was almost too much for her.

She nodded in reply to his silent question, since it turned out she couldn't speak either.

But it didn't matter. In a few moments they were inside.

"Luke?" she remembered to ask.

"Sleepover."

As soon as the front door closed behind her, he backed her up against it. Heat enveloped her, his body crowding close to hers as he peeled off his jacket and tossed it aside. He hiked up her legs and wrapped them around his waist. His hard erection pressed against her sex. She'd been ready ever since he'd first kissed her next to the Jeep. Now the sensation of heat and pressure, right where she needed it, made her moan.

"Oh God, Roman, that feels so good." The words came from some husky place deep in her throat.

"Hell, yes," he muttered as he pushed up her shirt. He ran his thumbs across her bra-covered nipples, which gave her an electric pleasure. Good Lord, if it felt so good now, what would it be like without a bra? In the next second she found out, as he undid the front clasp and filled his hands with her freed breasts. Oh sweet Lord above—the heat of him, the roughness of his palms, the maddening pull of his fingers, plucking, arousing, sent bolts of lightning straight to her belly.

Digging her hands into his shoulders to pull him closer, she ground her pelvis against the ridge of his cock. Even through both their layers of clothing, the shocking pleasure mounted, higher and sweeter and brighter, as if they were flying into a blazing sun.

He murmured something gruff and commanding, the sound touched a place deep inside her, and she broke apart into a blinding flash of orgasm. Stunned, uncomprehending, she came and came . . . the waves of sensation so intense as to be nearly painful. She buried her face in his shoulder as her body shuddered against his. The last spasms still hadn't faded when he whirled her around and strode to the bedroom, the house a dim blur to her dazed vision. Inside the bedroom, he kicked aside a chair and a few stray pieces of clothing.

Then he tossed her onto his enormous bed and stood over her like a conquering warrior.

She lay on her back, breathless from the whirlwind trip through his house, not to mention the astonishing climax just before that. He'd nailed her to the wall, she thought hysterically, and hammered her senseless. A goofy grin spread over her face as giggles spurted from her mouth.

"You're laughing." Roman narrowed his eyes as he tore off his shirt. "Am I that funny-looking?"

"No," she said, through uncontrollable giggles.

"You're ssss . . ." She struggled to get the word out through her gales of laughter. Why was she laughing? It made no sense. Nothing made any sense. She'd come through two layers of clothing, his and hers, without any other contact. When did that ever happen? "You're sexy."

"Glad you think so." Roman still looked suspicious as he dropped his pants. Sabina's laughter came to a sudden, choking halt when he stood before her completely, breathtakingly naked.

It was as if Roman redefined the word "man." It would never mean the same thing to her again, she knew, not now that she'd seen him in his full magnificence, from his pitch-black, wildly mussed hair to his powerful thighs and the thick rod of flesh that reared between them. He was fiercely, proudly, arrogantly aroused.

"Come here," she whispered hoarsely.

"God, how I want you," he answered, striding to the edge of the bed. "Why, for all that's holy, are you still dressed?"

"I have no idea." She brought herself to a kneeling position. The two of them fumbled with her clothing with equally shaky hands. She flung it all willy-nilly across the room until she knelt, completely naked, on the bed. After a long, reverent, scalding look that made her nipples tighten, he joined her like that and they sealed their torsos together, flesh to hot flesh, his cock nesting between her open thighs.

"God, Roman." The feel of his strength, his heat, his power, his skin against hers, robbed her of all logical thought. Need pounded through her blood. *Mine. Inside. Now.* She thrust her hips toward the erection burning against her thigh, then reached a hand down to circle it. He felt hot to the touch, swollen and ready to burst.

His hands went all over her, stroking her back, curving along the indentation of her waist, cupping her buttocks. His strokes made every part of her purr with desire.

She whimpered into his shoulder, knowing with one part of her brain that she'd abandoned all dignity but not caring one bit. Not when his touch felt so incredible. Not when he looked at her with such hot lust, as if he wanted to devour her from head to toe. Not when he claimed her mouth for a kiss that seemed to last for a year.

"I'm going to take you now," Roman said in a voice so thick with lust she barely recognized it. "Make you mine."

"Yes," she choked. "Hurry."

He picked her up, flipped her onto her back, and spread her arms wide. "Wait right there. Just like that." The command in his voice sent bright shivers through her system. He leaned over to the bedside table and found a condom. She watched the muscles moving under his skin with a kind of sharp craving. She wanted him to pour every bit of his strength and power into her body. Into her being. And she wanted him to want *her* with the same degree of intensity.

When he turned back to her, his black eyes drinking her in as if she was water in the desert, she knew he *did* want her the same way. She wasn't alone in this frenzy of physical need. They were in it together.

"Please," she whispered. "Now."

"Oh yes. Now." His big, warm hands spread her open. She started to come even before he penetrated her with one long, sensual thrust. She clamped down on her oncoming orgasm, not wanting this to end too soon. His eyes half closed as her tight passage sucked him inside.

"*Dio,* Sabina. How can you feel so fucking good?" A shudder racked his powerful body and the muscles of his arms went rigid as he braced himself over her, straining to hold himself back.

Fuck it. She didn't want his restraint. She wanted his wildness, his lust, his roughness. "Don't hold back," she hissed. "Do it. Now."

As if she'd unleashed something, he reared up, then waited one long moment, while the spinning of the earth seemed to stop. Then, with a strong thrust, he plunged his cock into her, all the way to the hilt. Explosions detonated deep inside her, the shock waves traveling to the ends of her fingers, the curling tips of her toes. It was too much, too good, too far . . . and not enough. *"More."*

Over and over again he impaled her. He'd turned into a wild creature released from its chain—a beast claiming its mate. Each primal thrust sent her higher and higher into a realm of white-hot pleasure she'd never experienced before. She screamed and thrashed her head back and forth, gripping the sheets with unconscious fingers.

His wildness set her free to be just as wild—to grunt and moan and fuck and glory in the sheer physical bliss of being next to each other, inside each other, surrounded by each other.

He was making some kind of sound too, but she could barely hear it over the ringing in her own ears. A triumphant shout, a harsh cry, a *"mamma mia,"* or maybe it was *"Madre di Dio,"* some kind of glorious Italian mumble of gratitude, a long spasm as he arced over her. Then he tumbled onto the sheets next to her, maintaining contact through tangled legs and a heavy hand on her hip.

As the bright shimmers of her orgasm receded,

other senses returned to their usual jobs. She inhaled the scent of coffee and leather that clung to Roman, now mingled with the richness of sex. She licked her lips, tasting the salt of her own sweat and probing the swell left by his ferocious kisses. She became aware of the quiet of the bedroom, its orderliness, its tame decor.

Something about his bedroom reminded her of her own house—the blandness, the lack of personality, the anonymity. Maybe he had a bit of refugee in him too.

Oh Roman, she thought as she snuggled her face into his side. *Maybe we're more alike than we realize.*

Then she fell into a deep, satisfied slumber.

Roman watched Sabina sleep with a sense of hushed awe. He didn't question what had just happened. He'd been swept up in a kind of madness that only this one particular woman brought out in him. Why Sabina? Why here, why now? His fatalistic side didn't question it. And he ordered his conscientious side to shut up for the moment. They'd worry about the consequences later. For now, he traced the fine slope of her arm, felt the little poufs of breath from her parted lips, and marveled.

"What are you staring at?"

Too relaxed to be startled, he smiled. "The work of art that happens to have landed in my bed."

"Landed?" She snorted. Her eyes had opened a mere slit. They gleamed with silvery laughter in the moonlight filtering through the window blinds. "I was virtually carjacked, then dumped on your bed like a sack of potatoes."

"Technically not a carjacking since it was my car. You might get away with calling it kidnapping."

"Not that I'm complaining," she said, her lips curving. "Best kidnapping ever."

"It had its moments." His cock tightened as a couple

of choice memories came flooding back. *Dio,* she'd completely knocked all sense out of him. He cleared his throat. "How . . . uh . . . how are you feeling? I wasn't too rough on you, I hope."

"Excuse me?" She sat up and poked him indignantly in the chest. "Why would you say that?"

"Well . . ." The truth was, Maureen had preferred things a bit more . . . civilized. But it didn't seem appropriate to bring her up. "I was just checking in."

"Well, thanks for the thought, but if my unholy screams of ecstasy didn't clue you in, I'm not sure what would." Her face went pink—though it was hard to tell in this light. "Sorry if I . . ." She trailed off.

He experienced a sense of fierce satisfaction. So he wasn't the only one feeling a little awkward at how carried away they'd gotten. Not that he regretted it. But it had been so long since he'd lost control like that. He'd always been so restrained with Maureen.

"Don't you dare apologize for anything," he ordered, softening the command with a tender smile . "I loved every hot, sweaty second. I'm already planning how I can ravish you again. It'll be easier this time." He nuzzled her soft neck. "No kidnapping required."

She wriggled under the tickling of his tongue. "That's too bad," she teased. "That caveman technique has a lot going for it."

"Can't have you thinking I'm always a brute." He pinned her hands over her head and licked his way down her down her collarbone with delicate strokes of his tongue, as if it were a paintbrush. "I'm also a sensitive guy." He took her nipple between his teeth, not hard enough to hurt, and felt it stiffen. God, what a rush. He swiped his tongue over it and felt her shudder. He spoke around her nipple, loving how it responded to his hot breath and the movements of his mouth. "I like to take it slow sometimes. What's the rush? Why not savor every inch of your incredible body?" He gave her swollen nipple a long suckle.

"You're killing me." She dug her hands into his hair.

He smiled, rolling her nipple in his mouth. "Now that's what I like to hear." He pulled back and gazed at the wet morsel of flesh, now swollen to the size of a large raspberry, and just about the same color. "You are so beautiful." His eyes traveled down her lovely flesh, opened to him like a ripe apricot. The light patch of hair at her sex surprised him, until he remembered Taffy had been known for her reddish-gold hair. Sabina must dye her hair this shade of brown. He brushed his hand over the soft thatch and felt her wetness.

Slowly, he raised his eyes, knowing he couldn't hide what was in his heart. Couldn't hide what she did to him, how she turned him into a slavering beast.

Her lips curved in a smile of pure, wicked invitation, she rolled on top of him, surprising him with her strength. She straddled his hips with that supple, responsive body of hers. Her soft skin shone with a light sheen of sweat. Her breasts were sweet champagne flute curves, her aroused nipples calling to him like sirens. Obediently his cock rose and bobbed against her butt.

"My turn. I intend to get to know every bit of your fine and sexy body. And you'll just have to lie there and take it."

He took it. Without complaint. He watched with heavy-lidded eyes as she nipped and tasted her way across his chest, twirling curls around her finger, tweaking his nipples, teasing and exploring. It wasn't until she reached his cock, already hard again, and took it into the warm shelter of her mouth, that it dawned on him.

Life as he knew it was over. Making love to Sabina had changed everything.

Chapter Nineteen

To Sabina, every minute of the rest of the night seemed to exist outside the normal definition of time. Some moments passed extremely fast, so they'd look at the clock and realize it was three in the morning. At other moments it would seem impossible that they could cover so much ground in such a short amount of time. How could she feel so close to this man when they'd been intimate only a few hours?

Several incredible times in those few hours, but still . . .

They did much more than roll around on his king-size bed. He asked her why she was so adamant about leaving her Hollywood life behind. Since the question came from a Greek god of a man with his head braced on one elbow and his feet tangled with hers, it took her a moment to adjust to the new topic.

"I don't think 'life' is the right word," she said, tangling her fingers in a black patch of chest hair. "You know how transsexuals say they're trapped in the wrong kind of body?"

"Don't you dare say anything bad about your body," he growled. "I'd have to spank you."

She wrapped a curl around her finger and tugged. "Then you'd have to be prepared for revenge."

"I'd look forward to it." His laugh made his chest rumble under her hand. The vibrations traveled up her arm directly to her heart, which turned fluttery as a trapped moth. "But go on. You lost me at transsexual. You didn't like being stuck in this beautiful, delicious, sexy, desirable, strong, flexible, sensual . . . I'm out of adjectives. I need a thesaurus."

He stroked the slope of her hip with his fingertips, then dipped down to the valley between her hipbones. "Go on."

She shivered but soldiered on. "I always felt like I'd stumbled into the wrong existence. I was a tomboy. All I wanted to do was run wild and play."

"Like Taffy."

"Yeah, her character was a lot like me. But *playing* Taffy was boring. Memorizing lines and standing around while they set up the shots. I wanted to be *doing* something. I used to watch TV for the commercials because that's how I thought ordinary people lived. You know, the Tide mom tossing her little boy's muddy baseball clothes into the washing machine. That sort of thing."

"A TV star watching commercials to see how the other half lives, huh?"

"I know, it sounds weird. I never had anyone to really talk to. My mother . . . well, you have some idea of what she's like. My only other friends were kids who were on the show, and they came and went. Once one of the lighting guys brought his daughter to work and we got to be friends, but my mother didn't approve because she wasn't very pretty and had no future in show business."

"Seriously?"

"She's very single-minded. Especially back then, the only thing that mattered to her was furthering her career. Our career, since we were cast as a mother-daughter team." That sounded too harsh, so she added, "She loosened up a little once the show became a hit and we had some money. Does it sound like I don't love my mother? Because I do, I swear. We were so close for all those years. So close. I wish we could . . . " She shook off the wistful thought of having her mother back, without the Hollywood trappings. "I can't go back to her world."

He nodded gravely. She wondered if she sounded selfish, too worried about herself. "People think it's glamorous being on TV, but I didn't like it at all. You're always worried about what you look like. And people have all these funny ideas about you before they've even met you. Then they do meet you and they don't want to get to know you. They just want Taffy. The first time I walked into the Firefighter Academy and no one recognized me, I nearly cried from relief. I know it's hard to understand."

He put a finger under her chin and lifted her face to his. "Relax. I'm not judging you. I just want to know what it was like."

Sabina lost herself in those dark eyes as they scanned her face in a slow, thorough scrutiny. He really meant it, she realized. He wanted to get to know her. *Her.* Not Taffy, not Annabelle's daughter, not the wary, guarded firefighter, but her.

Strange thought.

"Do I sound like some spoiled Hollywood actress babbling on about myself?"

He snorted. "You're off base with that one. You want to make me happy?"

"I've been trying," she purred, caressing his leg with her foot. "Haven't I been succeeding?"

"Hell, yes. I can't argue with your methods." He smoothed his hand across her chest, spanning her nipples with his hand. A helpless, melting sensation made her limbs feel heavy. "But what I'd really love is some more of that babbling. I want to know everything about you. I want to know how you came out of such a crazy upbringing with your head screwed on right. I want to know if you liked anything at all about Hollywood. I want to know your favorite commercial besides Tide. Everything."

"You're serious?"

"Don't make me tease it out of you." He held one nipple between his thumb and forefinger and gently rolled it until her vision blurred.

"If you put it that way . . ."

So she obliged him and dredged up some Hollywood memories, discovering in the process that she hadn't hated everything about her old life. Working with Beau Bridges had been pretty cool. Not to mention the PSA she'd done with Clint Eastwood. She'd been to Skywalker Ranch and Neverland, though she'd never witnessed anything unusual there. She was a huge fan of Julia Roberts, who'd always been very nice to her. If she'd been born a little later, she would have loved to star in a Harry Potter movie. "Even a little part, like a Hufflepuff student or a Quidditch player."

"So you like movies."

"Of course I do. Just because I don't want to be in them doesn't mean I don't want to watch them."

"I see what you mean. Just because I like putting out fires doesn't mean I want to be in one."

"Right." She seized the chance to change the subject. Time for his turn in the hot seat. "What was your first fire—"

"Speaking of fires, I feel like starting one right now."

Playfully, he flipped her around so she lay on her stomach and tickled her sides and the tender skin of her ass until she begged him to stop. Her attempt to get him to talk disappeared in an all-consuming sexual blaze.

He settled himself over her, spreading her open and seeking her heat with his strong fingers. She bit the sheets to keep from moaning too loud, but she couldn't help it, it felt so good the way he moved his fingers against her sensitive flesh. When a thumb snuck inside and skillfully pressed a spot she didn't even know existed, she bucked hard against his hand, twisting and groaning while he wrested the last spasm of orgasm from her body. Then he eased himself inside her—God, he felt even bigger from this angle—and reduced her to helpless babbling with a few feral strokes of his cock.

After he exploded into his own intense, groaning orgasm and rolled next to her, she drew her knees to her chest, curling up like a baby. How many condoms had they gone through by now? They couldn't seem to get enough of each other. It was almost scary.

"We should take a break," she whispered raggedly. "Get some sleep."

"I can't." He flung an arm across his eyes. His chest rose and fell, his breath coming in great, jagged bursts. "Damn you."

"You're blaming me?"

"I can't stop looking at you. And when I look at you I want to touch you. And when I touch you I want to make love to you. It's all your fault."

She sighed, too wrung out to argue. After that they must have slept for a bit. When she woke up the sky outside the window was starting to get light. A bolt of panic brought her upright.

A new day meant a return to the rest of the world. They were both off for the day, but Luke would be back, and she probably shouldn't be here when that happened, because how would they explain this to him, how would they explain it to anyone? They couldn't, not if they both wanted to stay at the San Gabriel firehouse. This could never happen again, could it?

She burrowed her head into the great hunk of hot male flesh next to her. Never before had she realized what a comfort it was to have a man sleeping in her bed. She'd always maintained a wary, no-strings attitude toward relationships. Intimacy meant sharing secrets, and she couldn't do that. But Roman already knew her secret. He knew all about her now.

But she didn't know anything else about him. She'd done all the talking.

She made a move to get out of bed, but a heavy arm flopped across her waist and pinned her down.

"Where do you think you're going?" Roman rumbled sleepily.

"Um . . . bathroom."

"Come right back. It's cold in here without you."

"Okay," she whispered, and slipped out of bed. In the bathroom, she stared at herself sternly in the mirror. The smartest thing would be to hightail it out of there and not get in any deeper than she already was. She'd opened herself more tonight than she ever had. And he'd told her exactly nothing in return. She didn't know much about relationships, but that sounded like a recipe for heartbreak.

But the thought of walking away from the warm

nest of his king-size bed and his emperor-size body was simply intolerable. Not when she'd been alone for so long.

She'd give herself this one night. Surely her heart would survive one night with Roman.

Back in his bedroom, she snuggled next to him, wrapping his arms around her and glorying in the heat radiating from every part of him. Roman put out a lot of BTUs. Maybe they could measure a man's hotness with thermal units, and if they could, he'd be off the charts . . . and she needed his heat, after an entire lifetime of being cold . . .

She fell asleep again.

Night snuck out of the house like a restless guest on its way to another party. Roman had no idea how much rest either he or Sabina had gotten, but it couldn't have been much, in between delving into Sabina's past and savoring her luscious body. He found both those activities dangerously addictive. He could happily watch her talk and move and sleep for a thousand more nights like that.

But, judging by the peach-pink light filtering into the room, the sun had risen. The incessant murmur of mourning doves greeted the new day. Any minute now the neighbor's sprinklers would go off. Newspapers would land on sidewalks with a thump. Cars would begin leaving driveways, life would go on.

Last night, or another one just like it, would probably never happen again, though he could barely form the thought without pain. She'd been so generous with her confidences, allowing him a glimpse inside the true Sabina, sweet and open and lovable. Why hadn't he done the same? Why hadn't he told her about Maureen, about the most important events of his life?

He didn't know why. Maybe it was because he wasn't much of a talker. Ask Luke. Ask any of the counselors who'd offered their help after 9/11. Ask his parents, his crew. Even Maureen would have agreed. Talking wasn't his style. But he could do something else for her.

He swung his legs over the edge of the bed, pulled on a pair of loose cotton drawstring pants, gave the sleeping Sabina one last lingering look, and made for the door. In the sunny kitchen, he ground some of his favorite coffee beans and tossed olive oil into his best cast-iron pan. Not just any olive oil, of course. Extra virgin olive oil straight from Lucca, Italy, where he was convinced the very best olive oil was pressed.

He chopped some black olives—Greek, because, he had to admit, the Greeks out-olived the Italians. Wild mushrooms, scallions, some goat cheese, tomatoes . . . oops, he'd forgotten the toast. Back in New York, he often went to his favorite bakery, Pietro's, for a baguette first thing in the morning. He hadn't yet located such a place in San Gabriel, but there was still hope. He was pondering the possibility of luring Pietro to California for the sunny climate—he was getting old, after all—or maybe sending Anu to Brooklyn for some baking lessons—when a sleepy voice greeted him from the door of the kitchen.

"If only the guys could see you now."

He looked over his shoulder at her. She'd located one of his New York Fire Department T-shirts and wore it like a dress. Below the hem, her long legs emerged. The plain cotton and her bare limbs made an intoxicating contrast—innocence and sin. He raised one eyebrow. "Is that a threat? You planning on blackmailing me?"

"I think it's weird that you can cook like a demon

but don't take a turn in the cooking rotation. They'd love you forever if they could taste your tomato sauce."

He turned back to his omelet and flipped it over. "I don't let just anyone taste my sauce."

She snorted. "That sounds so naughty."

"Don't get me going." He shot her a dangerous look over his shoulder to drive home his point. The woman was going to drive him mad. Especially when she was rubbing one foot against the back of the opposite calf in that slow, seductive way. "Seriously. I'm cooking you an omelet here. They're tricky."

She dropped the provocative stance and hopped to his side. "Can I watch? No one's ever cooked me an omelet before. Well, no one I knew personally. Anu doesn't trust eggs."

He held up a hand as a barrier. "You can watch, but give it some space. Omelets can be very sensitive. I make mine with extra egg whites to make them fluffy."

"Fluffy." She made a sound suspiciously like a snicker.

"Is that funny?" Intently, he lifted one edge of the omelet and let the liquid spill over.

"It's not every day you hear a big, sexy hunk of a fireman say the word 'fluffy.'"

He frowned. "Why not? Fluffy bunny, fluffy hair, fluffy snow. Fluffy fluffy fluffy."

She let out a hoot of laughter and jogged his elbow, making the spatula tear the just-forming omelet. After that he banished her to the kitchen table until she could get control of herself.

Dio, she was fun to be with. Every moment in her company made him realize how lonely he'd been since Maureen's death. How isolated. He hadn't joined any counseling groups, any 9/11 widowers' groups. He hadn't wanted Maureen to be defined by the way she'd died. He'd kept his horror and grief private, even from his family and the guys at the firehouse.

His way of honoring Maureen had been to keep doing the job they'd both loved. Raise their son, put out fires, keep putting one foot in front of the other. All the joy in his life had come from Luke. He hadn't had another adult to laugh with until . . . well, now.

Roman had gone quiet while he finished the omelet. Sabina could practically see an imaginary wall being erected around him. Not that she'd complain about the fact that a bare-chested, gorgeous man was making her breakfast. She couldn't keep her eyes off his ass, those tight buttocks draped in thin cotton, unless it was to travel up the smooth curve of the ridged muscles along his spine to the broad, powerful shoulders bent over the stove.

Incredible smells drifted from that stove. Earthy mushrooms, rich butter, virile man . . . Mouth watering, she feasted her eyes on him.

He flipped the omelet onto a plate and added a piece of buttered toast. Sabina licked her lips as he brought her his masterpiece.

"Do you know the first time I ate actual butter was after I left home? My mother had very strict policies about dairy products."

He shuddered. "Life without butter. I don't want to think about it." After arranging a parade of jam jars in front of her, he poured her a cup of coffee. "Cream?"

"Hell, yes."

"That's the attitude. By the way, this omelet is known as a Rapscallion Omelet in my family."

"A what?"

"I learned how to make it from my Zio Paolo, my

uncle, who used to call me a rapscallion. I thought he meant the scallions he threw in the omelet."

"Cute." She smiled a little sadly—she'd always wanted uncles and aunts and cousins—and took a bite. Her eyes closed in bliss. "I never knew a rapscallion could taste so good."

"You make that sound so naughty."

She laughed through her mouthful of omelet, then put up a hand calling for silence. She didn't want anything to distract from her single-minded appreciation of his creation.

"You like it?" He sounded so vulnerable, so eager, like a little boy asking for his mother's approval. So endearing, she could barely stand it.

"Um . . . yeah. I like it. I love it. It's incredible. You're incredible." She dropped her eyes, embarrassed, and spooned a dollop of cream into her coffee. Her first sip elicited a new groan of ecstasy.

"You know, nothing is quite as satisfying as watching someone enjoy my cooking. Not even putting out a fire."

"You must be very satisfied right now."

"Oh, I am." He waggled his eyebrows at her in a piratical leer that made her stomach tighten. He went back to the stove to make his own omelet. They ate the rest of the meal in reverent, companionable silence. A sense of utter rightness and harmony made Sabina's heart sing. Sitting here with him, eating the omelet he'd made for her from a family recipe, an omelet with a family joke name, was a dose of heaven.

It took the edge off the fact that he hadn't opened up to her last night the way she had.

Maybe the Rapscallion Omelet and Zio Paolo would be the just the beginning. Maybe soon she'd know all his secrets too, and the invisible wall around him would topple.

When Roman finished eating, he sat back with a sigh and reached for the remote. "Let's see if they had any calls last night."

When he clicked on the little TV that sat on the kitchen counter, Ella Joy's perfect face appeared. Sabina squinted at the banner headline at the bottom of the screen. " 'Scandal at the Firehouse'? What's she talking about?"

"Can't be good." Grimly, Roman turned the volume up.

"A fellow Lush patron caught the entire incident on his cell phone." The TV screen filled with a blurry, grainy video of Roman slamming his fist into Vader's jaw. Damn, he'd hit him hard.

"Battalion Chief Ricardo—Rick— Roman and Firefighter Derek Brown are seen here duking it out in a local bar. Not just any bar, but one of San Gabriel's best-known gay bars. Clearly, there's a story here, but no one's talking, including Fire Chief Rent-a-Mirr—that is, Fire Chief Renteria. Attempts to reach Chief Roman have been unsuccessful. Brown's only comment consisted of a profanity we can't repeat here, per FCC regulations. But"—the anchorwoman winked—"it began with an F, ended with an F, and had two words." Ella Joy paused, giving viewers time to figure it out. "More to come on this developing story as the day progresses."

"I believe the phrase she means," said Roman, hurling his toast at the television, "is 'fuck off.' "

Chapter Twenty

"Did I somehow give you the idea that you were hired to make things *worse*?"

Grimacing, Roman held the phone away from his ear. He couldn't blame Renteria for his angry rant. He just wished he had something to offer in the way of an explanation.

But the fire chief didn't even pause to listen to the lack of one. "On Channel Two they're saying the two of you were fighting over a woman. On Channel Six they're hinting at a homosexual affair. I'm surprised someone isn't saying two-headed aliens were involved."

"None of that is true," said Roman, fighting to hold on to his calm. "I believed one of my firefighters was in danger. It was my error. The three of us have already sorted it out."

"That's cozy. Any advice for the rest of us who have to deal with the media wolves?"

"I'll step down if it helps." If anyone were to take the fall, it ought to be he. No one had asked him to follow Sabina and Vader into that bar. No one had asked him to rush to her defense, or carry her off like a savage beast . . .

Neither Sabina nor Vader should have to pay because he let his dick call the shots.

"No." Chief Renteria gave a dry laugh. "Bet you wish it was that simple. You're sticking around, Roman, like it or not. And you're in for a shit storm. Reporters are camped out outside the firehouse. They already cornered Firefighter Brown at the gym."

"I saw that."

All the channels had shown the shot of Vader leaving the gym with a small entourage of beautiful girls. Channel Two wondered if that meant Sabina was home nursing a broken heart. Channel Six speculated that he might be trying too hard to quash the rumors.

None of the stations had footage of Sabina. She was an expert at hiding from the media, after all. And from him too, apparently. After she'd left the house, white-faced and horrified, she hadn't answered any of his calls. Hopefully he'd see her back at work. Hopefully he'd be able to keep his hands off her, and not stare at her all day like a lovesick puppy dog.

Talk about a scandal.

"Straighten this mess out the best you can." Chief Renteria was wrapping it up now. "I'm starting to wonder if there isn't something to this curse."

"Sir?"

"Might as well be a soap opera over there. Never seen anything like it. Have you?"

"Not exactly, no."

"All right. Carry on. Keep me posted."

"Will do."

After he hung up, Roman dialed Sabina's number again. Not that he had much more to say about the situation, but he longed for some connection with her. If the feel of her sleek skin and the jasmine scent of her hair weren't available, her husky voice would have to do. Even if it was nothing more that her outgoing message.

"I'm unavailable. Please leave a message."

Short and to the point. And quite accurate. Sabina Jones was unavailable, at least to him, Battalion Chief Rick Roman. He'd made a huge mistake giving in to his craving for her. Things were more complicated than ever now. Fortunately, things weren't too far gone. They'd just have to forget what happened and focus on getting life back to normal.

If there was such a thing as "normal" in San Gabriel.

Baseball cap, check. Sunglasses, check. Generic T-shirt and jeans, check. The life of a media refugee came back so easily. Sabina was able to tune out the madness while she went jogging at a park on the other side of town. Afterward, she stopped at a coffee shop she'd never been to before. She kept her braid tucked under her cap and didn't say much to anyone. No one recognized her.

The same couldn't be said for Chief Roman. When she switched on the TV for her daily dose of reality—make that surreality—she saw a swarm of reporters mobbing him outside San Gabriel Middle School. With his face set in his most intimidating scowl, the one she remembered from that Reno intersection, he shepherded Luke through the crowd.

She ate up every frame of the shot, noticing how he kept his hand on his son's back, how he stood a head taller than everyone else, how his black hair and strong features made him a casting agent's dream. She wasn't surprised when Ella Joy followed up with a mini-feature on the hunky new San Gabriel training officer, a single father whose wife was killed on 9/11.

"Chief Roman has a reputation for being extremely strict but fair. But his short tenure at San Gabriel Station 1 hasn't been smooth sailing. Quite a change from New York, where he reportedly buried himself in his work after the tragic loss of his wife."

They showed a picture of Maureen O'Keefe Roman, a pretty redhead who looked much too young to die. At least San Gabriel's viewers were spared yet another shot of the Twin Towers collapsing. It was the Sunny Side of the News, after all.

"Officials are maintaining a strict 'no comment' policy, but the questions remain. Why were three San Gabriel firefighters duking it out in a bar? Can Chief Roman effectively do his job after this incident? When will Fire Chief Renteria finally crack down on the crew? Stay tuned for more on this story, including an exclusive interview with Annabelle Hatfield, mother of the San Gabriel Bachelorette."

Sabina groaned and threw a pillow at the TV set. Of course her mother would jump all over this. She must be in movie-star comeback heaven right now. They'd interviewed Annabelle next to a huge bouquet of flowers sitting on a grand piano. Why a grand piano? Why not?

"It's certainly no surprise that my daughter, Sabina, has two gorgeous men fighting over her. Which one has the edge? It's anyone's guess." Light laughter. "If she asked for my advice, I'd say exactly what Peg McGee told Taffy when two boys got into a snowball fight over her. Go for the one with the biggest snowball." She winked cheekily at the camera.

Sabina clutched at her aching head. This wasn't happening. It couldn't be happening. But it was. On every channel.

Finally she turned off the TV and crawled into her bed, which seemed small and lonely compared to Roman's. She kept replaying the image of Roman shielding Luke with his arm over his son's face, and the photo of Luke's mother.

Maureen O'Keefe Roman. Firefighter, wife, mother, 9/11 hero. Roman hadn't mentioned her once, not in all the hours they'd spent together. During all those magical, out-of-time moments, Roman had kept quiet about what must be one of the most important parts of his life.

Why? It was obvious. What they'd experienced together wasn't real life. It was a one-night fantasy.

After all, what did she really know about him? Oh, she knew the highlights. Skilled firefighter, outstanding leadership qualities, excellent father, incredible lover, great cook. But what about the real stuff? How could she fall in love with a man who'd never so much as mentioned his tragically deceased wife?

And yet . . . how could she not, when that man was Roman?

Luke seemed really shaken up by their encounter with the newspeople outside his school. He didn't say anything until they'd reached the batting cages at Los Feliz Park. Roman scanned the area carefully before allowing him out of the car. When the coast seemed clear of reporters, they picked the most secluded cage and took turns whaling away at the balls spitting from the machine.

With the temperature in the low sixties, a pleasant breeze playing at the backs of their necks, Roman remembered why they'd moved to Southern California. For exactly this. The *thwack* of bats hitting balls, a warm breeze in mid-December, baseball year-round. Luke's idea of heaven. He could put up with all the rest for Luke's sake.

It wasn't until they took a soda and hot dog break that Roman realized Luke's unusual silence wasn't just because of the reporters. As they sat on the bench, legs stretched out, gulping Seven-Up, his son suddenly said, "It's a lot different here than in New York."

"I'll second that."

"Do you ever think we should move back?"

Roman did a double take. Of all things he expected to hear from Luke, that hadn't made the list. "I thought you loved it here."

Luke gave him a sidelong look from under his sandy eyelashes. Roman noticed new freckles from all the sun. "I do. Mostly. But that's okay. We don't have to stay here."

Finally it clicked. "You're worried about me."

"Well . . ." He took a bite of hot dog and spoke through it. "It's kind of weird here."

"You mean because cameras are following me around. And everyone's talking about the firehouse. And one of my firefighters was a TV star. And her mother's a movie star. And I punched a guy out in a bar."

"Don't worry, I beat up Ralphie when he said you were gay."

Roman spurted out a mouthful of soda. "You know my philosophy on violence. It's a last resort."

"Like in the bar?"

"Well . . . yes, I suppose. I thought someone was attacking Sabina. It was a mistake, and look at all the trouble it's caused."

"But it wouldn't have been a mistake if Sabina was being attacked."

"Right." Roman frowned. He wasn't delivering the lesson quite the way he wanted to. "Maybe. Depends. Guys like you and me, Lukey, we're strong, so we have to be careful. I can really hurt someone. On the other hand, when I see someone in trouble, I know I can help."

Luke kicked at an old popcorn bag the breeze had piled against his feet. "Not everything."

Ouch. "Nope. Not even close."

"Do you know Carly's mom?"

"No." Conversations with a thirteen-year-old always seemed to go in unpredictable directions. "Why?"

"Nothing."

Of course it wasn't nothing. Luke wanted to say something, but Roman couldn't tell what. And he didn't know how to ask.

"I think . . . well, I think maybe Carly . . ."

"Yeah?"

"Forget it. It's good she has Sabina, that's all. And Papa?"

Roman silently cursed. But at least Luke hadn't said, *You wouldn't understand*. "Yeah?"

"I don't want to leave here."

"Hey, we're not going anywhere. We're tough New Yorkers, remember? We can put up with a few cameras and nasty rumors and movie stars and so forth."

He used the phrase "so forth" to invite Luke to say more about Carly. But Luke switched his attention to a sparrow with a hankering for hot dog bun crumbs. How was Luke supposed to learn to talk about the important stuff when his own father couldn't do it?

Roman made a mental note to ask Sabina if something was going on with Carly.

But first he owed Vader more of an apology than he'd offered so far. He tracked him down at Toned, a gym that had become popular among the off-shift firefighters ever since Ryan Blake had married the owner's sister.

He found Vader working his delts while glowering at the three TV sets, all showing some version of "Scandal at the Firehouse."

"Buy you a Red Bull when you finish up?"

Vader didn't look happy to see Roman, but could hardly reject an invitation from a battalion chief.

Fifteen minutes later, Vader heaved himself onto a bar stool at the juice bar, leaving one stool empty between him and Roman. Roman slid a Red Bull his way.

"I'm not going to beat you up again, Vader."

Vader bristled. "You didn't beat me up the first time. I never got a chance to get my shots in. Good thing for you."

"No doubt." Roman's peacemaking smile didn't come easily. This man had forced an uninvited kiss on Sabina.

"If I'd known there was a camera around I would have gone for it, dude. Do you notice how they keep replaying that one shot where my head goes back and nearly hits the guy behind me?"

"I saw that," said the waitress, appearing with a menu. Roman did a double take, wondering why she was dressed like a belly dancer, but Vader didn't seem to think it was odd. "I do shiatsu massage when I'm not working here, so if you need some work on your neck . . ."

"My neck is fine," gritted Vader.

Roman figured he must still be upset if he was ignoring offers of massages from pretty girls.

"I came here to apologize for that. I lost my head," said Roman. "If I'd realized it was you I wouldn't have gone nuts like that."

Vader guzzled down the Red Bull, crushed the can

in his fist, then rested his elbows on the counter. He dropped his head to his hands. Under his T-shirt, the veins on his biceps stood out. "No, you were right, dude. I shouldn't have done that to Sabina. If I'd seen someone mauling her I'd have knocked him out too. What a fucking mess. All I wanted was to prove I wasn't homophobic. Now I'm on every channel in town getting beat up in a gay bar. The things you'll do for a chick, you know?"

"I hear that."

"And you know the worst thing?"

"What's that?"

He lowered his voice. "I think I *might* be homophobic. I freaked out, man. Kissing Sabina like that, it wasn't cool."

Not cool at all, if you asked Roman.

"Cherie's probably laughing her head off along with everyone else in town."

"Well, you're in good company." Roman tilted his blueberry–bee pollen smoothie as a toast and sipped deeply, then nearly gagged. Apparently bee pollen didn't taste like honey. They ought to warn you about that.

Vader was tapping his crushed can against the counter. The waitress pranced toward them, practicing some kind of dance move that made her gypsy skirt jingle, but he waved her off.

"Chief?" Vader looked right, then left, checking for eavesdroppers.

Oh shit. Roman braced himself for a confession from the younger guy. He'd never been that sort of captain, the kind who cared about his crew's feelings. As long as they did their jobs, he didn't get involved in their personal lives.

Vader leaned over the empty stool between him and Roman. "How do you convince a chick you're not the way you seem?"

"Come again?"

"I'm more than a ripped body. I got a mind in here." He tapped his head. "Just because I don't know any Tori Amos songs doesn't make me stupid."

"Let's hope not."

"I want her to see the real me. I can be sensitive. I have feelings. Dreams. All that shit. It's all trapped inside here. Waiting to get out." He thumped his chest. "How do I get it out?"

You're asking the wrong guy, Roman wanted to say. *My shit's all locked up tight.*

But he owed Vader. "Maybe you could think of it like a backdraft."

"I'm afraid of backdrafts."

"Everyone is. Backdrafts are extremely dangerous. That's why we take the fire axe up on the roof and ventilate. You have to open up a hole and let some smoke out, right? Prevent a backdraft."

"Yeah." He furrowed his forehead. "Backdraft. I like how you put that. Open a hole."

"There you go." He tossed back the rest of his bee pollen. Emotional conversations really took it out of a man.

"Thanks, Chief."

"No problem." Holy Mother of God, had he managed to offer good advice to a fellow fireman? Maybe California was getting to him. "So we're cool?"

"Well . . ." Vader hesitated. "One more thing. That bar fight. That left hook."

"I said I regretted it—" What more did Vader want from him?

"Do you think you could do that again? Except in a ring with a bunch of people watching? Maybe some cameras?"

"What?"

"I want another chance, Chief. I think I could take you. And I want witnesses so everyone knows I can throw a punch as good as the next guy. It's only fair."

Roman put some money on the counter and gestured good-bye to the waitress, who was now gyrating and snapping her fingers in the air. "No way, Vader."

Vader swung around on the stool with an outraged glare. "What do you mean, no way? You gotta give me another chance."

"I mean, no way could you take me. I haven't lost a fight since the age of five. And I'm not in the habit of turning my best firefighters into bloody pulp. Sorry."

"Dude." But Vader looked too impressed to be pissed. And then the compliment sank in and a smile spread across his bony face. "Hey, thanks."

"See you at the station."

When Roman was halfway to the exit door, Vader came hurrying after him. "One other thing, Chief."

All of Vader's goofiness had been replaced by utter seriousness.

"What is it?"

"About Sabina. You better not hurt her. If you do, you'll have the whole firehouse after you."

Roman stared at him. What had Vader seen that night? His mind raced back to the Jeep, Grove Street, the Christmas lights, Sabina's beautiful eyes dancing with midnight sparkles . . .

"I've seen how she looks at you. Just about every fireman on the crew wouldn't mind that look from Two. But she's always been strictly about the firefighting. She's like your favorite sister combined with a gutsy firefighter who's smart and hardworking, plus she's hot as hell. Who wouldn't crush on her? She keeps her private life off-limits, even with me, and I'm her best friend at the station. But I know her, and she's not as tough as she acts. I've seen her looking at you, and Chief, you'd better not hurt her. Or I'll take my chances with that left hook of yours, for real. You see where I'm coming from?"

"Yeah. I see," answered Roman mechanically.

"Then I'll see you at the station, Chief." Vader headed for the parking garage while Roman stood like a zombie amid a swirl of girls arriving with yoga mats. Hurt Sabina? That's the last thing he wanted to do. She seemed so confident, so independent, so self-sufficient. He knew how much she prided herself on those qualities. But of course she was a human being and could be hurt like anyone else.

To quote Vader, what a fucking mess. They couldn't really date each other, since department policy forbade it. He could leave the department—but he'd just promised Luke they'd stay in San Gabriel. Besides, he couldn't leave this mess behind. Renteria had ordered him to straighten things out and that's what he intended to do. He was stuck at Fire Station 1 until further notice.

Worse than that, he was stuck at Station 1 with Sabina. Might as well lock an alcoholic in a wine cellar. Or lash a siren to the mast right next to Odysseus. How was he supposed to forget the taste of her, the turquoise flash of her eyes closing in bliss, the feel of her supple body coming apart under his?

And if he did manage the superhuman feat of forgetting, he'd be hurting her, according to Vader.

They had to back off, now, before things got any more complicated.

Chapter Twenty-One

When Sabina walked into La Piaggia, Anu took one look at her face and hustled her into the kitchen. The cook and his assistant buzzed around, preparing for the dinner crowd. Both of them stole secret looks at Sabina, but one ferocious glance from Anu stopped them cold.

"First you must tell me everything. Then I must tell you something."

Anu pulled her into the far corner of the kitchen, where the big pots were stored and no one could overhear. She wore a wine-colored sari with a pattern of gold-stitched paisleys and smelled pleasantly of sandalwood incense.

"It's a total nightmare, Anu." Sabina had never felt so miserable in her life. "It's like I'm jinxed. Every time I think it's getting better, something else happens and it gets worse. And now Roman . . ." She trailed off. She trusted Anu completely, but if any hint of their night together got out, the current media madness would go up another big notch. And for all she knew the cook had superhuman hearing.

"Now Roman's going to be in trouble," she said.

Anu put both hands on Sabina's shoulders. "I will set aside the fact that you didn't tell me anything about your dreadful secret and ask you if you are 'hanging in there.'"

Sabina smiled wanly; she knew Anu used that Americanism on purpose to cheer her up.

"Of course I'm hanging in there. So what did you have to tell me?"

"You sure you are ready?" Anu checked her watch.

"Is it something bad?"

"I cannot say." She bustled over to the little TV that sat on the counter and switched it on. "Your Chief Roman called a press conference."

"A *what*?"

"Perhaps he decided to fight fire with fire, so to speak. Now *shush*!"

The wobbly picture on the TV stabilized to show Roman at a bank of microphones. He towered over the other people there, the reporters and bystanders. Behind him she saw her beloved Station 1, a plain, tidy brick structure that didn't deserve all this craziness. A sick feeling tugged at her belly. Had Roman decided to resign his position? From the grim, forbidding look on his face, it sure looked like it.

Roman swept a long stare across the sea of reporters in front of him. "I'm going to make a brief statement today regarding the incident at Lush, then I'll take a few questions. I'm doing this in the hopes that shedding light on the situation will put the gossip and speculation to rest. Two of San Gabriel's firefighters, during their off-duty hours, were enjoying a drink at a local bar. I was under the mistaken impression that one of them was making advances on the other. I stepped in to put a stop to it. Though I was following my protective instincts, my actions were wrong and misguided. I've apologized to the firefighters involved and sincerely hope that will be the end of this."

Sabina's fingernails dug into her palms. He hadn't mentioned anything about leaving San Gabriel.

"He looks quite handsome, does he not?" said Anu. "He hasn't come to cook for ages. I believe he's avoiding us, more's the pity."

A reporter shouted out a question. "Word on the street says you've been asked to step down."

"Is that how you get your information?"

"Is it true?"

"No. I offered to resign, but the fire chief expressed his faith in me and so I will continue on in my current position at Fire Station 1."

Sabina nearly staggered with relief. *Roman isn't leaving. Roman isn't leaving.* She hadn't ruined his career.

Roman continued. "I hope this will bring an end to all the absurd speculation. The San Gabriel Fire Department is a top-notch organization and you should all be very proud of their work."

"Nice words, but quite pointless," said Anu. "Speculation is so enjoyable. It's human nature."

The reporters began tossing questions like hand grenades. Sabina could practically hear the sizzle.

"Lush is well-known as a gay bar, isn't it?"

"Why were Jones and Brown at a gay bar?"

"Are they dating, or is one of them gay? If so, will that cause problems in the firehouse?"

Roman held up a hand to stop the flow of questions. "I'm glad you asked that. The sexuality of my firefighters is none of my business and certainly none of yours.

If you have a problem with that, I suggest the next time your house catches fire, you stop the firefighters who are putting their lives on the line for your sake, and interrogate them personally."

That silenced the crowd. That, along with the harsh stare he aimed at each and every one of them.

Only one reporter dared to raise her voice. Ella Joy might be many things, but she didn't scare easily. "But Chief Roman, if it's disruptive to the firehouse—"

"It's my responsibility to keep order in the firehouse." He seemed to catch himself. "Mine and the other station commanders'. If we fail, we'll answer to the fire chief. End of story."

Sabina snorted. "He's so used to being captain, he doesn't know any different."

"But Chief Roman, what about Sabina Jones? It looks as if you and Derek Brown were fighting over her. So either one or the other of you must be dating her. If firefighters get romantically involved, won't that cause a problem?"

Sabina gnawed on her thumbnail. Was Ella Joy just throwing things out there or did she actually know something? Maybe the notorious anchor was underrated as an investigator. She had a way of showing up in the middle of everything.

"The department has policies regarding relationships between firefighters. We will adhere very strictly to those policies," Roman was saying. "Again, it's part of my responsibility to enforce them and I will do so. I can't speak for the captains, but I'm sure they'll do the same." His eyes flickered toward the camera, as if he knew Sabina was watching. "I can assure you the San Gabriel firefighters are completely dedicated to their jobs and that there's no threat to the public safety."

Sabina made a face at the TV. "Message received, Chief."

"What message?" asked Anu.

Never again, that was the message.

"That we'd all better watch our asses," she said vaguely.

"One more question!" a reporter shouted. "Did you ever think this was part of the Bachelor Curse?"

Roman shot him an incredulous look. "No."

"Don't be so sure, Chief Roman," said Ella Joy. "We've seen the curse in action a couple times here in San Gabriel."

"Well, I'm from New York, and if I can't see it, touch it, or hear it, it's going to be hard to convince me it's real." For the first time, humor lit his face. "Maybe that's why they hired me."

Laughter rumbled through the crowd of reporters. Roman could turn on the charm when he had to, realized Sabina. Not that she was surprised.

"Thanks for coming by, and the next time I see you, I hope it's at a fire." He winced, apparently realizing how that sounded. "That is, I hope I don't see any of you for a good long while."

The crowd laughed again. Roman strode away from the microphones. The camera followed him; Sabina could have sworn it zoomed in on his ass, just a bit. Then Ella Joy's exquisite face filled the screen and Anu turned off the TV.

"Well. Most interesting."

"Just another day on the job at the Bachelor Firehouse." Sabina groaned. "Maybe it's time I put in for a transfer. To Mars."

"Oh come now. It's nothing some chai tea won't cure. Come along." But before Anu could settle her into the only chair in the kitchen, Sabina's cell rang.

Excitement danced up her spine and made her pulse pound in her throat. It had to be Roman. She answered without looking at the readout. "Good job out there. And don't worry, I got the message."

But the voice on the phone belonged not to Roman, but to Max.

"Which one? I've left a few dozen."

She groaned and dropped into the chair. Anu bustled off, hopefully in the direction of tea—or liquor.

"I don't have to talk to you."

"Let me paint you a picture, munchkin. On one hand, cameras everywhere you go for the indefinite future. On the other hand, two weeks behind a camera, pfft, you're done."

"I'm hanging up."

"Why are you so damn stubborn about this?"

Sabina took the phone away from her ear and mimicked knocking it against the counter, over and over again. Finally she put it back to her head. "Because neither you nor Annabelle can be trusted. Because it would be only the beginning. Because my privacy would be gone forever."

"It already is," he said smugly.

"I swear to God, Max . . ."

Suddenly the phone was being snatched from her hand. Anu spoke into it, her vowels even more clipped than usual. "Who is this and what are you to Sabina?"

Sabina stared at her, goggle-eyed. Anu gave her a don't-worry hand gesture.

"Well, Max the Agent, I am Anu the All-Knowing and I happen to be completely confident in the fact that my client, Sabina Jones, has no interest in appearing on your silly TV show ever again. Please be so kind as not to bother her about this trivial matter in the future, as she will be busy doing important things such as saving houses. Good night!"

She held the phone away from her ear, ignoring the blast of cigarette-roughened ranting, then handed it back to Sabina. "He wants to talk to you again."

Sabina numbly took the phone. "Yes?"

She could practically hear the steam coming out of Max's ears. "If I ditch the Hatfield family, you're to blame. Stubborn as a freaking goddamn mule. You're just alike, you and your mother. You're both obsessed with your careers. At least hers brings in the big bucks. You, I don't get."

Now that hurt. "Bye, Max." She clicked off the phone and glanced up at Anu. "Thanks for sticking up for me."

"I enjoyed it. Are you okay?"

"Yes," she said, although some of his words had cut pretty hard. Obsessed with her career? Just like her mother? How dare he?

With a rustle of gold bangles, Anu handed her a mug of fragrant chai tea. Sabina inhaled the exotic cinnamon-cardamom scent, but shook her head. "I'm not sure tea is going to do it. They don't make chai vodka, do they?"

"I don't believe they do. But if you find yourself with neither a firefighting nor an acting job, we should consider it." A rich chuckle made her face light up. "I've been praying to Ganesh on your behalf."

"Ganesh?"

"Remover of obstacles. He has the head of an elephant. Stubborn fellow. Now drink up."

Lineup the next morning had to go down in San Gabriel history as the most awkward on record. Vader looked miserable. Chief Roman looked as if he'd been carved out of rock. The other guys seemed to have trouble keeping the smirks off their faces. Sabina tried to act as if nothing unusual had happened over the weekend, but her rusty acting skills weren't up to the challenge.

She didn't say anything as Captain Kelly told them about the EMT recertification rotation coming up the next two weeks. The vacation schedule went by in a blur. The warning to not speak to the media made her cringe. Then someone asked a question about the dinner rotation, which made her think of food, which made her think of Roman.

Her gaze, which had been firmly fixed on a screwdriver someone had left on the long kitchen table, flew to meet his. She didn't intend to look at him, in fact she'd been avoiding it all morning, but now she was stuck like a fly in honey. He seemed to feel the same way. He tried to look away but instead only managed a ferocious frown.

The memory of the breakfast he'd made for her came back in little sensory snatches, the scent of buttery mushrooms, the soft saltiness of goat cheese, the slide of cream into coffee. The slide of him into her.

A slow wave of heat crept up her face.

His jaw tightened.

Her knees threatened to wobble; she locked them in place.

Was everyone looking at them? Did anyone else exist? It felt as though the two of them were floating inside a bubble as the Munchkins of Oz watched and marveled.

As lineup broke apart, Roman spun on his heel and stalked into his office.

Vader tugged Sabina into the backyard. "You owe me," he said as soon as they were out of earshot. "It was your stupid idea to go to that bar."

"I know. I'm sorry."

"Here." He savagely punched numbers on his phone. "I'm calling Cherie, and you'd better figure out what to say to her."

"Me?"

But he just snarled at her until the call connected, then thrust the phone at her.

"Vader, this is crazy," Sabina hissed at Vader, who now had his arms crossed over his chest so he looked like Mr. Clean on guard duty.

"Talk."

Sabina swallowed. "Is this Cherie?"

"Yes." Cherie had a soft voice with whiff of delicious Southern accent. "I thought this was Vader's phone."

"This is his friend Sabina. I just want you to know that Vader's a good guy and he's not . . . um . . . *completely* homophobic . . ."

Vader glared and flexed his pecs.

"I also want to point out that he's not forcing me to make this call out of guilt or anything." Vader dragged a hand through his hair. "But seriously, it took a lot for him to leave his comfort zone and walk into that bar, but he did it. For you. So I think you should give him a chance."

There came a long pause on the other end of the line, followed by a deep sigh. "Would you put that big, silly goof on the line?"

For the first time since she'd seen the "Scandal in the Firehouse" story, Sabina felt a smile cross her face. She covered the phone with one hand. "Vader, if you screw it up with this woman, I'm never speaking to you again. Got it?"

He snatched the phone away from her. "Cherie? Babe?"

But Sabina's attention had switched to the tall, magnetic figure who now stood in the doorway. Roman jerked his head toward the side patio where they kept the grill. Cautiously she headed that direction. Could they speak without giving anything away to curious onlookers?

They stood on either side of the grill, as if the presence of a hunk of carbon-coated metal would prevent mischief.

"You okay?" he asked, his voice neutral but his eyes traveling her body, a quick down and up, as if to reassure himself she hadn't been beaten up by paparazzi.

"Of course," she said stiffly. "I saw your press conference. You did a good job. You explained everything very well." Especially the part about adhering strictly, *strictly*, to the rules.

His mouth tightened, ever so slightly. "It's too bad this has gotten so crazy. I've never experienced anything like it."

She swallowed. The way his deep voice dropped on those last few words, going husky, set off a pleasant vibration in her belly. She didn't need pleasant vibrations. They meant trouble. "I haven't either." She cleared her throat. "It's completely out of control."

He nodded and clasped his hands behind his back, as if to make sure he didn't lose control himself. "I called you a few times."

"I know. I . . . uh . . . it's better if . . ."

"Of course." He put up a commanding hand. "No need to say any more. I did want to ask you something, however."

"Uh-huh?" It came out as a squeak.

"Have you noticed anything different going on with Carly? Luke was trying to tell me something the other day but he couldn't quite spit it out."

Sabina frowned. That had certainly come out of left

field. The last time Sabina had seen Carly had been at Chili's when all the parents had mobbed her. "Nothing unusual, no. Except she seems to be hanging out with Luke a lot. She usually doesn't bother with boys."

"What about her mom? Luke asked if I knew her."

"Her mother's a bit of a binge drinker. But most of the time she keeps it together pretty well. Carly knows I'm always available if things get nasty."

He studied her for a long, sober moment. "That's good. Will you keep me informed?"

"Well, I don't know if I feel comfortable with that, Roman. It's her private family life, not mine. She needs to know I'll keep her confidence if she tells me something. If I got wind of something seriously wrong, I'd call the organization."

He snapped to his full height, his spine straight as an iron rod. "Of course. I hadn't thought of it that way. Very good, Firefighter Jones. You should be very proud of what you're doing there. Carry on."

She stared after his huge, powerful form as his long legs ate up the distance between her and the door to the firehouse. The man was one mystery after another. Each one made him even more fascinating. And more out of reach.

Chapter Twenty-Two

Sabina decided to join Fred on engine-polishing detail. Her nerves couldn't handle any more encounters with Roman, and Vader had hung up with Cherie in an even worse mood. As she ran a rag over the chrome fittings of the headlights, she could tell Fred was struggling to keep his questions to himself.

He lost the battle. "I've never seen Vader like this. Is he okay?"

Sabina shrugged. "He probably feels like an idiot."

"Maybe someone should talk to him."

"Be my guest."

That silenced him. For a moment. "You're his best friend."

"This isn't junior high, Stud. We're firefighters. If you've got something to say to Vader, feel free to say it."

His round, M&M's brown eyes went wide. The little sprig of hair that made him look so boyish seemed to jump up like an exclamation point. He tossed his rag over his shoulder and straightened. "You're right, Two. I'm going in." He hopped down from the engine and hurried out of the apparatus bay. "If I'm not back in ten minutes, you might want to call for help."

"Oh shit," Sabina muttered. If Stud messed with Vader in a mood like this, who knew what bloodshed might result. She ran after him. Psycho, emerging from the bathroom, perked up at the sight of potential action.

"What's up?"

"Don't know yet. Whatever it is, it's none of your business," snapped Sabina.

"The hell with that." He fell into step beside her.

In the workout room, Stud placed himself squarely in front of Vader, whose biceps were quivering and clenching from the effort of holding three hundred pounds of metal over his head. With a roar, he dropped the weights onto the padded mat on the floor. He roared again, glaring at Stud, who took an involuntary step back. The blood that swelled in Vader's muscles made him look even bigger than usual, and about twice Stud's size. He looked like a cartoon version of some mad scientist's mutant creation.

Fred quailed before this mighty vision of manhood. He looked like he might run, but instead he stood his ground and tapped his ear.

Vader scowled at him.

Stud mimed the action of taking off headphones. Vader grunted and shifted one of the earpieces behind his ear. The tinny sound of AC/DC echoed through the workout room. By now everyone was watching—Psycho, Ace the rookie, and a couple of the A shift guys who'd come in to work out.

"Vader, I just wanted you to know it doesn't matter to us if you're . . . you know."

Vader clenched his jaw until the muscles stood out like baseballs. "Shut the fuck up, Stud."

"No. It's too important. I won't shut up."

Vader's mouth fell open. Sabina braced herself. If Vader decided to pound Stud into the mat, she'd have to step into the line of fire along with him.

"Look, Vader, I know you're not gay like they're saying on Channel Two, but if you were, it wouldn't matter."

"I'm not," Vader ground out. "Some chick messed with my head, that's all."

"Well, I kind of wish you were."

"What?"

Sabina took a step forward, but Psycho held her back. "Oh no, you don't. This is too good." Glee lit his bright blue eyes.

Fred turned the color of a brick. "Not because . . . nothing like that . . . I mean so we could, you know, set an example. Be a beacon of tolerance. Use all the publicity to make a point."

Vader screwed up his face in a what-the-fuck-are-you-talking-about way, but at least he hadn't yet snapped Fred like a twig. "Beacon, my ass."

"No, I've been thinking about this, Vader. It's an opportunity to make a statement to the media. You know, since they're all paying attention to us."

"You're nuts, Stud," Vader growled. He picked up a gym towel and wiped the sweat off his face. "That attention's good for one thing only. Getting chicks."

Fred's face crumpled. He looked down at his feet, then back up, then did the whole routine a couple more times until Vader finished with the towel and slung it around his neck. "Vader," he burst out. "I'm disappointed in you. I know you act like a dumbass steroid freak, but I thought you had more depth than that." He shook his head with disgust and turned to go, nearly tripping on the mat.

Sabina whispered to Fred as he passed. "Give him some time." She knew perfectly well that Vader had more depth, if that's what you wanted to call it, than he let on. With the guys, he always acted the gonzo and party boy. Only with her did he relax and act like a normal guy.

"Hey, bozo." Vader picked up a free weight as if he was going to lob it at Fred. Sabina flung out an arm to protect him, but Fred pushed it aside.

"I can handle myself, Two," he said fiercely.

Vader launched into a rapid series of lifts. "Don't you know not to mess with a steroid freak?" He snarled like a rabid dog about to go on the attack.

The rising tension was shattered by a long, loud tone from the intercom. Everyone went still to focus on the intercom. "Reported structure fire for Task Force 1, Task Force 5, Engine 6, Truck 9, Battalion 1. Location is 1220 North Walnut. Incident number 324. Time of alarm is 9:32. We're receiving multiple calls."

Before the announcement had finished, the firefighters had poured out of the gym and hurried into the apparatus bay. Quickly, efficiently, Sabina thrust her feet into her boots, pulled up her turnout pants, and snapped on the suspenders. She donned her hood, jacket, and breathing apparatus, checked her pressure gauge, donned her helmet, then put on her gloves.

Roman, battalion chief on duty, was already settling into the passenger seat. Double D jumped into the driver's seat, and Vader and Captain Kelly launched themselves into the backseat next to Sabina. The door of the apparatus bay opened and, sirens sounding, they cruised out the driveway onto Main Street.

Roman punched up the GPS. "Looks like it's on a corner."

"I think I know the one. Big, at least six thousand square feet," said Double D, who probably knew every house in San Gabriel. "Lots of other houses right nearby."

Right on cue, the dispatcher clicked on. "Be advised, the next-door house is now involved in that fire on 1220 Walnut. Repeat, 1224 Walnut is also involved."

"That's the house to the south," said Double D, turning a corner as cars scattered to the sides of the road. "That one's even bigger. Seems to me they added a floor just to piss off the neighbors. Then the other guys put up a third floor, so the first one got themselves a cupola. "

"Winds are fifteen knots out of the northeast," said Roman, still looking at the laptop. "Any more houses that direction?"

"I don't think so. You got the two richest people on the block in a pissing match. Don't know why one of them don't just move."

All other issues forgotten, Vader and Sabina exchanged a glance. Fires and feuds made a suspicious combination.

"No assumptions," said Roman sharply. "It's a fire like any other."

Double D nodded, and they passed the rest of the trip in the tense, adrenaline-charged silence that always preceded a working fire. Sabina always felt a little sick to her stomach beforehand, sort of the way she'd felt before the assistant director yelled, "Action."

When they reached Walnut Street, several engines were already on the scene. Flames and smoke billowed from two huge, stately mansions. Visible waves of heat distorted the air. Even over the sound of the engine, they heard the roaring, insistent voice of the flames. On the dispatch channel, a calm male voice reported back with the initial size-up. "Dispatch from Engine 9, on the scene. 1220 Walnut. We've got a three-story, wood-frame single family dwelling with fire and smoke showing. Engine 9 will be known as Walnut IC. Engine 1, there's a plug on the southwest corner. The bravo side is heavily involved, flames spreading to the alpha side."

Double D spotted the fire hydrant and stopped the engine. Vader hopped out to hook up the hose. As soon as he gave the signal, Double D pulled forward, the hose stretching out behind them. He put on the parking brake, then they all jumped out of the rig. Sabina ran to her position at the nozzle of the hose and removed it from its housing.

Out of the corner of her eye she saw a knot of people clustered at the edge of the lawn. Two of them seemed to be yelling at each other, the others struggling to keep them apart.

"Fire department coming through," she yelled as she hauled the nozzle over her shoulder and got set to jog wherever the hose was wanted.

Commands crackled through the radio. "Engine 1, take the alpha side. Chief Roman, you're on safety-recon. Truck 1, you got ventilation. You will be known as Roof Division." Sabina spotted Psycho, fire axe in hand, jogging toward one of the ladders that had already been set up. He'd be responsible for hacking a hole in the roof to release the smoke before it built up inside.

"Anyone inside?" she yelled to a fireman coming to help her with the hose.

"Not so far. Still checking."

Captain Kelly kicked open the door and she hauled

the hose inside. A swirl of smoke burst toward them. She waited, adjusting her vision to the nightmarish, surreal state of this formerly elegant home. The ruthless nature of fire always shocked her. Fire didn't care how much money you put into your decor, or how many treasured family heirlooms you'd accumulated. It didn't care if you had a cat or a goldfish or a meth lab.

This didn't look like the type of place to have a meth lab, but you never knew. The firefighters sweeping the interior for residents would be keeping an eye out for meth labs, grow rooms, propane tanks, funky wiring, anything that might explode in their faces.

"Firefighter Callahan from Roof Division," came Psycho's voice. "We've got one hole opened up."

"Good job," said the incident commander. "Join your crew on the alpha side and get those flames out, would you?"

"I'm on it."

Sabina gave the signal and aimed the nozzle toward the heaviest smoke, which was coming from what was most likely the kitchen. She reached up and switched on her headlamp. Before her first fire, she'd never realized how dark it got inside a working fire. Dense gray smoke obscured her vision, and not even the occasional leaping flames offered enough illumination to make a difference. She could see other firefighters moving around, and the outlines of priceless pieces of furniture, soon to be charred heaps of junk.

Over the sound of the water hissing on the flames, and the constant, underlying roar, she could barely make out the pieces of vital information being communicated over the tactical channel.

"Upstairs is clear. Downstairs is clear."

So no one was left in the house; very good news.

"Might need another vent hole on the delta side."

"This looks like a grow room down here."

"Those are tomatoes."

"Any dangerous chemicals used in tomato gardens?"

Sabina smiled. With no people in the house, the fire crews could worry a little less, even though they were still working just as hard. It was no longer a life-and-death situation, although that could certainly change if something went wrong. But so far things were running smoothly.

Until the next blip from the radio.

"Fire's running the walls," said someone over the radio. "Damn, this is one stubborn-ass fire."

"Let's open up the ceilings. Fire's running the walls and the attic."

Sabina looked up at the ceiling. Pulling these cathedral ceilings would be a piece of work. Psycho and the others would love the challenge. As she looked back at the flames, something caught her eye through the murk. A flash of golden brown, the exact color of a golden retriever. "Take this!" She handed the nozzle to Vader behind her. "Think I saw something move. Do they have a dog?"

"Make it zippy," said Captain Kelly. "Truck crew's coming in with the pike poles."

"Two steps, here and back." She stepped forward into the gloom. The flames didn't bother her—they weren't bad on the alpha side—but the visibility sucked. But if there was an unconscious dog in there, no way was she going to leave it there to burn to death. Stan would never forgive her.

Well, if the incident commander had ordered her to leave, she would have. But he hadn't.

The two steps had been a slight exaggeration. Three long strides and she'd reached the stairwell. She crouched down and peered into the smoky, dusty haze. What had she seen? Certainly not a dog. All she found was an ottoman upholstered in beige suede sitting in a little nook under the stairwell. Relieved, she started to get to her feet.

Before she could straighten all the way, something fell across her back. *What the hell?* She started to turn, but something else crashed next to her. Damn it. The staircase. It was collapsing. She flung herself away from it, but it was too late. A heavy chunk of marble spun through the air and bounced off her helmet. A sharp crack echoed through the metal and she fell to her knees. For a moment she saw nothing but blackness and confusion.

"Stairs coming down!" she yelled into her radio. "I'm coming out!"

"Partial collapse of the staircase!" someone else said over the radio. "Jones, are you there?"

"Here!" she croaked. "On my way."

"No communication from Firefighter Jones," crackled the radio. It sounded like Vader. "Stairs are still coming down. She might be trapped underneath. Can't see a freakin' thing."

"I'm not trapped," she yelled, but the sound was lost amid the tumble of wood crashing around her. She put her arms over her head to protect it, and felt it wobble. Good Lord. Her helmet was broken. Split right in half. Which meant her radio mic must be out.

Never mind that. *Hold tight*, she told herself. *Protect your head. Wait until the sky stops falling, then get the hell out.*

It seemed to last forever, the staircase tumbling down itself with the maniacal glee of a little boy sliding down a banister. Chunks of wood and bits of plaster rained down on Sabina's back and arms. Even through her padded firefighter's coat she felt them bouncing off her. She was going to have some bruises tonight, no doubt. Then something big and bulky knocked her over so she lay on her side, her ankle twisted under her.

Cruel pain rocketed through her foot all the way up her leg. Mother of God, it burned. She cried out even though no one could hear her. More debris pelted her cheek and neck. She pulled herself up onto her hands, gritting her teeth at the agony in her ankle. She had to get out of here. Now that the staircase had collapsed, the flames would leap toward this new source of oxygen. The foyer would turn into an incinerator in no time.

But when she tried to move, she realized she was pinned. Whatever had landed on her ankle wasn't budging. She tried to tug her foot free, but went dizzy at the fresh onslaught of slicing pain.

Think, Sabina, think. Try the mic again. Shout. See if someone could hear her.

"Emergency Traffic, Emergency Traffic, firefighter down," she yelled. "This is Firefighter Jones from Engine 1, I'm trapped under the debris from a collapsed staircase on the alpha side. I think my ankle's twisted. Request immediate assistance."

When she heard no response, it dawned on her that she hadn't heard anything from her radio for some time. Her radio *reception* had gone dead too. All her communication was out. She was trapped, injured, and completely isolated.

It hit her. Holy crap, she was going to die. Horribly. By some incredible stroke of luck, whatever had fallen on her head with enough force to break her helmet hadn't killed her. No, instead it had left her conscious enough to understand that she was about to get burned alive—along with the remains of an extremely expensive custom marble and teak staircase.

It's a stairway to heaven, she thought hysterically. The

melody danced through her mind, though the words were fuzzy. *I'm buying a stairway to heaven.*

Her head spinning, she mouthed the words like a chant until a kind of black calm settled over her. This was death, inevitable, relentless death. Firefighters faced it every day. She'd always known the risks. Every firefighter did. But . . .

Not yet. Please, not yet.

Sorry, Annabelle . . . Mama.

Not yet, not yet. She hadn't done nearly enough before checking out. Not nearly. If she'd known it would come this soon, she would have skipped some of the jogging and spent more time . . . well, maybe she'd have a kid. Yes. A kid. The closest she'd allowed herself to get was Carly. What was wrong with her, why had she been so stupid?

No kid, no man, no family. All those bountiful, luxurious years had come down to these last few moments . . . and she'd never let herself love someone, and have a baby with him, and now it was too late and what the fuck had she done with her life?

Love. The word echoed again as Roman's dark, fierce, beautiful face filled her mind's eye. She feasted her eyes. *Thanks for being here. I appreciate it. You're a sight for sore, dying eyes.* One of Roman's black eyebrows swooped up. Oh, he was going to be furious about this. He'd probably call her into his office and pin her with that blistering black gaze, then maybe he'd throw the rule book out the window, snatch her up in his arms, and kiss her until the room spun six ways to Sunday and . . .

Time's up.

Immersed in Roman's kiss, she surrendered to the Grim Reaper, who took her into his rough arms and carried her up the stairway to heaven.

Chapter Twenty-Three

No thinking. Just act. Do. Run. Find Sabina. Ignore the smoke billowing around him. Ignore the flames grabbing for him. Dig through that pile of wood and marble trying to crush Sabina. He knew she was there. As soon as he'd heard the words, "Firefighter Jones might be trapped," he'd known. Because that's what happened when he wasn't around to stop it.

Not this time. This time, he was there and if he had to lift the entire freaking mansion with his two hands and his back, he'd do it. Other firefighters tried to hold him back, but they might as well have been cobwebs. He bowled past them, crashed through the doorway, and vaulted toward the collapsed staircase. With a roar, he lifted a big chunk of stone off the top of the pile and flung it aside. Next came a giant shard of wood, its underside smoldering. Holy fuck, one slight breath of oxygen and this whole stack of lumber would ignite like a bonfire. *Move fast, faster.*

The flash of movement caught his eye. Must be her. Get that stuff off her. Come on, move it, move it. The next chunk of marble moved easily, weirdly so, and he realized he wasn't alone. Vader was right there with him, helping him roll the slab aside. Yes, definitely movement, and the flash of the reflector stripe on every firefighter's coat.

"It's her. Hurry," he yelled to Vader. He didn't have to say it; the man was shifting debris like a madman.

Sabina moved again—it had to be Sabina—and he yelled to her this time. "Hang on, *cara mia*. Just hang on."

Vader shot him a funny look. Was that wrong, to speak to her in Italian? Give her sweet words? He couldn't remember. All he knew was Sabina was in trouble, terrible trouble, and he had to get her out.

More jagged pieces of wood cast aside, and now he could see her. Smart girl, she'd curled in on herself to protect her head and vital organs. *Vital organs*. Good God, every single part of her was vital as far as he was concerned. *She* was vital.

Then he saw something that chilled him to the core. Her helmet had split in two pieces, barely held together. Something had landed on her head and broken her helmet. *Head injury*, his brain screamed. If she was even alive. No, she had to be alive. She'd moved. And look, she was moving again.

"Sabina!" Desperately he scrabbled bits of wood and debris off her. As he did so, a blast of flaming gas burst around him like a dragon's belch. *Fireball*. He crouched over Sabina, using his body to shield her from the fiery threat. It blew past him, so fierce he felt its heat on his skin, even through the Plexiglas of his face piece. He gave a quick prayer of thanks to the scientists who had invented this gear, who had given him the bubble of clothing that offered firefighters their only chance in the deadly environment of a working fire.

"Help me get her leg free," he yelled to Vader. Between the two of them, they carefully rolled a huge chunk of marble; her left boot was wedged beneath it.

He bent low to Sabina. Her eyes were closed but her mouth was moving. He couldn't hear her. Her radio must have gotten broken along with the helmet. The eerie similarity screamed at him, along with thoughts he hadn't allowed for years. Faulty radio communication had killed Maureen. She'd been in that tower and hadn't heard the evacuation order due to a fucking repeater going out . . .

"Sabina, can you hear me? I need your help here. Raise your hand if you can hear me."

No response. She probably couldn't hear through his face piece. Should he take it off? No, that would be insane. He wouldn't be able to help her if he did that. Never mind. He'd just pick her up and get her out of here, with or without her help.

"Stand back," he told Vader. The other fireman backed away. Roman knelt next to Sabina. He pried one arm under her knees and the other under her shoulders. If she had a brain injury or even a concussion, moving her like this was problematic, but he had no choice. The room was getting ready to flash. He rolled her toward him, the tank of her breathing apparatus bumping against his arm.

When she was safely in his arms, he rose up on one knee, tightened his grip, then, with a guttural grunt, surged all the way to his feet. He swayed there for a moment, flexing his knees, as he got used to her weight. Sabina was tall and willowy, not a dandelion fluff of a woman at all, especially wearing all her gear. But it didn't matter what she weighed. He had her now and he wasn't going to let go, not if the entire house collapsed on top of them.

"We gotta go, Chief!" Vader yelled. "Call a Rescue Ambulance. Firefighter down."

Roman felt a hand at his elbow guiding him away from the pile of rubble. Blindly, he followed it. Flames fanned at his legs. He heard his own harsh breathing in the echo chamber of his helmet, the Darth Vader–like in-out through his mouthpiece. Through the murk of smoke and dust he spotted the outline of the doorway, the promise of sunshine outside. Just get her out, get her to the light. He stumbled once, twice, but willed himself to keep going.

And then the bright morning light embraced them, more firefighters surrounded them, the businesslike commands flowing. "All companies on the Walnut incident, back out, we are going defensive. Repeat, back out, we are going defensive."

Good call, Roman thought with the captain side of his brain. The house was too far gone. Time to put all their efforts toward saving the neighboring homes. But they'd have to do it without him. He had one mission and one mission only. Get Sabina to someone who could take care of her.

A faint moan reached his ears.

"Hang on, *cara*. We're almost there." An ambulance screeched to the curb, lights flashing. Paramedics dashed toward him. He scanned their faces. Did they look capable? Could he trust them? Never mind that. He didn't have a choice. He'd have to let Sabina out of his arms so the trained professionals could take over. But *Dio,* it hurt to hand her over.

"Her helmet cracked. She might have a head injury," he yelled to them.

The paramedic nodded. A gurney appeared. Two

guys helped him lay Sabina down. Immediately they checked her vitals and settled her onto a backboard and into a C collar. "BP 110 over 70, pulse is weak and thready," said a paramedic in a rapid-fire monotone.

She's alive, she's alive, Roman kept telling himself as he watched them at work, somewhat reassured by their brisk efficiency.

"Thanks to you," said Vader, still at his elbow.

Roman realized he'd been repeating the words out loud. He aimed a glare on the man. "Didn't they call all hands to the other house?"

"Yeah, they did, Chief. We better go."

Roman's glance told him where he could put that idea. "Go ahead. I got it from here."

Vader nodded and turned away.

"Firefighter Brown," barked Roman. "Good work." He said it over his shoulder, only tearing his gaze away from Sabina for a moment. Had her eyes opened? He thought he'd caught a flash of turquoise. But now they were closed, dark eyelashes fanning across her flushed cheeks.

"Yes, sir." And the man trotted off. Roman knew he should join him, and he would, just as soon as they got Sabina into the ambulance. He had to stay and make sure they were doing it right, that they didn't jostle her too much or dump her onto the ground. He wasn't letting her out of his sight until he absolutely had to.

Before he knew it, they whisked her away. She disappeared headfirst into the ambulance, the back doors closed, and the vehicle pulled away from him. The sound of its siren made him queasy. It felt as if a part of himself had been torn away.

Get a grip, Roman, he commanded himself. *You've got a fire to fight.* He jogged to the neighboring house, only to find it mostly under control. The crew of Engine 1 was reeling in the four-inch hose. He veered in their direction to help.

"Chief Roman," Vader yelled. "They got it from here. Captain Kelly said we can head to the hospital."

The hospital. He braced his legs as a wave of nausea struck him. The hospital. No. He couldn't. Burning building, yes. Hospital . . . "We'll just be in the way over there."

"Fuck that."

"You can go. We still have a shift to finish."

"But Chief . . ."

He took the hose from Vader. "Go. That's an order. I'll wrap things up here." Ignoring Vader's befuddled frown, he bent his concentration on the familiar task.

The doctors and nurses kept telling Sabina how lucky she was. An entire staircase had fallen on her head, and she hadn't even gotten a concussion. Her helmet had saved her. She had, however, suffered multiple abrasions, lots of bruising, and a broken rib, along with a broken left ankle that would take months to heal. She didn't even have any smoke inhalation, although her throat felt sore and her voice sounded extra raspy when she first used it to ask for water.

They kept her in the hospital for one night and most of the next day, just to be safe. During that time, Vader came to see her, as did Double D, Captain Kelly, Psycho, and Stud. Even Ryan came, bestowing kisses on various nurses' cheeks.

"Heard they have a new nickname for you," he said. "Iron."

"Iron?" she croaked.

"Because that's what your head must be made from to survive something like that."

"Crappy. Nickname."

"Sorry. It's got to be better than Zombie though. You're in the hospital, not sure what you can do about it. I'll try to put in a good word for you." He winked one summer-blue eye. She noticed how good that simple gold wedding ring looked on his finger, and how good he looked. Not just devastatingly handsome, which was a given, but, more importantly, happy and relaxed.

"Katie?" One-word sentences seemed to work best.

"Great." A smile drifted across his gorgeous face. "Greater than great. Hey, I heard Chief Roman pulled that staircase off you like a pile of pickup sticks. Carried you off in his own two arms."

She shrugged one shoulder, which hurt like hell. That's what Vader had told her, and Double D, who'd witnessed the entire event. Sadly, she hadn't seen hide nor hair of Roman, though she vaguely remembered being lifted into the air. "Haven't seen him."

"Well, when you do, give him a big kiss on the lips from me." Ryan winked. "Make it a sloppy one."

She scowled and shook her head violently.

"Word is he called you some Italian name when he was saving your life. The guys are checking the dictionary."

Her face heated. God, was she blushing? "Go away," she told Ryan. "Tired."

"Sure, Zombie. Whatever you say."

He strolled to the door in his slow-hipped cowboy stride. She threw a pillow at his backside.

She closed her eyes, thoughts racing. Maybe Roman hadn't come to visit because he'd called her something nice in Italian over the tactical channel. If he came to see her, the guys would talk. He was probably doing her a favor by staying away.

Bits and pieces kept coming back . . . the stairway to

heaven, Roman's dark face, his furious expression, the word "love". . .

No, no, she'd just been experiencing some strange hallucinations. Even so, nothing would feel right again until she laid her eyes on that big-bodied, fierce-eyed man again.

But the next time she woke up, Annabelle sat at her bedside. Her usual effortless makeup job couldn't quite hide the violet shadows under her eyes.

"You almost died," she said, with a sort of outraged anger when Sabina opened her eyes.

"Little. Dramatic." Sabina gestured for a drink of water. Annabelle handed it to her and Sabina took a long, grateful sip.

"So this firefighter thing. You actually like that. You *like* nearly dying."

Sabina closed her eyes, half hoping she was hallucinating and Annabelle would disappear. No such luck. "Yes," she said, simply, since short sentences still seemed best. "Mostly."

"I had no idea it was so dangerous."

Sabina raised her eyebrows.

"I never thought it through. They have all those big coats and boots and helmets and that thing on the back."

Sabina couldn't let that stand, no matter how tired she was. "Self. Contained. Breathing apparatus." She took another long swallow of water.

Annabelle looked affronted. "So technical!"

Revived by the water, Sabina dragged herself into a sitting position, ignoring the stabs of pain in her rib cage. "Firefighting. Needs technical knowledge. I had to study . . . hard for the exam."

"There's an exam?"

"A tough one." Sabina tried to express the rest of her thought, but didn't have the strength.

Annabelle pressed her lips together. A male nurse came in to check Sabina's blood pressure. His eyes kept darting back and forth from Sabina to Annabelle. He was good-looking in a beefcake sort of way, but for once, Annabelle seemed oblivious.

"The doctor's cleared you to go home," he said. "Do you have . . . uh . . . someone to take you?"

Sabina and Annabelle spoke at the same time.

"I'll call a friend . . ."

"I'll take her."

"Annabelle, there's no need for that."

"I'm taking you."

With an alarmed smile, the nurse hurried out of the line of fire.

"Hand me my phone," said Sabina.

"No. Sabina, you could have died. I didn't realize . . . it made me see . . . well, it all seems a lot more real now."

Sabina eyed her mother in disbelief. Speaking of real, were those real tears making her eyes shine like those of a cat caught in the headlights?

"I'm taking you home and I'm going to stay with you."

"What?"

"Yes. You're going to be on crutches for six weeks. Who else is going to take care of you? Vader?"

"You're staying for *six weeks*?" For a crazed moment, Sabina wished she was back under the collapsing staircase.

"Well . . . we'll see." Annabelle sniffed, clearly offended by Sabina's reaction. "Maybe we'll start with a few days."

Sabina sank back on her pillows. "Let me guess.

You've installed cameras in my house and we're actually going to be filming a reality show version of the *You and Me* reunion show."

After a long, astonished pause, Annabelle burst into laughter. Not her movie laughter, but her hearty, snorty belly laugh, the one Sabina hadn't heard in over twenty years.

"That's genius, kiddo. Should we call Max and set it up?"

But Sabina could only shake her head because tears were grabbing at the back of her throat, clamoring to get out. As if she were seventeen again, all alone and longing for her mother. But her mother had cut her off. Ignored her for thirteen years. Only returned when she needed something.

On the other hand, she'd nearly died. And she'd thought about her mother when the world had been collapsing around her. *Sorry, Annabelle. Mama.*

"You can take me home. But if you stay, you cannot mention the reunion show. And we'll take it a day at a time."

Annabelle dipped her head like a queen granting a bequest.

For Roman, the next couple of days passed in a surreal blur. He kept close tabs on Sabina's progress. He knew when the doctors discharged her. He knew when she left the hospital. He knew when her mother took her home. Hell, the whole world knew that, since the paparazzi had snapped photos outside the hospital.

"Brush with Death Reunites Hatfields," screamed the caption in the *San Gabriel Gazette*. Front page, no less. The newspaper lurked in his desk at the firehouse, taunting him with its glimpse of Sabina.

She sat in a wheelchair, her leg in a cast, bouquets

of flowers piled in her lap. They had all come from someone else; he hadn't sent a bouquet. Annabelle was pushing the wheelchair, oversize white sunglasses and a movie-star smile firmly in place as she waved to the cameras.

Roman stared at the photograph for what felt like a week, noticing every detail. Sabina's face looked a little thin. She looked irritated by the presence of the cameras. Or maybe by her mother. Or maybe by the fact that he hadn't visited her in the hospital.

He crumpled the newspaper and slammed it into the garbage can so hard he knocked it over with a harsh clang.

Stan lurched to his feet, gazed suspiciously at the garbage can, then went to investigate. When he sniffed at the balled-up newspaper, Roman snatched it away. "Sorry, Stan," he muttered. "I'm not done with the paper yet."

He smoothed it out and stashed it in the top drawer of his desk.

Chapter Twenty-Four

As Roman sleepwalked through the days that held no Sabina, it slowly sank in that something was bothering Luke. His son kept shutting himself in his room and blasting unfamiliar bands that made Roman's head hurt. He kept talking to someone on the phone in a low voice, and got quiet the instant Roman walked past.

When he drove Luke to practice, he forced himself to make the superhuman effort to discuss it. It took him the entire car trip to produce the first words, which finally came after he'd pulled up to the curb at the park.

"I'm sorry about Sabina."

Luke shot him an incredulous look. "Carly said she's fine. She hurt her ankle, that's all."

"That's not what I mean."

Luke waited, waving at the coach, who was hurrying past with the bag of bats. "What, Papa? I'm late."

"Well, I saved Sabina. I got her out."

"I know. You're a stud, Papa. Everyone says so." He jiggled his leg impatiently, an exuberant ball of energy trapped inside the metal cage known as a car.

"It doesn't bother you?"

"What? No." Luke looked at him as if he'd just arrived from Mars. "Can I go now? I really don't want to be late. I have to talk to someone before the game."

"Oh yeah? Who? What about?"

Luke paused. Roman saw hesitation, uncertainty, and confusion flit across his son's face. Like a roulette ball, he finally settled on impatience. "Later, Papa. Are you going to stay for practice? Cuz you don't have to."

That statement cut Roman to the quick. "Of course I'm staying. I'll go park. I'll be in the stands."

Luke nodded and ran off. Roman slammed the heel of his hand against the steering wheel. He'd handled the whole conversation wrong. He'd assumed he knew what was bothering Luke. That Luke was upset because he'd saved Sabina, but hadn't saved Maureen. Of course it should bother Luke, because it bothered—

His mind shied away from the thought. No sense in thinking about Maureen. Or Sabina. *Keep it simple, Roman. Work, Luke, work, Luke.*

He started to pull away from the curb, then nearly crashed back into it at the sight of Sabina, on crutches, swinging her way across the green expanse of the park toward the baseball field. She looked so beautiful in cutoffs and a sky-blue T-shirt. The white cast on her ankle set off the pale gold sheen of her long, taut legs. The bright sunshine picked out glints of marigold in the long braid down her back. Was she letting her natural color shine through? She looked lithe and nimble, like a ballerina on stilts. The way her hips swung with every step made his cock pulse. Christ Almighty, only Sabina could make crutches look sexy.

He kept the Jeep in idle. This was the perfect opportunity to act like a normal person and ask her how she was doing. He could help her into the stands, fetch her a soda, fall to his knees and cry in her lap from sheer gratitude that she'd survived. He could tell her how it had felt to nearly lose her, and how strange undertows of emotion were tugging him this way and that, and how he didn't understand any of it. How he couldn't sleep and how he kept obsessively staring at that newspaper photo.

Or he could put his car in gear and spare her an embarrassing scene. If she only knew what a goddamn fool he was, she'd thank him for staying far away from her.

No doubt about it, Roman was avoiding her. Everyone kept telling her how he'd charged into that house and dug through the rubble with his bare hands to rescue her.

"Bare hands? What about his gloves?"

"Don't interrupt, I'm telling a story," Double D scolded when he dropped by her house to bring her ice cream and ogle her mother. She shut up. She owed him, after all.

In fact, the story got more dramatic every time she heard it. The chunks of marble grew to the size of boulders. The flames were magically flaring all the way from the back of the house to the stairwell. Roman was completely blinded by the smoke and needed Double D to dart inside the house and lead him to the doorway. That detail appeared only in Double D's version, but no one dared dispute it.

What no one could explain to her was why Roman would go to the trouble of risking his life, retrieving her nearly lifeless body from under a pile of rare Moldavian marble, only to ignore her utterly ever since then.

She thought about asking Vader when he stopped by the house, but he was still so upset about the whole thing she didn't have the heart.

"You could have died. What the fuck, Sabina?"

"I'm sorry. I didn't mean to. How're things at the station?"

"I don't know. I've been off. Fire chief's happy, though. Roman made us look good. They wanted to give him an award or something, but he said hell no."

"Really?"

"Said he was just doing his job."

Right. Just doing his job. Of course that's all it was.

Vader pulled one of her beige armchairs close to the couch and propped his forehead on her upper arm. "I didn't know I'd be so messed up if you got hurt. Do you think . . . ?"

"No, I don't."

"Dude, you don't know what I was going to say."

"Sure I do. You're having crazy thoughts that you might be in love with me. You're not. We're friends. Don't go all mushy on me, Vader, or I'll drop a free weight on your foot next chance I get."

Vader straightened up, looking hugely relieved. "Thanks, Two. Because Cherie says I'm in love with her."

"Cool. Good choice. Is she okay with your potential homophobia or is it reverse homophobia now?"

"She worked up a whole program to cure me. It's like school, Two, with lessons. Lesson sixteen is watching *Brokeback Mountain* without closing my eyes. It's nuts. But she smells so good, like strawberry cheesecake. So I put up with it."

Sabina laughed so hard, her ribs nearly cracked all over again. "Good luck with all that. Invite me to the graduation party."

"Vader." Annabelle stood over them, hands on slim hips. "What are you thinking, making her laugh?"

"I didn't mean to."

"It's okay, Annabelle. I needed that."

Vader got to his feet. "I better go anyway. Big meeting at the firehouse."

"Thanks for coming by," Sabina told him quickly, before he said anything more about the station. It hurt to hear about everything going on without her. It hurt to hear about Roman, busy running drills, training the crew, doing everything *except* coming to see her.

"I'm going to order some chicken soup from Murray's Deli. You hungry?" Annabelle poised her index finger over her phone.

Sabina stared up at her, bemused. "In all those episodes where you cooked for Taffy, didn't you soak up any information?"

Annabelle bristled for a moment, as if she didn't know whether Sabina was teasing. "I can make hot cocoa. And I can probably remember grilled cheese. That was always your favorite."

"*Taffy's* favorite. We didn't eat cheese, remember?"

"Yes. Taffy's. Your favorite was . . ."

Sabina raised an eyebrow, waiting. If Annabelle remembered her favorite food, she'd eat her pillow. Her mother had been unexpectedly tolerable the past few days. She'd ordered takeout, refilled prescriptions, and even helped Sabina shower. She hadn't mentioned the reunion show once. Still, the fact remained that Sabina was stuck on the couch, unable to work, and at times had the nightmarish sense that she'd never managed to leave home at all.

"Steamed dumplings with lots of soy sauce," Annabelle announced proudly.

Sabina's jaw dropped. "You *do* remember."

"Is that so strange? You're my only daughter. A few details stuck with me."

The glint of humor in Annabelle's tilted eyes did something funny to Sabina's stomach. She wasn't sure she liked it. Is it possible she'd . . . well, not misjudged her mother, precisely, but . . . underestimated her?

"Annabelle . . . ?"

"What?" her mother asked when she trailed off.

Questions piled up in Sabina's mind. Why hadn't she acknowledged the money Sabina had given her? Why had she chosen to cut her off? Had she ever missed Sabina? But frankly, Sabina feared the answers. "Let's order Chinese. For old times' sake."

The next day she couldn't take it anymore. She had to get out of the house. Breathe some firehouse air. Remind herself that she was a firefighter. Talk to some members of the male gender for a change. Real, red-blooded, muscular men.

See Roman.

She borrowed her mother's Volvo, which was an automatic, unlike her beast of an El Camino. It felt wonderful to do something on her own, to drive herself instead of stewing in the passenger seat. Driving was a little uncomfortable, but right now, absolutely necessary.

The whole crew was excited to see her. They gathered around, clapped her on the back, teased her, called her Iron Zombie until she threatened to kneecap them with her crutch. They asked when she was coming back. Told her, in detail, about every fire she'd missed. Recounted the prank Psycho had pulled on the rookie. While poor Ace had been in the bathroom, Psycho had snuck the rescue dummy into his bed. Ace had freaked out when he crawled back into bed to find it occupied.

He'd gotten some serious ribbing the next morning about his wild night with a sex doll and all the crazy sounds he'd made.

Sabina listened, laughed, chatted, but not one moment passed that she wasn't hyperaware of the closed door of Roman's office. Did he even know she was there? Did he care?

Finally, when she was just about ready to leave, the door opened and Roman appeared, a mountain of smoking hot male filling the doorway. He looked just as good as she kept remembering every restless, tossing night. Better. From all the way across the room, she could pick up his scent, black coffee and potent man.

Good thing she was on crutches.

"Chief Roman," she said, hoping her voice didn't sound as weak as she felt.

"Firefighter Jones. How's the recovery?"

"Speedy. I hope to be back on the job very soon."

He hesitated, his dark eyes boring into her. "No need to rush it."

Oh really? So he didn't want her to hurry back? The man had some nerve, rescuing her and then ignoring her. Outrage stiffened her spine. "Chief Roman, may I speak with you privately?"

His fierce eyebrows pulled together. He didn't want to be alone with her—she could tell. Too bad. She was still a member of Fire Station 1 and had the right to talk to her own training officer.

Reluctantly, he jerked his head in assent and held the door open for her. Ducking under his powerful arm felt like passing through a field of radiation. Sexually charged radiation. Every particle of her body responded to him. Even her ankle throbbed.

Or maybe that was because she'd been upright too long.

He noticed. Of course he did, with those black eyes that scoured every inch of her body. "Are you all right?"

"Fine," she said.

"You're hurting."

"I'm fine."

"Sit down."

She wanted to object to his bossy command, but she really needed to get off her ankle, so she swung over to the chair. Instantly Roman was at her side. He took her crutches and held her elbow as she sank into the chair. A sound escaped her, a sort of moaning wheeze. She knew what it was—shocked pleasure at the touch of his warm hand. But to him it must have sounded like pain.

Roman's brows drew together in a worried scowl as he knelt next to her. "You should be in bed, not hanging around here."

"I'm tired of being in bed."

They stared at each other. The words "in bed" hung in the air between them, heavy and tantalizing. Deep in his eyes, a flame lit. She felt the same flame in the pit of her stomach, in the tips of her fingers, at the base of her throat.

She broke the spell by clearing her throat. "Word is, you rescued me. Thank you."

It was as though a shutter slammed closed over his face. He looked down at the cast on her ankle. "It was nothing."

"Nothing?" What the fuck did that mean? "You ass. It wasn't nothing to me."

She stared stubbornly at him, willing him to meet her eyes.

"Sabina . . ." His voice was thick and black, like tar running over gravel. "I . . ." Finally his eyes lifted, and she sucked in a breath. Pain radiated from him, a sorrow so deep and nameless she felt it like a punch in the stomach. "Are you sure you're okay?"

Unable to say a word, she nodded.

"Because if you weren't—" He broke off, his mouth tightening.

"I'm fine," she whispered. "Promise."

He got to his feet and stood looking down at her, head bent. She felt embraced by his concern, as if surrounded with warm, steady light. Her head swam. If only she could live in that place, in this moment, in the crosshairs of Roman's attention. She could imagine no safer, more blissful place to be.

Someone knocked on the door. "Captain, we got an issue out here. Stan's running in circles around the training room sounding like a chew toy."

The moment shattered. Roman straightened his head, the corners of his firm mouth curling in amusement. He strode to the door and cracked it open. Stan shot in. He whirled around the room, sniffing frantically, then skidded to a halt at Roman's feet. Tail wagging, he panted until Roman reached down, way down, to scratch him between the ears. His moist brown eyes closed and his tail pounded on the floor.

Watching Roman's long fingers work their magic, Sabina knew just how Stan felt.

"He likes you now?"

"Apparently so. Guess he just needed some time to warm up to me."

Sabina pushed herself to her feet and grabbed her crutches. "I'd better go." She hadn't said what she'd wanted to say, which was something along the lines of *Why are you pretending I don't exist?* But she'd gotten her answer. He knew she existed, all right. He just didn't know what to do about that fact.

Neither did she, for that matter.

Roman gave a brisk, formal nod. "Hang in there with the recovery. Do whatever the doctors say, don't push anything. We look forward to having you back with us."

Sabina gave him a half smile and stumped toward the door. He opened it to usher her through. On her way out, she leveled a long stare at him. "You don't fool me, Roman," she said softly. "Not anymore."

He straightened, surprised.

"I take back what I said before. If you really were an ass, Stan wouldn't have anything to do with you."

She felt his stare drilling the middle of her back all the way out through the kitchen, across the training room, and out the door. The tingle didn't go away until she was safely in her mother's Volvo, heading for the only person she could stand to talk to at the moment.

At La Piaggia, Anu sat her down and made her some Kapha tea. Sabina, she explained, had too much Pitta and needed to strengthen her Kapha to help her heal. Sabina had heard the terms before, when one of the makeup artists on the show had gotten into ayurvedic aromatherapy.

"If you weren't actually from India, I wouldn't put up with this for two seconds," grumbled Sabina as she sipped the twig-flavored tea.

"That's because you have too much Pitta."

"Please stop saying that."

"You Pittas are stubborn and have no patience. How are you doing? Paparazzi aside?"

Sabina heaved a sigh. "Confused."

"Confused, eh? That's good. My tea is working. Pittas never admit to confusion."

Sabina barely stopped herself from rolling her eyes.

"So tell me, what has Chief Roman done to confuse you?"

Sabina put down her teacup with a sharp clink. "How do you know it's about him?"

"Because he seems equally confused. He left out the oregano in his arrabiata the other day."

"*What?* He's still cooking for you?" Every hair on her arms stood up, as if Roman might be in the kitchen right now. Which was ridiculous, since she'd just left him at the station.

"On occasion. It seems to relax him. Right now, he needs a great deal of relaxation. What did you do to him, Sabina?"

"Excuse me? Why are you blaming me?"

"Because he makes sensational meals for my customers and now they are not so sensational as they were." Anu drummed her fingers on the table. "As a matter of fact, I'm a bit worried."

"You're worried about him? I'm the one with the broken ankle, cracked ribs, and multiple abrasions. Shouldn't you be worried about me?"

Anu regarded her with those lively brown eyes. "Should I be?"

"Yes, you should be." Because she was in trouble, bad trouble, trouble she didn't know how to fix. "Oh Anu, it's bad. I'm . . ." The words clawed at her throat. "I'm . . ." The truth battled to get out, like the alien trapped inside Ripley's stomach. "I'm in . . ."

Anu leaned forward, her entire body poised at attention. "Yes?"

Sabina exploded with a groan of pure frustration.

"Arrgh! Anu, it's terrible. I think I'm in . . . in *love* with Roman."

"Well, of course you are."

"What?"

"Chief Roman is an extraordinary man. And I'm not referring only to his good looks."

He was. He truly was. Which made everything a million times worse. Now that the words had come out, Sabina kept on going. "I can't stop thinking about him. Ever. Daytime, nighttime, doesn't matter. And he's avoiding me. Wants nothing to do with me. Well, except for saving my life. Even if he feels something, he's pretending he doesn't. And I don't even know if I want him to. He's my superior officer. We can't do this. There's no future. I know it, he knows it. What can I do?"

Anu shook her head in that fatalistic Indian way of hers. "Disaster, indeed."

Surely Sabina deserved a prize for not tossing her Kapha tea at her friend.

Chapter Twenty-Five

Roman drove his Jeep through a lovely wooded subdivision in a section of San Gabriel he hadn't seen before. With its graceful eucalyptus and cypress trees lining the streets, it had the feel of being out in the country. Following the directions he'd been given, he pulled in at a newish-looking two-story home. Off to one side, a silver Airstream trailer glinted in the evening sun.

Captain Brody had invited him to dinner and he'd accepted. He wasn't sure why, since the last time he'd seen the man, Brody had tried to challenge his authority. But his crew revered him, and that one brief encounter had certainly made an impression on Roman. Lord knew he could use allies. Something told him Chief Renteria's good opinion could vanish as quickly as he'd gained it.

A lovely, green-eyed woman who looked to be about five months' pregnant answered the door. She offered a quick smile and a surreptitious scrutiny that he pretended not to notice. "Hi, I'm Melissa, Captain Brody's wife."

"Rick Roman. Nice to meet you." They shook hands, sizing each other up. He handed over the bottle of Brunello from Montepulciano that he'd brought. She accepted it graciously.

"No wine for me, though," she said, patting her belly.

"I didn't know. My congratulations."

She gave him a stunning smile. "I guess the crew's been slacking in the grapevine department."

"I'll straighten them out."

She laughed. "I've been curious about you. You sure have shaken things up over at Station 1."

"I just do my job. The rest is out of my hands."

"I know what you mean." She led him into the kitchen, where Captain Brody was stirring a pot of beef stew, judging by the delicious aroma of rosemary. "Things do tend to get out of hand over there. Sweetie, Chief Roman's here and he brought us some wine."

"Glad you could make it, Roman. Here, have at it." Brody tossed him a corkscrew, which Roman deftly caught. He busied himself with opening the wine and filling the glasses Melissa retrieved from a cupboard.

He nearly choked on his first sip of wine when Melissa asked, "So what's your take on the curse?"

"I have no take on it."

Brody cast an affectionately scolding glance at his wife. "He's not here to be interviewed. She's a reporter," he explained. "They're always on the job. Watch what you say."

Melissa, who was passing behind Brody on her way to the refrigerator, pinched his butt in revenge.

Roman made a mental note not to say anything incriminating. "Can't say I'm a big fan of your profession at the moment. Can you get them to lay off the firehouse? And especially Sabina Jones?"

It felt good to say her name, as if doing so conjured her vivid, elegant face and supple body into the room with them.

"Sadly, I'm not Queen of the Media. And Sabina can handle herself." A wailing cry came from another part of the house. "Dani's awake. Be right back." Melissa put the cheese and cracker plate she'd assembled on the table and hurried away. Brody gave the stew one last stir and then joined Roman at the table.

"That was a hell of a rescue," he said, sitting down and resting one ankle on the opposite knee. "As Sabina's former captain, I'm extremely grateful. She's a fine firefighter and a pretty exceptional person."

Roman couldn't argue with that.

"She worked her ass off from day one," Brody continued. "Never seen anyone so tough on herself. Stubborn as a wildfire in a windstorm. I just sat back and watched her take on the doubters, one by one. I have huge respect for that woman."

Something in Brody's tone made Roman go still. "Hold on. Did you know? Who she was?"

"I did. Don't tell her, though. People are entitled to their secrets. She always kept a certain distance."

Roman had thought the same thing at the Starlight in Reno. It seemed a million years ago now.

Brody put a slice of cheddar on a cracker. "At any rate, I wanted to thank you in person."

"Just doing my job."

Brody didn't miss a trick, with that penetrating charcoal-gray gaze, but he let it slide. "Sounds like things are settling down at the station."

"Is that what the guys say?"

Chuckling, Brody lifted a hand in mock-surrender. "I'm not checking up on you, I swear. You know how firehouses are. I hear things. And what I hear tells me you're just what the place needs. I'm glad you're there."

Roman felt himself relax. Brody was a straight-up guy. Something about his level gray eyes and authoritative manner inspired trust. "I don't know," he muttered. "Things haven't exactly gone the way I expected."

"They never do, especially over there. Curse or not, it's not your ordinary firehouse."

Roman couldn't argue with that. How many firehouses had former child stars on the crew, or famous movie stars wandering through? "No, I suppose it isn't. I'll probably get used to it eventually."

But would he get used to working alongside Sabina? Or without Sabina? The past few days without her had been deadly dull. He'd felt like someone out of her zombie movie sleepwalking through his shifts.

"Is it a big change from New York?" Brody was asking.

"Yes and no. Same structure and discipline, different personalities. In New York—" He broke off. It occurred to him that no one had asked him about New York since he'd been here. Maybe they were afraid to touch a sore spot or make him think about 9/11. He cleared his throat. "It was time for a new start."

Taking a sip of wine, Brody nodded. His calm attentiveness drew something out of Roman, something completely unexpected.

"I'd been . . . in a rut since my wife died. On 9/11."

Brody tilted his head.

"The Pile took her." He shook his head, astonished at himself. Those four words were more than he'd uttered on the subject since just after it happened.

"She was in the North Tower?"

"Yeah. She never heard the evacuation order. Repeater was out." Brody, like every other firefighter in America, probably knew what had happened in the North Tower. Maureen and the others had gone in to clear the building. They never got the order to get the hell out. "I was home with Luke. We took opposite shifts so someone was always with him. I was in fucking Brooklyn when it all went down. I left him with a neighbor, but by the time I got to the Towers . . ."

Roman tipped his wineglass to his mouth. It was practically empty, but he needed something to hide behind. *Dio,* he hated talking about this—exactly why he'd never gone to any touchy-feely counseling sessions. It was damn uncomfortable. The last thing he'd wanted was someone trying to make him feel better.

But Brody didn't do that. He said nothing, just sat there as if reliving the memory right along with Roman.

"You did the right thing, coming to San Gabriel," Brody said finally. "Gutsy move. If you shake things up, anything can happen, except for one thing."

"What's that?"

"The same old, same old. I'm afraid you guaranteed yourself a roller-coaster ride, my friend." Brody raised his glass in a toast. "And you're definitely getting one."

"I'll drink to that." Roman finished his wine, feeling oddly lighter than when he'd arrived here.

"I'll tell you something funny," said Brody, brushing cracker crumbs off his jeans. "If we'd been having this conversation two years ago, and you'd told me that I'd just met the love of my life at a bachelor auction and that she'd turn my life inside out and I'd wind up with a beautiful child and another on the way, and the life I'd written off as impossible, I would have booted you off the premises."

Roman didn't know what to say to that, other than, "Bachelor auction?"

"Long story."

After that, Melissa came in, their little girl, Dani, trailing after her, and the conversation turned to the San Gabriel mayoral race and everyone's plans for Christmas. Roman couldn't remember the last time he'd had such a comfortable, relaxed evening with people he'd just met.

Brody was all right, he decided. The kind of man who'd have your back no matter what.

After dinner, Roman walked, whistling, to his Jeep. They were good people, Brody and Melissa, clearly deeply in love with each other, excellent parents to their adopted daughter, Dani. For a while after he'd lost Maureen he hadn't been able to spend time with other couples.

But tonight it hadn't bothered him at all, except that he kept imagining Sabina with him. Pictured meeting her mischievous glance over a shared private joke, touching her knee under the table, listening to her passionate and entertaining account of a structure fire. Maybe it was the Italian in him, but he loved the way she told stories, putting her whole body into it.

Why not go see her? She could probably use some company, not to mention some help maneuvering around the kitchen with those crutches. Not that she would ever admit it, of course. Sabina was so damn independent.

Yes, he should go see her. As a concerned friend, not as someone who couldn't get her out of his mind, of course. Luke was spending the night at Ralphie's again. Not that he would expect an overnight invitation, of course.

On the other hand . . . his blood surged at the thought

of Sabina's bed, of Sabina *in bed*. With him. He'd stretch himself out while she prowled toward him on hands and knees, silky hair loose around her naked body, desire in her smoky turquoise eyes. At the image, he went rock-hard. God, he wanted her. Her hair would drift around them like an intimate curtain and she'd lower her temptress's body over his, brushing the tips of her breasts against his chest, and his cock would rise up like an iron pike and . . .

Oops, he'd forgotten about her injuries. Quickly he revised his fantasy. He'd gently lay her down and surround her with soft pillows. He'd pet her and caress her—maybe restrain her so she couldn't hurt herself when she abandoned herself to the pleasure he'd give her. *Keep still*, he'd whisper, *let me give you everything you need*. And she'd do what he ordered—for once—because he'd make her feel so good, he'd lick her until she shivered, he'd taste every secret morsel of flesh, wring every helpless moan from her lips.

Somehow his Jeep had found its way to Sabina's house. He hadn't been inside before, but once they'd passed it on a call and she'd pointed it out. That piece of information had apparently lodged irrevocably in his brain.

He pulled up to the curb a few houses away. Was he going to do this? Really? Shouldn't he keep his distance? But talking with Brody had stirred something up inside him. He needed to see Sabina. Needed it. To hell with everything else.

Sabina lay on the couch with her ankle propped on a pillow and a pile of scripts next to her.

"You swear none of these is for the reunion show? I'll throw it right in the fake fire."

"All this suspicion is bad for your health," Annabelle said imperiously. She presented Sabina with an armful of tinsel and pine boughs. "Which do you prefer?"

"For what purpose?" Sabina asked suspiciously. The fresh scent of pine filled the room.

"For my new burlesque routine, of course."

"My my, Annabelle. You're getting so sassy."

"Christmas is in less than a week. In your house, it might as well be Saint Patrick's Day."

"I've always preferred to decorate for New Year's." She flipped the pages of a screenplay called *Six Ways to Sunday*. Despite the hokey title, the dialogue seemed sharp.

"Well, point me to the decorations, I'll put them up for you."

"They aren't much to speak of. Bottle caps, Cheetos crumbs, and hungover firemen."

Annabelle sniffed. "Hardly festive."

"When did we ever celebrate Christmas, Annabelle? I mean, really celebrate, rather than try to impress some producer with our mother-daughter bond?"

"Well . . ." Annabelle pursed her lips, clearly searching for a comeback. "I'm sorry," she finally said, in a dignified way that made Sabina feel like a jerk. "I can't redo the past. But I can put up some pine boughs for you now."

"Fine. Pine boughs it is." She breathed deeply, wondering why she was being so hard on her mother. Annabelle was trying, wasn't she? Or at least, trying to try? "They smell nice, actually."

The doorbell rang. Sabina sat up eagerly; visitors were the highlight of her life lately. After her trip to the firehouse the doctor had lectured her on the necessity of rest, so she'd taken up residence on the couch. Maybe her mother should drape her with tinsel.

"Lie back down," scolded Annabelle. "Honestly, Sabina."

Sabina groaned and settled back on the couch. Maybe one of these scripts had a female Nazi prison guard role—it would be perfect for her mother. Not that she wasn't grateful . . . mostly.

At the sound of a deep, black coffee voice, she bolted upright again. *Roman.* She looked down at her ratty tank top and pajama pants stained with coffee . . . or was it blackberry jam? And really, the word "ratty" didn't quite describe the top. Originally pink, it was now a sickly grayish-salmon color. It drooped around her armpits, all its elasticity gone. The only reason she'd put it on was that her mother's caretaking attempts didn't extend to laundry, and at least this shirt was theoretically clean, though no one would ever guess it.

She looked around for a blanket or a throw to hide under, but couldn't find one. Annabelle's surprised murmur and Roman's deep rumble were drawing closer. Damn it. Desperate, she grabbed the only thing she could think of and began piling her mother's scripts on her chest and thighs.

When Roman entered the room, she saw the hitch in his stride as he spotted her buried under a pile of paper. Confusion flickered across his face. Annabelle, on the other hand, smirked from behind Roman's big frame. Of course her appearance-conscious mother would immediately see the problem.

"I'll get us some lemonade," she said sweetly, apparently channeling Donna Reed, or maybe some demented mother from a Tennessee Williams play.

"Please don't," said Sabina. "Chief Roman's a grown man. Maybe he'd like an adult beverage. Coffee or something."

"Nothing for me," he answered. "I just stopped by to see how you're feeling." He eyed the scripts covering her body with an uneasy expression.

"I'm fine." Brazen it out. What choice did she have? "Catching up on some reading. Would you like to sit down?" She gestured toward an armchair.

He sank into it, then gave a deep sigh. "Nice place."

"You think so? Everyone teases me about it. Vader says it looks like a call girl's hotel room."

"Well, he would probably know."

She smiled. God, he looked good in that chair, like an emperor in a beige throne. His long legs, clad in black jeans, stretched before him, nearly reaching the coffee table. He wore a lightweight charcoal-gray sweater that barely contained his muscular chest. He brought the scent of wine and a winter's night with him.

She wasn't sure how long she'd been staring at him when Annabelle came in with a tray of water glasses and a pitcher of water. More importantly, she had a heathery cotton throw draped over one arm.

"Here, honey," she said as she passed the couch. "You must be chilly." Sabina, with a wary look inspired by the word "honey," something her mother never said, grabbed the throw and wrapped it around her shoulders. She sat up, feeling the scripts tumble inside the blanket. Roman looked more puzzled than ever. Distraction. She needed a distraction.

Annabelle unintentionally provided exactly that. She perched on the arm of the couch, crossed her legs gracefully, and addressed Roman. "I didn't like you much at first, Chief Roman."

"Excuse me?" Sabina looked from her mother to Roman, whose face held no expression other than a simmering amusement deep in his black eyes.

"I refused to suspend you on command," he explained.

"What?"

Annabelle gave an apologetic little shrug. "I'd convinced myself you'd be better off away from that station." She turned back to Roman. "If you'd suspended her, you wouldn't have had to save her life later on."

"No, because she probably would have strangled me with her bare hands before I had a chance to save her."

Annabelle tossed her head, conceding the point.

"Not cool, Annabelle—" Sabina began hotly.

Annabelle interrupted, still focused on Roman. "But since you did save her life, I'm rethinking my opinion. Which is *not* something I normally do, let me tell you."

Sabina considered the relative merits of beaning her mother with a pillow or a script, the only two weapons at hand.

But Roman seemed unfazed by her mother's bluntness. "Very generous of you."

"We'll see. The jury's still out."

Roman gave a rumble of laughter. "Saving your daughter's life only goes so far, does it? Do I have to unbury her from a pile of paper too?" He gestured to one of the scripts, which had fallen out from under the throw. "What are those, movie scripts?"

Annabelle widened her cat's eyes in amazement. "You've never seen a screenplay before?"

"Can't say that I have. I wouldn't mind taking a look though."

Roman picked up *Six Ways to Sunday* and read a line out loud. *"When's the last time you got your pool cleaned, lady?"* He lowered the script. "What kind of movie is this?"

Sabina snorted.

Annabelle bounded to her feet and peered at the script. "It's a comedy. I'm up for the part of Belinda. Comedy was always my specialty, right, Sabina?" Without waiting for an answer, she put one hand on her hip and lowered her head provocatively as she read the next line. *"Well, see, my last pool boy quit. He couldn't handle my . . . deep end."* The over-the-top purr in her voice made Sabina spew a mouthful of water onto the throw that covered her.

Roman raised one eyebrow, but forged ahead. *"That's because he was a pool boy. See, what you need is a pool man."*

Sabina laughed so hard her ribs ached, but she didn't mind. Roman and Annabelle continued with the script, a broad comedy about an older woman's affair with her handyman. Roman had no acting skills and looked like a smoldering hunk of testosterone no matter how much he aimed for goofy. Halfway through the scene they were all laughing so hard at his pathetic attempt at a Southern accent they had to skip to a different scene.

This time Roman played the envious best friend of Annabelle's character. When he read the line, *"That's not a pool boy, that's a hot little ticket to cougar heaven,"* in a high-pitched voice, the three of them laughed until tears ran down their faces.

Finally, Annabelle collapsed into an armchair, blotting the tears from her cheeks. "I haven't laughed this much in . . . well, Sabina must have been little. Before the show."

"Yeah. That's when all the fun and games ended."

Annabelle sobered with a sigh. "Thanks for indulging me, Chief Roman. It's been a while since I acted in anything."

Roman got to his feet. "Thank *you* for putting up

with my incompetence. It was fun, but I think I'll be keeping my day job."

"It might be best," said Annabelle, giggling like a girl.

Roman said good-bye then. After he left, the house seemed suddenly tiny and tame.

"That," said Annabelle, into the subsequent quiet, "is a very, very attractive man."

Sabina nestled into her pillows. "He's all right." She let her eyes close, feigning exhaustion, and didn't open them again until her mother had gone back into the guest bedroom. What was Roman doing, showing up like that, displaying a whole new side—a lighter side, that of a man who didn't mind looking ridiculous? How dare he come and disturb her peace of mind, just when she'd accepted—almost accepted—that a safe distance was best?

Damn that very, very attractive man.

Chapter Twenty-Six

So the evening hadn't gone the way Roman had fantasized. Sure, Sabina had been horizontal, but there'd been no tangled sheets, no cries of passion—unless you counted winces from Annabelle at the way he massacred his lines. But he'd had fun. Just being in the same room with Sabina made his blood fizz like a bottle of fine Asti Spumante. He loved seeing her eyes sparkle, her stubborn mouth curve in a mischievous smile. Her hair was reverting to its natural color, that autumn-brown color giving way to a burnished bronze with naughty glints of hell-raiser red.

He'd gotten his Sabina fix, but already he wanted more. The firehouse lost all its joy with Sabina out until further notice. The big talk revolved around the ski trip planned for the day after Christmas and a firehouse meeting that Roman had missed.

"D'you hear about the cookbook?" Psycho jogged

backward down the corridor as Roman strode toward his office.

"Nope."

"It's going to be on the news later. Stud's idea. We voted on it and Vader lost. He wanted a weight-lifting marathon or some testosterone-heavy shit like that."

"What the hell are you talking about?" He hadn't even had coffee yet, and Psycho was bouncing around like a blue-eyed version of the Joker.

"Stud had stroke of genius and thought we ought to take advantage of all the media attention to raise some money. Go to Vegas."

Roman stopped in his tracks.

Psycho jogged in place, laughing maniacally. "Too early for jokes?"

"By about an hour and two pots of coffee."

"Sorry, Chief. Just wanted to give you a heads-up."

"Why?" They entered the kitchen, Psycho still backpedaling. He veered just before slamming into the couch.

"Can't say. Sworn to secrecy."

"Drills in one hour," Roman barked. "Fucking circus," he muttered, swinging into the kitchen, where the A shift had already started the coffee.

"By the way, Chief." Psycho headed toward the backyard, where he liked to do speed push-ups before everyone else showed up. "I took Italian in college. See ya at lineup, *cara mia*." And he was gone.

Roman slammed coffee into a cup and headed for his office to tackle a report for Renteria. Damn radios, damn his impulsive Italian nature, damn Princeton. He needed to crack the whip on these guys. They were too loosey-goosey, too fun-loving, too . . . fucking quirky.

He conducted the toughest drill yet, running them through their paces on rapid intervention with a downed firefighter, who was played by a dummy. In coat and breathing apparatus, each firefighter had to race against the stopwatch to locate the hidden dummy, with nothing to guide them other than the sound of the alarm. They had to pull hose, then stop and listen for the alarm, knowing that each passing second made the situation more dire. In a dark, smoky environment it would be even more difficult. But no matter how much he drilled them, making them run it again, and again, and again, still he caught sidelong glances and the occasional smug smile. But he had to hand it to them—they performed well despite their smirks.

"Nice work," he said, grudgingly, when they'd finished the twelfth run-through flawlessly.

"Ella Joy's on!" someone yelled. And that was it. The entire crew went running for the training room. Roman took his time ambling back inside, enjoying the balmy December air, the pleasant scent of sagebrush. Maybe he and Luke should go horseback riding. Camp out. Roast marshmallows.

By the time he got inside, Ella Joy, wearing a sprig of holly in her hair, was launching into her report. He almost decided to ignore it, but the dreaded words "Bachelor Firemen" caught his eye, plastered across the bottom of the screen.

"The Bachelor Firemen of San Gabriel have a special treat for you this holiday season." Ella Joy beamed like Santa Claus's pretty younger sister. "Did you know that firefighters are not only heroes out on the fire lines, but in the kitchen too? That's right, they take turns making their own meals. This year, San Gabriel's Bachelor Firemen have put together a cookbook that contains some of their favorite recipes. If there's anyone in your life who likes to cook, they might enjoy an inside look at what firefighters prepare for their meals. Here's Firefighter Fred Breen with more about *Cooking with Heat: Favorite Recipes from the Bachelor Firemen of San Gabriel.*"

Stud, all eager brown eyes and wide smile, blinked at the camera. "First of all, I'd like to say that every penny you spend on this cookbook goes to charity. You probably want to know which charity, right, Ella Joy?"

Ella, who was leafing through the cookbook, jerked her attention back to Fred. "I was just about to ask that. Which charity will the cookbook benefit, Firefighter Breen?"

"Well. We had a hard time deciding which charity because there's so many good ones. Poor children, sick children, sick animals, the environment, refugees, really, it never ends. But as soon as we thought of this one, we knew it was the perfect choice. In honor of our new training officer, Chief Roman, all proceeds from this cookbook will go to the 9/11 Firefighters Fund."

Roman gripped the edge of the counter that separated the kitchen from the training room. He felt the blood drain from his face.

Fred switched from buoyant to serious. "Three hundred and forty-three firefighters and paramedics died in 9/11, and a lot more have health issues from the aftermath. Chief Roman lost his wife. We want to stand behind him. Even though we weren't there on September 11, in spirit we were, and we just want the chief and all the others to know, we'll never forget."

Ella was giving Fred her full attention now. "I'm sure our viewers will find that tribute very moving."

With the solemn part out of the way, Fred perked up again. "And they'll get some killer recipes. Ryan

Blake's Thai chicken curry is in here, and so is my personal specialty, meatball chili. We even included Chief Roman's recipe for the blackest coffee you ever tasted. That's on page five, in case you're wondering. It ought to come with a warning."

"What I'm really wondering is what these photos are." Ella peered at the cookbook and flipped to a page, which she held up to the camera.

Fred turned a fiery pink. "We threw in some snapshots of us cooking. In case you ever wanted to see a fireman wearing oven mitts."

"And nothing else, it seems."

"Well, he has pants on."

Roman squinted at the screen. The photo showed a bare-chested Vader checking a pot roast. He actually managed to flex his pectorals while sticking a thermometer into a hunk of meat.

"Looking good, Vader," said Psycho.

Vader stood up and flexed his biceps instead of bowing. "Someone had to put some testosterone into this thing."

Ella Joy continued. "If you'd like to give someone this festive and flirtatious holiday cookbook, you can order it online at the San Gabriel Fire Department's Web site, and at our station's Web site. If you order today, you might even receive it by Christmas. Speaking for myself, I don't even cook and I wouldn't mind a copy." She winked at the camera.

Someone switched off the TV. Roman knew the sound had disappeared, knew Ella's exquisite face had vanished, but his thoughts hadn't really caught up. The crew had voted to donate all proceeds to a 9/11 fund as a tribute to him. To express their solidarity with *him*—the most hard-assed, coldhearted captain on the Eastern seaboard.

A cookbook, no less. They didn't even know how appropriate it was. Not a single one of them, other than Sabina, knew of his secret kitchen skills. From day one, he'd refused to cook for the crew.

The other firefighters seemed just as tongue-tied as he was. Roman heard one of them clear his throat, another whisper something. Then Fred jumped to his feet like a big puppy. "How'd I do? Did I sound like a jerk? Being on TV is a lot harder than it looks, dude. I kind of went blank at first. Hey Chief, what'd you think? Did I do okay?"

Roman gazed down at those eager brown eyes. He felt like a glacier, slowly thawing under the sunshine of the kid's enthusiasm, the unexpected affection of these guys. He cleared his throat. "You did good, Stud." He glanced around the room, at the blur of faces watching him. "You all did good. It's . . . uh . . . appreciated. Now get back to work. The rigs need cleaning."

He wheeled around and strode into his office. That pile of paperwork needed to be off his desk by the end of the shift. It would happen a lot faster if he could get that goddamn speck of dust out of his eyes.

Dio, this place was really getting to him. At this rate, they'd banish him from Brooklyn and stick him in a freaking Disney movie.

A few days before Christmas, the Dane brothers held their baseball clinic for the Little League of San Gabriel. Luke had been chattering about it for days, as soon as he'd found out the twin minor leaguers were coming. To him, it was even more exciting than Christmas. What could be better than star pitcher Jake and home run king Todd Dane working with the team, one on one? The new laptop Roman had gotten him came in a distant second.

For Roman, it felt like early Christmas as well, since there was a good chance Sabina would be there with Carly. He hadn't seen her since the impromptu acting lesson. One visit from her training officer was understandable. More than that and people would talk.

He'd heard enough whispered *cara mia*s at the firehouse to last a lifetime.

So he had to rely on stolen glimpses of Sabina, like pieces of sea glass washed up by the ocean. La Piaggia was one of his favorites. He'd seen her at the restaurant once. He'd been experimenting with a new veal and porcini mushroom dish and the sight of her had made him forget he'd already added pepper. She'd given him a polite smile as she thumped through the kitchen on her crutches. She'd cut her hair so it swung like a sheet of hammered gold against her bare shoulders.

Before he could offer her a taste of his veal, she'd gone. She hadn't even said good-bye.

He'd turned back to the stove, cursing himself in two languages. He'd blown it, first by never visiting her in the hospital, then by never explaining himself. Maureen had always accused him of burying his feelings. He'd never told his wife this, but he suspected he did so because his feelings were so powerful. Practical Maureen would never have understood.

Maybe he should have given Maureen a chance to understand, something inside him whispered. Maybe he had a second chance now. A chance to let a woman really see inside him, see all the intense, unpredictable currents that swirled through his soul.

Just like that backdraft scenario he'd offered up to Vader. Open a vent hole. Let a bit of himself out.

On the day of the clinic, Luke bolted ahead of him, leaping across the park like a windup kangaroo. A sizable crowd had already gathered for the clinic. Roman, sunglasses safely in place, didn't even need to scan their faces to spot Sabina. She sat on the lowest rung of the bleachers, legs stretched out, leaning her elbows on the bench behind her. Her head tilted back so the sun made a halo out her tawny hair. A slight smile curved her mouth as she savored the hazy sunshine.

At the mere sight of her, he got hard, embarrassingly so. It wouldn't do to stroll up to a family event with a massive boner leading the way. He paused, collected himself, put his notorious iron will to work on his equally stubborn cock.

Maybe this was a bad idea.

Too bad. He was greedy and selfish and not about to pass up a chance to be in Sabina's presence just because his primitive side didn't know how to behave itself.

For the first time since Luke started playing baseball, Roman didn't sit on the upper left-hand bleacher seat. He joined Sabina on the lowest bench, his arm brushing against hers. With deep pleasure, he watched goose bumps rise on her skin, the dark teal of her irises turn black with surprise.

"Hey, Chief."

"Jones."

The sliver of air between their bodies vibrated. Roman leaned forward to prop his elbows on his knees, brushing her skin again in the process. She felt soft and fresh as a daisy petal. She smelled like marigolds and sunshine. Everything in him, body and soul, wanted to claim her, take her into him, and brand her as his.

Crazy. He was a fireman, not a damn pirate. "How's the ankle?"

"Healing, but it's slow. I think it's been about two years already."

"Ribs?"

"Still sore, but half the time I forget about them. Not a problem. I could strap on a tank, easy."

"Not happening," he said flatly.

Her eyes flared at him. "No need to get all bossy."

He shrugged one shoulder. "Goes with the territory."

"Chief territory?"

God, that little gleam in her eye made him want to roll her around on the grass right then and there. "Not exactly."

Sabina couldn't seem to catch her breath. Ever since Roman had descended onto the bench next to her, she'd felt as if she'd been running wind sprints along with the Little Leaguers. She could swear he was flirting with her. He kept giving her those little sideways looks, with that suggestive light in his eyes. It took her right back to the hours she'd spent in bed with him. That night was scorched onto her brain in any case, never to be forgotten if she lived to a hundred.

"I saw the cookbook the guys did. Pretty nice gesture."

He turned his head toward the field.

Jake and Todd were rounding up all the young players after their warm-up. Katie Dane, or maybe she was Katie Blake now that she'd married Ryan, handed out Tucson Breeze caps to the kids. The twins split the kids into two groups. Luke and Carly wound up on different teams.

Roman waited so long to answer that Sabina had almost forgotten about the cookbook and was about to tease him about his terrible acting.

"I still can't get a handle on it," he finally admitted. "I thought they all hated me. You all."

"Yes, but only at first."

That devastating groove dented his stubbled cheek. "Glad I managed to talk you out of it."

"I'm not sure you did. I mean, you're not a big talker, are you?"

"I wouldn't say that."

"Um . . . I think you just proved my point."

His chest rose and fell with a deep chuckle that set her nerves to dancing. "Maybe I have other ways to get my point across."

A full-body flush passed over her. Other ways . . . such as making love to her until her brain turned to Roman-obsessed mush? Or such as digging through rubble to save her life? "I see what you mean."

"Do you?" He gave her an intense, sideways look and lowered his voice. "Sabina, I . . . this isn't easy for me to say."

She sat up straight as a shaft of electric fear passed through her. He was going to break up with her. She knew the drill. It was exactly what had happened with Greg Harrington when she was sixteen and he was seventeen. He'd taken her out for a few "dates"—more like photo ops. She'd helped him pick out a puppy at the shelter. They'd hit a Dodgers game and eaten gigantic hot dogs. She'd dreamed of him every night, until that last horrible one when she wouldn't have sex with him in his swimming pool.

The next day his driver had picked her up and she'd joined him in the backseat as they drove around Beverly Hills and he dumped her. "Nothing personal," he'd said, "but my fans think you're a little young for me. You feel me?"

Oh yeah, she knew that look in Roman's eyes. She could practically write the script for him. *Nothing personal, we work together, neither of us wants to leave the sta-*

tion, we both knew it was a mistake . . . He was going to break her heart, right here and now in front of the San Gabriel Little League and most of the Dane family.

"Don't worry about it," she said, hurrying to fend off the inevitable. "I feel the same way. We're on the same page."

He frowned behind his sunglasses. "We are?"

She lowered her voice to a whisper, even though everyone else's attention was on the field. "We had one fun night, no need to make more of it than it was."

He flinched, as if she'd jabbed him with a toothpick. "That's it, huh? One fun night."

"Exactly." Now came the hardest part, the part she'd been wrestling with late at night when her ribs ached. "I figured out why you never came to visit me in the hospital."

Roman, who had been listening with absolutely no expression, finally raised one eyebrow in question.

"Obviously you didn't want to give me the wrong idea about us. You didn't want me to be misled by the fact that you saved my life. And that's fine. I get it. I agree with you. You were just doing your job."

Roman leaned forward, elbows on knees. Sabina followed his gaze. On the field, Todd was working with Carly. He made an adjustment to her swing, lifting her elbows higher up. Carly nodded and gingerly swung the bat.

Was Roman even listening to her?

"The situation's a little awkward, but I think if we're both totally honest with each other, we can still work together just fine."

Roman lowered his head so he was looking at the ground between his knees. His voice came in a low, ominous growl. "Honest?"

"Yes. Honest. That's the key."

"Honest?" The muscles in his forearms jumped as he flexed his fists. "You haven't said one honest word in the past two minutes."

"What?"

He swung his head toward her. "One fun night? Wrong idea? What kind of crap are you trying to dish out?"

She gaped at him as he rose to his full height, six and a half feet and two hundred plus pounds of virile, potent male. Eyes ablaze, he scorched her with one long, comprehensive glance.

"If you want honesty, Sabina Jones, you come find me. But be prepared for the real thing." And he stalked away from the bleachers.

Sabina gripped the edge of the bench, feeling the chipped green paint come off in her hands. *Oh my God.*

Little shock waves ran through her, up and down, head to toe.

Breathe, Sabina, breathe.

Chapter Twenty-Seven

The rest of the clinic passed in a blur of swings and misses and catches and skinned knees. Rather than count strikes, Sabina went over every moment of her encounter with Roman a thousand times. The man was a freaking mystery. One day he was saving her life, the next ignoring her, the next acting goofy with her mother, the next . . . well, she didn't know what had just happened.

It had sounded like a challenge.

Katie Dane Blake plopped onto the seat next to her. "Was that the famous Chief Roman Ryan keeps talking about? That black-haired giant with the killer ass?"

"Katie, I'm shocked. You're a married woman."

"As if I could forget." She darted a tender look toward the field, where Ryan was gathering up bats. "So do you guys have something going on?"

Sabina had to laugh at Katie's typically direct approach. "You aren't working for *Inside Edition*, are you?"

"Nope. For my brother Todd. He thinks you're cute. And he's a little shy."

"Shy?" She looked at the two lean, rangy men on the field, tall as maple trees in a field of worshipping sunflowers. The Little Leaguers were gazing up at them as though they were gods. "Which one's Todd?"

"I told him you'd say that." Katie chuckled. "Todd's the one with the lighter hair. He's the nice one. Jake's the demon seed from hell."

"They both look normal enough." And attractive. A month ago, before that stoplight in Reno, she would have been extremely interested.

"So whaddaya say? Are you available? Interested? Secretly married to Chief Roman? I have to warn you, neither of my brothers has a clue about relationships. But they're decent enough."

Sabina eyed Todd, who met her gaze over a seventh-grader's head and smiled hopefully. He had nice hazel-green eyes and a troublemaker's smile. If he was the nice one, she had a feeling the pair of them were a handful.

"Let me think about it."

"Aha. It's the hot guy from New York, isn't it?"

"No." She drummed her fingers on the bench. Why was she letting one confusing man rule her thoughts like this? Maybe a date with Todd Dane was exactly what she needed. A simple, no-strings-attached evening of fun with a nice baseball player. A play date that wouldn't roil up her insides and make her all swoony. Sabina Jones was *not* the swoony sort. Not at all. "Sure, I'll go out with Todd."

She sent him a sweet smile and a thumbs-up, which made him laugh, his eyes crinkling at the corners. He was cute.

Katie scowled suspiciously. "Are you sure? I saw the

way Roman looked at you. Like he wanted to eat you alive."

"Well, he does have a way with a lecture. And I have a way of pissing him off."

"Not that kind of eating alive. I thought the two of you would burst into flames right there on the bleachers."

Sabina flushed hot enough to burst into flames all on her own. "Nothing's happening between me and Chief Roman. Nothing can and nothing will. Now go tell your brother he'd better take me someplace nice. I have to take Carly home. I've barely seen her since I got out of the hospital."

But Carly wasn't on the field. No one could remember seeing her in the last few minutes. She wasn't in the bathroom, a charming structure assembled from blocks of concrete. Nor was she under the bleachers looking for stray balls. Maybe Luke knew where she was.

But she couldn't find Luke either. Maybe he'd gone home with Roman; but that was impossible. Roman had left early and Luke had stuck around for the rest of the clinic. He was probably catching a ride with one of his buddies. But she was Carly's ride. Carly wouldn't have skipped out on her. Had some pervert been watching the game? Had he lured Carly away with candy and balloons?

She tried to quell her sense of rising panic. Carly wasn't six. It would take more than balloons to fool her. It would take chloroform and a white van with tinted windows, and even so Carly would know what to do. She'd practically grown up on the streets.

Just as she was starting to get seriously worried, she felt someone tap her on the shoulder. Whirling around, she let out a *whoof* of relief. Carly stood before her, grubby and bruised.

"Hey, Sabina."

"Where have you been?"

Carly frowned at Sabina's panicky tone. "I helped the coaches take the gear to the van. Sorry, it must have taken longer than I thought."

Sabina brushed some grass off Carly's shoulder. "I didn't even think of that. Don't mind me, I'm a little scattered lately. I can't even use painkillers as an excuse anymore."

"You don't need to worry about me." Carly leaned on one hip, her typical sassy stance.

"I know. You can handle just about anything."

"And have."

True enough. Carly had seen a lot of crap in her short years. "You ready to go?"

"Yep. All ready." Carly shouldered her gym bag and winced.

"Are you all right? Let me take that."

"Yeah right, you're on crutches, Sabina. Besides, it's nothing. Happened when Todd Dane was showing us his trick for stealing second." She set off for the curb where Sabina had parked her mother's Volvo.

Roman's words came back to her, his question about whether something was up with Carly. Since the fire she hadn't had much time with Carly. Was she missing something? She picked up the pace, swinging faster on her crutches, but by the time she caught up with Carly at the Volvo, the girl had launched into a detailed comparison of the Dane twins, which one had better fielding skills, which one's jokes were funnier, which one's hair was a nicer color. Carly was entering the dreaded teen years, that was all. Everything was just fine.

Roman rapped on Luke's door, the door that had been shut tight far too often lately. Inside, a bass line throbbed.

After some thumping around, Luke opened it. His room was, as always, a mess—the floor a carpet of discarded clothes, school binders splayed facedown in the corner, old Transformers pieces popping up like neglected monsters. Roman, with his firehouse training, always winced at the sight of Luke's room, but he'd learned to keep his mouth shut.

A man's room was his castle, he'd told Luke early on. He could do what he liked there, as long as he stayed within the rules.

Luke still wore his San Gabriel Hardware team T-shirt, but he'd changed into his jeans. Roman remembered the time his son had gotten David Cone's autograph on a cap and worn it nonstop for the next month.

"Tell me you haven't made a vow to never change your shirt now that Jake and Todd Dane have been in its presence."

"Huh?" Luke blinked wide brown eyes at him. He looked distracted, a little spacey.

A terrible suspicion filtered into Roman's mind. Was his sweet, innocent boy doing drugs? Maybe Ralphie had gotten him into pot, or—his brain went into a wild spiral of fear—crack. Was that why Luke kept locking himself in his room, why he was keeping secrets from his own father?

He seized Luke's chin and tilted his head up so he could examine his son's eyes. Dilated pupils, that was a sign of drugs. Bloodshot eyes. What else? If Luke was doing drugs . . . He'd drag him back to New York, that's what he'd do. No wiggle room on that rule.

Luke's eyes looked not only perfectly clear, but perfectly furious. Luke jerked his head away. "What are you doing, Papa?"

"Just checking something," Roman mumbled, embarrassed.

"Geez, Papa. What, you think I'm doing drugs?"

They stared each other down. Roman blinked first. He cleared his throat. Should he apologize? Why did he never know what to say to Luke anymore?

"What do you want, Papa?"

"I just wanted to see how the clinic went after I left. Coach take you home?"

"No, I hitched a ride. With a drug dealer."

"Very funny. So how was it?"

Roman waited for Luke to invite him in, but he didn't. Instead he stood, gripping the edge of the door, clearly waiting impatiently for this father-son moment to pass. "Cool. Jake said if I keep working hard I can probably play for USC. He thinks my fastball needs some work. Too easy to read. I have to disguise my motion more."

"Good. Let's do it. I'll get my glove."

"He didn't mean right this minute." Luke glanced over his shoulder, where his computer was displaying a manic field of stars. "I'm busy right now."

"Later then?"

"Sure." Luke gave him a furtive look, something Roman had never seen on his face before. "That'd be great."

With a firm hand, Roman kept the door open one moment longer. "Luke, if something was bugging you, you'd tell me, right?"

"Of course." Luke rolled his eyes with some of his old spirit, but it didn't fool Roman. Something was definitely up. He resolved to keep an extra close eye on his son for the next couple of days. "By the way, Papa, did you hear that Todd Dane has a crush on Sabina? He asked her out."

"What?"

But Luke was already closing the door, and Roman wasn't about to make a fool of himself asking questions like a sixth-grader.

He wandered into the living room and flicked on the TV. He wasn't sure what made him feel worse, the scene with Luke or the news about Todd and Sabina. So what if Todd had a crush on her? Who wouldn't? Didn't mean anything. A good football game, that's what he needed. Or maybe a boxing match. When everything on TV seemed to be a sappy Christmas movie, he tossed the remote aside and stretched out, arms behind his head. He gazed up at the plaster ceiling with the smoked-glass light fixture and turned this new information over in his mind. It didn't take long to come to a very firm decision.

Sabina couldn't go out with anyone else. Absolutely not.

The idea of her holding another man's hand as she walked into a restaurant, the man taking her coat, letting his fingers linger in her silky hair, giving him one of her sparkling smiles . . . no, no, no. Not going to happen. Not up for debate.

He had to call her right away and communicate this important message. He snatched up his cell phone and punched her number. He'd figure out what to say once she answered. Maybe something like *You're mine, woman, all mine.*

He snorted. She might roll her eyes at the caveman approach. Maybe he should work on something with a little more finesse.

Sabina's outgoing message answered the call. Her husky voice told him, "You've reached my cell. I'll get back to you. Eventually."

Eventually. Not good enough. Savagely, he ended

the call without leaving a message. What could he say? *If Todd Dane even thinks of asking you out, I'll beat his ass into the outfield and back again. You come here where you belong. In my bed. I'll let you out when I'm good and ready.*

God, he was a primitive beast of a man. Sabina was an independent, intelligent woman who wouldn't appreciate playing prey to his hunter. *Finesse, Roman, Finesse.*

He dialed her home number. When Annabelle answered, he nearly hung up, since he had no idea how to express any of this to Sabina's mother. Feeling like a teenager, he said, "Hi, Annabelle. I'm looking for Sabina. Is she around?"

"Is this Todd Dane?"

"No."

"Not . . . Greg Harrington, is that you?"

Roman's teeth hurt from clenching his jaw too hard. *Greg Harrington?* The action star? "No, this is Roman. *Battalion Chief* and Section Commander Roman," he added for extra impact, to make up for the lack of car chases in his life.

"Oh. My, that's quite a title." She sounded far too amused. Enjoying this, was she?

Roman summoned all his patience. "May I speak with Sabina, please?"

"No, I believe she had plans tonight."

He kicked his footstool, sending it toppling. "Thank you." He hung up before he could say something inappropriate, like *You crazy lady, how the hell did Sabina come out so levelheaded?*

And compassionate.

And strong. And heroic.

And beautiful. Well, that part wasn't a surprise. But she could so easily have made a life by trading on her looks. Instead she'd chosen something uniquely hers. The San Gabriel Fire Department was lucky.

But he wasn't about to let Todd Dane get lucky.

Sabina gazed into Todd's non-black eyes, which held not a hint of midnight blue in their depths. She admired his hair, the color of Malibu beach sand—most definitely not black as a pirate's. Nor was his physique, though fit and trim, anything like the massively powerful body of . . .

But she'd sworn not to think about Roman tonight. Not to let him tie her up into knots any longer. She smiled at Todd, who answered with a delighted grin.

"Did I do okay? Katie said I had to prove up and pick someplace worthy of you."

"Worthy?" Uh oh, he wasn't seeing her as Taffy McGee/Sally Hatfield, was he?

"You're a firefighter. According to Katie, the firemen of San Gabriel walk on water. If anyone has a bad word to say about any of you, they'd better keep it to themselves around her."

Sabina laughed. "As my aunt used to say, 'She's a pistol.'" Well, the aunt on *You and Me* said that. Frequently. "And yes, you picked the perfect place."

He'd chosen an upscale Thai restaurant with ivory tablecloths, candles nestled into little bronze elephants, well-trained waiters, a rippling jazz piano in the background. The only thing missing was . . . but she wasn't going to think about *him* right now.

Todd twirled some pad Thai around his fork. "Is it difficult being a female firefighter?"

Score one for Todd Dane. He actually looked interested in her answer. He wasn't what she'd expected in a baseball player. For some reason, she'd assumed he'd be like the actors she'd dated, except he'd talk about his stats rather than his latest reviews. But he was funny and down-to-earth and hadn't once mentioned his batting average. And every woman in the restaurant was eyeing her with envy. He was a good-looking man, the kind any sane, single woman would want a play date with.

"It was hard at first," she answered. "I had to prove myself. And I had to get used to the firehouse atmosphere. They teased me a lot. Tested me. But they were never mean or unfair. Now I love them all like brothers."

Well, with one glaring exception. But she wasn't going to think about *him.*

"I heard Brody switched to the academy. How's the new guy?"

Had he read her mind? A slow wave of red started at her neck and cruised up her face. No matter how she tried, she couldn't stop it. She held a napkin in front of her face, hoping her blush would fade before it became too obvious.

But Todd was no dummy. "Ah," he said. "I had a feeling."

"No. It's not like that." She felt horrible suddenly, as if she'd led him on. But she hadn't. She'd intended to have fun with him, enjoy his company, flirt a little.

But now that he'd invoked the image of Roman, she knew it was impossible. Her smile dropped away. She lowered the napkin with a resigned sigh. "I'm sorry. I thought . . . I don't know what I thought. You're a nice guy and Roman . . ."

Todd held up a hand. "Never mind. No details required. I'm still glad I got to know you."

"Me too." She gave him a lopsided smile. "Can you excuse me for a moment? Restroom."

In the ladies' room, she splashed water on her face, disgusted with herself. She'd been willing to use a perfectly nice, gorgeous man as a way to forget about

Roman. Sure, he would have been a willing accomplice, most likely. But it wasn't cool. It was the kind of thing she'd sworn never to do when she left Hollywood. No games, no using people to further a career, no playing with people's emotions—none of the things that had been done to her.

She'd sworn to be real. Real and honest and true to herself. And yet, here she was, on a date with a man she wasn't interested in, after the man she wanted—craved—had thrown down his challenge.

If you want honesty, you come find me. The words still ricocheted through her mind, just as thrilling as ever.

Digging around in her purse, she pulled out her cell phone. She'd turned it off when Todd had picked her up, which was another of her post-Hollywood policies. Now she turned it on, her fingers trembling with impatience. She had to call Roman. She couldn't wait one more minute. She needed to hear that black coffee voice more than she needed oxygen.

When her screen lit up, she saw that Roman had beaten her to it. He'd called three times. The first time he hadn't left a message, but the second time, about ten minutes ago, he had.

"Sabina, it's Roman. Call me immediately, as soon as you get this message. It's urgent."

The next message, which he'd left two minutes after the first, shocked her to the core.

"Sabina, Luke is gone. He left with Carly. I don't want to call the police until I talk to you or her parents. He wouldn't have done this without a good reason. But I can't wait any longer. Call me when you get this and if I'm still nearby I'll pick you up. Otherwise, get hold of her parents and see if you can get any information. Thanks." His voice roughened. "I . . . please call."

Chapter Twenty-Eight

Todd insisted on waiting with Sabina outside the Green Elephant. Even though it was the gentlemanly thing to do, she had to grit her teeth to keep from telling him to go home. All she could think about was Luke and Carly off together somewhere. Where? Why? None of it made any sense.

While she waited for Roman, she called Carly's mother, but got no answer. She left a message with an urgent request to call back right away. Other than that, she had no brilliant ideas.

It didn't take long for Roman's Jeep to come screaming up to the curb. He must have sped the entire way. He started to get out, but Todd stopped him with a hand gesture. He took Sabina's crutches while she got in the passenger seat, then opened the back door and inserted them in the backseat.

"I hope you find them," he said, addressing both

Sabina and Roman. "Let me know if we can help. Any of us. We're a big family."

"Thanks, Todd." Sabina smiled at him. "And thanks for dinner."

"My pleasure." His wistful smile held a little sadness, but Sabina didn't feel too guilty. She had a feeling Todd Dane would be just fine.

Sabina stole a glance at Roman as he pulled away from the curb. He looked about as cheerful as a rock mountain surrounded by a thundercloud.

"So how do you know Luke's with Carly? Did he leave a note or a message?"

"E-mail."

"What did it say?"

"Here." Roman tossed her his smart phone, which was displaying Luke's e-mail. Sabina scanned it quickly.

Dear Papa,

I'm sorry but I have to do this. Carly needs my help. I promise to be very careful. I'll call you as soon as I can. Please don't call the police. Carly says they're even worse. We're going to find her father, then she'll be safe.

Your loving son,
Luke

"Carly's *father*? He left when she was little. She's never even seen him." She handed his phone back. "Have you tried Luke's cell phone?"

"Off."

"I tried Carly's mother, but she isn't answering."

Sabina could see a muscle working in Roman's jaw.

"It sounds like Luke is trying to rescue Carly from something. What's her family situation?"

Sabina felt sick to her stomach. Had she missed something? "Crappy. Her mother goes on a bender every so often. The boyfriends come and go. She's had to grow up fast, but I didn't think anything unusually bad was happening. But I haven't . . ." She shook her head helplessly. "I haven't seen her much since the fire. Whenever I asked, she said things were fine."

"Same with Luke. *Damn it.*" Roman's knuckles went white on the steering wheel. He looked wild in the glow from the dashboard. "He sneaked out on me. He knows I hardly ever check my e-mail at home. When I do, it's first thing in the morning, never at night. But I was checking on a Christmas present I'd ordered and saw Luke's message pop up. I thought he was in his room. I'd talked to him earlier in the evening. I even heard him go to bed. He yelled, 'Good night Papa' and turned everything off. When I got his e-mail I thought it was some kind of joke. But I ran into his room and he was gone. Out the back fucking window."

"Roman." She reached out to grip his shoulder, so tense it felt like a hunk of iron. "He can't have been gone long. Get ahold of yourself."

He gave a desperate sound, half laugh, half cry. "I don't know how, Sabina. I keep telling myself the same thing, get a grip, calm down so you can think, but this is Luke. My Luke. The only—" He broke off. His throat muscles worked. Sabina's heart ached for him. She kept her hand on his shoulder until she felt him relax. Glancing at the street ahead, she wondered if he should be driving in this state.

"Where are you headed?"

"The hell if I know. Police? Luke didn't want that. Little peckerhead. *Dio,* what am I saying?"

Good Lord, the poor man was losing it. She kept her voice calm and practical.

"Anyway, this is a clear case of a runaway. We'll spend hours making a statement."

"Fuck."

"Let's go back to your house and see if we can find something that gives us a clue. Have you checked his computer?"

"No, I just . . ." He rubbed the back of his neck. "Lost my mind. Got in the Jeep and came to get you."

"Good. You did exactly the right thing. You drive. Head for your house. Here, I'll do that." Sabina pushed his hand off his neck so she could massage the tense tendon that stretched between his neck and his shoulder. "They're both smart kids. Carly's dealt with dangerous situations before. And Luke's from New York. They're street-savvy, they know where they're going. It's not like they've been kidnapped."

Roman said nothing, but she thought his neck muscles eased just a bit. God, she prayed everything she'd just said was true.

She must have made sense to Roman, because he took the next turn, which led to his house. When they got there, he flung himself out of the Jeep, grabbed her crutches for her, tore inside, and went right to the computer.

"He's got a Facebook page," he muttered as he moved the mouse around on a pad with a picture of Nolan Ryan on it. "He thinks I don't check it, and usually I don't. But now . . ."

The Facebook search turned up nothing. Neither did a search of Luke's e-mail. But the cached searches turned out to be a jackpot. Luke had recently searched for the name Raphael Sandovar, the California State

Public Defender's office, and the Rancho Berendo State Penitentiary in Bannon.

"Maybe that's Carly's father," said Sabina, reading over Roman's shoulder. "I didn't know he was in prison. But it makes sense."

"Is her last name Sandovar?"

"No, it's Epps. Carlotta Epps. But why else would Luke do this search? I bet you anything they found out he's getting out of prison and they're going to meet him."

"At a *prison*? Hell no."

Roman surged to his feet, sending Luke's chair skittering across the room. "You ready?"

"Wait. He also checked the Greyhound schedule to Bannon. Two buses a day, last one left at six."

"Two hours ago." He groaned and ran a hand through his hair.

"So let's get moving." Sabina headed for the door, flicking aside a pair of shorts that threatened to trip her crutches.

"Wait." Roman settled his big hand on her shoulder. "What am I thinking? I'm being selfish. You don't have to come. You should be resting your ankle, elevating and icing and—"

"Fuck that, Roman." She aimed one crutch at him. "I've got crutches and I know how to use them. I'm coming with you."

He studied her with those black eyes, the overhead light picking out hints of deep midnight blue and stark fear.

"Besides, you need me, you big jerk. You're not thinking straight."

A wisp of a smile loosened the deep grooves next to his mouth. She noticed the black stubble already starting on his jaw. The taste of his lips came back to her with sudden erotic intensity.

"I thought of you, didn't I?" he said.

She swallowed. "Yes. That was smart. Now don't get stupid on me. Let's be practical here. Do you want to grab anything before we go? It's a long drive out to Bannon. We may have to spend the night."

"Spend the night," he answered blankly, running his hands through his hair.

"Well, we don't know when or where we'll find them. It might be three in the morning by the time we do. If you want to bring a toothbrush, now's your chance. Maybe we should bring Luke's laptop. A picture of him. That sort of thing."

"Right. Laptop. Picture. Toothbrush. But what about you? Your toothbrush?"

"Don't worry about me, I'll pick one up."

"But—"

"Are we really going to argue about toothbrushes? Come on, get the stuff and I'll meet you in the car. Really, it's a damn good thing you called me. Someone's got to think of these things." She swung past him with a cheeky wink—anything to keep that hunted, terrified look off his face.

They drove east, into the desert. Sabina gave him extra-precise directions that would have been irritating under normal circumstances. But Roman didn't mind. He appreciated her "In a hundred yards, turn right onto the highway" and "You have three seconds to beat that light." Ever since Luke's e-mail he'd felt stuck in a time-warp nightmare; the only thing that cut through the fog was Sabina's bright presence.

As soon as they left San Gabriel, the dark-as-velvet night closed around the Jeep, lending it an atmosphere of intimacy that Roman found both soothing and arousing.

Sabina punctuated the silence with brisk commands—they too were both soothing and arousing. "You drive while I watch the road for hitchhikers. Hopefully they're on the bus, but they might have decided to hitch. And if you start freaking out again, I'll distract you with random lines of Taffy dialogue."

He growled at her. "I don't 'freak out.' But I might if I get some Taffy McGee out of it."

She slanted a skeptical look his way. Fine. He'd freaked out. No sense in pretending otherwise. This was Luke. His son, his entire life. Alone on a desert highway heading for a fucking *state penitentiary.*

This was his fault. He should have talked to Luke more. Opened up to him. He should never have let Maureen go to work that day. He should have stayed in New York where his parents could help watch over Luke. He shouldn't let him play baseball or own a computer.

He didn't share any of these crazed thoughts with Sabina. Instead they piled up inside like thunderclouds.

After a couple of hours, Sabina directed him to a rest stop where the buses usually took a snack break. No one had seen anyone resembling Luke and Carly.

"That's okay," she reassured him as they stocked up on peanut butter cups and big bottles of iced green tea. "They probably didn't get off the bus."

"Maybe they're on a different bus."

"Remember, we checked the schedule? There's only one bus they could have taken."

What if there was a different bus line? What if they'd gotten on the wrong bus and were headed for Mexico? What if someone hijacked the bus and drove it into a . . . *Stop. This isn't helping. Listen to Sabina.* She was talking again. He hung onto the bright, confident sound of her voice as if it were a rope dangling in a subterranean cave.

"Back in the Jeep. The bus is too far ahead for us to catch up with it. We'll have to look for them in Bannon. Come on, move it, Roman."

It took three more hours to reach Bannon. Sabina kept up a stream of talk designed to keep him alert. She told him crazy stories from the set of *You and Me*. She told him about her own father, a bit actor she hadn't seen since she was little. Roman told her a few disjointed anecdotes about the Roman family—how they were descended from the rulers of an Italian city-state and seemed to have leadership bred into their bones. Luke had the gene too, maybe that was why . . . But as soon as he mentioned Luke he started to lose it. So Sabina launched into more Taffy routines, cute Taffy voice and tomboy mannerisms included.

"I wouldn't do this for anyone else, you know," she told him. "Once-in-a-lifetime opportunity."

It was after one by the time they crossed the city lines of Bannon. Everything was closed except a 7–Eleven and a Motel 6.

"Let's check at the 7-Eleven," Sabina said. "I bet they got hungry on the bus."

Roman nodded tightly. He couldn't imagine sleeping, but he knew he ought to try. His eyes stung from staring at the dark road. His neck felt tight as a drum. Poor Sabina must be even more exhausted, but no one would ever know it from her confident manner.

She hadn't mentioned her ankle once, but it had to be hurting her. Tenderness flooded him as he pulled into the parking lot of the 7–Eleven. "I'll go in. You stay here and rest. Any requests while I'm in there?"

"I'll take a snack. Anything, your choice."

When he slid back into the driver's seat, he felt like a new man. "The clerk saw Luke and Carly. They're definitely here. He said they were staying at a motel in town, he didn't know but he guessed the Motel 6, since it's the closest. But they're fine. Having an adventure, it sounds like. They bought beef jerky and pink Sno Balls. And a gallon of water."

"Oh, thank God." She slumped against the seat, her eyes closing for a tiny, revealing instant.

Dio, she'd been just as worried as he was. But she'd put all her energy into keeping his spirits up, keeping him on track—getting them to Bannon.

"Oh, Sabina," Roman said, cupping her face in one hand. "Why didn't you tell me?"

"Tell you what?" She blinked at him wearily, her eyelashes brushing his palm.

"Shh. Never mind. I got it from here." Now that he knew Luke was okay, the whole world looked different—bright, wonderful, and inhabited by the incredible woman in the passenger seat. He drove to the Motel 6, then made her stay in the Jeep while he booked a room and talked to the clerk.

In the lobby, he showed the sleepy clerk his driver's license and a picture of Luke. "Is my son staying here? He would have checked in with a dark-haired girl."

When the clerk made noises about guest confidentiality, Roman pulled out his fire department credentials, a ferocious scowl and a mutter about runaways. That did it. Room 232.

"They're fine," said the clerk anxiously. "The girl's ID said she was eighteen. Looked like they were having a lark, is all. No harm done. Nothing fishy. You want to wake them up?"

Yes. He wanted to wake them up and yell at them.

Then hug them. Or maybe the other way around. He followed the clerk to Luke's room. A soft knock on the door got no response. The clerk inserted the key card and ushered Roman in.

One lamp was still on. Like a beam of heavenly light from above, it illuminated the sleeping face of his son. Luke sprawled across one bed, Carly snuggled in the other, turned away from the lamp. Both slept deeply, as if they were utterly exhausted. Roman drank in the sight of his son, his mouth half open, his arms wrapped around a pillow. Sweet relief swamped him, a kind of bone-deep gratitude.

He put his finger to his lips, warning the clerk not to make a sound.

His first instinct was to wake them up and read them the riot act. But something—maybe their deep sleep—held him back. He stepped softly to Luke's bedside and bent down. As he reached over to shake his son awake, a sheet of notepaper on the nightstand caught his eye. It lay haphazardly across the faux-walnut surface, a pen abandoned nearby.

In the dim light from the parking lot, he could barely read it. Some lines were crossed out as if he were trying to get it just right.

Papa, I'm really really sorry. ~~I was trying to help a friend.~~ *I had to protect my friend. She needed me. Don't be too mad.* ~~It's okay if you ground me~~. *If you want to ground me,* ~~that's okay~~. *If you ground me, I won't complain. I'll take it like a man. I'm more grown up than you think.*

At that point, the writing trailed off. Luke must have fallen asleep while writing it, and never switched off the lamp.

Roman took a deep breath, gazed at his son for one more long, lingering moment, then backed away from the bed.

Outside, he gestured to the clerk, who followed him down the hallway.

"I'm going to let them sleep. But I don't want them leaving the motel without me. Are you here all night?"

"Until six."

"I'll be up before then. If they try to leave, don't let them. Keep them in the lobby and call me. Put me in the room closest to them."

The clerk nodded doubtfully. "I'll do my best, sir."

Back in the parking lot, he slid into the driver's seat and met Sabina's anxious look.

"I saw them. They're fine. Sleeping. Separate beds, not that I was worried about that. Luke was practicing what he's going to say to me when he fell asleep."

The relief on her face mirrored his. "You okay letting them stay the night?"

"No. Not really. But they need their sleep. They have to deal with *me* first thing in the morning."

He took her hand and squeezed it tightly, unable to express all the emotion welling through him. "Thank you for being here. Thank you for coming with me."

"Of course, Chief. Where else would I be?" She gave him a bright wink, as if trying to lighten the moment. He lifted her hand to his lips, pressed a kiss into it, then let her go.

When he'd parked the car close to their room, he came around to open the passenger door.

He held out his arms. "Come here."

"Excuse me?"

He maneuvered her out of the passenger seat and into his arms, holding her like a baby. A slightly outraged baby. "I've done this twice before, you know. And once you had all your gear on."

"Yes, but . . ."

"Shh."

He carried her inside the motel, used the key card to enter their room, and placed her gently on the beige striped bed. He put a pillow under her ankle. "Elevate before sleep. You want a blanket? Are you cold? Hot?"

She threw a pillow at him. "I'm fine. I'm not your ailing Aunt Mildred."

"That would be Zia Maria. No Mildreds in the Roman family. I'll be right back. Gotta get your crutches. Which reminds me . . ." He folded his arms across his chest and speared her with a stern look. "Todd Dane . . ." He couldn't finish the sentence.

The corner of her mouth twitched in a way that made him want to fall on her like a junkyard dog. "It's nothing."

With that settled, he went back to the Jeep to collect her crutches and the overnight bag he'd brought. In the parking lot, he stood for a long moment, breathing in the clear air of this desert dot-on-the-map. Luke was okay. *Grazie a Dio,* he prayed silently. And *grazie* to Sabina, who'd guided him here like the North Star. Without that bright-eyed, truehearted, clearheaded woman in there with her foot on a pillow, he'd still be driving around San Gabriel like a lunatic.

Grazie, grazie a tutti gli angeli.

Back inside the motel room, Sabina had fallen asleep. Carefully, tenderly, he extracted the bedcovers from under her body and settled them over her. Then he took off everything but his boxers and crawled in next to her.

They'd offered him a room with two beds, but he hadn't seen the point of that, since the chances that he'd be able to keep his hands off her . . .

He settled one hand on the warm curve of her hip.

Zero.

* * *

Sabina woke up next to a radiator. A breathing, rumbling radiator. She felt warm all the way to her core, inside and out. The long, broad body next to her belonged to Roman, and it was exactly where it ought to be. Next to her. The only thing wrong was that she had way too many clothes on, and so did he.

A few fumbling, broken ankle–impaired moves later, she was naked. She pressed herself against him, nearly delirious at the divine sensation of his bare flesh. She snaked one hand under the waistband of his boxers. But before she could find out if that particular part of him was awake, a hand clamped onto her wrist.

"Oh no, you don't. You're injured."

"So?" She wanted to cry from frustration. After all the nights she'd dreamed of being with him like this again . . . now he was going to go all protective on her?

"So . . . you just lie back. Let me do the work. I got this."

"Work?"

"I pride myself on my work." He reinforced his sexy growl with a menacing raised eyebrow.

She giggled, unable to stop the goofy sound. After the long, drawn-out tension of that endless drive across the desert, to be in bed with Roman, naked and joking, was some kind of miracle. And then the miracle soared into a whole new realm. Roman rose above her, tenting the covers over them. He bent to her lips and kissed her from the furthest depths of his soul—or at least that's how it felt to her dazed brain. On and on went the kiss, until her blood ran like honey and her skin prickled from the oncoming storm. She kissed him back with everything in her, every dream from every lonely night, every fantasy she'd ever indulged, every moment she'd longed for him, since she'd met him . . . and maybe even before.

The depth of her response frightened her.

She tore herself away from his kiss. "Why didn't you come see me in the hospital? Everyone else did. Even One dragged her ass in."

He stilled, then touched his forehead to hers. The intimate touch, as if they were thought to thought, made her shiver. "Oh, *cara*. I thought about you the whole time. Every second."

"Tell me why." She poked him in the chest. "You said, if you want honesty, come find me. Well, here I am."

He lifted his head and searched her face. Stubbornly she held his gaze. The air between them seemed to sizzle. Finally he dropped his head. "I . . . I couldn't. I haven't been in a hospital since . . . since Maureen died. I went to every single one in New York, looking for her. The morgues too. Never found her."

Oh God. A vise seemed to tighten around her throat. Why hadn't she thought of that? She was an idiot a thousand times over. Someone ought to just shoot her now. "I should have known. I'm sorry."

Mortified, she tried to slide out from under him, but his immovable body kept her right where she was.

"No, Sabina. I'm no good at this shit. You started this, now stay still and let me finish."

"Good at what shit?"

"Vent holes."

Vent holes? She went still, letting herself be captured by Roman's dark, deep tractor beam of a gaze.

"I got to you in time," he said in a low growl. "But not her."

She sucked in a sharp breath. Everything in her wanted to flee. *Out, out*, she wanted out, wanted to run while she still had a scrap of self-defense left.

But Roman kept her caged between his powerful arms and his massive chest. "Fuck, this is hard. Maybe if I'd done all those counseling sessions I'd know the right words. It's in my blood. I'm the leader. I'm supposed to lead the way. Take the fall. I'd sacrifice myself for any one of my crew. And Maureen was my *wife*. I would have put myself in her place in a second, so she could live and Luke would have a mother. It should have been me in the Pile, not her."

"Oh, Roman." Tears slipped down her face. What did her selfish feelings matter compared to a loss like that? "You don't have to talk about this. It's okay."

"I'm not done, damn it. When you were in that falling-down building, I was like a wild man. No one could have kept me out."

Her heart was doing funny things, speeding up, jumping, perhaps stopping entirely. She tried to breathe evenly, but it was no use. "That's what they said. People kept telling me about it."

"Well, they didn't know this part." He leaned in even closer, so his warm breath surrounded her and the feral light in his eyes outshone the dim glow filtering through the curtains. "There was no way in living hell I was going to watch another fucking pile of concrete take a woman I love."

Chapter Twenty-Nine

Had Roman just told her he loved her? Through the roar of the blood racing through her veins, she wanted to rewind the moment, make sure she'd heard him correctly. But he gave her no time. His mouth was devouring hers again, and this time there was no possibility of tearing herself away. He touched her with ravenous need, filling his hands with her breasts until she arched against his hard body. An urgent chant pounded through her . . . get close, touch, lick, pleasure, inhale. She wanted to breathe him into her being, make him part of her.

He met her motion for motion, cry for cry. He traveled her body with his tongue and big hands. They were a devastating combo, his hands taking hold, claiming, keeping her prisoner while he ravaged her with his devilishly clever, wickedly warm tongue. This was no leisurely sensual journey. Oh no. He was a man on a mission, which was apparently to render her so mindless from desire that she'd spread her legs apart before he even reached them, push her hips up to urge his tongue to her sex, even beg him with little incomprehensible whimpers.

"Roman, Roman, please," she moaned, when he took a side trip to the quivering skin of her inner thigh. "You're trying to kill me." His head shook with a laugh, so his hair brushed against her sex. "Oh my God," she sobbed. What if she came against the top of his head? She forced herself to hold still and concentrate on the meandering swirls of fire he was planting on her skin, sweet trails of sizzling heat.

"Just relax, *cara*. I got this," he murmured, sending a breath of heat wafting against her sensitized flesh.

"Relax?"

"Lie back. I'll take care of everything." And he stroked his thumb against the aching nub crying out for his attention.

She bit back a sob of joy that something could feel so good. The least she could do was follow his suggestion. Or maybe it was an order. Didn't matter. She relaxed her body and surrendered to the wicked things he was doing with his tongue and mouth. And thumbs. And fingers. Two went inside her, one after the other, seeking some spot of nirvana, using her moans and twitches and "Oh Gods" to track the way. When that devil finger found what it was after, it got busy, pressing and circling. The wet, warm weight of his tongue picked up the pace too, with sucks and nibbles that made her scream out loud.

The entire lower half of her body lost every shred of control. Her hips thrashed against the bed. If he'd been any less strong, the two of them would have tumbled to the floor, but he kept his grip firm and immovable. There was nothing for her to do but let him taste her and pleasure her and lap her up. Nowhere for her to go except straight into the sun.

And that's where she went, diving toward the bright, beckoning explosion, reveling in the sweet flash of climax that went on and on under the powerful urging of his hands and mouth. While the spasms still shook her, he poised his thickly aroused cock at her entrance.

"This doesn't hurt you anywhere? Ankle? Ribs?" The effort of restraint turned his voice harsh as sandpaper.

"No," she gasped. She'd forgotten she was injured. Maybe she'd feel it later, but right now every part of her body pulsed with well-pleasured delight. "I want you. Come inside, please."

When he pushed inside her, claiming her completely, it felt as if a bright light spread throughout her being. The light pushed away all the tension, the sadness, the loneliness. In that moment, a brilliant flash of knowledge formed like a perfect crystal: until now, she'd been alone. Entirely, comprehensively alone.

When he was fully embedded in her body, he lowered himself so his chest brushed against her breasts. "I meant what I said before. I love you."

She nodded, knowing it wasn't enough. She should say it back. Tell him what she felt, what he made her feel. She even opened her mouth to do so. But nothing came out other than a groan of pleasure.

That was enough, apparently. He flexed his hips, taking her deeper into the velvety darkness as she closed her eyes. She felt every movement of his cock all the way to her fingertips. Her scalp tingled, her mouth flew open. "Roman, I . . . I . . ."

"I know, *cara*."

He gathered up her hips, holding her steady while

he began a determined, relentless assault. Sparks spangled behind her eyelids. She grabbed his shoulders, feeling his muscles flex and tense. The wild scent of aroused, primal man rolled off him in waves, the smell of sweat and need and salty skin. She lifted her head to lick his shoulder. The taste of him made her crazy for more. She darted her tongue at his neck, his collarbone, every square inch of him she could reach.

"Sabina." He let out a desperate groan. "I need you. You don't know how much."

"You got me," she whispered. "I'm right here." She licked the underside of his chin, feeling the stiff stubble abrade her tongue. Taking his chin into her teeth, she gave it a little nip. "There isn't a single part of you that doesn't turn me on," she murmured, then reached for his lips with hers. He tilted his head to make it easy for her. She ran her tongue across his firm mouth, then kissed him with all the savage hunger he aroused in her.

That sent him over the edge. He thrust deep, deeper, so deep all the barriers between them melted away and they seemed to become one being surging toward ecstasy. His body shook from the powerful spasms, he tilted his head toward the heavens and howled his release. She held on tight, like a boat rocked in a storm, until she too got swept into a whirlpool of sensations, down, down, until nothing was left but purest bliss.

Surfacing took a while. But it was so sweet to find herself held tight in Roman's arms, his cock still inside her, her face pressed against his strong chest with its *thump-thumping* heart. Roman's heart. The heart of a lion. A big, black-furred, courageous, true-to-the-bone lion. And he'd said he loved her. Loved her . . .

After a while Roman gingerly rolled off her, onto his back. He pulled the blankets over them, then snuggled her into his arms. Sleep tugged at her, but before she could drift off, Roman spoke.

"No condom," he said, his voice still raspy. "I got carried away. I'm sorry. But if it helps, I haven't had unprotected sex since Luke was born."

She turned her head and blinked up at him. "It's okay. I hardly ever have sex." In her relaxed state, the admission slipped out before she could think it through.

He smiled with the smugness of a conqueror. "Why is that?"

"Cautious. Wary, I guess."

"Because you used to be on TV?"

"Well, I lost my virginity to someone who saw me as a ticket to the tabloids. It worked for him. Not so much for me. Then when I joined the force I had to be even more careful. I wanted people to focus on my skills, not my gender. I didn't want to sleep with other firemen." She gave him a lazy push on the arm. "So much for that plan."

A rumble of laughter shook his chest. She flattened her hand against it so she could feel it rise and fall under the mat of curly hair.

"I guess we've ruined each other's plans then," he said.

"What plans?"

"I assumed I'd spend the rest of my life raising Luke. No girls allowed. For me, at least. I'm sure he'll be wanting a girl. Maybe he's found one."

Sabina felt oncoming sleep weigh down her eyelids. She struggled to focus. "I don't know. I don't think it's like that. It seems to me he wants to help Carly. You Romans. Always rushing off to help the damsels in distress."

Tenderly, he cupped her cheek. "In distress? You?"

She had been in distress, though she hadn't fully realized it until that crystal moment in which she'd seen her life, seen what Roman meant to her. But right now, she couldn't explain. Too sleepy . . .

"Right," he said. "That pile of marble I rescued you from."

No, that wasn't it. He'd rescued her from something much harder than marble. Her eyes closed halfway. "Marble is nothing compared to . . ."

Compared to what? She'd mumbled something after that, but hell if he could tell what.

He knew what she hadn't said. She hadn't said she loved him.

Dio, he'd rushed it, bumbling, boneheaded fool that he was. How could he expect her to share his feelings when he'd barely figured them out? He hadn't expected to declare himself so suddenly. Must have been his impulsive, romantic Italian nature taking over.

But he'd meant it, every word. He did love her. Still didn't know what to do about that fact, but fact it was, and knowing him, fact it would stay. He wanted her. All to himself. Forever.

He froze.

What was he talking about, forever? That kind of talk meant . . . But he wasn't ever going to marry again . . . No, marriage was out of the question, it would be disloyal . . . He'd never even thought about it after Maureen was killed. That part of his life had ended after it had barely begun . . .

Growing up, he'd always assumed that he'd marry and have lots of kids. He loved kids, loved toting around the little ones and building forts with the older ones. He'd always imagined his life would be filled with children. More skeptical about the idea, Maureen had agreed to one child so they could see how they handled being a two-firefighter family.

They hadn't had much time to try it out before that sunny, cruel day in September.

Since then, he hadn't given any more thought to his old visions of children, marriage, happiness. What did that mean for him, for Sabina?

As Sabina snored gently next to him, he watched the light at the edge of the curtains grow dishwater gray. Not a single brilliant answer came to him.

At a quarter to six, he shook her awake. "We should get moving."

Like a good firefighter, she woke instantly and swung her feet over the edge of the bed. And winced.

"You okay?"

"Yeah. I keep forgetting." She yawned and stretched, her torso making a taut, achingly lovely line in the morning light. Her nipples were beautifully high and rosy, her skin flushed from sleep. He wanted nothing more than to throw her back down on the bed.

But Luke and Carly came first. He snagged her clothes off the floor and handed them to her.

"I wish I'd brought another pair of underwear," she grumbled. "I guess I'll go commando today."

He groaned. "Don't tell me that."

She batted her eyelashes at him, the gray light bringing out sparks of pure green in her eyes. His chest hurt, she was so beautiful. If he didn't put some physical distance between them, he'd never get out of here to find Luke.

"Come on," he said roughly. "I'll meet you in the lobby. Should I grab you a coffee?"

"Sure. I'll be right behind you."

* * *

Sabina pulled on her clothes as quickly as she could. Of course Roman was in a hurry. He wanted to snag Luke. She shouldn't read anything into his distant manner this morning. Even though last night seemed like a dream, it wasn't. He'd said those words, he'd made powerful, passionate love to her. It had all happened, every erotic, liquefying moment.

The two of them were combustible. Incendiary. Impossible.

In the lobby, Roman looked like he was about to explode. "The damn clerk missed them. He was on a bathroom break and when he came out, they were getting into a taxi. Come on, we gotta go."

They hurried into the Jeep. Sabina concentrated on the early morning desert landscape, the sun rising behind a light fog the color of mustard. She ignored the increasingly awkward silence. If he wanted to be all business, fine with her. At the steering wheel, Roman scowled at the road, virtually deserted at this hour. "I'm taking away his computer. No, grounding him from baseball. Maybe that'll teach him."

"Why don't we just wait until we find them?"

"I am waiting. But as soon as we do, I'm grounding him. You should ground Carly."

"I'm not in a grounding kind of position. And her mother still hasn't called me back. Something really bad must have happened. I just wish she'd told me about it."

"We'll know soon enough."

"Let's hope."

That ominous statement hung in the air until they reached the vast complex of the Rancho Berendo State Penitentiary. It was made from massive concrete blocks, with square watch towers anchoring the corners and wire sprouting off the outer walls. Everything about it was large and intimidating and no place for two young kids.

And yet, there they were, two figures waiting outside the front gate. Luke wore his father's black leather jacket, Carly a blazer that made her look easily eighteen.

Swearing, Roman screeched the Jeep to a halt and jumped out. He ran to Luke, who swung around, wide-eyed, a frightened kid too skinny for his dad's jacket. Snatching him up, Roman hugged his son so tightly to his chest the boy's feet dangled above the ground.

Sabina followed more cautiously. Would Carly be mad at her for interfering? But when the girl burst into tears, Sabina moved as fast as she could on her crutches until she reached her side. "Are you okay, Carly?"

"Ye-es." Her voice wobbled. Sabina was used to the tough, I-can-handle-anything Carly. She'd never seen her so frightened. Balancing on her crutches, she opened her arms and Carly collapsed into them. "But this place is so scary and I don't want to be here anymore. I don't know what I was thinking. Stupid, stupid, dumb me."

"Stop that. It's okay. Everything's going to be okay." Sabina hugged her and whispered soothing things until the girl's shaking subsided.

"Can we go?" Carly wiped her face. "This was a stupid idea. I just want to get out of here."

Sabina glanced over at Roman, who still hadn't let go of Luke. His face was buried in his son's hair, his arms wrapped around him. Sabina's heart stuttered. She knew what she was witnessing—pure, raw, unconditional love. Not something she was used to. Beneath the hardass Chief, the strict parent, the stoic widower,

Roman, at his core, was a man who knew how to love. The sight humbled her.

Finally, Luke wriggled free. His sneakered feet hit the pavement and he swiped at the wetness on his cheeks. As Roman gazed down at his wayward son, his expression shifted to one Sabina knew all too well—Training Officer on the Rampage. But before he could say a word, Luke spoke up.

"I know you're going to yell, Papa. But can we eat first? I think I'm going to throw up."

Carly gave a shaky snort. "He's not too used to junk food."

Over the kids' heads, Roman and Sabina's eyes met with helpless mirth. After the fear and worry, it all came down to junk food.

And just like that, their closeness from last night was back.

They drove back to Bannon, the kids quiet in the backseat. Once they'd found a Denny's and settled into a booth, the whole story came out. Carly's mom had gone off the deep end, drinking herself into a stupor every night. She kept threatening to kick Carly out of the house. But the worst part was her boyfriend, who'd announced that he was sick of working for the city sanitation department and wanted to give pimping a try.

"He didn't mean . . ." Horrified, Sabina couldn't finish the sentence.

"He keeps giving me funny looks, is the thing. I started wondering about my father. I knew he was only in for selling pot. He's not violent or anything. Maybe he could take care of me. So Luke helped me find out where he was. We were just going to talk to him. But I didn't think the prison would be so scary. I can't believe my father's inside there."

She fixed her gaze on her untouched English muffin.

"Why didn't one of you consider talking to an adult? Luke?" Roman scowled at his son, who went a little pale.

But Carly's head snapped up. "Don't get mad at Luke. If he hadn't gone with me, I would have gone by myself. He was trying to make sure I was safe."

Roman stopped her flow of words with one upheld hand. "I'm asking my son."

A long, pulsing silence followed.

Then Luke put down his forkful of French toast and lurched to his feet. "Papa, you treat me like a little kid. Like I can't handle anything. I just wanted to . . . wanted to . . . Arrgh." Like a punctured balloon, he sank back onto the booth. "Forget it. It was pretty stupid."

Roman opened his mouth, then closed it again. He stared long and hard at his son. Before, Sabina would have thought he was angry. Now she knew he was working things out deep inside that huge heart of his.

Sabina stirred fake maple syrup into her oatmeal. "Carly, why didn't you come to me? Maybe I could have done something."

"Well . . ." Uneasy, the girl pushed her hot chocolate around the table. "I know you're my Big Sister and all, and that's really cool, but it's not like . . . I mean, you're not responsible for me. You're not my parent. It was my problem. No one else should have to fix things for me."

"But . . ." Sabina trailed off, hearing a disturbing echo of herself in Carly's words. She'd never wanted to rely on anyone either. And Carly was right, a Big Sister didn't have parental responsibility. But still, it stung.

"Anyway," said Luke, starting to look more cheerful. "It wasn't all bad. It was kind of fun up until we saw the prison. The bus ride was so cool, and we watched movies in the hotel room and . . ."

Roman held up his hand. "Not the right direction for avoiding punishment."

"I'm not trying to avoid it." Luke swallowed a giant bite of French toast and glared at his father. "I'm going to take it like a man. As long as it's fair."

Seeing Roman's ominous expression, Sabina quickly changed the subject. "Can you guys explain why they even rented you a room? You're underage. Didn't they check your IDs?"

"I took my cousin's." Carly dug into her pocket. "She's eighteen and I look exactly like her." She plopped the card on the table.

"And Luke?"

"They didn't ask for mine. Besides, I'm tall for my age. And I borrowed Papa's jacket."

"Okay, that's it. There goes the computer," snapped Roman.

Luke winced, then nodded. "Okay. How long?"

"That depends on what other nasty details come out."

Luke clamped his mouth shut as if to stop them leaking out without his permission.

Roman brandished his fork in the air. "And I will—repeat, will—hear every detail. Have no doubt about that."

"Dude, you're strict." Carly gazed at Roman with something approaching awe, as if she'd never seen a parent exercise authority before. Which perhaps she hadn't. "I mean, Chief," she added hastily.

"Dude is fine." He caught Sabina's glance, humor simmering in his midnight eyes. Then he sobered. "But right now, we have to figure out what's next. It sounds like you can't go home until things get sorted out. Do you have any other family you can stay with, Carly?"

Carly's head drooped as she twisted her hands together. The poor girl looked so crestfallen, Sabina wanted to cry. Her Little Sister thought she had to handle everything by herself. But no one should have to.

No one.

Before she knew it, Sabina's mouth opened and the most astonishing words came out. "You can stay with me, Carly."

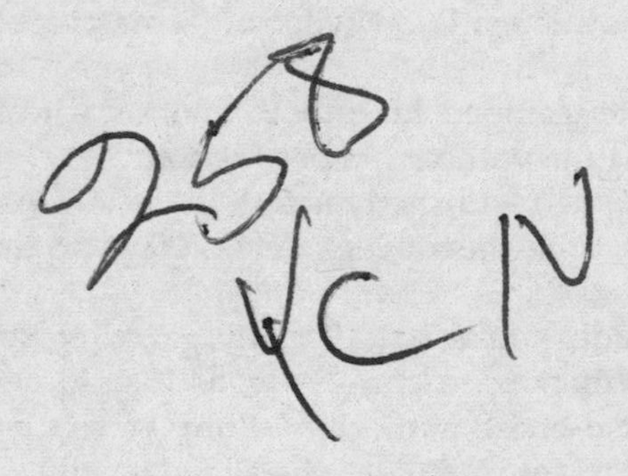

Chapter Thirty

Sabina could barely believe her own ears, but there it was. And there was Carly, her hot chocolate halfway to her mouth, which had dropped open in complete astonishment. Luke gave Carly a high five, which missed its mark and hit her shoulder, spilling a bit of hot chocolate.

What had she just done? After years and years of living solo, she was about to share her home with not only a difficult movie star, but a moody thirteen-year-old. Why, why, when all she wanted to do was fight fires and be left in peace?

But maybe that wasn't all she wanted. The warm, arrested look in Roman's eyes made up for a lot.

Anyway, she couldn't back out now, not with Carly exchanging behind-the-back low fives with Luke. "We'll have to talk with your mother first," she reminded the girl. "And it's just temporary."

"I know." Mention of her mother brought the minicelebration to a crashing halt. "Can you come with me to talk to her? If you're there it'll go better."

"Of course."

In the end they all went. Roman wanted to see for himself what Carly was dealing with, and he didn't want Luke to leave his side.

In a tiny Fern Acres apartment, with bars on the windows and broken lawn chairs out front, they found Carly's mother, Amarinda, just emerging from a three-day binge. Empty rum bottles littered the filthy carpet, along with old copies of *Travel* magazine.

"She likes to plan trips when she's drinking," explained Carly, her face dusky red from mortification. "And she cries a lot. *A lot.*"

Amarinda squinted at her daughter. "How was school, baby?"

"I haven't been at school. I went to prison."

"Que?" She slipped into Spanish.

Sabina interrupted before things got ugly and explained what Carly and Luke had done, and why. Luke, nudged by Roman, stepped forward and introduced himself, then offered a grudging apology.

"Sorry for what we did. But you shouldn't let that man near Carly."

"Hell, boy, I wasn't even conscious. Save your sorry for someone who deserves it." Amarinda swiped her hand across her streaming eyes.

"Mami, don't start crying," groaned Carly.

She sobbed. "I let you down, baby."

Carly rolled her eyes.

Roman, who'd stayed in the background, stepped forward with the commanding manner Sabina knew so well. "Ms. Epps, I'm Battalion Chief Roman from Fire Station 1. We need to talk about your daughter's future."

"A chief? Am I in trouble?"

Roman flicked a glance at Sabina, who shrugged. If Carly's mother was going to accept a fire chief's authority, why not go with it? "I think we can work things out, as long as we keep Carly's best interests as our top priority."

"Sure, mister. I mean Chief."

And so they made a deal. Amarinda promised to spend two weeks in rehab and gave Carly permission to stay with Sabina until she got out. She also vowed to never let the aspiring pimp in the house again.

After packing up some of Carly's clothes and her baseball gear, they drove Amarinda to a detox unit at Good Samaritan. Roman told her not to worry about the money; she didn't argue because he said it in such an authoritative way. Privately, he told Sabina he'd figure something out.

Next, Roman drove everyone to Sabina's house. Annabelle had gone out, which gave Sabina a chance to get Carly settled in before breaking the news to her mother. Luke and Roman made lunch while Sabina got Carly set up in her bedroom.

When they all finally sat down at her tiny kitchen table, Sabina could barely believe her eyes. "This is what you whip up for lunch?"

A savory, tenderly steaming casserole sat on the table. They all inhaled the mouthwatering scent.

"Mushroom risotto. More or less." He shrugged. "I did what I could with what you had in the kitchen. Not a lot you can do with instant rice and ramen noodle soup."

"Don't look at me. I'm an invalid. My cooking efforts are on hiatus." She winked and brushed her good leg against his thigh. He responded right away, hooking his leg under hers to draw it closer. Warmth spread all the way to her core. It felt so intimate, sitting in her kitchen with two runaway kids and a lionhearted fireman. It felt like a dream, as if everything that had happened since she'd left the Green Elephant was part of some kind of fantasy.

"Whatever you need me to do while I'm here, you just tell me," Carly promised fervently. "I like doing laundry. I'm good at folding. I do all the cooking at my house. Not as good as Chief Roman though."

"There's one problem with Roman's cooking," Sabina said. "He doesn't live here." His strong thigh moved against hers, radiating heat. "I suppose we could invite him over to cook for us now and then."

That suggestion made Carly and Luke clap their hands in delight. Roman cast a severe look at his son.

"Luke and I are going to need some family time for a little while," he said. "We still have a few things to settle. I'm not sure losing the computer for a week is a strong enough consequence when I think of how many things could have gone wrong with that cockeyed plan."

Luke held his tongue with a visibly painful effort. Soon afterward, Roman pushed back his chair and gestured for Luke to follow. Sabina swallowed hard as she rose to her feet to see them out. After spending every second of the past twenty hours with Roman, it felt strange, wrong, to separate.

Outside, Luke ran ahead to the Jeep while Roman lagged behind. "Give us a minute, Lukey, all right?"

"Sure, Papa."

Roman pulled Sabina around the side of her porch, behind a camellia bush that gave them some privacy. The fresh scent from its early morning watering rose around them. He turned his body so she was shielded from the street and examined her closely, until she thought she might faint under his intent gaze. "Are you sure about what you're doing here? With Carly?"

Sabina fought back her disappointment. She'd thought he was going to say something about their night together, and those amazing words, "I love you." She was starting to wonder if she'd imagined the whole thing. "She needs a place to stay."

"And it's generous of you to step up. But the more I think about it . . ."

"What?"

"Well, that night I came over and made an ass out of myself with that movie script."

"I remember."

He made a little face. "It seemed you and your mother were getting along pretty well. Mostly."

"She's been okay."

"Seems like an opportunity."

She poked her crutch at a brown-edged camellia rotting on the ground. "To what? Bicker? Relive our sorry past? Disrespect each other's careers?"

"Sabina. She's here, isn't she? Give her a chance. Don't use Carly as a distraction."

Sabina felt her nostrils flare. "You don't know anything about me and Annabelle."

He pulled back, just a little, but she caught it. "I know enough."

"Then you should know to stay out of it."

He held up his hands to show his innocence. "I'm not getting into it. I was just suggesting . . ."

"Well, don't suggest."

"*Dio,* you're stubborn. Are you going to shut her out your whole life?"

She tore her arm away from his grasp. "I said, *keep out of it.*"

He took a big step back, then another. From a distance of about four feet, he stared at her with the intensity of a blowtorch.

"Is that what you do? Shove people away and keep them there?"

The shock of that accusation rippled up her spine. "How dare you?"

"How dare I?" He wheeled around, stalked away a few feet, then spun around to face her again. "This is how. Last night, I told you how I felt. You looked right in my eyes and didn't say a word in return. And before, you said it was just one fun night. I didn't believe you meant it, but . . . I get it. Now I get it."

Wordless, she stared back at him. He ran his hand over the back of his neck, then forced out a crooked grimace of a smile.

"I get it," he repeated in a low voice.

By the time she snapped out of it, he'd made it all the way across her front yard to his Jeep.

"Roman," she croaked, but he was already inserting himself into the car, turning the key in the ignition.

Disappearing down the street.

"Sabina?" Carly called from the front door. "Can I take a shower?"

"Sure." She slowly stumped her way inside the house, thoughts crowding her mind like a swarm of voracious gnats. Annabelle . . . Roman . . . *I love you* . . . fear . . . joy . . . confusion . . . that crystal moment . . . what was it again? . . . fear . . . need . . . Roman.

"Papa." Luke poked Roman in the ribs as they drove away from Sabina's house. "You're such a dork."

"Huh?" Roman scowled at his son, who was looking pretty cheeky for someone facing an unknown punishment.

"You didn't even kiss her good-bye."

Roman nearly drove off the road. Of course he hadn't kissed Sabina good-bye. They'd . . . well . . . had a fight. "Why would I do that?"

"Why wouldn't you? You like her, don't you?"

"None of your business."

Luke snorted. "And you want her to like you. I don't know why she would, though, the way you keep frowning at her and yelling at her."

Roman took a turn that put them heading directly into the sun. He grabbed his shades from the visor and slid them on. That little extra bit of protection gave him the guts to continue with the conversation. "Sabina and me . . . well, don't worry about it."

Luke put his hand out the window to play with the onrushing wind, a move that always made Roman nervous. He gritted his teeth and suppressed the impulse to make him stop.

"Did you break up with her?"

"There's nothing to break up."

"Yeah, right. You're different with her, Papa. I can tell."

Roman suppressed a sigh. Kids always picked up much more than you realized.

"Doesn't matter. It takes two, son."

"Carly says Sabina's in love with you. That she's never seen her act like that with anyone."

Roman tightened his grip on the steering wheel. Right now, after what had just happened, he didn't need to hear that. "Can we change the subject?"

"Why? Why can't we talk about Sabina?"

"Because I don't want to." He ground his teeth together.

"Well, geez, Papa, that's a big surprise. You never want to talk about anything." And he subsided into his own thoughts.

Roman silently cursed a blue streak the rest of the way home. Damn his sleepless night, the stress of two days of anxiety, the mouth that said all the wrong things—too much to Sabina, too little to Luke.

When they pulled into the driveway, the sight of their squat little bungalow swept Roman back to the state of mind in which he'd left the night before—the stark terror of no Luke. That horrifying black pit opened under his feet again.

What was worse, losing Luke or talking to Luke? Maybe it was time for another little vent hole.

"Okay, Lukey, you asked for it. I love Sabina, even though it tears me up inside because of your mother. I told her I love her, but she didn't have much to say about that. And just now I said something she didn't like too much. So that leaves us pretty much nowhere."

He stared ahead at the little garage, at the fence that separated the front yard from the back, the glossy-leaved orange tree studded with exuberant fruit. A sick feeling grabbed his throat in a suffocating grip. He'd said too much. Luke couldn't handle all that. He braced himself for an explosion: *What about my mom? Did you forget about her? How come you get to find someone new while she's dead?*

Instead, he felt his son's hand clap onto his shoulder.

"You'll work it out, Papa," said Luke confidently. "You just have to hang in there. Sabina loves you back. Carly said so and she knows all kinds of girl stuff like that."

Whaaat?

The slam of the car door penetrated his shocked trance. He watched his son lope across the lawn toward the front door. Of all the ways he'd imagine his son reacting, man-to-man advice hadn't come up. Maybe his son had grown up more than he'd realized.

"Hang on a second there, buddy," he called, jumping out of the car and striding after him. "We still have a consequence to discuss."

Luke sat down on the front stoop and propped his chin on his folded hands. Roman settled opposite him. Eye level; that was different. He was used to looming over his son.

"Maybe I am a little overprotective. I couldn't help it after your mom and . . ." *Spit it out, bozo.* "The attacks."

Luke fixed wide eyes on him, as if Roman was the oracle or something, when he was only a tongue-tied man trying to spit a few words out. Roman scratched at the back of his neck.

"I can't let anything happen to you," he said flatly. "The worst punishment I could think of would be for you to feel, even for one second, what it was like to get that e-mail and find your room empty. Nothing I lay down can even come close."

Luke went so pale his freckles glowed. "I'm sorry, Papa. But . . ." He chewed on his lip.

"I hear you. I do. You're getting older. You want me to give you some slack."

Even though it killed him to say those words, the hope dawning in his son's eager brown eyes made it worth it. "Yeah. I'm pretty smart, Papa. I didn't want you to worry too much. That's why I sent the e-mail. And I didn't want to lie. I could have just said I was spending the night at Ralphie's."

"I'm glad you didn't lie, but that doesn't absolve you of the rest of it."

"I know, I know. I said I was sorry. Like a million times. But Papa . . ."

"No buts."

"But . . ."

"That's a but."

"I know, I know, but . . . I mean, nevertheless . . . Arrgh!" Luke threw back his head in frustration and yelled. "I just wanted to help her. I couldn't just do nothing, or let her go off by herself. Would you? No way."

"Are you blaming this on me?"

"Papa! You're twisting it. I always try to think what you would do. You're my hero! I guess . . ." He buried his face in his arms. "I guess I just got it wrong this time."

"Aw, son." Roman put a hand on his son's shoulder. All his worries, and his son's problem was an overactive need to protect. The apple didn't fall far from the tree. "You could have done worse. You both came back safe. But next time, come to me first. That's what I'm here for."

"No, but . . . Carly doesn't know you the way I do. She didn't want me to say anything to you. She's actually kind of scared of you. Or she was."

"Well, I am terrifying. Especially when I'm telling you no Internet, Wii, or any video games for two weeks. That includes the time we're in New York."

"Two *weeks*?"

"After the two weeks, we'll talk about lightening up on some of the rules."

"Really?" The eager look on Luke's face made Roman cringe. Had he been that strict?

"Yes. But you have to talk to me, not go off and do crazy things like this."

Luke nodded. Even his freckles looked serious. "I will."

"And before we leave for Christmas, you have to clean up your room. That gives you two days."

"Clean up my *room*? What does my room have to do with anything?"

"It has to do with the fact that Sabina nearly ate it with her crutches when we checked your computer."

Luke gulped. "Sabina came into my room?" Roman could practically see the wheels spinning, Luke trying to remember all the potentially embarrassing things he'd left strewn about the room.

"Got a problem with that?"

"No," he said in a small voice. "Can we go inside now?"

"Sure. I love you, son."

"Yeah. I better get to work. It's gonna take me the entire two days to clean my room."

Luke dug out his keys and trudged inside the house. Roman headed to the Jeep to grab his bag. Truth to tell, he was proud of his son. Luke had gone about it wrong, but his intentions were good. He'd been trying to protect Carly. He was a Roman through and through.

No, scratch that. He was fifty percent an O'Keefe, which meant double the trouble. Maureen had possessed the gene too, the one that compelled you to throw yourself in front of a moving car to save a pedestrian, or into a dying building to save the panicked office workers inside. Maureen would be proud of Luke too. He was a good kid.

Our son thinks I'm a hero, Maureen, he thought. *Even though I couldn't save you.*

In his mind's eye, he imagined Maureen laughing. *I held my own, big guy, all the way to the end. You worry about saving your own ass.*

Saving his own ass? What did she mean by that?

Chapter Thirty-One

To Sabina's surprise, Annabelle didn't mind the new living arrangements. She drew Carly into her orbit, treating her like some combination of personal assistant and makeover project. No one had ever coddled Carly before, bought her lip gloss and cute bras. Carly tolerated it, though she drew the line at mascara.

"I'm an athlete," she informed Annabelle. "Pitchers don't wear mascara."

"They do if they're on the Olympic softball team and doing a spread for *Sports Illustrated*."

"Semi good point," Carly conceded. She allowed one swipe of mascara, no more.

Sabina wondered if Carly was better off with her binge-drinking mother, but on the other hand, it was fun to see her scoff while Annabelle pored over *People* magazine and told her embarrassing secrets about all the stars.

It gave Sabina time to think about everything Roman had said to her.

For a while she felt nothing but fury. Roman had no business meddling in her life. Acting as if she'd done her mother wrong. Annabelle was the one with something to answer for, not her. And yet he talked as if Sabina was heartlessly pushing her mother away.

As if she pushed everyone away. She didn't do any such thing, did she?

On Christmas Eve she got a phone message from Roman. "Luke and I are headed to New York for Christmas. I hope you . . . well, season's greetings."

Season's greetings? What kind of thing was that to say after he'd declared his love both with words and physical demonstrations of the most unforgettable sort?

It's more than you said to him, her conscience whispered.

Christmas passed in a blur. In San Gabriel the holiday always had a goofy, surreal quality. The next-door neighbor put up a plastic snowman surfing on the green lawn. Reindeer pranced across a roof with no hint of a chimney—wearing hot-pink boas around their necks.

Sabina got gift certificates for everyone. Annabelle ordered a decadent spread from her favorite restaurant in Los Angeles. Sabina could barely enjoy the chestnut-stuffed pork medallions and chocolate terrine, though Carly's suspicious prodding of the unfamiliar dishes offered some entertainment.

What if Roman's right? Would it kill you to give Annabelle a chance? But after so many years of putting everyone at arm's length, anything else felt nearly impossible.

You shove people away and keep them there.

No, I don't. Do I?

She went to bed early, while Annabelle and Carly played a late-night game of Monopoly. *Don't let Carly become a distraction,* Roman had said. But what did he know? What gave him the right to lecture her?

Because he cares, that annoying voice in her head pointed out. She pulled a pillow over her head with a hopeless groan. Pillows were no use at all, since they reminded her of Roman. Roman, propping her foot on a pillow . . . Roman, nestling her into a pile of them at the Bannon Motel 6 . . . Roman, smiling into her eyes from the next pillow over in his heavenly king-size bed.

The week between Christmas and New Year's passed with the jerky dissonance of a very long hangover. Sabina knew she had to do something. Things couldn't go on as they were. But a sort of paralysis gripped her, as if she was still trapped under that pile of marble inside a burning house.

On New Year's Day, Channel Six aired a *You and Me* marathon. Annabelle popped the cork off a bottle of champagne and settled into the armchair, curling her legs under her. Carly's teammates had called an impromptu practice in the park. She'd ridden off on Sabina's mountain bike, her glove stashed in her backpack. For the first time since the big prison adventure, Annabelle and Sabina were alone together.

Well, Annabelle, Sabina, Taffy, and Peg.

From her usual position on the couch, Sabina took a sip of champagne and squinted at the TV. The familiar opening credits played across the screen, the theme song giving her nostalgic little palpitations. "This may require a drinking game of some sort. Take a drink every time Peg says, 'Why Taffy Bannister McGee, what were you thinking'?"

"I said that about six times an episode."

"Sounds about right to me. Or maybe a drink every time Taffy slams the door. Remember how that picture kept falling off? It fell on my toe once."

"I believe it was helped along by the art director."

"What?"

"You drove him crazy. He had to keep coming up with new paintings." Annabelle reached for a truffle from a box spread open on the coffee table.

"I *had* to slam the door. It was in the script."

"But that hard?"

"Yes. It was the only fun I ever had on that set." Although she'd started that statement lightheartedly, by the end it had taken on a woebegone wobble. Quickly she hid behind her champagne flute.

Annabelle rolled her eyes as she bit into her truffle. "Always with the exaggerating."

Sabina gulped a mouthful of champagne, the bubbles prickling her throat. Let it be. What was the point of getting into another fight after all these years? But maybe . . . well, what the hell? Annabelle was here, and what if she never got another chance? "I'm not exaggerating. Being on that show was incredibly boring for me. We kept having to do the same things over and over again."

"But that's how it's done. We shot on film, not live."

"I know. That doesn't it make it fun."

"But—" Annabelle scraped a polished fingernail along her champagne flute. "It *is* fun. I can't imagine anything more fun. All those people, everyone coming together to create something, everyone looking at you, listening to you. Applauding when it's a wrap."

"That was definitely my favorite part. It's a wrap."

Annabelle set her champagne flute on the coffee table with a sharp click. She gazed at the TV, where

Taffy was climbing up a ladder to the roof. "You always looked like you were having fun," she said wistfully. "I suppose you're a good actress. You should consider—"

"No."

"Pardon?"

"I'm not going to consider anything having to do with acting. I don't like it. I never want to do it again."

Annabelle shot her a dry look. "I've picked up on that by now."

Sabina swallowed another overlarge gulp of champagne. Maybe it was the alcohol, but she was starting to feel a little like a passenger on a listing cruise ship. "I'm never going to do that reunion show."

"I know. That's what I told Max."

"But . . . I thought you wanted to do it. Desperately. That's why you came here. You destroyed my privacy with all those ridiculous interviews. Ruined my life."

"For goodness' sakes, Sabina, you're blowing it all out of proportion! I didn't ruin anything. You were hiding out like a . . . a criminal on the run."

"Well . . . maybe I was. But that's how I wanted it! My choice. My life."

"You want to live your life all alone with no one knowing who you are?"

The ship was seriously tilting now. Sabina held on to the cushions of the couch as though she might slide off. Was her mother actually making some good points? "This isn't about me. It's about you and how ruthless you are. Are you denying you came to San Gabriel to get me to do the show?"

"Well, of course not. At first, anyway. But after all that media attention, people started sending me scripts. Decent ones. A good script means a lot more to me than money." She poured herself more champagne and toasted the TV screen. "Rest in peace, Peg McGee."

Sabina wanted to slap the champagne flute from her mother's hands. "So that's it? As long as you're getting good scripts, everything's cool? I was just a means to an end for you, wasn't I? When I left the show, you had no more use for me. See ya!" She mimed a wave. "Wouldn't want to be ya!"

Annabelle went white. "How dare you?"

Sabina got up from the couch, grabbing her crutches for support. "You never once tried to reach me after I left."

"Max told me not to. He said you wanted all communication to go through him."

"What?"

"Besides, I was furious with you. The tabloids ate me alive. 'TV mom's daughter files for emancipation.' Do you have any idea what I went through?"

Sabina winced. She'd managed to block that part out—she'd had to, in order to keep going. Still . . . "Why is it always about you, Annabelle?" Her voice rose; she couldn't help it. "What about me, stuck at the stupid show for my entire fucking childhood? I was just a prop to you. A royalty machine."

Quick as a spitting cat, Annabelle jumped to her feet. Her red hair crackled around her head like firecrackers going off. She stood toe to toe with Sabina. "Well, excuse me for giving you the chance to become a star. You could be rich and famous by now. A millionaire."

"Sure, if I hadn't given you all my money!"

"What are you talking about?"

"The money I gave you! From the show!"

"You never gave me any money! I had to sell the Brentwood house after the show ended. I lived off residuals and voiceover work."

Sabina shook her head, utterly bewildered. "Annabelle, I signed all my earnings over to you. Every single cent. I sold those diamond earrings you gave me and lived off them until I did *Zombie Nights*. I wanted you to be okay financially after the show ended. Max said he'd take care of it."

"Oh my God."

They stared at each other, realization dawning. Sabina slammed her crutch against the couch. "That weaselly little rat bastard."

Into the stunned silence filtered dialogue from *You and Me*, voices from mother and daughter, circa a lifetime ago.

I told you not to touch that stove!

But I wanted to roast marshmallows and you said not to make a campfire.

Why, Taffy Bannister McGee, what were you thinking?

Annabelle grabbed the remote and turned off the TV. "When's the last time you heard from Max?"

Sabina tried to focus her whirling brain. "It's been a while. Not since the fire. Not since you took me home from the hospital."

Annabelle snatched up her cell phone and began scrolling through her contacts. "I'm calling him. And a lawyer. And maybe a hit man."

Sabina sank back onto the couch while her mother dialed. After a minute, Annabelle tossed the phone aside. It landed on the coffee table with a clatter. "His cell's been disconnected."

"He doesn't have access to any of your money, does he?"

"I don't think so. Good Lord." Annabelle sank into

the armchair with a lack of grace she'd never have allowed if she weren't so upset. "This explains so much. When you left with no word, I thought you hated me."

"I didn't hate you. I hated my life."

Annabelle rubbed her forehead, as if trying to chase away frown lines. "I know. I knew you hated it."

"Then why did you make me—"

Impatient, Annabelle waved off the question, her rings sending sparkles through the room. "Obviously, I didn't think I could do it without you. I thought my career would be over. I'd only gotten the tiniest roles before I brought you in for that audition."

The familiar, sickening guilt slammed Sabina in the chest. "I'm sorry," she said through dry lips. "I didn't mean to—"

"Oh stop. I'm a grown-up." A self-mocking smile quirked one corner of her mouth. "I admit it took me a while." She smoothed down a stray lock of hair and drew a deep breath. "I don't do this often, so savor it, kiddo. I should have listened to you. You were outgrowing the show in any case. I shouldn't have fought it so hard. And I shouldn't have outted you at the station, even though it was bound to happen sooner or later. But how do you think I got from nowhere land to TV star? I'm one stubborn bi—broad."

Sabina blinked at her mother. Her image wavered, then came clear. Hardheaded, electrifying, driven Annabelle. A woman who would always surprise.

Annabelle gave her old snorty laugh, and it felt like a fist squeezing Sabina's heart. "Here." She stood up, picked up her glass of champagne, and toasted Sabina. "To my stubborn only daughter, who's more like me than she would ever want to admit."

Sabina took in those eyes, so much like hers, the color of the stormy Caribbean, and that full Merlot-tinted mouth. She raised her glass. "To my only mother, who's pretty freaking amazing."

"I'll drink to that."

They clinked glasses.

"And to making Max pay," Sabina added.

"Oh hell." Annabelle drained her champagne. "You can count on that. No one messes with my kiddo and gets away with it."

Sabina's throat went so tight, she couldn't have said anything with a gun to her head.

Annabelle put down her champagne. "But maybe I ought to thank him. I got a real-life reunion with my daughter the firefighter." She pulled Sabina into a hug, the first they'd shared in about a million years.

"No," her mother said in Sabina's ear. "I'll make him pay first. Then maybe I'll thank him."

Maybe it took a return to New York for Roman to finally figure things out. It felt like a trip back in time, as if he were a visitor from the future who couldn't quite communicate with the people he knew. Even his parents could tell something was different.

"You did the right thing, moving to California," his father said as they walked down the block toward the church on the corner. "It did you good. Same for Lucio." He refused to call Luke the Americanized version of his name.

"The bagels in San Gabriel are a disgrace. And their idea of Italian cooking is spaghetti mixed with clam chowder. Olive oil's not bad, though."

"You teaching those West Coast boys how we fight fires in New York?"

"They know what they're doing."

"I heard they're under a curse."

"You watch too much TV."

His father leaned in close, reaching a big-knuckled hand to cover his. "Son, it never pays to ignore a curse. Have you been having trouble in the love department?"

"*Babbo,* please." He and his father never discussed such things.

"I'll light some candles at the church. If you're fighting a curse, you need all the help you can get."

"I can handle it without help from above, thank you."

"Foolish boy."

Roman chuckled. Only his father, Brooklyn firefighting legend, could get away with calling his six-foot-five-inch battalion chief son a foolish boy.

"I saw her on TV. *Bella ragazza.*"

"Let's not talk about this. Not right now." They had reached Saint Ambrose's, a small church built of soft gray stone and adorned with simple scrolls and a lovely Madonna. Roman had grown up attending this church; Maureen had loved it.

"You can make it home okay?" Roman asked his father.

"I do this walk twice a day, son. Take your time. I'll have some prosciutto e melone waiting for you."

Roman kissed his father on the cheek and opened the side gate of the tiny churchyard. A sense of tranquillity enveloped him as soon as he stepped onto the lovingly tended path that hugged the side of the church. The sounds of Brooklyn faded, honking horns replaced by cheerful birdsong.

After Maureen had died, once the uncomprehending grief had faded, he'd gone to Ground Zero, to the site of her last moments, but the place had stirred up too many terrible emotions. So he'd come here instead, and begged for help from the priest.

Now, in the tiny cemetery, he knelt down next to an

exquisite headstone with the name Maureen O'Keefe Roman carved in bold strokes. Bold suited her, as did the rest of the words. Wife. Mother. Firefighter. Hero. He put his hand on the stone. Its rough surface, warmed by the sun, tickled his palm. A peaceful calm settled over him.

"Luke is doing great," he murmured. He looked around, feeling silly, but saw no one else. He had the place to himself. "There's someone I need to tell you about. Someone who's come into my life."

As soon as he said the words, he knew they weren't needed. Wherever Maureen was, he had her blessing. "I think you'd like her, Maureen. I know you would."

The thought of Maureen and Sabina hanging out together made him smile. Two kickass, gutsy, firefighting babes. Though they might not appreciate that description.

"The problem is, well, there's a couple problems. I may have pissed her off. I know that doesn't surprise you. I'm pretty sure I can make that right. But the other . . . We worked it out pretty well, both of us on the force. Two-firefighter family. But I don't know if I want to put Luke into that situation again."

And maybe that was the purpose of saying things out loud, of speaking them in words, rather than confused thoughts that bubbled beneath the surface. Because as soon as he said them, something fell into place.

"Oh," he said to the headstone. "Oh."

Tenderly, he traced the letters of Maureen's name, then sat back on his heels. "Now why didn't I think of that?"

Roman and Luke headed back to California fully stocked with certain essential items such as black olives and his favorite brand of Parmesan. When they stepped off the plane, the warm, smoggy air embraced him like a long-lost friend. The snowless streets, inhabited by smiling passersby who weren't wearing winter coats and elbowing each other out of the way, welcomed him kindly.

Surprise, surprise, San Gabriel had become home.

They barely made it back in time for Luke's first day of school and Roman's first shift. He swung by Sabina's house before his shift started, but it was far too early to knock on the door. He'd have to wait, which seemed impossible. The need to see Sabina drummed in his blood. But maybe it was better. He had something to do at work first.

At the firehouse, the early relief guys were reminiscing about the Christmas ski trip to Big Bear and boasting about the record-breaking sales of *Cooking with Heat*. They weren't the only ones talking about it. Chief Renteria had left a message on his voice mail.

"Every time I turn on the TV, I see another story about those cookbooks. Good job, Roman."

"Hear that, Stan," he said to the dog, who'd been flatteringly glad to see him. "I finally did something right. Even though I had nothing to do with it." Stan wagged his tail and held his Christmas present, a ball in the shape of a cartoon bomb, between his jaws.

At lineup, Roman dropped his own bombshell. "Where are we on the dinner rotation?"

"Stud's up."

"Stud, mind if I fill in?"

Everyone's jaws dropped.

"You, Chief? I mean, sure, of course," said Stud.

"Good."

"Chief, if you need ideas about what to cook, we have some copies of *Cooking with Heat* left. Only a few, though, we're practically sold out, if you can believe it."

"I'm good. I have cooked before, you know."

No one seemed convinced, and he got a lot of funny looks throughout the day as he did his prep work in between calls. It was an unusually busy day at Fire Station 1. Usually they fielded an average of three to five calls per twenty-four-hour shift. This time, they got called out eight times before dinner. The cannellini soaked a little too long thanks to an electrical fire at a local hardware store. His Parmesan cheese grating got interrupted by a San Gabriel High linebacker's broken leg. Then there were the mushrooms to soak in white wine, which meant bending the rules against alcohol in the firehouse just a tad.

Stan kept him company the whole time. Roman convinced himself it was out of love and not the bits of pancetta he occasionally dropped in the dog's vicinity. Stan had good taste, he figured, until he saw the mutt get equally excited about a bit of Styrofoam packaging.

Finally, it was time for dinner. First, he set out plates of bruschetta made with Italian bread he'd brought back from New York. The guys had never tasted anything like it.

"Dude, how can bread, garlic, and tomato taste so freaking good?"

"Where'd you learn to do this?"

"We gotta reprint the cookbook, man. Special edition."

Stan didn't care for it, but then he'd never been a big fan of garlic.

"Now for the soup course," said Roman with a flourish. He unveiled the magnificent pot of pasta e fagioli con rosmarino that had been simmering most of the day.

"I had to turn it off during that car fire. Hope it's okay."

"That wasn't a car fire," said Vader. "That was a *Mustang* fire. Had to have been the ex-girlfriend. Who else would set fire to a 1978 Mustang convertible? Hell, this is great, Chief." He slurped a big spoonful. "What are you, like the Iron Chef or something?"

"That's it!" Fred pounded his fist on the table, making the plates rattle. "The chief's nickname. Iron Chef."

"Finish the meal first," said Roman. "Tonno con caponata."

"Con who?"

"Just try it."

A reverent silence descended as the firefighters dug into their tuna steaks with caper-garlic-vegetable sauce.

"Good golly, Miss Molly," said Double D, who seemed to be forgetting all about his new diet.

"Holy Mother of God," breathed Psycho. "Who *are* you? How did you make this? This is—"

"Un-fucking-believable," said Vader. "And I don't even like French food."

"It's Italian," corrected Roman, who was otherwise completely enjoying the crew's reaction. "This recipe is from Southern Italy, as a matter of fact."

"Is that where you learned it?"

"It's a family recipe, mostly. I changed a few things. Little less olive oil, little more capers."

"What the hell are capers?" Vader frowned at his fork.

"Little fish," said Fred.

"No, they're flower buds," Roman corrected again. "Pickled flower buds from the caper shrub. Did you guys really put out a cookbook?"

"Yeah, but our hardest recipe was fish tacos. How come you been holding out on us, dude?" Psycho took another bite and moaned with appreciation.

"Well, that's a good question." Why had he kept his tenderhearted side to himself? Maybe he'd been waiting for this moment. Roman took a deep breath, the kind required when one is about to jump off a cliff, and rose to his feet. "I'm leaving the station."

Chapter Thirty-Two

While Sabina was in the shower, her phone buzzed with an incoming text message. Then another one. And another. Something big was happening. Extracting herself from the shower was no easy feat, and she was swearing by the time she grabbed her phone off the edge of the bathroom sink.

All the texts were from Vader.

Holy fuck. Roman's out.
He's ditching the station.
Can't believe you're missing this.
Dude can cook.

Sabina didn't know she could move so fast on crutches, but before she knew it she was out the door, her hair in a wet tumble down her back, and diving into Annabelle's car.

"Take my car if you need it," she called to her mother, who stood in the open doorway, her phone forgotten. Two producers wanted her for their next movies, and she had to hire a new agent, fast.

Then Sabina was flooring the accelerator with her good foot, zooming toward San Gabriel Station 1 as if a fire had broken out on the premises. Roman couldn't leave, not like this, not until she told him the most important thing in the world.

When she reached the station, she swung her way through the side door that opened onto the apparatus bay. She stumped down the corridor, the familiar scent of diesel and varnish and bleach mingling with something absolutely heavenly. Something savory and rosemary-flavored and mouthwatering. Something that could only have been created by Roman.

When she burst into the kitchen, the crew was sitting around the long table. Roman stood at the head, his back to her, his powerful form towering over everyone else. A blur of faces turned in her direction—Vader, looking from her to his cell phone, mystified, as if she'd time-traveled her way here. Stud, a spoon halfway to his astonished face. Double D, in the middle of loosening his belt.

"Roman," she said loudly. "No. You can't."

He swung around. She ate up the sight of him—how long had it been, a couple of weeks? Too long, far too *stupidly* long. Never let that happen again. His black eyebrows swooped upward in astonishment. "Sabina?"

"You can't leave San Gabriel," she repeated, tightening her grip on her crutches. The feel of his eyes on her, that smoldering black gaze, made her wobbly in the legs. "I have to tell you something first."

The kitchen went utterly quiet. Everyone was looking at her, of course. What else should they look at when a still-wet woman in denim shorts, tank top, and an ankle cast stormed into the room? A drop of water plopped onto the floor, then another. She was dripping all over the firehouse.

Roman waited, a slight frown denting his forehead. He made no move to invite her into his office to discuss this privately. Then again, he had no idea what they were about to discuss. She opened her mouth to suggest retiring to his office, but suddenly . . . it didn't matter. So what if the whole B shift was watching? She'd had enough of keeping everything hidden. No more wariness. No more arm's-length. And no more delay—not one single second more.

She squared her shoulders, took a long breath for courage, and laid bare her heart. "Roman, I love you." There, it was out. Like diving into a cold lake, not so bad after the initial shock. "So you can't leave. I should have told you before, because it's been true a really, really long time. But I'm a stubborn idiot. Ask the guys. They'll tell you."

But no one said a word. The silence felt excruciating. Another drop of water plinked into the growing puddle at her feet.

"You were right about me, before. And about my mother. But it only took me two weeks to figure it out, unlike my mother, who waited thirteen years, but I'm not going to be like that." What was she talking about now? She had no idea. Neither did anyone else, judging by the puzzled looks they were exchanging. "The point is, I love you. And you said you loved me before, but maybe you changed your mind after I was such a jerk, and maybe that's why you're leaving, but please, don't . . ." She trailed off because Roman was now striding toward her. He crossed the room in three long steps and swooped her into his arms. Her crutches clattered to the floor.

"No one in the apparatus bay for the next ten minutes," he growled over his shoulder to the crew.

A chorus of "No, sirs" and "Go get 'ems" followed them down the corridor. Sabina clung to Roman's broad shoulders, wondering dizzily what she was in for. Was he angry? Overcome with lust? Unwilling to reject her in public? But right now, it felt so good to simply inhale his scent, breathe in the all-male, rosemary-infused aroma of Battalion Chief Ricardo Roman.

He opened the door of Engine 1 and plopped her on the seat, her legs dangling over the edge. Bracing his hands on the vinyl on either side of her, he leaned in so she was completely encompassed by his passionate gaze. "First of all, I'm not leaving San Gabriel. Second, when I say, 'I love you,' it doesn't change overnight. Or in two weeks."

"It doesn't? I mean, you do?" A supernova expanded in her heart. She was sure beams of light must be radiating from her chest. "You still do?"

"I still do. Ask me in five years, you'll get the same answer. And in ten. Twenty. Thirty. I love you, Sabina. For good."

She gave a breathless hiccup of sheer relieved joy. "I didn't screw everything up then?"

He smiled, a sheepish, almost boyish expression. "I thought I had."

"No. No. You didn't. You couldn't. But . . ." She grabbed on to the twin iron ridgepoles of his arms. "Vader said you're leaving."

"Leaving the station. Yes."

She shook her head, not getting it.

"I'm leaving the force. I'm not going to be a firefighter anymore."

"*What?* But firefighting is your life . . ."

"No. My life is Luke. And you, I hope."

She drew in a long, astonished breath. "I don't understand."

He ran one hand up her arm, raising a trail of goose bumps. "I'm not very good at explaining things like this. After 9/11, after Maureen died, everything went dark. The whole world sort of . . . collapsed in on me. Nothing made sense. All I knew how to do was keep going to work, keep doing the job, keep being there for Luke. Luke was it, the only thing that mattered, the only thing I could see." He paused, flicked a glance up at her. She waited, breathless. "Luke's real name is Lucio, which means 'light.' It was supposed to be a play on fire." He shrugged one massive shoulder, glancing around the gleaming engines in the apparatus bay. But Sabina couldn't drag her gaze away from him, this powerful, beautiful man telling his story.

Roman cleared his throat and forged ahead. "But he was my Lucio, in every way. After 9/11 he was my light in the tunnel. He kept me going through all that darkness. But it was still a tunnel. A bleak, sad, one-step-at-a-time tunnel. Until I met you and the tunnel . . . crumbled away."

Tears sprang to her eyes, but he wasn't finished yet.

"And there I was, in the light. With you."

"Oh, *Roman.*" Overwhelmed, she cupped her hand around his cheek, feeling his jaw muscles work. He turned his head to drop an infinitely tender kiss into her palm.

"I love you, Sabina. I want to marry you. I want to live with you and look at you and talk to you and be with you and touch you. I'd like to have more children, if you're interested in that."

Tears spilled over onto her cheeks.

"But I don't want to be part of a two-firefighter family again. It works for some people, but not for me. At first I thought I couldn't bear to love another female firefighter, ever again. I nearly lost my mind when you were under that staircase. But that's who you are. You're a firefighter and I fell in love with you and I can't change any of that. You deserve to keep your career. I know what it means to you."

"Not as much as—"

"Stop. You don't have to choose one or the other. *I'm* choosing. For many good reasons."

Her voice caught. "Oh, Roman. I love you so much. I've been so lost without you. Just . . . empty and awful. I know I'm stubborn and hold people away, but I don't want to do that anymore. Especially you, because, God, Roman, I love you so, so much. When I thought you were leaving . . . and me on crutches . . . I would have stumped all the way to New York if I had to."

"Oh, *cara*." Then they were kissing, and it felt like no other kiss in the world, impossibly, rapturously glorious. Touching him again, after all that time apart, felt nothing short of miraculous. With Roman, she'd never be alone again, never be one stubborn woman against the world. With Roman, she'd be loved, through and through, and even better, she could open her own heart and let all her piled-up love pour out. She put every last bit of gratitude and passion and sheer, shivery delight into that kiss.

When he finally pulled his mouth from hers, the expression on his face sent a jolt of awareness shivering down her spine. He looked outrageously lustful, as if he'd ravage her right there in Engine 1, although their ten minutes of solo time must be up now.

Which reminded her . . . "If you're no longer going to be a firefighter, what are you going to do?"

The entire B shift of San Gabriel Fire Station 1 came to the grand opening of Lucio's Ristorante Autentico Italiano, formerly known as La Piaggia. So did Luke's baseball team. Carly's mother brought her; she'd left rehab a few weeks earlier and hadn't relapsed yet.

Anu and Sabina greeted each customer while Roman turned into a raving lunatic in the kitchen. With all the banging of pots and clanging of knives, there seemed a strong chance of blood being spilled tonight. The kitchen staff was used to Roman, but now that he owned the place, he demanded the kind of instant obedience a fire crew gave him. Sous-chefs, it turned out, were a different story.

Some of the arrivals were confused. "Wasn't this always an Italian restaurant?"

"Yes, but now it's a *real* Italian restaurant," answered Anu, who had agreed to stay on to help run the place. "*Autentico*, that means authentic. I can personally vouch for the wonderful creations you are about to experience." She lowered her voice. "And if you do not like the new dishes, I will secretly heat up some SpaghettiOs for you. I used to do that, you know, when I was feeling particularly lazy," she confided to Sabina.

"So are you glad your parents sold the restaurant to Roman?"

"Quite, quite glad. They've purchased a taco truck but they promise to sell naan as well. Now, tell me. Are you glad you became engaged to Roman?"

Sabina smiled. "Oh yes. Although my mother's terrified I'll embarrass her with some grandchildren."

"Is she here?"

"Yep. Camera crew in tow." She indicated Annabelle, radiant in a gold lamé dress, on the far side of the room. A cameraman and soundman were at her heels.

"Cameras! Have you broken your policy on privacy then?"

"Call it an engagement present. She's in the running for a great role and needs a little publicity. Harmony for the Hatfields . . . good story, right?"

"Certainly harmony is quite desirable. But what's in it for you?"

"Oh Anu. So cynical. I worked it out with Chief Renteria. We agreed that the best use of my newfound, thought-I'd-gotten-rid-of-it, now-it's-back-again fame is to make a few public service announcements for Big Brothers Big Sisters."

"How wonderful!"

The arrival of Vader interrupted Anu's ecstatic clasping of hands. A pretty redhead wearing cat's-eye glasses and a vintage fifties sweetheart dress hung on his arm. "Two, meet Cherie. Cherie, this is Two, also known as Sabina or Sally Hatfield or Taffy—"

"Call me Sabina," she interrupted, smiling at Cherie. "Are you sure you know what you're getting into here?"

"With Vader, you mean?" She ran a hand along his bulging biceps. "Oh, I'm just peeling back the layers, right, hon?"

Vader's brow jutted, his jaw clenched, his pectorals quivered through his muscle shirt. "Layers? You talking about getting laid?" He winked at Anu, who was already backing away, looking slightly horrified.

Sabina and Cherie burst out laughing. "He's a keeper, Cherie. Just keep him away from Anu."

Cherie winked from behind her rhinestone-studded glasses. "Let's get us some wine, honey. Sabina, is that your fiancé, Chief Roman?" Roman was beckoning to her through the diamond-shaped window of the kitchen door.

"Not a chief anymore," growled Vader.

"Whatever he is, he's something else," sighed Cherie.

Sabina agreed wholeheartedly. "And more so every time I set eyes on him. Be right back, you guys. Enjoy the party."

From behind the swinging kitchen door, Roman watched his beautiful fiancée pick her way through the mob. Even though she no longer needed crutches, she still favored her left ankle. But she did it so gracefully that she could probably set a trend. People would be copying her sexy moves even if they had no injuries. But they couldn't mimic that vivid glow in her eyes, that naughty promise that made him groan at the thought of everything he'd do to her later that night.

He beckoned her into the kitchen, where Luke was waiting with his proposal. "Luke has an idea he wants to run past you. A fund-raising idea for Amarinda's rehab bill. Since I'm not with the department anymore, I can't really give him a yes or no."

Sabina aimed her bright smile at Luke, who beamed back. All things considered, he'd adjusted pretty well to Sabina's presence, though Roman made sure he and Luke still did things like batting practice together.

"Sure, what's up, Luke?"

Before Luke could speak, a knock sounded at the

back door. Captain Brody and Ryan Blake stuck their heads in. "Fire department here," said Brody. "All your fire extinguishers in order?"

Ryan winked. "Nothing personal, but I always feel the need to check before I eat anywhere."

Roman had heard about Katie's bar, and the series of mysterious fires that had kept Ryan busy. He beckoned them inside. "What are you so worried about? I heard the Hair of the Dog fires brought you and Katie together."

"Yep, they helped me break the curse."

Luke piped up. "You're both still firefighters, right? San Gabriel firefighters?"

"Yes," answered Brody. "Why do you ask?"

"Because my baseball team would like to hold a special fund-raising event to help out the mom of one of our teammates, Carly Epps, I mean, her mom's name is Amarinda and she's been in rehab. Now she has to pay the bill but we want to help her out because we're a team, you know?" Luke's speech came out in a tumbling rush, a little nervous, a little excited.

"Teammates ought to help each other. So we were thinking maybe we could have a bake sale, but not a regular bake sale. We'd make the recipes from your cookbook, *Cooking with Heat*. And maybe some of you guys could come help out on the bake sale day, and then all the TV stations would come too, and then more people would show up. And it would be good for the fire station too because the bake sale customers might want to buy the cookbook, which would mean more money for the 9/11 fund, which is good too."

"Kid," said Ryan, visibly impressed. "That's some genius thinking."

"You like it? Can we do it?"

Brody spoke in his measured, authoritative way.

"I'd say the firehouse should put it to a vote. But I'm sure they'll say yes. Sabina, what do you think?"

Sabina's vivid eyes shimmered mist-green with tears. "I think they'd love it. *We'd* love it. Count me in. Great idea, Luke. Makes me proud to be a San Gabriel firefighter."

Roman's chest swelled with emotion so intense, it hurt. How could one man feel so proud and happy? He put his arm around Sabina and she slid into his embrace like a fish into water. Exactly where she belonged. By his side, forevermore.

Luke ran off to tell the team the good news.

Still riding that wave of emotion, Roman scowled at Brody and Ryan. "While you're both here, I'd like to put this curse rumor to rest for good. Look at me. I was a poor, lonely, single guy until I came to San Gabriel. That's when I got my woman."

"Your *woman*?" Sabina squirmed under his arm, but he tightened his grip; she wasn't going anywhere.

"Yes, but didn't you have to quit to get her?" said Ryan.

Sabina spluttered. "Excuse me, I'm *right here*. I have a name and it's not 'her.' "

"We're just making the point that Roman was no longer with the San Gabriel Fire Station when he sealed the deal with you. In fact, he had just announced his resignation when you barged in and told everyone you loved him."

Roman smiled broadly. Best moment of his life.

"But *I* was still a firefighter," Sabina pointed out. "I didn't have to quit to get my man." She poked him in the ribs with her elbow.

"True," said Ryan.

"A helluva firefighter," agreed Brody.

"The best active-duty firefighter in the Roman-Jones

family." Roman felt another poke in the ribs, followed by a warm hand nestling into his.

Then Brody spoke, slowly. "But hang on a second. You weren't on active duty then, Sabina. You had a broken ankle." They all looked at one another.

"It's spooky, you gotta admit," said Ryan.

But then the two waitresses rushed in with the first orders. Roman gave Sabina a long, hard kiss on the lips—for luck, and because he loved her with all his heart. Then he sent everyone out of the kitchen so he could concentrate on making Lucio's the spectacular success it deserved to be.

As he filled a plate with veal piccata, he kept thinking about the "curse." Did it really matter if it was real? Then he remembered his father's advice to never ignore a curse.

Why tempt fate?

"Constancia Sidwell and Virgil Rush," he muttered. "Sorry it didn't work out for you two."

The sous-chef gave him a suspicious look over his sauté pan of veal reduction.

"But Sabina's stuck with me. You'll just have to go curse someone else. And you might want to go a little easier on the next guy. Then again . . ." He filled a plate with penne al'arrabiata. "Do whatever you have to do. It was all worth it."

Next month, don't miss these exciting new love stories only from Avon Books

What Happens in Scotland by Jennifer McQuiston
When Lady Georgette wakes up with a wedding ring on her finger and next to a very handsome, very naked Scotsman, she does the only sensible thing: runs for it. All James MacKenzie knows is that his money is missing and the stunning woman who just ran from the room is either his wife or a thief . . . or possibly both.

The Duke Diaries by Sophia Nash
Would bedding the duke mean wedding the duke? Even though Lady Verity's reputation is in peril, after a wild night with the Duke of Abshire, there are far graver worries that plague her: like being unmasked as the author of the infamous Duke Diaries. And if that happens, no one can save her . . . except perhaps the man of her dreams.

Night Resurrected by Joss Ware
On a quest to safeguard the powerful crystal that is her family's secret legacy, Remy dares not trust anyone, even a man like Wyatt. With nothing left to lose, Wyatt has no reason to let anyone in. But as he joins Remy on her dangerous journey, the last thing he expected was for her to find a way past the walls he'd built around his heart . . .

Funny, poignant, sexy and totally outrageous fiction from *New York Times* bestselling author

SUSAN ELIZABETH PHILLIPS

Just Imagine

978-0-380-80830-4

Kit Weston has come to post-Civil War New York City to confront the Yankee who stands between her and her beloved South Carolina home.

First Lady

978-0-380-80807-6

How does the most famous woman in the world hide in plain sight? The beautiful young widow of the President of the United States thought she was free of the White House, but circumstances have forced her back into the role of First Lady.

Lady Be Good

978-0-380-79448-5

Lady Emma Wells-Finch, the oh-so-proper headmistress of England's St. Gertrude's School for Girls knows only one thing will save her from losing everything she holds dear: complete and utter disgrace! So she arrives in Texas on a mission. She has two weeks to lose her reputation.

Kiss An Angel

978-0-380-78233-8

How did pretty, flighty Daisy Deveraux find herself in this fix? She can either go to jail or marry the mystery man her father has chosen for her. Alex Markov, however, has no intention of playing the loving bridegroom to a spoiled little featherhead.